THE
RANSOM

Book **Seven** in the
Munro Family Series

CHRIS TAYLOR

LCT Productions Pty Ltd
18364 Kamilaroi Highway, Narrabri NSW 2390

ISBN. 978-1-925119-14-5

The Ransom is a work of fiction. Names, characters, places, brands, media and incidents either are the product of the author's imagination or are used fictitiously. Any resemblance to actual persons, living or dead, events, or locales, is entirely coincidental.

Published in the United States of America

Oh, what a tangled web we weave, when first we practice to deceive...

When Ellie Cooper married Clayton Munro six years ago, she hoped his daughter Olivia would accept her into her life, but despite all of Ellie's efforts, the ten-year-old has rejected her at every turn. When Olivia is kidnapped while shopping with Ellie, she's beside herself with guilt. To add to her devastation, Clayton's blaming her for not taking proper care of his daughter.

Detective Senior Sergeant Lane Black of the Chatswood State Crime Command is put in charge of the case. A child is missing and time is of the essence. To further complicate matters, the New South Wales Attorney General's youngest daughter was present at the time of the kidnapping. The girls look very much alike. Could it be a case of mistaken identity? Could the abduction be politically motivated?

When interviewing the Attorney General, Lane's disquieted by the man's nervousness. His oldest daughter, Zara Dowton, is also on edge. Immediately drawn to her exotic beauty, Lane does his best to remain unmoved and impartial, despite his body's urgings.

What are the Dowtons hiding...and why?

THE MUNRO FAMILY SERIES

THE PROFILER
(Book One—Clayton and Ellie)

THE INVESTIGATOR
(Book Two—Riley and Kate)

THE PREDATOR
(Book Three—Brandon and Alex)

THE BETRAYAL
(Book Four—Declan and Chloe)

THE DECEPTION
(Book Five—Will and Savannah)

THE NEGOTIATOR
(Book Six—Andy and Cally)

THE CHRISTMAS VIGIL
(A Munro Family Series Novella)

THE RANSOM
(Book Seven—Lane and Zara)

THE DEFENDANT
(Book Eight—Chase and Josie)

THE SHOOTING
(Book Nine—Tom and Lily)

THE MAKER
(Book Ten—Bryce and Chanel)

DEDICATION

This book is dedicated to Kylie Griffin, who from my very earliest days,
encouraged and supported me in my dream to be an author
and as always, to my sexy, real life hero, my husband, Linden.

ACKNOWLEDGMENTS

As usual, no book comes into being without a lot of help and support by my friends and family. A world of thanks must go to my friend and fellow author Angela Bissell, critique partner extraordinaire, and a girl who loves the Munro family as much as I do.

To Pat Thomas, the best editor in the world. I love working with you. You turn my humble offerings into something truly amazing. I couldn't do it without you.

To Alisha of damonza.com, thank you for yet another fantastic cover. To my sister, Nicole Guihot, thank you for your excellent editorial comments and suggestions. Nic, I hope you like the final result.

To Grace Anselmo, a quirk of fate has brought us together and I now can't imagine writing a Munro Family story without your input. Thank you for all of your suggestions. They are highly valued.

To Detective Superintendent Michael Kilfoyle, thank you once again for all of your technical expertise. Any mistakes are wholly my own.

To Amy Atwell and her dedicated staff of miracle workers at Author EMS who are so much more than book formatters. Amy, once again, heartfelt thanks for working your magic.

To the fantastic writer organizations such as Romance Writers of Australia, Romance Writers of America and Romance Writers of New Zealand for all the help, support and encouragement they offer new and aspiring writers, including me.

To my readers, thank you for your support and love for the Munro family. Your encouragement and enjoyment make this journey all worthwhile.

And lastly, to my friends and family, especially my husband and children. Thank you for putting up with late dinners and even later conversations as I've emerged day after day from the sometimes scary but always enthralling world I've created on my computer.

Prologue

Sydney, Australia
Saturday, January 13, 11:45 p.m.

Rivulets of cold sweat tracked a path down the sides of her head and leaked into her eyes, ruining her carefully applied mascara. The salt of her perspiration burned into her pupils, as did the bright, round flashlight that shone in her face. Her tightly bound hands ached, both from fear and a lack of blood flow.

Despite the physical discomfort, she eyeballed the man who loomed over her with a confidence she was far from feeling. "Tying me up, Draco? Is that really necessary?" She followed her truculent tone with a well-rehearsed pout.

To her chagrin, he remained entirely unaffected. If anything, his expression got harder. "Where. Is. My. Money?"

Each word was bitten off and spat at her, accompanied by the vile stench of breath rank with nicotine and a lifetime of dental neglect. He leaned over, his face inches from hers. Anger reverberated off him in palpable waves. She no longer recognized him.

"I'll-I'll get it, Draco. I promise," she stammered and silently cursed the fear in her voice.

The slap snapped her head backward and she gasped. Her cheek erupted into flames. She bit her lip and stifled a sob. It could have been worse. Much worse.

Draco eyed her with contempt, his upper lip turning up in a snarl. "Two weeks."

"That's not enough time," she protested. "We're talking about a million dollars."

"Two weeks. *Or else.*"

Chapter 1

Two weeks later
Sydney, Australia
Saturday, January 27, 9.35 a.m.

The Westfield Mall in Sydney's leafy northern suburb of Chatswood appeared ahead of Ellie and Olivia Munro and Olivia's friend Brittany Dowton as they made their way on foot from the car park. After an unseasonable week of wet weather, the sun had at last made an appearance and the general atmosphere of the mall was light and positive. It was so far removed from the mood between Ellie and her stepdaughter that it took all of the self-control Ellie could muster not to call the scheduled shopping expedition off and come back another time.

She stared at the stiff retreating back of her stepdaughter and bit back a sigh. The girl might only be ten years old, but already, she'd perfected the sulky pout and could flounce away with all the attitude of a teenager. It was only early, but with Olivia already in a mood, the day promised to be beyond trying.

As if she could read Ellie's mind, Olivia came to a sudden halt in front of her and swung around, a mutinous expression on her pretty face.

"I want more credit on my iTunes account."

Ellie bit her lip and curbed her anger, hoping to avoid

another eruption of the argument that had begun last night. Drawing in a deep, steady breath, she forced herself to remain calm.

"Olivia, we've already talked about this. We agreed your pocket money would be set at ten dollars a week. And that's only if you do your jobs," she added.

Olivia's eyes narrowed. She crossed her arms and stared Ellie down. "Ten dollars isn't enough. I've already spent this week's allowance and I only got it yesterday."

"Well, then you might need to learn how to budget, so that it lasts longer."

The young girl stamped her foot. Sun glinted off the bling on her silver Havaianas flip flops.

"None of my friends gets a measly ten dollars a week," she whined. "Even Brittany gets fifteen."

Ellie shot Brittany a look. The girl flushed and averted her gaze.

"I don't care what your friends get. Your father and I spoke to you about this last night and again this morning and now you're raising it for the third time. I don't want to talk about it again. We're here to buy you a swimsuit. Summer break's nearly over. You're back at school next week and you're going to need it. Can we please just get on with it?"

Without waiting for a reply, Ellie pushed her way past the girls and headed toward the entryway to the mall. Olivia called out to her, raising her voice above the hubbub of the crowd around them.

"Ellie, I can't download any more music off iTunes until you pay me again. I *have* to have the new One Direction song. I just *have* to!"

Grinding her teeth together, Ellie ignored the use of her first name and wished she could be as dismissive of Olivia's rudeness as Ellie's husband, Clayton, was. Determined to remain unruffled, Ellie swung around to face the recalcitrant child.

"No, Olivia. I told you last night. You'll have to wait."

"No, Olivia. I told you last night," Olivia mimicked in a sing-song voice, rolling her eyes as she did so.

Fury erupted in Ellie's chest and gushed through her veins. Her hands clenched into fists in an effort not to lash out and connect with her stepdaughter's smug face. She'd never struck the girl, ever. But she'd never felt such an uncontrollable urge to do so, either.

Keeping a tight rein on her temper, Ellie turned away from the girls and forced her feet forward. *How on earth was she ever going to survive Olivia's teenage years, when hormones would be running rampant around the girl's body and she actually had an excuse to be a bitch?*

Ellie bit back a sigh and prayed Clayton would be up to the task, or at least show her a little more support than he had in the past twelve months. They'd been married nearly six years. She'd known from the outset there would be some adjustments. Olivia had been four when Clayton and Ellie married and even though she was the only mother Olivia had known, Ellie hadn't deluded herself into thinking it was going to be easy.

Until Ellie's arrival on the scene, Olivia had been the center of her father's world. Ellie had been acutely aware of the need to ease her way into the little girl's life and had been determined to win her over.

It had been tough, but over time, Olivia had come to grudgingly tolerate her. With Clayton's love and support, they'd managed to form a fragile bond, but even after six years, Ellie still felt a distance. Lately, it had become a chasm.

Living with a ten-year-old who could barely bring herself to speak to her stepmother with even a modicum of courtesy was taking its toll. The days when Ellie wished she were still a detective for the New South Wales Police Service were becoming more and more frequent and that scared her. She hated to admit it, but she was almost on the verge of giving up trying to connect with the child.

She wished she could talk to Clayton, like she used to in the early years of their marriage. Back when she could count on him to be there for her, to understand and care about her needs and to want to do something to help. But lately, he'd been drifting away, physically and emotionally, and she didn't know what to do about it.

A little over a month earlier, Clayton's father, Duncan Munro, a former District Court judge, had suffered a ruptured brain aneurysm. For more than twenty-four hours, he'd been in a coma and no one had known when or *if* he'd wake up, but even the hospitalization of his father hadn't gone far in bringing them closer and it seemed they were both at a loss with how best to deal with Olivia.

It was Clayton who'd suggested the move to Sydney. Ellie had jumped at the opportunity to return to her hometown. Both of them hoped that the change of city would be good for Olivia. The girl had lived in Canberra her entire life. Sydney would be a fresh start—a place for new memories, new experiences untainted by whatever memories she thought she had about her mother.

They'd moved straight after Christmas, but if anything, Olivia's belligerence had gotten worse. Ellie could only hope that Olivia's budding friendship with the sweet and accommodating Brittany Dowton would make a difference in her attitude. So far though, it hadn't happened.

Ellie sighed and tried to push the depressing thoughts away. The automatic doors of the shopping mall slid open on a whisper of sound at her approach. Stepping inside, she was enveloped by the temperature-controlled air conditioned comfort of the mall and sighed again, this time in relief. With a deep breath, she turned to wait for the girls. Surly reluctance was evidenced in Olivia's every step.

With the girls trailing behind her, Ellie made her way into Myer and headed straight for the swimwear section. Now her goal was to get the shopping expedition over with as quickly as possible. Finding a rack with brightly colored full-piece swimsuits, Ellie chose a couple and turned around to face Olivia.

"How about these?" she asked, plastering a smile on her face.

"I want a bikini."

Ellie tried not to show her shock—or her anger. "You're ten years old. I'm not buying you a bikini."

Olivia's bottom lip jutted out and her expression turned sullen. "I want a bikini."

"You're not getting a bikini." She held up the swimsuits in her hands. "Now, which one of these do you like?"

Olivia pushed past her without responding and walked over to a nearby rack. After sliding several swimsuits out of the way, she selected a tiny, hot pink bikini. Smiling triumphantly, she lifted it up and waved it before Ellie.

"This is the one I want."

Fury once again flooded Ellie's veins. "I'm not buying you that, Olivia," she ground out.

"Then I'll get Daddy to buy it," the girl said flippantly.

"No, you won't."

"You're not my mother. You can't tell me what to do."

Ellie gasped and tried to ignore the hurt her daughter's words caused. "I'm the only mother you have and yes, I *can* tell you what to do." Taking hold of the girl's arm, she steered her in the direction of the change rooms. Shoving the swimsuits she'd selected into Olivia's arms, she said, "Go and try these on. *Now.*"

"I hate you! I wish you were dead! As dead as my *real* mother."

Ellie's mouth dropped open in shock. Olivia threw her a lethal look and stormed off toward the change rooms. Brittany shrugged apologetically and followed her.

Ellie spun away in an effort to escape the venom in her daughter's eyes and stumbled blindly past racks of clothing, her head spinning. Dragging in oxygen, she plowed through startled shoppers, averting her eyes to avoid their curious gazes.

"Sorry. Excuse me. I'm sorry." Aimed in the vicinity of the bodies around her, the mumbled apologies that fell out of Ellie's mouth barely registered in her mind. The only thing she could think of was to get as far away as possible from the young girl who was slowly driving her insane.

Taking refuge behind a high display of fine cotton sheets,

she tried to slow her breathing and still the trembling in her limbs. Shock rendered her brain numb. All she could see was the hatred in her daughter's eyes as she'd hurled those vile words in Ellie's face.

How had she let it get to this? How had *Clayton* let it get to this? He was her biological father. He bore even more responsibility for his daughter's attitude and actions than Ellie did. No matter how often they said they were equal in the parenting stakes, they both knew she was no match for the blood tie. There had been more than one occasion over the years when he'd stepped in and overruled a decision of Ellie's in favor of his daughter.

Although it hadn't happened often, the few times when it had, Ellie had been wounded to the core and had become more and more reluctant to make decisions concerning Olivia without his consent, even common-sense ones. It was a struggle and a situation she was far from happy about, but it had gone on for so long, she no longer knew how to change it.

She'd had no idea when they'd married, that six years later, she'd still be battling to befriend Clayton's only daughter. When the boys had come along, she thought they would soften Olivia's antagonism, that they would help her feel like she was part of a real family. But it seemed to have made things worse.

Although her half-brothers Mitchell and Damon adored their older sister, the feeling seemed less than mutual. Ellie knew a ten-year-old didn't have much in common with a pre-schooler and a kindergarten child, but she'd been certain a couple of siblings would help Olivia feel they belonged together.

Olivia had only been fourteen months old when her mother died. Ellie knew the child didn't have any real memories of the woman and yet she clung to her mother's idealized memory with an almost unsettling fervor. It didn't help that Clayton had recently allowed his daughter to install a life-sized image of her mother in her bedroom. It hung on a huge canvas and took up most of one wall.

Ellie had bitten her tongue when the portrait made an appearance though she believed it was unhealthy to so blatantly feed Olivia's obsession with her late mother.

Ellie didn't know if informing Olivia that her mother had committed suicide would make any difference to the girl's adoration, but it wasn't Ellie's place to say anything and so far, Clayton hadn't shown any inclination to enlighten his daughter to the truth. Not that Ellie blamed him, but his daughter's fixation was going beyond the boundaries of normality and there was no question it was interfering with Ellie's ability to connect with her.

Knowing that the issues between them weren't going to be solved today, especially given the mood Olivia was in, Ellie took a deep breath, squared her shoulders and headed back toward the change rooms. There was no attendant near the entrance, so she walked on through. To her left and right stood a row of cubicles. Most of them were curtained off.

"Girls, how are you doing in there?" she asked. Her question was met with silence. Trying to stem her irritation, she lightened her tone and tried again.

"Olivia? Brittany?" She walked further inside the change room. "Olivia, I know that you're mad at me, but let's just find a swimsuit and get out of here. If you like, we can stop at Wendy's for an ice cream on our way home."

She hated offering the bribe, but right now, she was almost out of options. Short of opening each and every one of the curtains, she didn't know how else to find them.

"Come on, Olivia. They can't look that bad. Come out and show me."

There was still no answer. Ellie frowned and moved further along the left side of the change room. About halfway down, she glanced down and spied a sneaker-clad foot. It was twisted sideways and was just visible beneath the bottom of one of the curtains.

Although the shoe wasn't familiar, long-dormant instincts kicked in and her stomach clenched in premonition. She reached instinctively for the gun at her hip and came up empty.

It wasn't there. Of course it wasn't there. It hadn't been there for years. She'd given up being a detective right before Mitchell was born.

Heart pumping, she drew in a quick breath and tried not to jump to conclusions. With her jaw set and her lips compressed, she pulled back the curtain and gasped. Brittany Dowton lay slumped on the floor. Blood oozed from a nasty gash across her forehead.

Adrenaline surged through Ellie, propelling her to the floor. She immediately checked for a pulse and sighed in relief when she found one.

"Brittany? Honey, wake up. It's Mrs Munro." She slapped her lightly on the cheek, but the girl remained motionless.

She looked around the small cubicle. The full-piece swimsuits hung on a hook above her head. The hot-pink bikini lay crumpled on the floor. Olivia was nowhere to be seen.

"Olivia?" She tried to keep the panic from her voice. It wasn't easy. "Olivia?" she called again, striding into the corridor. She moved along the aisle, ripping open the curtains which covered the other cubicles. In one, a half-naked elderly woman gasped and tried to cover herself. Ellie mumbled an apology, barely noticing.

One after the other, she furiously tore back the curtains of every cubicle. *Nothing.*

"Olivia? Oh, my God! Olivia? Where are you? *Olivia?*" Her heart pounded. The sound of it echoed in her ears, surpassed only by the panic that thudded through her veins.

She stumbled back to the entry way and spied a young saleswoman. Clutching hold of the girl's arm, she cried, "Did you see her? My daughter? She's ten years old? About this high?" Ellie held her hand up near her chest.

The saleswoman frowned and shook her head back and forth, her gaze darting around in confusion. Desperation flooded through her.

"There were two of them. Two girls. You must have seen them go in. They came right past here. Blond hair, brown eyes. They both look fairly similar. They came in here to try on swimsuits. You must have seen them," Ellie uttered, more as a plea than a question.

"Right, now I remember. They went into room three."

Ellie's heart skipped a beat. "One of them came out. Did you see where she went?"

The woman shook her head. "No, I had to return some stock to the shelves. I was only gone five minutes though. Are you sure they're not still in there?"

Icy fingers clutched at Ellie's heart. She grabbed the woman by both arms and shook her, knowing she was frightening her, but unable to stop.

"She's *not* in there. My daughter's not in there. Her friend's in there and she's bleeding from a head wound. You need to call an ambulance. The police. Hurry! Something's happened. Someone's taken my baby!"

Releasing the saleswoman and shoving her out of the way, Ellie bolted through the store screaming Olivia's name. Years of training dissolved into mindless panic and she was beyond thinking rationally.

People stared at her, their eyes clouding with equal parts concern and curiosity. Confusion, fear and panic overwhelmed her. Her gaze snapped back and forth, searching, searching, searching...

Nothing. A wild keening sound started at the back of her throat and ripped through her mouth. With her legs no longer able to support her, she collapsed in a heap on the floor.

CHAPTER 2

Saturday, January 27, 9:50 a.m.

Detective Senior Sergeant Lane Black of the Chatswood Local Area Command scanned the half dozen new emails loading onto his computer screen and sighed. The usual assortment of jokes forwarded at least fifty times filled his inbox. He deleted the emails without giving them a second thought and wondered for the umpteenth time why people never bothered to write personal messages anymore. The jokes had been sent from various colleagues and friends—some of whom he hadn't seen for over a year or more and yet, they hadn't taken the time to type even a line or two of greeting or news.

He swallowed his irritation, knowing that it had become quicker and easier to simply forward the jokes rather than actually taking the time to write something meaningful. That's was just the way it was. Every day, technology made it easier to communicate and yet people seemed to be saying less and less.

An email from Katie Leeds, a detective stationed at the nearby station of Artarmon, caught his eye. He'd taken her out a few times and was he still gauging his interest. She was keen, but he wasn't the kind of guy that did commitment. The premature death of his father had seen to that. He never wanted to put himself in a position where he could be forced to abandon someone who relied on him. Besides, he still didn't know if he wanted the complication of getting involved with a work colleague.

Not that Katie worked for the State Crime Command, like he did, but the police who worked the streets of Sydney's northern suburbs were a close bunch and frequently socialized together. If things turned sour, his life could get difficult.

Still, it might be worth it. Katie was definitely a looker, with killer legs and bumps and curves in all the right places. Teamed with a smart mouth that hinted at a keen intelligence, she was pretty much the full package. A rare find, indeed. And yet, there was something holding him back. Refusing to contemplate that further, he clicked on her email and read the contents.

Saturday night, eight o'clock. Your place or mine?

Blood rushed to his groin. His cock hardened. Tugging his keyboard toward him, he replied with a single word.

Mine.

"Lane, got a minute? You too, Jett. My office."

Lane stared at the retreating back of Detective Superintendent Michael Collins. His boss was always taciturn. It wasn't the handful of words he'd spoken that snagged Lane's attention. It was the way he'd said them. And the look on his face. *Something was up.*

He shot his partner a questioning look. Detective Jett Craigdon pushed back the hank of black hair that had fallen across his forehead and shrugged, looking as mystified as Lane felt. Pushing away from their desks, the men made their way to the boss' office.

Michael's face was grave. "Emergency call just came in. Young girl's gone missing from Myers at Westfield in Chatswood. Kid's clothing department. Level three. Ambulance is on its way."

Lane frowned. "Ambulance?"

"Yeah, another kid was injured in the attack."

"We got any names?" Jett asked.

"Brittany Dowton and Olivia Munro."

Jett pursed his lips. "Dowton. Any relation to the State Attorney General?"

Michael gave a brisk nod. "His daughter. But it appears she wasn't the target."

A cold feeling of foreboding stole into Lane's veins. "Who's Olivia Munro?"

"She's the daughter of Clayton Munro."

Lane's heart sank, but he had to make sure. "The criminal profiler from the Australian Federal Police?"

Michael's lips compressed. "Afraid so. Been with the AFP more than a decade. Relocated to Sydney earlier this month. One of the finest profilers in the country. More than that, he's a damned nice bloke."

Lane's head spun. "He's a friend of mine, along with his wife, Ellie, and his brother, Tom. Tom's a police negotiator based in North Sydney," he muttered.

Michael looked grim. "Both of you get on over there, ask questions. Given the people involved, as of now, we're treating it as a kidnapping at best." He paused and eyed them solemnly. "At worst, an act of terrorism."

Lane tapped the steering wheel of his unmarked police vehicle and waited for the traffic to clear. Even with his lights and siren blazing, the Saturday morning traffic remained obstinately heavy. A car accelerated beside him, blocking his path and he bit back a savage curse.

"Easy, partner. We don't want to arrive in pieces."

With compressed lips, Lane tossed a sideways glance toward Jett who filled the passenger seat with his bulk.

"I'd be happy just to arrive. Did you see that asshole? What the hell are we coming to when lights and a siren don't even make an impact?" He shook his head in wordless disgust.

Jett turned to stare out of the window. "Do we know who else is at the scene? Has it been secured?"

"The boss said a couple of general duty officers responded to the call. They should be there already. Let's hope they've done their job."

Swinging into the bus terminal situated on the lower level of the shopping mall, Lane pulled up alongside the curb. He flung off his seatbelt and climbed out of the car, heading toward Westfield at a jog, Jett right behind him.

Lane caught sight of Ellie Munro, seated near the change rooms of the children's department and moved quickly toward her. She turned and spied him approaching and leaped to her feet. Racing to his side, she grabbed his sleeve.

"Oh, thank God! Lane, you have to help me. Someone's taken my baby. Someone's taken Olivia!"

Despite her years of police training and more than her fair share of horrifying experiences, Ellie was ashen. Black rivulets of mascara ran down her cheeks. Her breath came fast. Panic clouded her eyes.

Lane fought back the urge to hold her. Though she was the wife of his friend, right now, she was a witness and he was the lead investigator. As gently as he could, he removed his arm from her grasp and led her back to the chair she'd vacated. A young female store clerk stood nearby, wringing her hands.

Jett came up beside him and murmured, "The paramedics have already taken Brittany Dowton to Royal North Shore Hospital. We'll have to speak with her there."

Lane frowned. "They didn't waste time. Is she all right?"

"Yeah, apparently she's conscious but she has a nasty graze on her forehead. They're taking her in for observation. Given who she is—"

"Of course. They'd rather play it safe. I guess that's understandable." Lane indicated Ellie with his chin. "That's Ellie Munro, Olivia's mother. See if you can round up any staff members that were in the vicinity at the time the girl disappeared. You never know who might have seen something. I'd start with that young girl over there."

He looked toward the young store clerk who had remained standing near Ellie's chair. "And get someone to locate the security vision."

"Sure thing." Jett moved away and tugged a notebook out of his jacket pocket. Lane drew in a deep breath and let it out slowly, steeling himself for what was to come. He walked back to Ellie and kneeled beside her. Taking her hands in his, he gave them a reassuring squeeze.

"Ellie, you need to take some deep breaths and listen to me. Have you called Clayton?" Her gaze lowered and she nodded.

"I take it he's on his way?"

"Yes, yes of course. He's been at home with the boys. I-I was supposed to be taking Olivia shopping."

Her voice caught on the last word. Lane felt for her, but right now he had a job to do.

"Ellie, I need to know everything. Everything you saw. Everything you heard. Can you tell me?"

She stared down at her hands where they were clenched in her lap, and finally nodded.

"Get out of my way! Where the hell are they?"

Ellie's head snapped up and her eyes widened in distress. Clayton Munro stormed toward them, his eyes dark with barely concealed panic.

Ellie slowly came to her feet. Lane stepped forward and held out his hand in somber greeting. Clayton shook Lane's hand, his expression grim. "Lane. Thank Christ you're here."

Lane nodded in acknowledgement and looked from him to Ellie. She'd moved a short distance away and now had her arms folded across her chest, her gaze pinned to the floor. Nervous tension radiated from her in waves.

Glancing back at Clayton, Lane cleared his throat and directed his first question to Ellie. "I have to ask you what happened. I need you to tell me every detail you remember."

He moved closer to her and tugged out his notebook. Without warning, Clayton turned on her.

"See, this is what I don't get. How can you lose a child on a *shopping* trip? For Christ sake, how does that *happen?*"

Ellie shook her head and pushed her fist against her mouth. Lane gaped in surprise. Tom had hinted the two of them were having difficulties, but the confronting anger in Clayton's eyes came as a shock. Fear made people react in extraordinary ways, but Clayton was a trained police officer, with years of experience. He ought to know better than to let his emotions take control. Lane cleared his throat, a little nervous at the thought of what he was going to have to do.

"Ellie, I'd like you to have a seat and take some time to think about what you saw. It's very important you think about everything you remember, no matter how insignificant. I'm going to give you a few moments alone while I talk to Clayton. Is that all right?"

Ellie nodded, her eyes wide and uncertain. The instinctive urge to offer her comfort rose up inside him again, but he resolutely pushed it away and focused on what had to be done. He led Clayton a short distance away and took advantage of a wide rack of clothing to muffle their conversation.

"Talk to me, Clayton. What's going on?"

Clayton paced the short confines of the aisle beside them, anger apparent in every line of his body. Running a hand through his disheveled, blond hair, he groaned aloud his frustration.

"It's Ellie. She and Olivia haven't been getting along. They've been arguing about the stupidest things every minute of the day. Every time I turn around, they're at each other. I had no idea it had gotten to this; that Ellie couldn't even be bothered to watch out for her."

Lane frowned. "That seems a bit harsh, mate. You can't possibly believe Ellie has anything to do with her disappearance? Besides, the last few times I saw Olivia, she wasn't making things easy."

Clayton cursed savagely. "She's ten years old, Lane. You

can hardly expect her to act with the maturity of an adult. That's Ellie's job."

"From what I saw last week when you were over at Tom's, it was Olivia who was the one pushing away. All she talked to me about was her dead mother."

Clayton closed his eyes. His lips thinned.

"Does Olivia know Lisa committed suicide?"

Clayton turned on him, his eyes blazing. "Of course not! How the fuck could I tell her something like that? She idolizes her mother!"

Lane forced himself to remain calm. "Her mother's dead."

"So?"

"One day, she'll find out how it happened."

"Not from me."

Drawing in a deep breath, Lane exhaled slowly and opened his notebook to a fresh page. "When Ellie called you, did she say anything about what happened?"

Clayton shook his head abruptly. "Just that they were in the swimwear department and she'd argued with Olivia about what kind of swimsuit she could have. Olivia went to the change rooms with her friend, Brittany Dowton."

"Brittany's been taken to the hospital." He held up his hand to ward off the questions he saw in Clayton's eyes. "She's fine. A knock to the head. They've taken her in as a precautionary measure."

"Thank God for that. David Dowton would have my balls if anything happened to his daughter."

"I'll talk to her as soon as I can and find out what she knows. Let's keep going. What else did Ellie tell you?"

Clayton turned away and resumed his pacing. "Ellie says she waited outside the change rooms. The first time she knew something was wrong was when she went in to check on the girls and found Brittany unconscious on the floor. There was no sign of Olivia."

"That's it?"

"Yeah, that's it. I called the neighbors and asked them to watch the boys for me and then I hightailed it over here."

Lane glanced across the top of the clothing rack to

where Ellie sat hunched over the chair. Her face was drawn and pale, her eyes red and swollen. Turning back to Clayton, he noticed the tension in his friend's jaw and the anger that still lingered in his eyes.

Lane's gut tightened. He hated to see them so at odds with each other. He'd known Clayton's older brother, Tom, for years. The two of them were stationed in neighboring Local Area Commands in Sydney. He'd spent many a night on the couch at Tom and his wife Lily's, recovering after a big night out.

It was through Tom that Lane had met some of Tom's brothers, including Clayton. As one of the country's top criminal profilers, Clayton was often seconded to assist some of the most difficult State investigations and had usually stayed with Tom during his visits to Sydney.

Although Clayton's first wife had died before Lane met her, he still recalled how shattered his friend's brother had been and how concerned the Munro family had been for Clayton's welfare.

He'd also been privy to Clayton's relationship with Ellie Cooper. Tom had shared the news of his brother's marriage to the New South Wales detective with unbridled joy. At last, his brother had come out from under the black cloud that had followed him since his first wife's death and had learned to love again.

It was something straight out of the movies and far too sappy for Lane to get excited about, but it had made his friend happy and had put a smile back on Clayton's face and for that, he was grateful to the woman who'd made it happen.

The obvious strain between them was so different from their usual happy family unit—tensions with Olivia aside. He was used to watching Clayton and Ellie interact with each other and had felt envious over their closeness, their ability to sense the other's needs without a word spoken.

He'd thought that kind of thing existed in the realm of fantasy, to be found only between the covers of sappy romance books, but he'd witnessed it himself and had come to the conclusion that it not only existed, but was worth waiting for.

But now wasn't the time to be wasting thoughts on things like that. A little girl was missing. Every hour she stayed away, lessened their chances of finding her alive. He cleared his throat and spoke again.

"I'm going to talk to Ellie. I'd prefer it if you stayed here, out of the way. I need her to remember everything she can think of. With you standing over her, glowering and ready to bite her head off any minute, she's likely to forget. You don't want us to miss something important."

Anger flared again in Clayton's eyes and his fists clenched. He opened his mouth as if to protest. Lane stared at him, hard. Clayton's mouth closed and he turned away. Spinning on his heel, Lane made his way back to Ellie's side. Kneeling again, he flipped over to a fresh page in his notebook.

"Okay, Ellie, let's start again. What time did you arrive at the mall?"

"A-about nine-thirty."

"And you came straight here?"

"Yes."

"Did you notice anything unusual when you walked into the shop?"

She shook her head and shrugged. "No, not that I recall."

"What about any men?"

"No one that stood out. We were in the children's clothing department. It's mostly filled with moms and their kids. I think I would have noticed a man."

Ellie had once been a well-respected detective with the New South Wales Police Service. It may have been a few years since she'd been on the job, but Lane had no doubt her observation skills were still sharp.

"You were shopping for swimsuits, is that right?"

"Yes." Ellie's lip trembled and tears flooded her eyes. "It's all my fault," she cried. "Olivia's missing and it's *my* fault!"

Lane stilled, wanting to offer her comfort, but at the same time, needing to know what had happened. "Why do you say that?" he asked, striving to keep his voice neutral.

"I was supposed to be looking *after* her! She was my responsibility!" Her voice cracked, but she sucked in a breath and continued.

"We had a stupid argument over a bikini. I let my anger get the better of me. Olivia stormed off with Brittany to the change rooms and I...I moved away. I had to put some space between us."

A sob escaped and tears coursed down her cheeks. She brushed them away and stood, turning away from Lane. Rubbing her hands up and down her thighs, she paced the length of the change rooms and then spun around to face him.

"I'm thirty-three years old! I should have had more self-control. When I calmed down, I was across the other side, over in the bedding department. By the time I got back to the change rooms, Olivia was gone."

Lane puffed out his breath on a sigh, his head reeling. "You haven't told Clay this?"

Ellie shook her head vehemently. "He already blames me for not taking proper care of her. If he knew I'd—" A sound of agony was wrenched from her throat. Her shoulders shook.

Lane got to his feet, unable to sit by another second and watch her fall apart. He gave her a hard hug then stepped away. Still, he continued to hold her gaze, silently urging her to overcome the emotion that tore her up inside.

"Ellie, listen to me," he said quietly. "I may not be speaking from experience, but anyone who's ever done it knows how difficult it is to raise someone else's child. From what Clayton's told me, things have been a little tense between you and Olivia for a while. It's not your fault, Ellie. You need to stop thinking like that and focus your efforts on trying to remember something, *anything* that might help us find her."

Ellie drew in a ragged breath and scrubbed her fingers through her short cap of dark hair. "Ever since it happened, I've been wracking my brain trying to think, rewinding the scene in my mind over and over again."

"Do you remember what Olivia was wearing?"

"White shorts and a pink Katy Perry T-shirt.

"What kind of shoes was she wearing?"

"A pair of Havaianas."

Lane frowned. "Havaianas?"

"Yes. An upscale flip flop. They're silver and have some sparkly faux jewels glued along the straps," she added.

Lane took note of the clothing. "Is there anything else you can tell me? Anything at all?"

Ellie shook her head, tears brimming in her eyes. "No. I wish there was. God, you can't know how much I wish there was."

Her shoulders hunched and sobs shook her body. Lane stood and caught Clayton's eye, motioning him over.

Clayton moved closer and came to a halt by Ellie's side, but made no move to offer her comfort. Lane broke the tense silence.

"Do either of you have any idea who might be behind this? Clayton, is there anything you're working on that could have upset someone? You've been involved in some pretty high profile cases recently."

Clayton cursed. "Yeah, but most of them are based in Canberra. I've barely had time to set up my desk in Sydney. Besides, what do you want me to say? The kind of scum I deal with every day..." He laughed without humor. "Pick a name, it could be any number of people. Kevin Fernandez, wife and baby killer, mouthed off at me with obscene threats only two days ago when I attended his sentencing hearing. Threatened everyone related to me. Do I think he was serious?" Clayton shook his head in disgust. "Of course he was, but no more serious than all the others."

Lane pressed his lips together and nodded. "All right, what about Olivia? Has she been having trouble with anyone?"

"Nothing that she's complained about," Ellie replied. "We've only been living in Sydney three weeks and she's been on school holidays all that time. Not that she'd confide in me if she was," Ellie added with a grimace.

Lane turned to Clayton, who shrugged. "Don't ask me, I'm just her father."

"What about you, Ellie?" Lane said, changing tack. "Can you think of anyone who might be bearing a grudge against you?"

She shook her head. "I've been out of the field for more than five years, Lane. I doubt it has anything to do with me."

Lane was inclined to agree with her. "I think you're right. If anyone's involved in this, I think it's more likely to be from Clayton's end."

Clayton ran a hand through his hair. "Christ, I can't believe I brought this on my daughter."

"I'm not saying that," Lane said. "At this stage, we don't know anything for certain, but hell, it's the most likely scenario."

Clayton's shoulders slumped in defeat. "As much as it pains me to say it, I think you're right." He sighed and moved closer to Ellie. "So, what do we do now?"

Lane closed his notebook. "I'll call the boss and get him to organize some phone taps. If this is about money, when the ransom call comes in, we want to be able to trace it."

Ellie stiffened and her eyes went wide. She shook her head in disbelief. Lane felt her pain. His voice softened. "I'm sorry, Ellie. I wish to God you didn't have to go through this." His look encompassed Clayton who stood silent and tense, his face like weathered granite.

"You know the drill," Lane added. "The techies should be at your house within the hour."

He offered his hand to Clayton, who shook it. "Thanks for coming, Lane. I'll go home and start looking into possibilities. We will narrow this down somehow."

Lane nodded and then turned and hugged Ellie again. "We'll find her. We're not going to rest until we do."

Ellie barely acknowledged his comment. Fresh tears flooded her eyes. Clayton moved closer and awkwardly patted her shoulder. With nothing further to add, Lane left them to their pain.

CHAPTER 3

Saturday, January 27, 11:55 a.m.

Lane strode into the station and tossed his keys onto his desk. Following close behind him, Jett threw himself down in his chair with a sigh and stacked his hands behind his head.

"I don't get it," he said. "How could one girl be knocked out and another completely disappear and no one see or hear a thing? How does that work?"

Lane sympathized with the exasperation that lined his partner's voice. He felt the same way. He looked up when Michael Collins strode toward them, his expression grim.

"Lane, Jett. How'd it go with the Munro case?"

Lane shook his head. "Not much, yet. I've interviewed Ellie Munro who was with the girls at the store. She didn't see the attack and so far, she can't remember anything useful."

"Ditto for the shop assistants," Jett added.

"We've asked the store manager to provide us with the morning's security tapes. He's getting them together."

"Pity there aren't any cameras in the change rooms," Michael muttered.

"Yeah," Lane said, "but we're hoping we may spot something out of place. The person or persons responsible must have entered the store some way—probably the same way they left. We know roughly what time Olivia Munro was taken. We might be lucky enough to spot them on camera."

"Good," Collins replied. "Let's hope so. I've organized for a group of technicians to head over to the Munro house. They should be there shortly. In the meantime, I want you to take a ride over to the Attorney General's house. He called a few moments ago. His daughter's been released from hospital and is now back home. He wants to talk to us. Something about him believing his daughter might have been the target."

Lane frowned. "Why would he think that?"

"Wouldn't say. Just asked for someone to go over to his house and talk to him. Pronto. His words, not mine. If there's a possibility the AG's involved, we'll need to form a joint taskforce with the AFP. Given that the child taken belongs to one of their own, I'm sure they'll be keen to be part of this, but let's find out what's going on first." He handed Lane a piece of paper.

"Here's the AG's address. Find out why he thinks his daughter could have been the target. I'll let him know you're on your way. Jett, chase up those security tapes. The sooner we take a look at them, the sooner we'll know who we're dealing with."

Lane glanced at the piece of paper he'd taken from his boss. The address was listed in Point Piper, one of Sydney's most prestigious suburbs. He stowed it in his shirt pocket.

"I don't need to remind you how sensitive this is, Lane," Collins added. "Having one of the AFP's top profilers involved is bad enough. Throw the AG into it and it's fast becoming a PR nightmare. Dowton's been in the media a lot lately spouting off about law reform and not everyone's happy about it. Until we know who's involved in this, we have to keep things tight."

Lane eyed him solemnly. "You can rely on me, boss."

———————

The midmorning traffic was heavier than usual, but Lane

made good time crossing the Harbour Bridge. He joined the flow of traffic heading toward Sydney's eastern suburbs. The sun shone clear and bright across the sapphire blue of the Pacific Ocean, sending blinding shards of light off the water. A scattering of yachts and the occasional iconic mustard-and-green-colored ferry decorated the harbor, packed with carefree weekenders.

It was a view Lane never tired of and one he wished he could afford. His two-bedroom condo, situated on the busy Pacific Highway only minutes from the Chatswood train station might have been convenient to work, but was a far cry from the luxury and old-world opulence of the lower north shore and eastern suburbs, where architecturally designed mansions with views of the harbor bunkered down behind high brick fences—with nary a train track in sight.

Still, his condo was comfortable and didn't stretch his modest salary to its limit and the double glazed windows took care of almost all of the noise from the busy highway below. Besides, with his crazy work schedule often comprising multiple twelve-hour shifts, it was really only a place to crash and recover for the next bout.

Not that he regretted his career choice. Being a cop was all he ever wanted. He'd entered the Academy straight out of high school and graduated a year later with honors, ready to conquer the world.

More than a decade later, most days he still felt invincible. He'd been smart and he'd been lucky. He'd worked hard and had come up the ranks with enviable speed and even though he'd been caught in some sticky situations, he'd managed to come out unscathed.

Well, relatively. Give or take a few cuts and bruises and the seventeen stitches he'd received in his bicep after coming up close and personal with a burglar high on crystal meth and wielding a razor-sharp machete.

He turned onto Stafford Drive, a cul de sac off New South Head Road and looked for the number Michael had written on the paper. It was the third house along, although to call it a house was an understatement.

Like all of the other houses in the street, there was only part of it visible from the sidewalk. A high rendered fence, painted in the same shade of taupe as the house, shielded most of it from view. A set of double, black iron gates guarded the driveway.

Lane turned into the entryway and came to a halt. Pressing the button located on a steel panel set at eye level on the gate wall, he announced his presence. Moments later, the gates swung inward on well-oiled hinges.

Huge Moreton Bay figs that looked more than a century old graced at least an acre of well-manicured lawn and provided shade to a number of symmetrical flower beds that burst with color. Two gardeners labored with hedge clippers and secateurs, their full-brimmed hats bearing the brunt of the noonday sun.

Lane's unmarked vehicle crept along the winding, paved driveway. He surveyed the grandeur of the house before him. Three storeys of brick and sandstone towered above him, looking like something out of Hollywood Hills. To his left, the driveway peeled off and led to a garage that was big enough to house four motor vehicles. He'd always assumed the Attorney General made a good living, but this was way beyond his imaginings.

Continuing along the right fork, he headed toward a parking bay situated outside the main building and brought the car to a stop. He climbed out and was assailed by the sweet scent of roses and honeysuckle that hung heavily on the air.

Almost immediately, Lane's nose twitched and his eyes began to water. He grappled for his handkerchief and caught the sneeze seconds before it exploded. He was still sneezing several minutes later when the imposing double entry doors opened inward to reveal a slight woman with graying hair and kind eyes. The white apron she wore over her navy uniform regaled her to the position of housekeeper.

"You must be the detective. Come in. Mr Dowton's expecting you. I'll let him know you're here."

"Thank you," he managed, wiping his eyes with the back of his hand.

The housekeeper looked at him curiously for a moment and then nodded in understanding. "Hay fever."

Lane nodded and grimaced. "Chronic."

The interior of David Dowton's mansion was just as impressive as the exterior. Original artworks from some of Australia's most reputable artists lined the sandstone walls. Sparkling chandeliers hung from the twenty-foot ceilings and an enormous Persian rug, in muted hues of cream and burgundy, covered the polished concrete floor that led from the entryway into a large, open concept living room.

Lane waited in silence for the housekeeper's return. A light breeze drifted in through an open window on the far side of the room, bringing with it the verdant scent of the garden. He braced himself for another bout of sneezes.

A few moments later, the woman reappeared, her rubber-soled shoes making no sound. "The Attorney General will see you now. Please, come with me."

Lane followed her through the living room and into what he assumed was Dowton's office. Floor-to-ceiling shelves laden with books lined one wall. An enormous, red cedar desk cluttered with an untidy assortment of papers dominated the room. Sunlight poured in through the tall windows and cast the face of the man who sat behind the desk into shadow. Although he'd seen the Attorney General countless times on the television, Lane had never met the man in the flesh. David Dowton stood as Lane entered and came toward him with his hand outstretched.

"Detective Black, thank you for coming. I appreciate your quick response."

Lane shook the proffered hand and eyed the Attorney General with interest. Of medium stature, Dowton's light-brown hair was liberally streaked with gray, but the strength in his forearm and the tautness of his belly beneath his tailored business shirt indicated a level of discipline rarely seen in men who had passed their prime.

"What can I do for you, Attorney General?"

"Please, call me David. And take a seat," he added, indicating a pair of richly upholstered, black leather armchairs that stood opposite the desk.

The Attorney General returned to his seat. Lane followed suit. His gaze snagged on a pair of matching photo frames that graced the overcrowded desk.

"My daughters," David supplied, noticing Lane's interest. Picking up one of the frames, the man turned it so that Lane could take a better look. "This is Zara, my eldest."

Lane looked at the photo and tried to contain his surprise. The girl looked about eighteen or nineteen and was unmistakably of Filipino heritage. Her midnight black hair framed an oval face and fell in long, straight waves to below her waist. She was smiling at the camera, displaying a set of perfect white teeth.

Unable to help himself, Lane reached for the photo frame and examined the picture more closely. His stomach somersaulted. The girl seemed to look right into his soul.

"She's beautiful," he murmured, handing the picture back.

The Attorney General took the photo and smiled with pride. "Yes, she is. This was taken a few years ago, on the night of her high school graduation. She finished top of her year."

"You must be very proud of her."

"I am. I'm proud of both of my daughters."

Setting Zara's picture down, the Attorney General picked up the other one. Staring at the photo, his lips compressed and his eyes filled with emotion. "And this is my baby. This is Brittany."

He handed the frame across the desk and once again, Lane was forced to contain his surprise. Brittany Dowton looked nothing like her sister. A cloud of golden blond curls framed the tiny heart-shaped face of a child who looked about four or five. The only similarity between the sisters was their dark brown eyes. Brittany stared out at the photographer, her eyes alight with mischief.

"I know what you're thinking. My girls, they're like night and day. Zara's mother was my first wife, Anna. She died in childbirth a few hours after Zara was born." He rubbed his forehead with the back of his hand. "God, I can't believe it's been twenty-five years."

Lane refrained from offering commiserations and waited for the Attorney General to continue.

"I met my second wife, Allison, eleven years ago. Brittany's our little girl."

Lane nodded and recalled the information he'd been supplied on his way to the scene. "She's ten."

"Yes, Britt turned ten a couple of months ago. As you can see, this photo was also taken a long time ago. I really should update them," he murmured, almost as an aside.

Lane sat forward, ready to get down to business. "Tell me what happened this morning."

Dowton sighed, his expression troubled. He steepled his fingers and rested his forehead on them, staring down at his desk. He didn't look up when he spoke.

"Brittany went to the Westfield Mall today with her friend, Olivia Munro and Olivia's mother, Ellie. Stepmother, actually," he corrected.

"Yes, I know them."

The Attorney General lifted his head, momentarily surprised. "Really? They haven't been in Sydney long."

"That's right, but I've known Clayton Munro for years, along with some of his brothers. They're all in law enforcement."

"Oh, then you know him better than I do. Brittany and Olivia became friends only recently. We met through mutual friends. The girls have been spending a lot of time together during the school holidays. I've only met Clayton a couple of times. It's usually Ellie who's in charge of the play dates. I understand Clayton's a highly respected profiler with the AFP?"

"The best in Australia," Lane agreed, regarding him steadily.

The Attorney General fussed over the papers on his desk. "Yes, well, I can't imagine what he and Ellie are going through. I mean, their daughter seems to have vanished into thin air. One minute she was there and the next, she was gone."

Lane kept his heart rate even. "You've spoken to Brittany."

Dowton nodded. "Yes, briefly. She's still quite shaken. I'm sure you understand."

"Of course," Lane agreed. "You'd better start from the beginning."

The Attorney General folded his hands on the desk in front of him and sighed. "Ellie called last night to invite Brittany to go to the mall with her and Olivia. It's something the girls have done at least three or four times over the holidays. They usually go to a movie. Ellie collected Brittany about eight-thirty this morning."

"Where were they going?"

"To Chatswood Chase. As far as I know, they were shopping in Myer when Olivia disappeared."

"I've already spoken with Ellie. She's verified your information." Lane cleared his throat, wanting to cut to the chase. "When you called Detective Superintendent Collins, you said you thought Brittany might have been the target. I agree that the girls look alike. Are you saying you think it's a case of mistaken identity?"

Dowton averted his gaze. After a slight hesitation, he nodded.

"What makes you think that? I assume Brittany's okay?"

"Yes, thank God!" The Attorney General's relief was palpable. "Apart from a graze on her forehead. She was given the okay by the doctors. I brought her home and then called your superior."

"Where is she now?"

"Resting upstairs. I asked Zara to sit with her." He pushed his hair back off his forehead and sighed. "Allison is visiting her sister interstate. I called her to let her know what's happened. She's anxiously waiting to catch the next flight home. Unfortunately, there's only one flight in and one flight out a day, but she'll be here as soon as she can."

"I'll have to interview Brittany."

"Of course. I understand. I'll send word up to Zara." He picked up the phone near his elbow and spoke quietly to the person on the other end.

Lane tugged a notebook out of his pocket and jotted down some notes. When the Attorney General had finished on the phone, Lane spoke again.

"You still haven't explained why you think your daughter was the target."

"I'm sure you've read it in the papers, or heard it on the news. I'm pushing for tougher controls on outlaw motorcycle gangs. They've had a free run in this State for far too long. It's time we clawed back whatever power we can."

"You won't get any argument from me. All of us are right behind you. The sooner the better."

"Yes, well unfortunately, not everyone feels that way. I'm ashamed to admit that if I'd had the slightest inkling my actions could cause so much angst, I'd have been a little more cautious."

Foreboding trickled through Lane's veins, followed by a surge of impatience. He wanted to shout at the man, to shake the words out of him. Olivia Munro was missing. Every second counted.

"I'm still at a loss to connect this with the disappearance of Olivia Munro. With all due respect, Attorney General—David—you need to get to the point. A little girl is missing. Her parents are sick with worry."

"Of course. I'm sorry. I'm not doing a very good job of explaining myself." He drew in a breath and scrubbed at his face with his hands.

"Last night, I-I took a call from an unidentified male. It was late. I was trying to catch up on paperwork. He warned me about continuing with my quest for the proposed law reforms. He told me there would be consequences. He implied my family was at risk."

Lane frowned. "Did you recognize the caller? Did you report the call?"

"No. The voice wasn't familiar. I couldn't place it. But the threat sounded legitimate. It shook me up. I couldn't sleep for hours."

"And you think he might have been a member of an outlaw motorcycle gang?"

Dowton shrugged, impatience in his eyes. "I don't know. You're the detective. But that's my guess. Who has the most to gain if these reforms disappear? No one has been more vocal about them than I have. What I do know is that last night I received a threatening phone call and the very next day, my daughter's attacked and her friend disappears."

"Why would they take Olivia?"

The Attorney General briefly closed his eyes and drew in another breath. "As I said, I think they made a mistake. The girls look alike." He spoke slowly, enunciating every word, as if he were talking to a simpleton.

Lane's anger stirred at the AG's tone, even though he understood the man's frustration. He thought back to the last time he'd seen Olivia. It hadn't been that long ago; the girls definitely shared a number of similarities. The photo of Brittany was dated, but he assumed her fair coloring and cloud of blond hair hadn't changed. To someone unfamiliar with either of the girls, it could have been a simple mistake to make.

"I'd like to speak with Brittany now, if you don't mind."

"Of course. I've already asked Mrs Harrow to let the girls know you're here. It might be best if we go upstairs. I don't think Britt's up to coming down."

"That's fine."

The Attorney General pushed away from his desk and Lane did the same. He followed Dowton through his office and into the airy living room. An ornate marble staircase stood off to the left. Their footsteps were muffled by a rich, gold-and-navy carpet stair runner. More valuable art works lined the wall. Lane wondered again about the Attorney General's prosperity.

"You have great taste in art, David."

"Thank you. Most of them I inherited from my father. He was one of the founding fathers of Sydney Legal. He was the reason I went into law. Among other things, he prided himself on having an eye for art. He was a collector."

Lane relaxed. Dowton came from old money. That explained the opulence. It wasn't at all what he'd been thinking.

Turning right at the landing, the Attorney General came to a stop outside the second door along and tapped his knuckles on the closed panel. It was opened almost immediately.

CHAPTER 4

Saturday, January, 27, 12:20 p.m.

Lane gasped. A strikingly beautiful woman who barely came up to his chest stared back at him. Although she bore a close resemblance to the photo he'd seen on her father's desk, Zara Dowton had done some growing up since her high school graduation.

She wore a knee length dress made out of some kind of floaty floral fabric. It was cinched in at the waist with a matching belt and caressed her slender curves. A pale gray silk scarf embroidered with fine silver thread circled her neck. The form-fitting bodice emphasized the generous swell of her breasts, but it was her eyes that held him arrested.

So dark they were almost black, their perfect almond shape widened at the sight of him and flared with an indefinable emotion. Lane stood rooted to the spot, unable to drag his gaze away. The Attorney General broke the spell when he cleared his throat and addressed her.

"Zara, this is Detective Black. He's here to speak with Brittany."

The woman angled her head in Lane's direction and offered him the slightest nod before she returned her attention to her father.

"She's still in shock, Dad. I don't know how much she'll be

able to help you." The last was directed toward Lane. He finally found his voice.

"I won't be long, but I'm sure you understand how imperative it is we find out what she remembers."

Zara nodded and turned away. Lane followed her into the room. The scent of orange blossom and jasmine trailed in her wake. It smelled as exotic as the woman who wore it. He filled his nostrils and then silently berated himself, hoping it wouldn't set off another bout of hay fever.

A blond-haired princess lay curled up on a huge four poster bed which was decorated in reams of pink and white fabric. An iPod dock sat on the white cane nightstand, along with a remote control, presumably to the huge flat-screen TV fixed to the wall opposite.

Lane approached the bed with caution, feeling more than a little out of his depth in the girly room. He was the oldest of four boys. Pink had not been a color of prominence in his family home. Even now, his condo reflected his solitary male existence. Sparsely furnished, it was a place to rest and recover from the events of the day. Nothing more, nothing less.

Occasionally, he'd let a woman sleep over for the night, but that was the extent of his willingness to cohabitate. It didn't do to get too attached when he had no intention of turning it into a permanent commitment. That was something that worried him about accepting another date with Katie Leeds. It was obvious she wanted to share more than a meal with him. It probably wasn't fair to let it go any further without having 'the talk.'

His gaze strayed to Zara and then flicked quickly away when she caught him looking at her. He quelled the sudden surge of interest that pumped straight to his groin, and attempted to focus on the girl in the bed.

"Hi, Brittany. My name's Lane. I need to talk to you about what happened this morning at the mall. Olivia's missing, Brittany. We need to find her. Do you think you can help me?"

A tiny nod was the only sign that she'd heard him.

"I know this is difficult for you, but it's really important that you to tell me everything you remember."

It took the young girl a few moments to respond. She turned her head on the pillow and looked toward her sister. Zara gave her an encouraging smile. Brittany's gaze slid back to Lane.

"I'll try," she whispered.

Uncurling her slight body, she reached for Zara's hand and clung to it. The older girl leaned over and smoothed back the golden halo of hair from Brittany's forehead.

"Just take it slowly, sweetheart," she murmured.

Brittany took a huge breath and exhaled with a shudder. Lane stepped closer and perched on the end of the bed, his notebook and pen at the ready.

"Your dad said you went shopping in Chatswood this morning with Olivia and her mom. Is that right?"

Brittany nodded. "Stepmom, actually."

Lane bit down on his irritation. No one could ask for a better mom than Ellie. Pressing on, he tried again. "Did you buy anything?"

Brittany shook her head.

"Did you stop anywhere? Like for an ice cream or a milkshake?"

"No."

"Tell me what happened," he urged as gently as he could.

Brittany compressed her lips, as if debating about whether to reply. At last, she spoke.

"We went to Myer. It was our first stop. Olivia wanted to get a bikini."

"Did she find one?"

Brittany shook her head. "Her mom—I mean, her *step*mom said she wasn't buying her a bikini. She made her try on some full-pieces. Olivia argued with her, but Mrs Munro wouldn't give in. Olivia snuck a bikini into the pile of swimsuits Mrs Munro gave her and we went to the change rooms." Brittany fell silent and turned her face toward her sister, clutching at Zara's hand.

"It's okay, baby," Zara reassured her. "It's okay."

"What happened then?" Lane asked, after the girl had calmed a little.

"We...we were in one of the cubicles. Olivia had just started to take off her T-shirt." She stopped and bit her lip. Tears glinted in her eyes.

Zara sat beside her on the bed and put her arms around her. Brittany sniffled and leaned into her.

"Did the cubicle have a door, Brittany?" Lane asked.

The young girl shook her head. "No, just a curtain," she whispered, her voice muffled against her sister's dress.

"What happened?" Lane asked again, trying not to rush her, but aware that every moment Olivia remained missing dramatically decreased her odds of being found alive. It was common knowledge the first forty-eight hours after a kidnapping were crucial. As far as he'd been able to ascertain, she'd already been gone for nearly three.

"Th-there was a man. He...he ripped open the curtain."

"What did he look like?" Lane urged.

Brittany shook her head back and forth in distress. "I don't know. I don't know. I don't know."

Lane bit down hard on his impatience. "Okay, Brittany. Let's take it slowly. Was he tall?"

The girl nodded.

"As tall as me?"

She nodded again.

"What color hair did he have?"

"None."

"What do you mean? Was he bald?"

"Yes. No. Kind of. I think his head was shaved."

"Did you notice his eyes?"

"No."

"Did he have a beard?"

"Yes."

"A heavy beard? All over his face?"

"No, a beard like Dad gets when he hasn't shaved for a while. But he looked scary. And mean."

Lane jotted the information into his notebook. "What was he wearing?"

"I-I can't remember."

"You're doing really well, Brittany. Take your time and think really hard."

The young girl squeezed her eyes closed. A few moments later, she spoke again, her voice quiet and uncertain.

"He...he wore a leather jacket. A black one. It was open."

"That's great, Brittany. Anything else?"

"A black T-shirt with some kind of picture on the front—and jeans. I remember thinking he must be hot in all those clothes."

Lane scribbled again. "What else can you remember, Brittany?"

She frowned. "He had weird skin. It looked really rough and had little holes in it. And a tattoo. A redback spider on his hand."

"That's great, Brittany. You're doing great. Do you remember which hand?"

"His left hand, I think."

Lane's gut tightened. Although not uncommon, it was a symbol used by one of Sydney's notorious outlaw motorcycle gangs. *Perhaps the Attorney General's on the mark?*

Pushing the speculation aside, he concentrated on the girl in the bed. "Okay, Brittany, you're doing really well. Now, this may be a little bit scary, but I need you to try and think as hard as you can about what happened next."

Brittany looked up at him, her eyes wide with fear. Lane kept his voice calm. "What did the man do when he came into the cubicle?"

"He...he pushed me hard out of the way and grabbed for Olivia. I stumbled against the wall and hit my head. That's all I remember. I-I think that's how I got this."

She lifted up a fold of golden hair and Lane caught sight of a small white bandage taped across the side of her forehead.

"Did he say anything?"

"No, he just kind of grunted. I-I think I cried out when he

pushed me aside, but I'm not sure what happened after that. The next thing I knew, someone was yelling for an ambulance."

Lane digested the information. It was better than nothing. In fact, her description of the attacker was better than he'd hoped. He closed his notebook and returned it to his pocket.

"You've done really well, Brittany. Thank you."

"Will you be able to find Olivia?" she asked quietly, hope igniting the depths of her eyes.

Lane shot her a confident smile he was far from feeling. "You betcha." He stood, keenly aware of Zara watching him. He looked at her, and again felt the impact of her eyes. "If she remembers anything else—"

"We'll call you," Zara finished.

Pulling out a business card from his shirt pocket, Lane scribbled his home number on it and handed it to her. Their fingers touched. The spark traveled between them again. Lane knew she felt it, too. His gaze locked with hers.

"Call me if she remembers anything else. Anytime." He dragged his gaze from hers and turned away. The Attorney General ushered him out of the room. Lane followed him down the stairs in silence.

At the foot of the stairs, Dowton turned to him and held out his hand. "Thank you for coming, Detective."

Lane shook it. "You let me know if you remember anything else about that phone call. I'll let you know when we find Olivia."

When, not if. He'd issued the confident statement deliberately and he was sure that sooner or later, the child would surface. His only hope was that she was still alive when that happened.

CHAPTER 5

Saturday, January 27, 12:50 p.m.

Zara Dowton stared down from the window where she stood in her sister's bedroom and watched the detective head toward his car. He opened the door and went to climb in when Emily McGregor appeared. The girl worked with Mrs Harrow and helped to keep the household running smoothly. She was also precocious and flirted outrageously with some of the male staff.

Zara was sure she didn't mean anything by it and no one seemed to mind, least of all the staff. Emily was barely out of high school. With her svelte figure and fun, flirty ways, she seemed to draw men to her with very little effort and Zara couldn't help but admire her for her confidence.

She saw the detective laugh at something Emily said and a pang of envy went through her. What she wouldn't give to be carefree and confident like Emily. To be witty and make someone laugh. She had the best part of half a decade on the girl and yet Zara felt awkward and uncomfortable whenever she was left in the presence of an eligible male. A casual flirt she wasn't, no matter how she wished she were different.

A few moments later, the detective offered Emily a cheery wave and climbed back into his car.

A minute later, his vehicle headed down the driveway

and disappeared from sight. She glanced back at her sister, now asleep on the bed. She'd urged Brittany to rest after her ordeal and had promised to stay with her while she slept. Her heart ached for the trauma and shock the little girl had endured and Zara thanked God she'd been spared the worst of it.

She didn't know the Munro family very well, but she felt their pain, deep in her chest. She couldn't imagine the agony of not knowing where their daughter was, whether she was hurting, whether she'd ever come home...

She fingered the business card given to her by the good-looking detective. *Lane.* That's what he'd told Britt. It was a nice name, a strong name, like him. With his long, muscular legs and broad shoulders, he'd towered over her. At her five-foot nothing, that wasn't hard for most men, but Lane carried himself in such a way and with such an air of confidence and determination—as if nothing would ever get in his way—that he seemed even taller than what she guessed him to be.

And he'd been so good with Brittany. The little girl had been scared to death, had sobbed without relief when she'd first arrived home. She had begged Zara to stay with her, but the detective had seemed to sense her fragile state and had gently coaxed her into giving him the information he needed.

At first, Zara thought he was going to change his mind about conducting the interview. The look of panic on his face when he'd entered Britt's bedroom would have been almost comical under less serious circumstances. He'd looked too big and too dark and too male amidst the fluff and flutter of her sister's fairy-tale bedroom. But he'd kept his composure and managed to get what he came for, without unnecessary stress on Brittany—and for that, Zara was grateful.

The memory of his gaze as it captured hers sent a shiver of awareness down her spine. Hazel colored and flecked with brown, his eyes had looked right into her soul. For an instant, the world had narrowed to just the two of them. He radiated strength and honesty and sex appeal and she'd been drawn to him like an arsonist to kindling.

And then her father had spoken and the spell had broken, but as the officer went about carefully and kindly eliciting answers from her sister, her gaze had returned to him over and over again.

She'd never felt so drawn to a man before. Of course, he was probably too old for her. From the creases lining his forehead and the crow's feet in the corners of his eyes, he'd either spent way too much time in the sun, or else had waved good-bye to thirty some time ago. Not that she had a thing about age. In fact, she didn't have any set of criteria with which to judge a potential boyfriend.

Always a high achiever, in high school she'd been too caught up in Pythagoras' theorem and solving quadratic equations to be bothered with boys. Attending a prestigious all-girls school hadn't helped. Opportunities to socialize with the male species had been limited to a school dance twice a year and the right to be partnered by someone to her high school graduation. In the end, she'd chosen a male cousin for the role, a choice her ever protective father had quietly applauded.

Even her university days had been filled with more work than play. Following in the footsteps of her forebears, she'd enrolled in a degree that combined economics and law. Having been awarded a full scholarship, she'd felt the need to put even more effort into her studies in order to pay tribute to the honor she'd been bestowed. And that had paid off. She couldn't deny her enviable university results had led to the numerous job offers from illustrious law firms right across the country in the weeks prior to her graduation.

Of course, she could have gone to work for the firm set up by her grandfather. Although her father no longer practised law, her choice to begin her career in the firm founded by her family would have been met with paternal pride and satisfaction. But, in the end, she'd chosen Breakers, a large law firm based in Sydney. It not only allowed her to put her exceptional legal skills to use, but also, the firm had an enviable reputation for philanthropy, an attitude and way of life she held in high esteem.

Zara had been raised with the knowledge her mother had been born in a tiny village in the Philippines where the majority of its residents were unemployed. Anna Mendoza's family had depended upon the mercy of charities and philanthropic entrepreneurs in order to survive.

Zara had always loved hearing the story her father told about how he'd traveled to her mother's village as part of a group of volunteers working for a charitable organization during his university days. Her father told her many times, that within moments of meeting Zara's mother, he'd known she would one day become his wife.

Two years after their initial meeting, the recently graduated lawyer returned to the village and claimed her for his bride. After marrying Zara's father, life became much different for Anna Mendoza, but Zara never forgot the stories her father told her about the poverty and desperation that had influenced her mother's early life.

It was one of the reasons why Zara gladly worked eighty-hour weeks and was rarely home before Brittany's bedtime. Part of every billable hour she recorded was donated by Breakers to charities around the world. It meant her social life was largely non-existent, but that was a sacrifice she was prepared to make. Over the years, she'd never had cause to lament her lack of boyfriends. *Until now...*until the arrival of Detective Black.

A wave of emotion surged through her, leaving her feeling fluttery and restless. With it came the wholly unfamiliar feeling of jealousy when she remembered the smile he'd given to the house maid. *So what if he'd flirted with Emily?* The girl might not have an original thought in her head, but she was pretty and fun and knew how to make a man smile. Zara had watched her in action with a few of the younger gardeners on more than one occasion. She could hardly blame the detective for being interested.

With a disgruntled sigh, she turned away from the window and paced the length of her sister's bedroom. She was more than content with her life. She was happy with how things were turning out.

She worked hard at a job she enjoyed. She was surrounded by a family who loved her. Well, maybe not so much by her stepmother, but no one's life was perfect. And yet, all of a sudden, she felt a yearning deep inside that things were different and it had everything to do with the very sexy detective.

Sliding his business card out of her pocket, she looked at it again. Her fingers moved over the plain black text that described his name and rank and the contact details where he was stationed. She flipped it over and stared at the handwritten scrawl on the back. *His home number.* Her heart fluttered. She pressed the small card to her breast and tried to slow her breathing.

She wished she had a reason to call him, to hear his voice again. Deep but gentle, it had caressed her skin like a whisper-soft kiss. She'd barely been able to concentrate on the content of his questions earlier, her distractedness something that secretly astounded her.

The description her little sister gave the detective of the attacker rang a chord of familiarity in her mind and her thoughts turned to the men she'd spied in her father's office a fortnight earlier. Such a contrast to those he usually met with—they were rough, dangerous looking men she'd never seen before. When she asked her father about them later, he assured her they were undercover police officers, but as he said it, he'd paled and she'd briefly recognized unconcealed fear in his eyes.

Now, she could only wonder if their visit had something to do with the disappearance of Olivia Munro. She wondered if her father had mentioned the visitors to Lane. She could call him and make sure. It would give her the excuse she was looking for.

Lane. Already, she was calling him by his first name.

Heat crept up her neck and suffused her cheeks. She bit her lip against the strange rush of desire that suddenly weakened her. She'd never felt this way before about any man, *ever*. Nothing came close. The scariest thing was, she didn't have a clue what to do about it.

She was a twenty-five-year-old woman who was well on her way to an illustrious career and yet she'd never known a man in the most intimate of ways. She'd never had the time to date anyone seriously; she'd never had the inclination. She didn't understand why her feelings about all that had changed in the seconds and minutes since she'd met Detective Senior Sergeant Lane Black of the Chatswood Local Area Command.

Her heart leaped with nerves and excitement at the possibility of talking to him again, but her head issued a cautious warning. Dark undercurrents tugged at her consciousness. A fortnight ago her instincts told her that all was not as it seemed and the feeling of dread hadn't diminished with time. After listening to Brittany's description of the man who'd attacked her, Zara's disquiet had magnified. *Why was that?*

Everything came back to her father, a man she loved more than anyone in the world.

She needed to speak to him. She needed him to explain to her a second time the reasons for the presence of the rough-looking men in his office. Her gut told her he hadn't been honest with her and she wanted to give him a chance.

A chance to tell the truth.

Chapter 6

Saturday, January 27, 1:03 p.m.

Olivia Munro curled herself tighter into a ball and tried to hold the sobs at bay. She didn't know where she was or how long she'd been unconscious. The only thing she could clearly remember was arguing with her stepmother about a stupid bikini. After that, there was nothing.

A rough-looking man dressed in dirty jeans had come and checked on her twice. Both times, she pretended she was still sleeping. He'd come over to where she lay on the floor and had shoved her with his boot, turning her onto her back to face him. Though he no longer wore the leather jacket, she recognized him as the man who'd kidnapped her. It had taken everything she had to remain silent and motionless.

Eventually, he'd sauntered out again, locking the door behind him with a jangle of keys. She groaned at the pain in her arms and wriggled in an effort to get more comfortable. The bindings around her wrists were tight and she'd lost all feeling in her hands. She swallowed a sob and tried to hoist herself upright, using the wall behind her for leverage.

With a grunt and a hard shove, she managed it. She was left panting from the effort, but at least her head was now off the floor and she was better able to take in her surroundings.

The single window had been boarded up and only the tiniest slivers of light escaped inward from underneath. It was barely enough to dent the dimness, but as her eyes grew accustomed to the dark, she slowly made out the rest of the room.

The space was smaller than her bedroom and was bare of furniture. Cobwebs hung from every corner of the ceiling, their long strands swaying gently from an unidentified source of moving air. They reminded her of the dark and scary caves she'd seen in the *Indiana Jones* movies she'd watched with her dad. All she needed was a gigantic, hairy spider to appear.

With a shudder, she lowered her gaze and tried not to think about it and wished her daddy was near. Dust lay thick on the floor. She looked down at her once-white shorts and grimaced, upset for a second that they were ruined. Then her situation really hit home. She was captive—she had no idea where—and guarded by the frightening thug who'd shown her no mercy. *How had all this happened?* From her fear, memories slowly began to emerge.

Her head was fuzzy. She wondered where Brittany was. *Had she been taken, too?* Perhaps she was here with her, somewhere in the house? The thought gave her hope that she wasn't alone with the short, thickset man who'd attended her earlier. Through her squinted eyes, she'd seen the bulging muscles in his arms and the array of tattoos that covered his skin. She'd also sensed the menace coiled inside of him and that terrified her. The danger of him had been there in the change room before he pressed a sweet-smelling cloth over her mouth and nose and the world went suddenly dark and blank.

Tears welled in her eyes and slowly leaked down her cheeks. She wanted her daddy. *Where was he?* Surely he knew she was missing? Her stepmother would never have kept something like this from him. She must have told him. He was on his way. He'd find her. He'd rescue her. She was sure of it.

The rattle of the key in the door once again stole her

breath. Heart thumping, she tried to slide sideways, to pretend she was still asleep, but though she tried, she couldn't get the impetus she needed to topple. Panic clawed at her throat. She watched, as in slow motion, the door opened and revealed the bulky shape of her captor.

CHAPTER 7

Saturday, January 27, 1.10 p.m.

Before she knocked on the door to her father's office, Zara took a deep breath and tried to quell the nerves that tumbled around inside her belly.

"Dad, it's me. May I come in?" Not waiting for a reply, she opened the door and found him at his desk, frowning behind a mound of papers. He looked up as she entered.

"What is it, darling? How's Brittany?"

"She's fine. She's sleeping. I think today's events and the visit from the detective wore her out."

"Not surprising, after all she's been through."

Zara nodded her agreement and took a seat opposite her father's desk. Needing to occupy her hands, she picked up a heavy glass paperweight and moved it from one hand to another.

Her father watched her in silence for a few moments. "What's troubling you, Zara?"

The nerves she'd almost managed to suppress returned full force, tightening her throat and turning it sandpaper dry. She licked her lips and tried to form the words. In the end, they came out in a rush.

"It's about those two men who visited you a couple of weeks ago. You heard Britt describe the man who abducted Olivia. The men who were here looked like him. I-I was wondering if they could have had anything to do with Olivia's disappearance?"

Her father stopped writing on the notepad in front of him and gave her his full attention.

"Why would you say that?"

Zara broke the eye contact, suddenly filled with uncertainty. "I don't know. They were dressed in much the same way and seemed so...so menacing."

With a nod of understanding, her father resumed writing. "I told you. They're police officers. They've been working undercover for a long time. Sometimes the lines get blurred and they forget who they really are."

He glanced up at her and grimaced. "It's a danger our undercover operatives constantly face and one we keep a close eye on. It makes them really good at their job, but the change can wreak havoc on their families."

Zara digested his explanation. It made sense—kind of—but something was still a little off. She continued to juggle the paperweight in her hands. Her father looked up at her again, an eyebrow raised in query. "Is there anything else?"

She drew in a deep breath and released it in a rush, needing to ask the question before she lost her courage. "If that's the case... If they were really undercover officers...why did they scare you?"

His eyes widened in surprise and then he laughed. "Don't be silly, darling. Of course they didn't. I've known those men for years."

"But—"

He came around the desk and pulled her to her feet. Putting his arms around her, he gave her an indulgent hug and pressed a kiss to her forehead.

"Thank you for caring about me, darling, but you have enough to worry about. Don't look for issues where there are none."

Releasing her, he stepped away. "Go on up and check on Brittany. I have a few things to do down here and I don't want our baby girl waking up and finding herself alone."

"Of course." Turning, Zara left the room. If she hadn't seen firsthand how much the men had frightened him, she would have been inclined to believe his explanation. Although it was unusual for officers to come to their home, it wasn't unheard of. She wished she could simply accept his explanation and forget about it. Perhaps, at the time, she'd imagined the fear she'd seen in his eyes? Perhaps, as he suggested, she was finding issues where there were none?

With a sigh, she headed up the stairs, hoping his reassurances would settle her concerns, but more than a little disturbed that they might not.

Lane scrolled through the entries on the computer screen in front of him. He glanced at the clock on the squad room wall and cursed. Another hour had passed since Olivia Munro had disappeared.

Although the security camera footage had identified a man who generally fit Brittany's description, the angle had been wrong and the camera too far away to make a positive identification viable.

There were still a number of general duty officers canvassing shoppers in the mall, but so far, they hadn't turned up a credible witness. Lane had reported back to his boss about Dowton's threatening phone call, but they still didn't have enough evidence to indicate his daughter was the target. So far, Lane's team was dealing with the matter on their own.

"What did you find?"

Looking up, Lane spied Jett walking toward him from the direction of the tea room, a cup of steaming coffee in each hand. Setting one on Lane's desk, he propped a hip on the adjoining desk and took a sip out of his cup.

"Thanks, mate," Lane murmured, sliding his coffee toward him and taking a grateful sip.

"Thought you could do with some caffeine. So, what's happening?"

Lane grimaced. "Not much. The officers at the mall still haven't come up with anything. I've run the tattoo through the database. It's come up with five hits." He grimaced. "It would be asking for too much to have just one."

"I think the redback spider image is pretty common, as far as tattoos go. I'm surprised that's all you got."

"Brittany Dowton said it was on his left hand. I think the location has narrowed it down some."

"Yeah, well it could have been worse. You could have gotten fifty." Jett leaned over the desk and scanned the names on the screen. "Some of those sound familiar."

"From Brittany's description of the attacker and from the tattoo, I'm running with the theory our guy's part of a biker gang. The tattoo search supports that theory. Three out of the five hits I got belong to members of the Redbacks."

Jett shook his head. "Surprise, surprise."

Lane took another sip of coffee and clicked on one of the names on the screen. A few moments later, the file opened.

"Here's the first one. Tim "Toothpick" Todd. A rap sheet as long as your arm for serious assaults, drug offences and robbery. Known associate of the Redbacks. Has a distinctive redback spider tattoo on his left hand."

He returned to the search file and clicked on another name. "Boris "Beefcake" Vukovic. Another prolific law-breaker. Did a stint in Long Bay for manslaughter. Just the kind of bloke you'd want to date your sister. Also a member of the Redbacks with a distinctive redback spider tattoo on his left hand. Last but not least, we have Draco Jovanovic."

Jett sidled closer. "Why have I heard that name before?"

Lane compressed his lips into a grim smile. "He's the president of the Redbacks. Surrounded by a club full of violent and lawless members, he's risen to the top."

"What's his form?"

"The usual. Assaults, numerous drug offenses, unlicensed firearms, intimidation of a witness, the list goes on. Several visits to the big house."

Jett shook his head again, his tone derisive. "And yet, we keep on letting them out."

Lane frowned. The remark triggered an idea in his mind, sending a surge of adrenaline through his veins. He sat upright and turned to his partner. "Let's print out the mug shots of all five and do an identikit up for Brittany. She might recognize one of them."

"Good idea. It might give us the break we need. I'll get right on it."

"Thanks, Jett. I appreciate it. Make sure you throw in a few extra headshots so that we don't get any hassles when this thing goes to court. I hate it when good evidence gets tossed out on a technicality."

"I'm hearing you, mate."

Lane reached for the phone. "I'll call Clayton and Ellie and give them an update."

CHAPTER 8

Saturday, January 27, 1:45 p.m.

Clayton stared out the window of his study and tried to ignore the dread that clawed at his gut. Every minute, every hour that crawled past was another hour they'd lost in their search for his baby.

The technicians had arrived and had made short work of setting up their equipment. Over cups of black coffee and murmured conversation, they manned the phones in the kitchen.

The sound of muted laughter in the backyard beyond his study window drew his attention. The afternoon sun bounced off the swing set where his young sons played. Ellie stood nearby, staring off into the distance, her face stark with uncertainty and barely controlled panic.

His heart ached. He hated to see her so troubled, but he seemed powerless to help her or offer her comfort. He was holding onto his own senses with an ever loosening grip. He had nothing to give her. The anger he'd felt earlier had long since dissipated, but he still couldn't comprehend how she hadn't seen anything. Or, at the very least, *heard* something during the abduction.

From what he understood, Brittany had received a reasonable injury to her head. *Surely the girl had screamed?*

Or, at the very least, called out? And yet Ellie remained adamant she'd heard nothing.

It was no secret Ellie and Olivia had been butting heads. His daughter was growing up; she was struggling with the rapidly approaching onset of puberty. He guessed most girls got into arguments with their mothers when hormones were running rampant and they were struggling to come to terms with the transition from child to young woman.

For some reason, in the last year or two, Olivia's loss of her biological mother had become more and more important to her. She'd barely mentioned Lisa over the last six years and then suddenly it seemed she slipped his first wife's name into every other conversation. He could only assume his daughter was lashing out at Ellie because she represented the mother she would never have; the mother she *couldn't* have—the one who had given her life.

He didn't condone Olivia's brattish behavior. It was rude and disrespectful and it was hurtful to the woman who loved her as her own. He realized, that as a family, they needed some intervention. He hadn't told Ellie, but he'd determined last month over Christmas while he'd been with his family in Grafton, to arrange for Olivia to see a counselor.

And then there was the other side effect of Olivia's increasing obsession with Lisa. Her repeated outbursts stoked the embers of the long-dormant guilt he thought he'd buried forever. His first wife had swallowed a bottle of sleeping pills while he'd been at work. The knowledge that he'd failed her had tortured him for years afterwards because in the months after the birth of his daughter, he'd failed to recognize that his wife was suffering from postpartum depression. He'd failed to realize she needed help. He'd failed her when she needed him most. And then, it was too late...

When Ellie came into his life, he'd been wracked with guilt, but her understanding nature and kind and gentle loving had prised open the claws around his heart and had lightened the burden of his shame. He'd never dreamed he'd be happy again, let alone fall in love.

And yet, he had and he loved Ellie more than he ever thought possible. He'd done his best to largely ignore Olivia's occasional eruptions or rude snipes at Ellie. Until recently he'd refused to acknowledge it could be more than a passing phase, but it seemed the last few weeks had been more than difficult. When his daughter begged him to allow her to enlarge a photo of Lisa to hang on her wall, he'd been startled at her request, but had reluctantly agreed.

Mulling it over later, in the privacy of his study, he'd acknowledged once again that there were several signs over the last year that Olivia needed help. Once again, he'd determined to do something about it, as soon as he found the time. But the time hadn't come and the appointment hadn't been made and now his little girl was missing. Pain speared through him. Once again, he'd failed someone he loved: This time, it was his daughter.

With a moan of despair, he clenched his fists and turned away from the window. Dragging in a breath, he tried to ease the tightness in his chest. The phone in his pocket rang and he snatched it like a lifeline.

"Clayton Munro."

"Clay, it's Lane. How are you holding up?"

"Yeah, you know," he managed.

"I take it there hasn't been a ransom demand?"

"No, not yet."

"Well, I may have something."

Listening to Lane's explanation about the tattoo and its links to the Redbacks, Clayton frowned and shook his head. "Lane, it's been more than two years since I had anything to do with biker gangs. Even then, I was involved in a sting against the Hornets up on the northern beaches, not the Redbacks, close to home. We both know there's no love lost between them. It doesn't make sense that the Redbacks would seek retribution on behalf of a rival gang."

"I agree. But we can't ignore the connection. According to Brittany, the man who attacked her had a distinctive tattoo on his left hand. Out of the five hits I've had on similar tattoos, three of them came back to members of the Redbacks. We know they have a substantial number of members in Canberra."

Lane paused and took a breath. "On top of that," he continued, "in the security footage we obtained from Myer, we've managed to locate a man entering the store shortly before the attack that matches the description given by Brittany. He's dressed in the standard biker gear."

Clayton's voice sharpened. "Have you identified him?"

"No, we're still working on it, but hopefully it won't take us long. This is the strongest lead we've had. The AG gave me some information that supports the idea that the perpetrator could be a member of an outlaw motorcycle gang."

"Why, what did he tell you? Just because someone's wearing a leather jacket doesn't make them a biker."

"You're right. What you don't know is that the AG received a threatening phone call last night. Although he couldn't identify the caller, the gist of the threat related to his recent quest to tighten controls on these gangs. The papers have been full of it. It's no surprise it's pissed some of them off."

"Fuck." Clayton mulled over the implications. A few moments later, he said, "Do you believe him?"

"About the phone call?"

"Yes."

Lane sighed. "I have no reason not to."

"That's not what I asked."

"It's as good as I can give you right now. Dowton's been more than cooperative. Until he proves himself untrustworthy, believing him is all we can do and you have to admit, it makes sense."

"Maybe. What happens now?"

"We're putting together a photo line-up to show Brittany which will include all five of our tattoo-wearing suspects. With a bit of luck, she might identify one of them. It might help us narrow down our search for the abductor."

"Call me as soon as you know anything. I want to be involved as much as I can. If you send me what you have, I can start putting together a profile. Something. Anything. This sitting around, just waiting, is killing me."

There was a pause on the other end of the line, almost as if Lane could feel the weight of Clayton's pain. And then Lane spoke again, his voice low but full of feeling.

"I understand, Clay and I appreciate your offer, but we need you right where you are. You want to be there if a call comes through for the ransom." Lane paused again. "And you need to be there for Ellie."

Clayton's shoulders slumped on a heavy sigh and he collapsed into the nearest chair. "You're right, Lane, and thanks. For everything."

"We'll find her, Clay. We've done it before."

Memories washed over Clayton and he bit his lip against a surge of emotion. Three years earlier, Tom's daughter, Cassie had been abducted. Thankfully, she'd been found in less than twenty-four hours, alive and relatively unharmed.

Lane was right. He had to trust the police. They'd done it once; they could do it again. They could find his daughter and bring her back to him, safe and sound.

After ending the call, he immediately dialed his brother's number. Tom would come over and help him. *Tom would know what to do.*

Zara tenderly brushed the hair off her sister's forehead, her heart filling with love and gratitude. For all that her heart ached for Olivia's parents, she was selfishly glad Brittany had escaped unharmed. Zara's relationship with Brittany's mother might be less than ideal, but she'd never felt anything but an overwhelming sense of love for and from her baby sister.

From the moment Allison and her father returned home with the squalling bundle wrapped securely in a fluffy, pink-and-white blanket, Zara had been in love. Most fifteen-year-olds were too self-absorbed to notice or care about a newcomer to the family, but for Zara, the feelings generated inside her by the tiny, red-faced infant with the swirl of velvet-soft golden curls couldn't have been more different.

That first night, alone with Brittany in the nursery, she'd vowed to protect her baby sister with everything she had. It was a promise she'd meant and had kept over the past ten years and although the little girl was now growing up and less inclined to seek out her much-older sister, their bond was as strong as ever.

Beneath the quiet stroking of Zara's hand, Brittany stirred. Her eyes blinked open and for one moment, they were unclouded by the day's events. Zara watched as realization slowly dawned and the light in the young girl's eyes dimmed. She reached blindly for Zara's hand and clutched it tightly to her face.

"It's all right, baby. I'm here. It's all right," Zara whispered in a lulling tone.

Brittany quieted under Zara's soothing hand. After awhile, the young girl drifted back off to sleep. Zara sighed. She got to her feet and stretched her arms above her head. They'd cramped from being in the same position for so long. Walking over to the window, she peered down at the parking bay below. *Had it only been an hour or so since she'd watched Lane walk away?* It seemed like a lifetime ago.

Lost in her thoughts, she didn't immediately notice the boy who pedaled a bicycle down the driveway. He'd passed the bed of begonias and the rose display before she spied his slight figure. She frowned and wondered at the reason for his visit.

The long hours she put in at work precluded her from knowing much about the children inhabiting the neighbourhood, though properties in Point Piper had remained in the same families for generations. She thought she knew most of the people in the vicinity but the boy who jumped off the bike and ran toward the front door wasn't familiar.

Perhaps he was a friend of Brittany's? From what Zara

could tell from this distance, he looked about the same age. She glanced back toward the bed and was pleased to see her sister's chest rising and falling in a slow, steady rhythm. It wouldn't do for Emily or Mrs Harrow to disturb her sister with a knock on the bedroom door.

Zara strode across the carpeted floor and slipped quietly out of the room. She eased the door closed and then hurried down the stairs. She found the puzzled housekeeper in the entryway. The woman held a folded piece of paper.

"Mrs Harrow, was that a visitor for Brittany?"

The woman turned in surprise. "No, at least, I don't think so. I've never seen the boy in my life. He knocked on the door and handed me this. He told me to give it to the Attorney General."

Zara stepped forward. "Here. I'll see that he gets it." Taking the paper from the housekeeper, she turned and headed toward her father's office. When Mrs Harrow disappeared in the direction of the kitchen, Zara opened the note.

Scanning the letter, her blood ran cold. Fear turned her feet to lead. It was like her life had become a slow motion movie and a horror one, at that. The words of the note seared into her brain.

Finding her breath at last, she screamed for her father.

CHAPTER 9

Saturday, January 27, 2.53 p.m.

Lane turned both the lights and siren on inside his unmarked police car and sped through the early afternoon traffic. Jett rode beside him, hanging on while Lane once again negotiated his way across the Harbour Bridge and headed toward the eastern suburbs.When they turned into New South Head Road and started climbing, Jett glanced across at him. "How much further?"

"We should be there in about seven minutes."

"What did Dowton say?"

"Not much. Just that he'd received a ransom note and we needed to get over there. Pronto." Lane grimaced. "It looks as though he was right about his daughter being the target. The kidnapper snatched the wrong kid."

Jett shook his head, frowning. "Shit, what a mess. I guess we'll get that joint taskforce, after all."

Lane nodded grimly. "Yep, now that we know for sure the AG's involved, we don't really have a choice. The boss was making the calls to the AFP as we left. No doubt the whole thing will be in full swing by the time we get back."

"Did you get a chance to take a look at the identikit photos?"

"Yeah, thanks for putting it together so fast. Too bad the

three Redbacks look so much alike. Skin heads with muscle. All we can do is hope Brittany recognizes one of them."

Lane swung the car into Dowton's street, keeping his foot on the accelerator. The tires squealed in protest. He turned into the paved driveway that led to the Attorney General's residence and pressed the intercom button. Before he could announce his presence, the imposing double gates opened inward. The two gardeners he'd spotted earlier were no longer in sight. The huge fig trees now cast long afternoon shadows across the driveway. Lane's gut tightened at the sight, acutely conscious of how much time had elapsed since Olivia disappeared.

"Wow, this is some kind of hacienda." Jett's voice was full of the same surprise and admiration that had filled Lane on his initial visit.

"Wait until you see inside. The place is full of expensive artwork. The AG told me his old man left him most of the paintings. His father was some hotshot lawyer from the old days. He must have been worth a fortune."

Jett whistled low under his breath and continued to take in the impressive property. "I'd like to be able to afford something like this on a government salary."

"That makes two of us." Lane parked the car where he'd left it a few hours earlier and tried to shrug off the feeling of déjà vu. Returning here so soon was a good thing. It meant they were making progress. Besides, a part of him also hoped he'd catch another glimpse of the AG's beautifully exotic daughter.

His gut tightened at the thought and blood rushed to his groin. Annoyed at his body's reaction and the path of his thoughts, he impatiently fixed his attention on serious police business. He had to remain focused on the case.

Bracing for another bout of sneezing, he rapped twice on the door. His knock was answered in less than a minute. The same housekeeper greeted him, but this time there was no smile. She stood back for them to enter. "No hay fever this time, Detective?"

Lane shook his head. "Not yet, anyway. I must be getting

acclimatized." He turned to indicate Jett behind him. "This is Detective Jett Craigdon."

The housekeeper took the proffered hand. "I'm Mrs Harrow. It's nice to meet you." She looked back at Lane. "Please, let me take you through to Mr Dowton. He's waiting for you."

"Has Mrs Dowton arrived yet?" Lane enquired.

"No, but Mr Dowton's expecting her later this afternoon. She's flying home from Queensland."

Lane nodded and in silence, they followed the woman across the room and headed in the direction of the Attorney General's office. Even with Lane's heads-up, Jett gaped at the opulence around them.

The AG met them at the door, his face waxen and drawn. Without a word, he handed Lane a single sheet of folded paper.

"It was delivered about an hour ago."

Lane tugged out a pair of latex gloves from the back pocket of his suit pants and slipped them on. Handling the note with care, he scanned its contents. It was typed in twelve point courier font, a commonly used font that was available on any computer.

> I want my money.
> One million by midnight tomorrow
> or the girl dies.

Lane's gut filled with dread, along with a disquieting suspicion: The note didn't contain any details for the drop or even how the kidnapper could be contacted. It was almost as if the author of the note and the AG knew each other. As if certain details didn't need to be explained because they shared some unwritten information. His misgivings ratcheted up another notch, even while he tried to remain outwardly calm.

Folding the single sheet of paper, he placed it in a plastic evidence bag. His gaze drilled into Dowton's. "How did it arrive?"

The Attorney General swiped at the perspiration on his forehead. "M-my housekeeper answered the door to a young boy. I-I'm not sure who he is. I assume he lives in the neighborhood. Mrs Harrow thinks he might be one of the Shearer boys, although she's not sure, but if that's the case, he lives in the next street over. Number twenty-two."

"I'll make the call," Jett offered, tugging out his phone.

"If it was, get someone over there right away," Lane added. Jett nodded and swung away.

Lane turned to face the Attorney General. Out of the corner of his eye, he caught sight of a movement...Zara. Despite his best efforts to remain unaffected, his heart stuttered.

The AG's eldest child was dressed as she had been earlier, but now an even deeper concern lingered in her dark eyes. He watched through the doorway while she moved with quiet grace down the staircase and positioned herself at her father's side.

Lane found his voice and managed to acknowledge her. "Ms Dowton."

She held out a hand toward him. He took it and returned the slight pressure, trying not to think about how soft her skin was and how tiny her hand felt engulfed in his.

"Please, call me Zara."

He nodded and dragged his gaze back to the Attorney General's. "We need to talk."

Zara lifted one of the matching leather chairs that stood opposite her father's desk and moved it to her father's side. After taking a seat, her gaze settled on Lane. He wore the same charcoal suit he'd appeared in earlier, but his navy-and-white striped tie now looked as though it had been tugged on more than once and his pristine white shirt was creased. His face disclosed little and the expression in his hazel-flecked eyes was hard. Nerves danced in her belly.

She stole a look at her father and her heart went out to him. Pale and trembling, he bore little resemblance to the confident, charismatic man she knew. This whole ordeal was taking its toll.

She silently castigated herself, knowing that what her family was enduring was nothing compared to the agony the Munro family must be suffering. Her sister was safe and sound upstairs in her bed. *Their* daughter's whereabouts and health status was anybody's guess.

"We need to talk about the ransom note," Lane stated, his voice flat. "First of all, you're going to explain why I sense the kidnapper had prior contact with you."

Her father dropped his gaze. He swallowed and moved the papers on his desk from one side to the other. Zara reached out and covered his hand with hers, stilling it.

Lane's expression turned grim. "Start talking, *David*. We can do this here, or at the station. You choose."

Her father shook his head from side to side. A deep red flush crept up his neck and stained his cheeks. "That won't be necessary, Detective. I'm sure you can conduct your interview here. I'll tell you everything I know."

Zara squeezed his hand and let it go and tried to relax against the back of her chair. Lane pulled out his notebook.

"Let's start with the note. You said it was delivered by a boy from the neighborhood. Did anyone ask who'd given it to him?"

"No," her father replied. "As far as I know, Mrs Harrow took the note and the boy left."

With gloved hands, Lane took the note out of the evidence bag and smoothed it open. He read it again.

"I'm curious, David. This isn't the first ransom note I've seen. Fortunately, there haven't been many, but what strikes me as odd is that the note demands money, but provides no details of how it's to be delivered." His gaze narrowed on his face. "Do you have any idea why the kidnapper might omit that?"

"No, no I don't. I don't know anything about these men."

"What makes you think there is more than one?"

Her father looked flustered. "Well, I'm-I'm not sure. It was merely a figure of speech. Don't these people usually work in groups?"

"Sometimes, sometimes not. The note refers to 'my' money. I would have thought that indicated a kidnapper acting on his own." He stared across the desk. "It's interesting that you don't see it that way."

"It-it's not that I don't see it that way," her father blustered. "You're putting words into my mouth."

"All right, well tell me what you make of the fact the kidnapper left no instructions on how to deliver the ransom money? He or she has given you until midnight tomorrow." He glanced at his watch and frowned. "Which is less than thirty-three hours away and yet they've not even left a phone number where they can be contacted."

He pinned her father with his gaze, his eyes now flint. Zara's breath halted.

"In fact, in every one of the ransom notes I've been privy to, I've never once seen a note that didn't offer a means of making contact. It's almost as if the person who wrote this *knew* that you'd know where to find him."

He pushed away from his desk and threw his arms up into the air. "That's preposterous!" he shouted, his face now mottled with purple. "Do you know who you're talking to? You'd better watch what you're saying, boy, or you'll find yourself out on the street, sweeping pavements."

Zara gasped at the implied threat, shocked at her father's outburst. Her heart thumped. *Could Lane be right?* Her throat was so dry she could barely swallow. She didn't know what was going on, but she had a terrible feeling deep in the pit of her stomach that her father knew more than he'd let on. Her gaze flew to Lane's. His face was granite and his voice was just as hard.

"I apologize, Attorney General. I didn't mean to offend you. My only motivation is to find a little girl who must be terrified out of her mind and take her back home to her parents. As a father, I would have thought you'd understand."

To Zara's relief, the tension in her father's shoulders dissipated and he walked back to his chair and sat down.

"I'm sorry, too, Detective," he offered. "I've been under a lot of stress lately and now, with this..." He shook his head. "It's hard to think rationally when my little girl's involved."

"I understand, Attorney General," Lane replied, the steel in his voice easing infinitesimally. "And I hope you can spare a thought for the Munros."

"Yes, yes, of course. That poor family. I can't imagine what they must be going through."

Lane drew in a deep breath. Zara watched in fascination as his chest expanded and then slowly contracted beneath his tailored business shirt.

"Do you have any idea why the kidnapper didn't provide you with a means of contacting him or a point he'd make contact again?"

Her father met the detective's gaze head-on. "No, I don't."

Lane stared at him for long moments. Her father was the first to drop his gaze. Lane flipped to a new page in his notebook.

"All right, we'll have to assume whoever it is will be in contact again with that information. Now, let's get back to your earlier theory that Brittany may have been the target."

Lane looked up at her father. "When I spoke to you this morning, you thought that the kidnapping might have been politically motivated. We've done some checking of the tattoo Brittany described and it appears it's a symbol used by members of the Redbacks, an outlaw motorcycle gang operating out of Western Sydney."

He paused, his gaze firmly on her father's. "Let's assume you're right about the fact Brittany was the target. Given the fact the ransom note was delivered here, I think it's a fair assumption to make. Your recent stance, proposing harsher laws to deal with outlaw motorcycle gangs, has been well publicized. You told us you took a call last night from someone demanding you back away. Correct?" Her father nodded and Lane continued.

"It's plausible that a member of the Redbacks decided to kidnap your daughter in order to bring pressure on you to drop the reforms. The only thing I don't get is why none of these demands are mentioned in the ransom note? In fact, if you hadn't told me about the threatening phone call, I'd think the kidnapping had nothing to do with your political stance. It appears no more than an unfortunate incident that thankfully happens only rarely in Sydney where someone has targeted you as a wealthy member of society who might very well be willing to pay an enormous sum of money to have his daughter returned. The fact that the kidnapper took the wrong child is tragic, but it doesn't change the essence of what happened."

Lane's breath came faster, but he wasn't finished yet. He leaned over her father's desk and eyeballed him. "The only peculiar aspect of that theory is why it would involve the Redbacks. I admit, they're a bunch of violent, lawless criminals, but kidnapping young children for the sole purpose of extortion isn't their scene. Something doesn't add up. What's your take on it, *David?*"

Zara's fingernails bit into her palms. She held her breath and waited for her father to answer.

His face was flushed. "If you're asking me whether I have ties to an outlaw motorcycle gang, the answer is a vehement *no*. Of course I don't have links to an illegal biker gang. The very idea is preposterous!"

He looked directly at Lane, who didn't flinch. "If you're asking me whether a member of such a gang could have a grievance against me, then I guess the answer's yes. You've already referred to my position in relation to the laws governing these gangs."

"Then why is there no reference to those laws, no mention of backing off, in the note? You said last night's caller made specific reference to your reforms. A child mistakenly believed to be your daughter is kidnapped, a note turns up, but makes no mention of the earlier demands. It doesn't make sense." Lane's voice was threaded with steel, as if daring her father to dispute that.

Zara listened to Lane's reasoning with a growing sense of unease. On top of her own disquiet, the possibility that her father was involved in something awful refused to go away. She watched him closely, hoping to gauge something from his response.

His eyes flashed at Lane with anger and his face turned red. His breath hissed between clenched teeth. Zara held her breath, praying silently for him to regain control.

"I don't know what you want me to say, Detective," he growled. "I received a phone call threatening my family with harm if I didn't back down from my current position. A day later, my daughter's involved in an attempted kidnapping. Call me stupid, but I can't help but think those incidents are related."

Lane moved slightly away and gave a brisk nod. "Okay, let's go with that theory. In fact, we've put together a photo line-up of convicted criminals who sport the redback spider tattoo in the position Brittany described. I'd like to ask her to take a look at it."

"What if the man responsible doesn't have a record?" her father asked.

"Then we have a problem. Our system only records the distinguishing scars, birthmarks, tattoos and the like of convicted felons. If our guy's never been convicted, then without another eyewitness, there's very little chance we'll find him." Lane's face reflected his frustration. "Let's hope it doesn't come to that."

Her father's shoulders slumped almost in a sign of defeat. He looked sideways at Zara. "Do you think Brittany's up to talking with the police again?"

Zara compressed her lips together, wanting nothing more than to spare her sister another round of questioning, but she thought of Olivia and her parents and knew she didn't have any choice.

"She was sleeping when I came downstairs, but I'll go and check on her again. I think it's important to do all we can to help."

Her father nodded tiredly. "Yes, of course. You're right."

Lane nodded a brusque thank you and pushed away from the desk. He strode toward the closed door of her father's office and flung it open.

"Jett, are you out there?"

Zara started forward and stopped when Mrs Harrow appeared in the doorway. She glanced around at the people in the room. "I'm sorry, Detective. Your partner left to interview Harry Shearer."

Lane frowned. "Harry Shearer?"

"The boy who delivered the note."

"Oh, I see. Jett's managed to identify him. That's good. Thanks for letting me know." Patting the pocket of his suit, he turned back to face them.

"Detective Craigdon prepared the photo line-up. Let's hope he hasn't taken the car to the Shearer house. The photos were on the back seat. I'll go and check."

Lane strode out of the office. Zara heard the click of his boots on the concrete floor. She turned to her father, concern and fear warring inside of her.

"Dad, are you sure the men I saw a couple of weeks ago had nothing to do with this? Is it possible they were working undercover in the Redbacks biker gang? You said yourself sometimes the lines get blurred."

The Attorney General shook his head. "They're from the Drug Enforcement Agency. I shouldn't be telling you this, but I know I can trust you. They're part of a taskforce investigating the illegal drug trade in Cabramatta. They have nothing to do with outlaw motorcycle gangs."

Zara sighed heavily in relief. His explanation made sense and it went a fair way to alleviating her concerns. It also explained the rough appearance and the air of danger that had surrounded both men. Living undercover in such a precarious and dangerous world meant total immersion. If the enemy they'd infiltrated had even the slightest suspicion that the two men weren't who they said they were, it could prove fatal. The more believable they were in their role as active participants in the world of illegal drugs, the better their chances of success and survival.

She couldn't imagine what it must be like to live like that and she could understand why they did whatever was necessary to stay alive. No wonder they'd appeared so menacing. No wonder her father had demonstrated fear, even if he refused to acknowledge it.Reassured, she sat back in her seat and awaited Lane's return. There was no point waking Brittany until Lane produced the photo line-up.

As her mind shifted to the good-looking detective, she once again felt an unfamiliar surge of desire. She recalled the feel of his palm against hers and how her heart had skittered and stuttered and then taken off in a gallop. The breathless anticipation, a feeling so unfamiliar and compelling that she marveled at its existence, was even now causing her chest to tighten and her pulse rate to increase.

Now that she knew her father wasn't involved, she could afford to ponder the detective's dreamy countenance without the strain of her concerns interfering. There was something very special about him. Even in the midst of the anxiety and desperation to find Olivia, he remained strong and calm and confident. He exuded capability. She was drawn to him like she'd never been drawn to another man. The feeling filled her with excitement and nervousness and anticipation and all kinds of delicious emotions that were totally foreign to her. It was like discovering and learning a new skill and experiencing the freedom that came with it. She yearned to find out more about him and get to know him better.

The sound of his footsteps crossing the living room floor had her pulse once again picking up its pace. She sat straighter in her chair and smoothed down her hair and waited for him to appear in the doorway.

"Here it is." Lane re-entered her father's office, brandishing a large envelope. "Jett left the car behind. I called him while I was outside. He only had to walk around the corner to speak to the Shearer boy. Unfortunately, the boy can't tell us much, other than it was a bald man in a car wearing a black leather jacket. The man pulled alongside him while he was riding his push-bike and asked him to deliver the note to the Attorney General."

David sat forward. "Did he give you a description of the car?"

"No, only that it was a white sedan."

"Plate number?" the Attorney General added.

"I'm afraid not. I guess the boy had no reason to suspect anything was amiss."

"What about a tattoo?" Zara asked quietly.

Lane's gaze locked on hers. Her heart pounded furiously.

"He didn't see a tattoo. Then again, unless the man's left hand was high up on the steering wheel, it probably wouldn't be visible from the driver's side. It's still possible the guy's a member of the Redbacks."

Zara nodded agreement and licked her suddenly dry lips. Lane stared at her. The moment stretched on. Unable to bear it another second, she dragged her gaze away.

Lane cleared his throat and addressed her father. "I'd like to talk to Brittany now, if that's all right with you?"

Her father stood and pushed away from the desk. "Of course." He turned to Zara. "Would you mind going upstairs and checking if she's awake?"

Grateful for the reason to escape the intoxicating pull of Lane's presence, Zara stood and left the room. Moments later, she reached her sister's room and eased open the door. Brittany had pushed herself up against her pillows and was focused on the television. A children's game show filled the screen.

"Hey, sweetheart. How're you doing?" Zara murmured.

Brittany offered her a weak smile. "I'm okay."

Moving closer to the bed, Zara reached out and laid her hand on Brittany's cheek. "This has been such a difficult day for you. I understand how much you've been through and you've been so brave and so wonderful, I can't wait to tell Olivia what a good friend you are."

Brittany's eyes clouded at the mention of Olivia. Zara cursed under her breath. She hadn't meant to upset the child. Goodness, she was trying to prepare her sister for another police interview.

To her relief, Brittany's mouth tilted upwards in the tiniest of smiles, her eyes full of hope. "Do you really think they're going to find her soon?"

Zara's heart clenched at the eagerness that filled her sister's eyes. "Of course," she replied with as much confidence as she could muster. "That nice Detective Lane's working as hard as he can to bring her back. In fact, he's downstairs right now. He'd like to ask you some more questions."

Brittany pulled a face and tugged the bedcovers up under her chin. Zara patted her knee.

"This is so tough on you, baby. But I need you to stay strong. Detective Lane needs your help and so does Olivia."

"Can I go downstairs?"

"Sure, if that's what you want."

Brittany nodded and pushed back the bedcovers. Still dressed in the clothes she'd worn that morning, she slid off the bed, brushing tendrils of golden curls out of her eyes.

"Here, put on your slippers." Zara held them out to her and waited for the girl to slip them onto her feet. With an arm around her sister's shoulders, she hugged her to her side and together they made their way down the stairs.

Lane and her father were still in his office. Lane had moved to stand near the floor-to-ceiling windows that looked out onto the lush gardens. He turned at the sound of their footsteps and smiled when he saw Brittany.

"Hello again, Brittany. Thank you for coming downstairs."

Brittany peered up at him shyly. "That's okay."

Tugging the envelope out of the inside of his jacket, he motioned for her to take a seat. She hesitated and Zara squeezed her shoulder reassuringly, silently urging her forward.

Lane moved closer and placed the envelope on the desk within Brittany's reach. He hunkered down beside her. Like the expression that filled his face, his voice was gentle.

"I have some photos I'd like you to take a look at Brittany," he murmured. "After we spoke about the man who attacked you, I went back to my office and my partner and I put together a page containing photos of men that look a little like the man you described. I'm hoping the man you saw in Myers might be one of them."

Brittany tensed beneath Zara's fingers. Zara bent and put her face close to her sister's. "It's okay, sweetheart. I'm here. It will only take a few moments. Remember what I said? Lane's trying to find Olivia. You might be able to help."

The young girl drew in a shaky breath and nodded. "Okay."

Lane opened the envelope and drew out a legal sized sheet of thin white cardboard. On it were two rows of male head shots. There were ten altogether and they were all physically similar. Zara stayed close to her sister while Brittany examined the photos.

"Take your time, Brittany," Lane said softly. "Have a good look. It's important that you're absolutely certain."

"Th-that's him," she whispered, pointing to one of the pictures.

Zara looked to the man Brittany had pointed to and gasped and then clenched her fist against her mouth, trying to push the sound back in. Her heart pounded. *It was one of the men she'd seen in her father's office.*

As if sensing something amiss, Lane's gaze zeroed in on her and then slowly looked at Brittany. "Are you sure?"

"Y-yes, I'm sure. That's the man I saw in the change rooms."

Zara was still doing her best to get her emotions under control. Her heart continued to thump hard. She could still feel Lane's assessing gaze.

"Who...who is that?" she rasped, pointing to a second man she recognized. Her blood pounded so loudly she was sure everyone could hear it. She didn't dare look at the detective—or her father.

Lane glanced at the man she'd indicated. "Draco Jovanovic," he replied, his lip curling with disdain.

"Jovanovic's the president of the Redbacks. He's done serious jail time. Why do you ask?"

Panic like she'd never known, suddenly seized Zara's chest and it was all she could do to keep breathing. She searched frantically around for something to say, but try as she might, she kept coming up blank. She drew in a surreptitious breath and swiped at the sweat that had popped out on her lip. Lane continued to look at her curiously.

"Who is he?" Brittany asked and once again pointed to the man she'd identified. The relief Zara felt when Lane's attention was drawn to her sister nearly caused Zara's legs to give out from under her.

"That's Boris Vukovic, another prominent member of the Redbacks," Lane replied and then turned to address her father, his expression grim. "It looks like it's just as you suspected: retaliation for threatening to tighten the biker laws."

Zara stared at her father. He'd paled beneath his perpetual tan and a frown left deep creases in his forehead. He exhaled on a heavy sigh.

"Do what you need to do, Detective. I'm not going to let these outlaws dictate how we run this State. It's easy for me to say because my daughter's not the one missing, but I'm prepared to put all available resources at your disposal so that you can find this scumbag and bring him to justice."

"Thank you, Attorney General. Fortunately, we're already in the process of forming a joint taskforce with the Australian Federal Police. They have more resources available to them than we do and given that you're a political figure, their expertise is not only required, but necessary. We'll also be calling on officers in the Organized Crime Squad and the New South Wales Crime Commission to assist. Their knowledge of these outlaw motorcycle gangs far exceeds ours."

Her father nodded and turned away. "Good, good. It sounds like you have everything under control, Detective Black. Keep me informed of your progress."

"Yes, sir. I will." Lane paused and then added, "About the ransom money, Attorney General. Did you have any thoughts in that regard? I'm sure you know the government's position on paying ransom demands and I understand it's not your child who's at risk, but—"

"I still feel responsible and I want to help. I'm sure I can get my hands on some of it at short notice. Whether I can find the full million… I'll have to see."

Lane started in surprise. "That's awfully generous of you, Attorney General. While we'll do our best to keep track of it, there's no guarantee you'll get it back. Olivia isn't your daughter—"

"No, but I'm the reason she's been taken. It's the least I can do for the Munros. This had nothing to do with them. If I hadn't been so vocal about my stance against the gangs, they would never be trying to retaliate. Besides, it could have just as easily been Brittany. In fact, if whoever has taken Olivia knew the girls better, it *would* have been Brittany…" His gaze drifted to his youngest daughter and he shuddered.

Zara watched him and burned with the strain of remaining quiet. She wanted to shout out the truth, but fear and uncertainty kept her silent. Her father knew better than she did that two of the men in the photo line-up were more familiar to him than Lane could ever imagine: A fortnight ago, the very same men had been sitting right there, in the Attorney General's office.

After promising to make the necessary phone calls to compile what he could of the ransom money, David asked the detective and his daughters to leave his office. He needed time alone to think. He needed to talk to Draco. With an unsteady hand, he pulled his phone out of his pocket and dialed the number. It was answered on the first ring.

"I see you got my note."

"What the hell are you doing? Are you *crazy*?" David whispered, hating the desperation in his voice.

Draco didn't seem to notice. "That bitch owes me. A million dollars. I told you a fortnight ago. I want it back."

"You'll get your money. These things take time. You didn't have to take the girl."

"Just be grateful Boris fucked up," Draco snarled. "Next time, you won't be so lucky. Besides, there's always your other daughter." His chuckle was pure evil. "Beautiful Zara," he crooned. "She's like a little china doll. So tiny. So perfect. All that black, silky hair... Me and my boys could have so much fun with her. Who knows? Maybe next time, we'll take both of them."

David began to shake so hard he had to lean against his desk for support. His heart pounded. Sweat popped out on his brow.

"You'll get your money," he wheezed. "Please, just leave my girls alone."

Chapter 10

Saturday, January 27, 3:55 p.m.

Olivia stared at the ugly man with the pockmarked skin and dirty jeans and tried very hard not to cry. He shone the flashlight he carried right into her face and the bright beam burned into her eyes. The man took another step toward her and terror pulsed through her veins.

"Please," she whimpered. "Please don't hurt me."

The man merely snorted and scratched at his beard-roughened chin. Closing the distance between them, he squatted beside her and smiled.

"You're a pretty little thing, aren't you?"

He reached out to touch her cheek. Olivia shied away from him, pressing herself up against the wall. The man chuckled and cupped her chin in his hand, forcing her to face him.

"I like 'em feisty, that's for sure." He turned her face this way and that, examining her in the yellow light. "You're a bit on the young side, but you never know, I might be able to be persuaded."

He leaned closer and the smell of unwashed body and stale cigarettes made her gag. She struggled with the bindings around her wrists, but they didn't budge. Fear clogged her airways. She gasped and choked and coughed, suddenly unable to breathe.

Her tormenter thumped her on the back. Hard. She gasped again and sucked in oxygen.

"Don't go all silly on me, girlie. Draco's entrusted me to keep you safe, at least until the ransom's paid. I can't have you dropping dead on me. Draco will have me hide. What's your name, anyway?"

Olivia stilled, hardly daring to believe that it wasn't in his immediate plan to kill her. The tiniest sliver of hope trickled through her and she prayed with increased desperation that her father would find her.

The man nudged her with his shoulder. "I'm Boris. Draco said you were Brittany."

Olivia gasped again and shook her head vehemently. "No, no, no! You've got it wrong! I'm not Brittany! I'm Olivia! I'm Olivia Munro!"

Confusion appeared in Boris' eyes, but then he shrugged as if it was of no consequence. "Brittany, Olivia—same difference."

"No, no! Please, it's not the same. I'm Olivia. I'm not Brittany! Brittany's my friend. You've got the wrong girl!"

Boris stared at her a moment longer and then cursed viciously. Pushing away, he spun on his heel and headed toward the door, taking the light with him.

Lane dialed Clayton's number on the way back to the station and quickly brought him up to speed. As Lane knew he would, Clayton exploded when he discovered Olivia hadn't been the target.

"You mean to tell me my daughter's been kidnapped because of a monumental fuck up by some brain-dead, drug-infested, scumbag biker gang member who has a grievance with the AG's politics?"

Lane grimaced. "Yep. At least, that's what it looks like. I'm sorry, mate—you don't know how much. This whole thing is screwed up. The only good thing is, now we know who we're dealing with and now that we know for certain the AG's involved, we can get a whole lot more people in on this. The boss has already contacted the AFP. He's putting together a joint taskforce as we speak."

"How long have they given Dowton to come up with the cash?"

Lane bit his lip, trying to delay the inevitable. "Midnight, tomorrow."

"Who's getting the money together?"

"The AG's offered to see what he can do. He feels responsible and he's making phone calls right now. Let's hope he gets it together in time."

"Well, I appreciate his support, that's for sure even if it is true that my daughter's life has been endangered because of his political views." Clayton sighed heavily. His voice was devoid of emotion when he spoke again. "One million dollars in a little over thirty hours. What are his chances?"

Lane chose not to answer. They both knew the outcome was far from certain. The first hurdle was to find the money. The second was to have the kidnapper fall for the trap the taskforce would set with it.

"I'm going to call Dowton. Ellie and I have access to a bit of cash put away for the kids' college fund. Not a million dollars, but between all of us, we might find it."

Lane pressed his lips together, but nodded. Clayton knew as well as he did that government policy dictated the police would never pay a ransom demand, but if it were his daughter, he'd do everything possible to get her back, even if it meant handing over every dollar he had.

"I want to do the drop," Clayton added, his voice rough. "I want to look this prick in the face when he hands over my child. I want to remember him for as long as it takes."

On the other end of the phone, Lane was already shaking his head before Clayton finished. "You can't be involved, Clay. As far as Boris Vukovic knows, he has David Dowton's daughter. It's the AG he'll be expecting, not you."

"What happens when this asshole realizes he's taken the wrong child?" Clayton's question was voiced in a tone that became softer and deadlier with every word, as if the reality of the situation had exploded in his head at the end of his chain of thought.

Lane's gut plummeted. He didn't even want to think about the possibilities if the kidnapper discovered his mistake—including the consequences for Clay's daughter. He remained silent.

"Fuck, fuck, fuck, fuck, *fuck!* What the *fuck* am I going to tell Ellie?" Clayton's agony reverberated through the phone.

Lane's knuckles turned white around the steering wheel. He squeezed his eyes shut against the surge of emotion that threatened behind his eyes. He let Clayton's anger and fear and frustration and pain run its course in an ever-increasing volume of oaths and curses and vowed with every breath he took to find the little girl who was loved more than she knew.

Boris Vukovic heard the sound of a key turning in the lock only moments before the Prez's impressive bulk filled the doorway of the safe house. Scrambling off the chair, Boris came to his feet.

His gut lurched with apprehension at the look in Draco's eyes. The Prez hadn't made it to the top by fighting fair and when Draco came toward him with narrowed eyes and moved each booted foot in a slow, measured tread, Boris couldn't help the shiver of unease that coursed through him. His fear skyrocketed when Toothpick made an appearance behind him, swinging a foot of loose steel chain.

"P-Prez, I wasn't expecting to see you here. Didn't you get my text? I told you I had the girl. Everything went to plan, just like I promised."

Draco's gaze turned meaner. Without taking his eyes off Boris, he whipped a pistol out of his jeans and fired off three rounds into the television set that blared behind Boris. Sparks flew out of the screen. Boris gulped and tried to remain calm.

"W-what's the matter, Prez? I did as you said. I got in and out with the girl and no one saw a thing. I—"

"You got the wrong one."

Boris frowned. His lip trembled at the steel in Draco's voice.

"B-but I got the one you told me about. The one with the blond hair. She—"

"She was with her friend. They *both* have blond hair, you fuckwit. You got the wrong fucking girl!"

Toothpick stepped forward. The chain swung back and forth in his hand. Menace glinted behind his eyes. Boris' bowels loosened. He groaned and dropped his head.

The first he knew of the blow was when he heard the crunch of cartilage. Pain exploded in his nose and across his cheek and quickly spread over his ear and up the side of his head. Blood gushed from his nose and sprayed across the wall.

"Fuck," he moaned, holding onto his nose in an effort to stem the blood. "What did you do that for?"

Toothpick lifted the chain again and Boris stumbled backwards. Draco raised his arm and Toothpick stilled. Boris gasped and gulped in air through his mouth, one hand holding his brutalized nose, the other one holding his head. He tried to stem the tears.

"Look at Beefcake," Toothpick sneered. "He's sniveling like a girl."

Draco's lips curled up in an imitation of a smile. "I'm sorry I had to do that, Beefcake, but your fuck up made me mad and you know what I do when I get mad."

He strode around the confines of the small kitchen/living room, his nose wrinkling in disgust at the sight of the half-empty pizza boxes and beer cans that lined every available surface.

"For fuck's sake, Beefcake, what are you? A fucking pig? You've been here for less than twelve hours and the place looks like a shit heap. Didn't your mother ever teach you any manners?"

Boris kept his head bowed and remained silent.

"The girl you grabbed doesn't belong to Dowton. She's the daughter of some fucking Federal agent. A fucking criminal profiler. It sounds fancy, but he probably gets paid shit."

Draco spun on his heel and strode toward Boris who instinctively pressed himself against the wall.

The president pushed his face close to Boris', his menacing eyes only inches away from Boris' face. "How the fuck's someone like that going to come up with a million dollars? Huh?"

"I-I dunno, Prez."

Draco hawked a globule of phlegm and spat it at Boris' feet. "You don't know. That's just fucking great." He turned to Toothpick who remained close by, eagerly awaiting instructions. "How about that, Toothpick? He doesn't know."

Moving surprisingly quickly considering his size, Draco grabbed Boris' shirt and shoved him hard against the wall. Boris cried out in surprise and fear, unsure whether his legs would continue to support him.

The president moved in close. "What are you going to do, cocksucker? What are you going to do now? And what the fuck are you going to do with the girl in the room next door whose usefulness just expired?"

Boris blinked rapidly in an effort to dispel his fear. "I'll...I'll fix it, Draco. I promise."

Draco released him, his lip curling up with disdain. "Oh, you'll fix it, all right. If it's the last thing you do. Get rid of her and do the fucking job properly this time."

"I will. I promise, Prez. I won't let you down again."

CHAPTER 11

Saturday, January 27, 5:15 p.m.

Clayton heard Tom's knock on the front door and his shoulders slumped in relief. He stood and met his brother halfway down the entry hall. Another brother, Brandon, was right behind Tom. Emotion tightened Clayton's chest at the sight of them.

"Clay, thank Christ you called me," Tom said, his expression grim. He closed the distance between them and hugged Clayton hard.

"I can't believe you've been trying to deal with this on your own," Brandon added. "Tom said Olivia's been missing since nine this morning."

Clayton swallowed the fear in his throat and nodded. "Yeah."

"Where's Ellie?" Tom asked, looking around the living room.

"She must be out of her mind," Brandon added quietly.

Clayton felt the weight of his guilt like a tonne of steel pylons. He closed his eyes against it. When he opened them again, his brothers stared at him with identical expressions of concern. "Yeah," he said, not able to manage anything more.

"Is she okay?" Tom asked.

Anger suddenly gripped Clayton. "Was Lily okay when

that asshole took Cassie? Were *you*? Of course she's not okay. Neither of us is. We're barely hanging on."

Brandon stepped forward and took hold of Clayton's arm and guided him to the couch. "Sit down, Clay and tell us what happened. After that, you're going to tell us how we can help."

Tom nodded, his expression grim. "Brandon's right. We need a plan." He stared hard at Clayton. "We're going to find her, Clay. We're going to find her and she'll be fine. Just like Cassie was. Trust me. I know what I'm talking about."

Clayton's anger dissolved with a heavy sigh. He held Tom's gaze, taking comfort from his oldest brother's confidence. Tom had been there before. Tom knew what it was like to have a child stolen from him. Tom and Brandon would help him. They'd help bring Olivia home.

"I'm just so fucking scared," he admitted with a harsh sob, his voice breaking. Tears burned behind his eyes. "I need to find her."

Tom's gaze burned into his. "We'll bring her back for you, Clay. We promise." He glanced across at Brandon, who nodded, his expression stoic. "Have we ever let you down?"

After Lane took his leave, Zara's father ushered her and Brittany out of his office and had then sequestered himself inside for the best part of an hour. Although she needed to seek answers from him, she didn't want to endure another round of bald-faced lies, so she hadn't confronted him again. She now watched from her bedroom window as her father's half million dollar LFA Lexus sped down the driveway and disappeared from view.

Undercover DEA agents, be damned. From the start, she'd suspected there was more to it than what he'd told her, but she'd wanted to believe him; hadn't wanted to think he could be involved in something so sinister. Her mind shied away from it every time she dared to consider it.

But she *had* to consider it. She *had* to think about it. The evidence was on the piece of thin white cardboard. The men she'd seen in her father's office were members of the Redbacks—and not just any members.

According to Lane, they were the worst of the worst; criminals who'd done lengthy time in jail. For what, she didn't want to know, but after Brittany had identified a Redbacks member as the man who'd attacked them, it had become more and more obvious they were involved in Olivia Munro's abduction.

Abduction. The word sent shivers down Zara's spine. She thought of the terror the little girl must be feeling and anger kindled deep inside of her. Her father had left the house without speaking up. As far as she knew, he had no intention of telling the truth. Meanwhile, Olivia's heart and mind must be terrorized as she wondered if she'd ever be rescued and prayed that she would.

Zara set her jaw in determination. She strode across the room and flung her bedroom door open. Hurrying along the carpeted hallway, she took the stairs two at a time. Within moments, she'd descended again and stood in front of the door to her father's office. Her breath came in short pants. She glanced around. When she was sure the way was clear, she drew in a deep breath and turned the knob.

The room looked just as it had when she'd left it except for the empty tumbler which now sat on her father's desk. She lifted it to her nose. The smell of scotch was still detectable. After what had occurred a little while ago, she understood his need for a stiff drink.

She set the glass back where she found it and went around to the other side of his desk. She rested her hand on the seat of his chair. The leather was still warm. With her heart in her throat, she pulled open the top drawer of his desk.

It opened easily and some of her tension dissipated. She riffled through an assortment of pens, paper clips, blank note paper, a legal pad and two packets of highlighters. She didn't know quite what she was looking for, but mundane office supplies certainly weren't it.

Closing the top drawer, she tried the bottom one. It was deeper than the first drawer and could hold something more substantial. She tugged at the handle. The drawer didn't budge.

She tried again. Nothing. *It was locked.* Her imagination went into overdrive. Why had her father locked one of the drawers of his desk? No one had any interest in accessing his space. It was his private domain, where he went to work without interruption or to take important work-related calls. The only times she'd entered were to seek him out for one reason or another. Before now, it never occurred to her to go in and look through his private papers or anything else he stored in there.

And yet, his bottom drawer was locked, as if to keep out prying eyes... *What could he be hiding?* Did the drawer contain evidence indicating her father's connection to members of the notorious Redbacks biker gang? Or was the locked drawer nothing more than a way to keep private government papers private? There was only one way to find out.

Knowing she couldn't break the lock, Zara hunted around for the key. In contrast to the mess of paperwork she'd spied on his desk earlier, apart from the empty scotch glass, a desk blotter and two family photographs, her father's desk was now scrupulously clean. She tried to think where he might have hidden the key.

It made sense he'd conceal it somewhere in the room. He'd never know when he'd want to access the drawer. Besides, his office had been the venue for his secret meeting with the Redbacks. Evidence of such a connection, if there was any, would be locked away, hidden from prying eyes. The key had to be here.

She pushed back the chair and strode over to the bookshelves, running her fingertips along the shelves. A faint line of dust coated the bottom of her fingers. She checked each shelf carefully, even taking the time to drag one of the armchairs over and stand on it in order to reach the highest shelf. They were all coated with dust. It was obvious none of the books had been disturbed for some time. She swiveled slowly on her heel and surveyed the room.

Apart from the paintings on the walls and the bookshelves, the enormous desk and matching armchairs were the only other furniture in the room. She pursed her lips in thought. *It had to be in the desk.* It was the only place that made sense.

Returning the armchair to its place opposite her father's desk, she sat back down in his chair. Leaning forward, she ran her fingers along the wood underneath the desk in front of her. Within moments, her fingers stumbled on something. A hard object was fixed to the wood in something soft and putty-like. Manipulating it with her fingers, she pulled it free.

Bingo. She'd found the key. It had been stuck to the desk with blu-tac. Simple, but effective, even if the hiding place wasn't exactly inconspicuous.

Zara pressed the key into the palm of her hand. Now that she had it, she was overcome with indecisiveness. *Did she really want to know what her father kept locked in his bottom drawer?* Once she opened it and discovered his secrets, there would be no going back. The memory and knowledge couldn't be undone. *Did she really want that burden?*

Images of Olivia as she'd last seen her—laughing, carefree, happy—reeled through her mind like a movie. Her stomach tightened. Dread weighed down her limbs, but she knew what she had to do.

With trembling fingers, she fitted the key into the lock, turned it and slid the drawer open.

———

The mood in the crowded squad room was charged with tension. Australian Federal Police officers and other police from the Crime Commission and the Organized Crime Squad milled around. Expressions were grim; conversation was muted.

Lane sat back in his chair and stared at the clock on the wall. It was already after seven. He still hadn't heard from the AG or Clayton about the money. AFP officers had been dispatched to the AG's house to keep watch and await the arrival of further instructions from the kidnapper.

Jett pushed away from his desk nearby and sighed. "Coffee?"

Lane grimaced. "Yeah, thanks."

A few minutes later, his partner reappeared with two cups in his hand. Gratefully, Lane reached out for one and took a sip.

Michael Collins appeared in the doorway of his office, his expression taut. "Now that we know the man who took the little Munro girl is Boris Vukovic, we can fine-tune our plan of attack."

Lane frowned. "It doesn't seem logical that Vukovic is acting on his own. For one, although he's a prominent gang member, he's never before taken the lead. In every single one of his convictions, he was the one following orders. If this is politically motivated like we suspect, it makes more sense that this is a prearranged attack orchestrated by the Redbacks as a whole and I'm certain that someone other than Vukovic is calling the shots."

"Like Jovanovic?" Collins asked.

Lane nodded. "Jovanovic's the Redbacks' president. He's bright enough to put together such an assault. He's made a lot of enemies over the last few months with his law reform platform and the subjects in his sights are not exactly afraid to take a stand."

Collins narrowed his gaze at Lane. "You don't sound convinced."

Lane acknowledged his boss with a brief nod. They'd worked together for nearly five years. There wasn't much Michael didn't know about him.

"There's something about the whole thing that's got me jittery and it's more than the fact that, as we speak, one of my mates is praying for the return of his little girl." He grimaced and took another mouthful of coffee before continuing.

"For one, the ransom note's suspicious. The wording of it is off. When I questioned the AG about it, he got all defensive and threatened my job." Lane shook his head in bafflement. "Why would he do that? Why would he feel the need? Given the evidence we're putting together, it was a natural question to ask and yet he went off half-cocked about me being out of line and that if I wasn't careful, I'd be out of a job."

A frown lined Michael's forehead. "You're right. It's odd. But then again, he's under a lot of pressure. Maybe he didn't mean it to come out like that?"

"We're all under pressure. It was more than that. Besides, why would a biker gang member demand a ransom of a million dollars? As far as the average Joe's concerned, David Dowton's an elected public official with job security only guaranteed until the next election. Not many people would think of a State politician and that kind of money in the same thought, not even one with as high a profile as the AG."

"You're right," Jett agreed. "I for one wouldn't have guessed he'd have access to enough money to be able to pay a million-dollar ransom."

"Exactly. Unless you knew Dowton personally or did some pretty in-depth research, you'd have no idea he was loaded. Until I got a look at his place of abode, I had no idea and I work for the man, sort of. And yet some run-of-the-mill member of an outlaw motorcycle gang knew enough about him to know that he could find that kind of money..."

"What are you suggesting?" Michael asked, his expression darkening. "That he may have some kind of previous connection with them? Like a drug connection or something? We're talking about the AG."

Lane moved restlessly. "I don't know. I really don't. But something like that. Maybe. The ransom note gave no details about where the drop's to take place, not even a contact number. It's risky for the kidnapper to make contact with Dowton again and yet, he has to if he wants the money to be delivered, unless he and the AG have some prior arrangement. It stands to reason there's a personal connection there, no matter how far-fetched it sounds."

Lane shook his head and blew out his breath in frustration. "I listen to what I'm saying and I can't believe it, but it's the only thing that makes sense. The boys from the AFP would know him better. We could get their take on it. They can probably also tell us more about his daughter, Zara. That's the second thing that's bugging me."

Michael frowned. "I thought the daughter's name was Brittany?"

"Yeah, she's the younger child. He has a daughter by his first marriage. Her name's Zara. I don't know how old she is, but if I were to hazard a guess, I'd say she's in her mid-twenties."

"What about her?"

Lane cleared his throat and chose his words with care. "Zara Dowton was present when I showed Brittany the photo line-up. Zara looked at it, too. I watched both girls closely and I noticed Zara's reaction. She looked like she was going to faint." Lane pushed away from his desk and began to pace.

"Granted, the guys who formed our line-up were a little on the brutish side, but even so, her reaction seemed over the top. I'm sure she recognized at least one of them. She specifically pointed to Draco Jovanovic and asked if I knew his name."

Michael frowned. "How would the daughter of the AG know a criminal like Jovanovic?"

"That's exactly what I wondered. So, I Googled her when I returned to the station," Jett offered. "She works for the law firm, Breakers. Her bio lists her area of expertise as commercial law and estate planning. She's never done any criminal work or other litigation. I can hardly imagine how she'd come into contact with the likes of the president of the Redbacks."

Michael's frowned darkened. "It's been a long time since Jovanovic's last arrest. It's not like he's been in the public eye recently. He's a big time supplier. He has a huge network of dealers. If the AG's daughter recognized him, you'd nearly have to assume it has something to do with drugs.."

Jett shrugged. "There's never been anything in the media about a possible drug connection to the AG. It hasn't even been hinted at and he's been in the game for a long time. He appears to be squeaky clean. You'd think, if that kind of thing was going on, at some stage someone would have gotten a whiff of it."

"That's what's driving me so damned crazy," Lane exploded, throwing his arms out wide. "My theory that Dowton is somehow involved in a drug deal gone bad sounds plausible, right down to the part where I look at the AG and his family and realize how ridiculous it is. I mean, they couldn't have been more helpful. It was the AG who told us about the connection to his daughter and how he thought Brittany had been the target. He gave us access to her and let her speak to us. He even called us when the darn ransom note arrived." Lane groaned aloud, his frustration evident.

"He didn't have to do any of that," he continued. "We'd never have known about the mistaken identity angle if he hadn't told us. We'd never have known that Dowton's daughter was the real target. We'd still be in the dark about the Redbacks, about Brittany, about all of it." He scrubbed at his hair and swore. "And every bloody minute we don't solve it is another minute we'll never recover, another minute that poor little girl lives scared to death."

A second or two passed. Michael broke the silence. "All right, what about Mrs Dowton? Isn't the AG married?"

Lane nodded. "Yeah. Her name's Allison. She's his second wife. I haven't met her, yet. She's been away visiting her sister in Queensland. Last I heard, she was waiting for a flight."

"Do we have any background on her?" Michael asked.

"No. Given that she was interstate when Olivia went missing, we haven't focused our attention on her."

Michael nodded. Another moment of silence descended before Lane's boss drew in a breath, an unwavering look in his eyes. "All right, this is what we're going to do. I'll talk to the AFP boys, but we need to tread very carefully. Right now, I want both of you to run some property searches on Vukovic and Jovanovic. I tend to agree with you Lane. Vukovic hasn't got the brains to pull this off on his own. Someone's feeding him orders."

He pursed his lips. "But, it was Vukovic who Brittany identified as the man who snatched Olivia. If he still has her, he must have her hidden somewhere. I've spoken to the boys in Organized Crime. They've given me a list of names of the other Redbacks' key players, including a man by the name of Tim Todd. It's widely believed by the blokes in Organized Crime that Todd is Jovanovic's right-hand man. Run property checks on all of them, in case Vukovic isn't the only one involved and track down the location of their clubhouse. I doubt they'd be stupid enough to stow her there, but you never know."

Lane and Jett nodded grimly and returned to their seats. Lane tugged the keyboard closer and started punching words into the computer. Determination surged through him and he narrowed his eyes at the screen. "Let's find this asshole's last known address. It's time we paid him a little visit."

CHAPTER 12

Saturday, January 27, 9:25 p.m.

Olivia licked her dry lips and yearned for a drink of water. The room where she was confined was close and hot and it had been hours since her captor had paid her a visit. Not that she wanted him to. His ugly face and mean, squinty eyes frightened her. But she would have given nearly anything for a drink and a visit to the bathroom.

She lay on her side, with her cheek pressed against the dusty floor. It was made up mostly of bare boards. She could also just make out scraps of old linoleum in some pea-green color, stuck in sporadic strips to the floor where it caught the paltry light that escaped under the boarded-up window. Not that any light showed now. She could only assume night had fallen.

Swallowing a sigh that was tinged with desperation, she wriggled her body in an effort to reach a strip of the linoleum, hoping it would provide a smidgen more comfort than the bare boards, but after a few attempts to roll over, she gave up, exhausted.

The numbness in her hands had traveled up past her elbows. Her shoulders ached from the unnatural position she'd held for so long. For the thousandth time, she strained against the bindings that held her wrists, but like every other time she'd tried it, they didn't budge.

A sob rose in the back of her throat and she clenched her jaw tight in an effort to contain it. Crying would get her nowhere. Crying only filled her eyes with tears and her nose with snot and she had no way of wiping away either of them.

She thought of her dad and prayed again that he was on his way to rescue her. He tracked down baddies for a living. He was the best in the business—so she'd heard from some of his work colleagues. Even her stepmother praised his achievements.

Olivia's chest tightened with anger at the thought of Ellie. If her stepmother had allowed her to buy that stupid bikini, she might never have been taken. She'd be safely home with her brothers, listening to music on her iPod and counting down the days until school started. She couldn't wait to start the fifth grade with Brittany.

Brittany. They'd only known each other for a few weeks, but they'd fast become best friends. Boris had smiled with a weird kind of pleasure when he told her a little while ago how he'd shoved Brittany out of the way and she'd hit her head as she'd fallen. He'd left her bleeding in the change rooms and seemed to be proud of it.

At least now Olivia knew her friend hadn't also been taken. She hoped Brittany was okay. *Surely Ellie would have found her before it was too late?*

Thinking of her stepmother again, a twinge of guilt pricked her conscience. It hadn't all been Ellie's fault. Olivia didn't even care that much about getting a bikini. She didn't know why she'd picked the fight with her stepmother, but it seemed lately that's all she did. Still, it wasn't like she did it without provocation. Every time she turned around, Ellie was telling her what to do. Or more importantly, what she couldn't do. It wasn't fair. She wasn't her real mom.

So what if Olivia had been a baby when her real mother died? It didn't mean her mom had never existed. It didn't mean she'd never held her or wanted her or loved her. Her real mom had gotten sick and died. It happened to people all the time. Admittedly, they were usually old when that happened, but it still happened.

People didn't simply forget all about them—forget they'd ever existed—and yet, that's what Olivia felt was happening to the memory of her mother: That everyone around her wanted to forget that her mother had once been alive.

It was one of the reasons she'd begged her father to enlarge the portrait. She wanted a picture of her mother hanging on her bedroom wall where she could stare at it and tell her things no one else could understand.

For as long as she could remember, everyone had told her that she looked like her mother. The resemblance made her happy. It made her feel close to the woman who'd given birth to her, but whom she'd never known. It made her feel connected to her—like they were one.

The rattle of the key in the lock intruded on her thoughts. A moment later, the door swung open and she tensed in fearful anticipation. Her eyes had become accustomed to the darkness and the bright flashlight that beamed in her direction seared her eyes.

The rancid smell of body odor and stale cigarettes preceded Boris into the room and her nose twitched at the onslaught. She turned her head away and breathed in the dust, by far the better option. A booted foot pressed hard against her side and rolled her over. She stiffened and ducked her head, anticipating a blow.

"Get up, you're comin' with me."

Zara stared down from her bedroom window at the empty courtyard below. Her father still hadn't returned. Her thoughts returned to the contents of the bottom drawer of his desk and the dread inside of her increased tenfold.

It had taken her awhile to find it. At first, when she opened the drawer, her shoulders slumped, both in relief and disappointment. There'd been nothing more than a pile of files. Riffling through them, she scanned the contents and found they contained notes and details of various party meetings and memos in relation to proposed policy changes. One file contained notes of a meeting between her father and the State Premier and a couple of other cabinet ministers, discussing the possibility of a threat to the Premier's leadership.

Whilst she didn't think the subject matter contained in the folders necessarily warranted a locked drawer, she could understand the sensitive nature of the memos and conceded that her father was probably wise to keep them under lock and key.

With a sigh, she'd arranged the files in the order she found them and returned them to the drawer. She was about to close it when a slip of paper snagged in the side of the drawer caught her eye.

Taking care to tug it free without tearing it, she smoothed out the single sheet of notepaper and tried to make sense of her father's handwriting. It seemed to be a record of a phone conversation. Although there was no date, the word "Draco" was written and underlined twice.

Her heart thumped. *Draco.* It was part of the name Lane had given her when she'd asked about the identity of the man on the line-up, the man she'd seen in her father's office. According to Lane, Draco was the president of the Redbacks. Written next to the name was an address in the western Sydney suburb of Milperra. Brittany had identified their attacker as a member of the Redbacks. Lane had also told her the Redbacks operated out of western Sydney.

Lane had questioned the contents of the ransom note and its failure to contain any contact or drop details. In fact, he'd expressly stated that it appeared as though her father knew the kidnapper. *Or his whereabouts.*

With a growing sense of conviction, Zara tore a sheet off her father's notepad and copied down the details from the note before returning it to the drawer. With shaking fingers, she locked the drawer again and pressed the key back where she found it.

Her mind whirled then—just like it was doing now, hours later. What if Olivia's kidnapper wasn't acting alone? What if the Redbacks' president was in on it, too? It appeared the address and Draco was connected. Could the address in Milperra be the drop off point? Had the rendezvous point been arranged earlier? Is that why the ransom note didn't include the kind of details Lane expected—like the meeting point?

Her mind spun with the possibilities. *Could the address in Milperra be the same place where Olivia was being held?* All of a sudden it seemed more than plausible.

She had to call Lane and tell him what she'd discovered. But then, she'd have to tell him how she came about the information and that would mean breaking her father's confidence and maybe even worse.

Over the intervening hours, she'd become more and more convinced her father was involved, but she couldn't be the one to point the finger at him. For the first fourteen years of her life, he'd been everything to her—father, mother and best friend. Then he'd met and married Allison and within a short frame of time, Brittany had arrived and the undivided attention Zara had enjoyed up until then had suddenly been vastly diluted.

Not that her father had loved her any less. She wasn't immature enough to think that. But things had been different. There were others with demands on his time. A new wife took precedence over a daughter and an infant daughter was just plain more fun.

Despite this, Zara had been happy for her father. She'd been pleased he'd found love again and if she'd had an inkling her stepmother had liked her new husband's daughter, Zara would have been satisfied.

But it hadn't worked out that way. No matter how hard Zara had tried, Allison hadn't warmed to her. Then when Brittany arrived, it seemed—as far as Allison was concerned—Zara no longer existed.

It had hurt; of course it had. It still hurt. But she'd learned to brush the hurt aside and focus on the good things in her life. Like her career. Like her sister. *Like her father.*

Indecision gnawed at every fiber in her body. Images of

Olivia flashed through her mind. They were replaced by images of Zara's father smiling tenderly, holding his arms out to his firstborn and pulling her in close for a hug. Then there was Brittany. Sweet, little Brittany.

Zara couldn't destroy her family. She just couldn't. But neither could she ignore another little girl's terror. If there was a possibility Olivia was being held at the address Zara had taken from her father's desk, she had to look into it. She'd never rest peacefully again if she discovered later that she'd had the information to find the child and had ignored it— out of fear, out of loyalty, even out of love. She couldn't betray her father, but neither could she have Olivia's safety or lack of it on her conscience.

Frightened by what she had to do, she turned away from the dark outside her window and stared at the piece of paper she'd stuffed in her pocket. *Thirty-seven Scarborough Road, Milperra.* A totally innocuous street address, in fact, it almost sounded pleasant.

What secrets lay behind its closed doors? She shuddered. There was only one way to find out.

————————

Lane checked his rearview mirror for the headlights of the three unmarked police vans that had followed him to the nondescript fibro and galvanized-iron shack and was relieved to see them pull in behind him one by one and park a short distance from Boris Vukovic's rented house. It had taken some doing and some clever searching, but they'd finally located his address. The building was set back on a small block surrounded by other housing commission homes, all in a similar state of disrepair.

Lane's gut churned with nerves. He glanced at Jett beside him. He was sure his partner's tense expression matched his own. Any raid on a dangerous criminal was an apprehensive and stressful event, no matter how well prepared and how well resourced the team.

Lane cleared his throat of the usual nerves. "Vukovic might not be the smartest one of the pack, but he's known to shoot first and ask questions later. Make sure everyone's wearing a Kevlar."

Jett nodded, his lips compressed. Lane watched him check his gear for the hundredth time. Being prepared kept you alive. It was as simple as that. The phone in his pocket vibrated against his chest. He tugged it out and checked the screen and then cursed under his breath.

Jett looked at him. "What is it? Has there been a change of plan?"

"No, nothing like that. It's a text from...someone I was supposed to meet at eight. She waited at my place for more than an hour before she gave up. I've had my phone on silent. I've been so caught up in all this, I forgot all about her." He grimaced. "Now she's royally pissed."

Jett shook his head and shot Lane a slight grin. "Too bad, mate. I hope she understands when you explain what happened."

Lane pursed his lips. He hadn't given Katie a thought since this morning, when he'd replied to her email. Since then, his head had been full of the kidnapping...and Zara Dowton. And now wasn't the time to think about either woman. He had a job to do.

Climbing out of his vehicle, he strode back to meet the other members of the taskforce and a handful of officers from the Tactical Response Group that had been put together with short notice to carry out the raid on Vukovic's residence. It was late and the street was quiet. Conversation was clipped and kept to a minimum.

Lane ran through their plan again, confirming that everyone understood the drill. He checked again that they were ready.

His gaze drifted back to the ramshackle house. Light spilled through the open window of the front room and onto a weathered porch. A small child's bicycle with the seat missing and a faded football stood in the shadows. A solitary streetlight illuminated the overgrown lawn and the piles of trash that were strewn across the front yard. Lane couldn't imagine the kind of people who came home to such a welcoming scene.

Turning away, he did a last check of his equipment. A moment later, he nodded to his men and prepared to enter the building.

CHAPTER 13

Saturday, January 27, 10:17 p.m.

"*P*olice! Open up!"

Lane gave the order and waited a few moments for the occupants of the house to respond. He was greeted with silence. He glanced at the team of TRG and AFP officers lined up behind him, armed with face shields, breast plates and fire power. Thumping on the door again, he yelled out for a second time. Not a sound emanated from inside.

He stepped back and glanced at the men around him. He spoke in a low voice. "All right, boys, we're going in." Speaking into the radio clipped to his shoulder, he checked with the officers who waited at the rear of the residence. After receiving their okay, he nodded to the men behind him.

"After three. One. Two. Three."

The steel battering ram hefted by two burly officers crashed against the wooden door. It groaned, but didn't give. Another ram and then another. The men grunted with the effort. On the fourth attempt, the door splintered with a squeal of hinges. Lane charged through the door, his weapon drawn. The others poured in behind him.

A baby playing with an old toaster and wearing nothing but a dirty diaper stared up at him in surprise from its place on the bare floor of the front room. Lane cursed and looked around. A faded couch with the stuffing ripped out of it, leaving the springs exposed, lay along one wall. A television stood on a scarred, low table in the far corner. It was switched on with the sound turned down. There was no one else in the room.

"Clear," he shouted.

He could hear his men plowing through the other rooms, clearing them as they went. And then the tone changed.

"Hands in the air! Put your fucking hands above your head!" It was Jett.

Lane's pulse leaped. Leaving the baby where it was, he pushed his way down the hall, now ablaze with light. At the end of the corridor, he came up short outside a bedroom. Jett and two TRG officers had their weapons trained on a woman dressed in a filthy nightgown who lay on an unmade bed. Her eyes were open, but unfocused. She squinted at them through the light. The smell of body odor, cheap perfume and unwashed bedclothes assaulted his nose. He forced himself closer.

"Get up!"

Struggling to a sitting position, the woman complained loudly about their presence in her home.

"Shut your mouth," Lane growled. "We're here for Boris. Where the hell is he?"

The woman shrugged and attempted to push the sleeve of her nightgown back onto her shoulder. "How the fuck would I know? I'm the last one he talks to around here."

Lane bit back his impatience and lowered his gun, indicating for the men around him to do the same. Tempering his tone, he spoke to her again. "What's your name?"

"Sandra," the woman offered grudgingly. "Sandra Welsh."

"All right, Sandra, we're here to speak to Boris. Where is he?"

"I already told ya. I don't fuckin' know where he is!"

Lane tried again. "You must have some idea. He lives here, doesn't he?"

Sandra turned away and shrugged. "When he feels like it."

"When was the last time you saw him?"

"I dunno. A night or two ago. I lose track of time."

"Did he say where he was going?"

"What, do I look like—his fuckin' mother?"

Anger surged through Lane. The woman must have seen something of it in his eyes because she quickly mumbled, "He said somethin' about headin' out west for a while. Had a job to do."

Excitement surged through Lane. He looked up and caught Jett's eye. His partner nodded in understanding.

"Whereabouts out west?" Lane asked.

"Out west, ya know. Fuckin' western suburbs. What am I? A fuckin' GPS?"

Lane drew in a deep breath and forced it out slowly between clenched teeth. "I want an address."

"An address? What the fuck would I want with that? I don't go out there. None of my fuckin' business what he does out there. Long as he comes home with some fuckin' gear, that's all I ask."

Shaking his head, Lane bit back his disappointment and disgust and shouldered his way out of the room. The baby sat where he'd left it. He spared it a pitying glance, then threw over his shoulder, "For Pete's sake, would someone call Family Services?"

He strode out of the house without another word.

CHAPTER 14

Sunday, January 28, 11:07 a.m.

Zara peered over her shoulder and once again checked that she wasn't being followed. She'd waited until after her father left for church before sneaking out of the house to her car. Brittany had been left to rest in her room. Mrs Harrow had assured Zara she'd keep an eye on the little girl in their absence.

It had taken her the best part of two hours' drive, but according to the GPS mounted to the windscreen of her Z4M BMW Roadster and the scrap of paper in her hand, the rundown weatherboard cottage with the overhanging wisteria vine and the rusted mailbox was the one she was looking for.

Thirty-seven Scarborough Road. The house looked innocent enough from the road. Mid-morning sunlight heated the rusted steel fence posts and wilted a patch of red geraniums battling for space amongst the tangle of overgrown grass. The house sat well back from the street, and apart from a general air of neglect, there was nothing to indicate unthinkable evil could be taking place inside.

She took a deep, fortifying breath and patted her purse, feeling the reassuring hardness of her can of capsicum spray. It was hardly a defense against a gun, but it was better than nothing. Now that she'd arrived, the nerves tightened like a tourniquet. On the way over, she'd tried to formulate a plan, but nothing stuck and she was no closer to deciding her next move. That she'd have to approach the house was a certainty. Even from her position out on the street, she could see the front windows were boarded up and wouldn't help her detect anyone inside.

Another wave of nervousness went through her.

What the hell was she doing?

This kind of thing was better left to trained police officers: people who knew what they were doing. People who were armed with more than a measly can of capsicum spray. People like Lane. She was insane to think she could launch a one-woman raid against a dangerous biker who may or may not have Olivia. And yet, here she was, squaring her shoulders and readying herself to do battle, in order to protect her father and find a lost, little girl.

She should have called Lane and told him. She should have given him the address. He and his team of properly trained officers could have searched the house last night. Olivia might already have been found if Zara hadn't sat on her findings.

A surge of guilt went through her. He'd been so kind and thorough and professional. He was only trying to help. But, he would have asked her questions and she would have had no choice but to answer them truthfully. She barely knew him, but somehow she could tell he wouldn't be fobbed off with vague references. She'd be forced to tell him what she knew and how she'd come by the information and in the process, she'd have to betray her beloved father.

Knowing to procrastinate any longer would only eat away at her determination and what little courage she had left, Zara opened her car door and stepped out. The air around her was hot and still, made even more so by the fact she'd driven out there with the air-conditioner on high.

Loosening the silk scarf around her neck, she looked down at her clothing and grimaced. She'd dressed in another light summer dress that ended just above her knees. It wasn't exactly practical for picking her way through high overgrown grass, but after a sleepless night, she'd been so focused on finding Olivia and anxiously waiting for her father to leave, she hadn't given a thought to what she wore.

Having never been to Milperra before, she'd also assumed the address would lead her to a tidy home on a well manicured street. She couldn't have been further from the truth, but now wasn't the time to be thinking about practicality. She'd have to cope as best she could, despite her poorly chosen attire.

Walking the short distance to the house's rusted front gate, she tried the latch and was relieved when it opened without too much effort. She estimated the distance between the fence and the house was a little over two hundred yards. Knowing no one could see her from the boarded front windows, she picked her way toward the house with a confidence that barely touched the fear and nervousness that coursed inside her.

Reaching the front porch was the easy part. It was the possibility of what might confront her inside that made her most apprehensive. She prayed silently that it wouldn't be deadly.

———

Olivia managed to squeeze a breath past the filthy lump of rag that had been forced into her throat and tried not to gag. The blindfold fastened across her eyes was tight and the knot that secured it dug deep into the back of her head.

The car she was traveling in hit a bump on the road and she bounced up and down on the back seat. It had been at least half an hour, maybe more, since Boris had blindfolded and gagged her and thrown her into the vehicle. *It felt like a lifetime.* She bit back the sob that threatened to choke her and tried not to lose hope.

Despite his announcement that they were leaving, she'd spent the night scared and uncomfortable, lying bound on the hard wooden floor of the house. The fact that another day had dawned, terrified her. She'd been missing maybe as much as a day and nobody had come to rescue her. *Surely, someone was looking for her?* Where was her daddy? The man who could find anyone? Didn't he care she was missing? Did he even *know*?

The sudden thought occurred to her and her heart stopped cold. *What if her stepmother hadn't told him?* What if Ellie hadn't been game to tell him she'd lost her and had spent the day at the mall, pretending all was well? He wouldn't have found out she was missing until her stepmother arrived back at home without her. What if Ellie had made some excuse, lied to him about Olivia's whereabouts? Her stepmother could even have told him his daughter was sleeping over at Brittany's. *Maybe that's why he hadn't found her?* Maybe he didn't have a clue she'd been taken?

Burning anger at Ellie replaced the fear and desperation and she clung to it with all she had. Deep down, she knew she was being unfair to her stepmother, but right then, anger was what she needed to sustain her.

Some time during the night, Boris had brought her a slice of cold, dried-up pizza and a small cupful of water. She'd swallowed the water greedily and had quietly asked for more. When he refused, she pleaded with him to free her, but he'd merely shaken his head. No amount of tears or pleading had budged him.

She'd been pathetically grateful when, earlier that morning, he'd allowed her another cupful of water and an opportunity to use the bathroom. He'd untied the bindings around her wrists and had stood careful watch while she used the toilet. Her wrists were so sore and she burned with embarrassment, but her relief at being able to pee, quickly overcame her humiliation.

She hoped his thoughtfulness reflected a softer spot in his character, but he dashed any such notions when he told her she was more valuable to him alive than dead and besides, he didn't want to risk her messing up the back seat of his car.

The knowledge that he wasn't going to kill her had given her spirits a lift. Even the excruciating pain in her arms and wrists as the blood flow had been gradually restored hadn't dampened them. But all too soon, the bathroom visit had ended and Boris had once again secured her hands. Now, bouncing up and down on the back seat of his car, she did her best to remain positive. They were on the move. Boris had refused to tell her where he was taking her, but she hoped it was somewhere closer to other people. Perhaps if she screamed loud enough someone would hear her. She tried to peer through the blindfold, but the thick cloth made vision impossible. She bit her lip against a surge of desperation and pain shot through her mouth.

She didn't know what time it was, but the sun had been hot on her face when Boris dragged her out of the house. The man in question turned on the radio and began to sing tunelessly along. The sound of it grated on her nerves, but she stilled when she realized a news bulletin had come on.

Straining to listen over the sound of the engine, she prayed for mention of her name. There was an emergency on the Harbour Bridge. A car had caught fire. All of the southbound lanes were closed.

A gang of youths held up a bank in the city and had been arrested shortly afterwards. The latest poll showed the embattled Prime Minister was gaining ground. Then the sports stories rolled and Olivia's shoulders slumped in despair.

Her daddy didn't know. It was the only conclusion she could draw. Either that, or he didn't care...

No! She immediately discounted that possibility. Her father would be worried out of his mind. She was his sunshine. For as long as she could remember, he'd told her that. Now that she was older, his open affection for her often left her embarrassed. She'd turn her face away and pretend she hadn't heard. It was even worse when he called her that in front of her friends. But now, not knowing how much longer she'd be held captive—scared and hungry and tired—she would have given anything to hear her name on his lips. Right now, she'd even be glad to hear from Ellie.

She sighed. At least she now knew the time. The newsreader had announced the eleven o'clock news. She'd been missing for more than a day. All of a sudden, the pressure behind her eyes became unbearable. She tried to hold the hot tears back, but they fell anyway. They came slowly at first, streaming down her cheeks, but within moments, they gained momentum and soon, uncontrollable sobs echoed in her ears. She cried like she'd never be able to stop. Even scarier was the thought that she didn't think she'd want to.

The vehicle swerved onto the shoulder of the road and lurched to a sudden halt. Olivia's stomach lurched with it. Her heart pounded. She strained to listen for the slightest noise that might indicate where they were, but all she could hear was the sound of her blood pumping hard and loud in her ears.

The passenger door opened. Something cold and hard was pressed against her forehead.

"Shut the fuck up, little girl, before I blow your fuckin' head off. I've had about enough of your blubberin'. Draco's wiped his hands of you. He's given you over to me. That means *I* get to call the shots. *I* get to say who lives and dies." He shoved the gun harder against her skin and she whimpered in terror against the gag. "Do you understand me?"

The last was yelled only inches from her ear and she nodded in panicked agreement. This Boris was a different Boris to the man who'd watched over her the past night and day. This man sounded fearful and unsure and scarily out of control. This Boris was even more terrifying than before.

She gasped with relief when she felt him move away. A second later, he hit her with something hard. Pain seared through her head. Her cry was muffled. Her chest was tight. She couldn't breathe. She couldn't breathe. She couldn't... Blackness descended.

Chapter 15

Sunday, January 28, 11:18 a.m.

Zara made it to the side of the dilapidated house without detection and paused to catch her breath. She could hardly hear a thing over the pounding of her heart. Much to her relief, the windows along the side of the house were also secured with boards. Stepping with care, she picked her way around the back.

Dry, yellowed grass up to her chest almost concealed the charred remains of a car a few yards from the back steps. Zara stared dubiously at the battered wooden porch and wondered if it would hold her weight. She stilled and cocked her head to listen, straining to hear whether the house was occupied.

If it were the Redbacks' hidey-hole and Olivia was inside, it was likely her captor would either have a companion, or at the very least, a television for company, but the only thing she heard was the breeze that had finally announced its presence. It picked its way through the stand of enormous gum trees fifty yards away and skimmed along the tops of the tall grass. The sound of a bird tweeting was incongruous amidst the danger of the moment but helped to ease the tension that held her shoulders stiff.

Slipping out of her sandals, she tiptoed up the steps and onto the dilapidated porch. Unlike the front windows, the two that looked out onto the backyard were not boarded, but were coated with thick dust and cobwebs. Padding closer, Zara rubbed one of them with a tissue in an effort to clean a space big enough to see through.

Meager light infiltrated the combined kitchen and living room. A table and single chair revealed themselves through the grime. Empty food cartons and beer bottles littered the table and spilled down over the floor. What had once been a television set sat up high on a wooden crate, its screen shattered. As far as she could see, the room was unoccupied.

Apart from the sounds of nature, silence continued to envelope her. The house had an air of abandonment, but her heart still skipped a beat at the thought of stepping over the threshold. She tugged at the scarf that hung loosely around her neck and tried to build up her courage. She'd come this far. She couldn't turn back. Not without knowing whether Olivia Munro was inside.

With one hand brandishing the can of capsicum spray, she eased open the rusted screen door. It creaked in protest and she winced. Praying the sound went unnoticed, she stepped forward into the kitchen, her heart pounding.

The smell of unwashed body hit her like a solid beam. She covered her nose with her free hand and breathed through her mouth. Creeping across the room, she moved into a darkened hall and checked in both directions to ensure the way was clear. Seeing no one, she continued forward.

The first room she came to was so dim she could barely make out that it was empty and she cursed herself for not bringing a flashlight. Wooden floorboards covered with dust and the remnants of old fashioned linoleum lay bare to her gaze. Like the kitchen and living room, it was also void of people.

With her breath still tight in her throat, Zara forced her feet forward. Another room, similar in size to the previous one, adjoined the first. It too, was bare of furniture and signs of human habitation. At the end of the hall stood a room with a toilet and another that housed a bath. Small windows in each room allowed enough light that she could see they were stained with age and neglect, and both thankfully empty.

Relief eased the tension that had taken grip of her body. Her shoulders slumped like a marionette puppet whose strings were no longer taut. *The house was vacant.*

Now that the danger had passed, disappointment surged through her. She leaned against the dirty wall behind her for support. She'd been so sure the house had held some relevance. Why else would her father have recorded the address next to Draco's name? It was obviously connected to something, just not to the disappearance of Olivia Munro.

With a sigh, she pushed away from the wall and half ran down the hall, back the way she'd come. Now that it was obvious her conclusions were wrong, she wanted to get as far away from the place as possible. Striding back across the porch, she swiped at the bottom of her feet in an effort to remove the dust, tugged on her sandals and headed for her car. Unlike her approach, now she couldn't get off the porch fast enough and made no effort leave as cautiously as and quietly she'd arrived.

Allison Dowton stared at her reflection in the mirror. For the moment, she was alone in the restrooms of the Port Douglas airport. Her plane would be boarding any minute and she needed all the time she could get to prepare herself for the upcoming confrontation with her husband. She'd already delayed her departure long enough. Telling him the only plane out yesterday was fully booked had bought her some time, but it hadn't made the inevitable altercation disappear. There was no other choice but to return. Besides, she wanted to see her daughter. She wanted to ascertain that her baby truly was all right.

She pulled out a tube of lipstick and did her best to apply it with a hand that was never quite steady.

"Damn it," she muttered, when she smudged the crimson gloss across her mouth. It looked like a slash of blood and her thoughts immediately returned to her daughter. Her knees went weak, like they had yesterday, when she'd been told the news. David had assured her their daughter was okay and she hoped it was true. She'd never forgive herself if anything happened to her baby. And she'd never forgive Draco. Anger surged through her. *Damn him for involving her family...*

She swiped at the smudged lipstick and did her best to reapply the gloss, wishing she had something to help her get through the next few hours. She riffled through her handbag on the slim hope she had a tablet, a joint—anything—to dull the torture of what was to come.

Nothing.

With increasing desperation, she searched again. Again, she came up empty-handed. Tossing the handbag aside, she clutched at her face and stared at her reflection in the mirror. Her eyes were wide, a prelude to the panic attack which lay right below the surface. *So much for the costly fortnight in rehab...*

A woman walked into the restroom and glanced in her direction. Allison drew in a deep breath and forced her hands away from her face. It was all right. She could get through this. David would understand. She was sure he would. He always had in the past...

CHAPTER 16

Sunday, January 28, 11:55 a.m.

Lane activated the lights and sirens on his unmarked police vehicle and floored the accelerator pedal. Adrenaline surged through him. Another round of property searches on Draco and a few of the other high-profile Redbacks, had revealed a house on the outskirts of Milperra. It was owned by the president of the Redbacks.

Draco Jovanovic had been the president for nearly a decade. Given what they knew of Boris Vukovic and his limitations, it stood to reason that Jovanovic might be involved.

Glancing into his rearview mirror, Lane counted the unmarked vehicles that streamed out behind him and fought the sensation of déjà vu. As soon as they identified the property off the State database, he'd reconvened the TRG squad and the AFP officers and planned their next raid—the house on Scarborough Road.

The rundown cottage looked sad and neglected from the roadside and was strangely reminiscent of Vukovic's hovel they'd raided the night before. Indicating with hand signals for his team to gather close, he ran through their plan of attack as quickly as he could, mindful of the minutes ticking by.

A short time later, they had the house surrounded. It sat

silent and still, but Lane was taking no chances. The Redbacks were notorious for their stockpile of illegal weapons and he wanted to ensure every member of his team came home alive.

Turning to face the men who waited silently behind him, he signaled for them to ready themselves. Moments later, he gave the order to charge.

———————

After ensuring the house was deserted and securing the scene, Lane strode through the building and surveyed the contents. From the food scraps and empty beer bottles strewn around the kitchen, it was obvious the place had been inhabited recently. The food, whilst dry and unappetizing, hadn't had the chance to spoil.

He stepped closer and ran his hand along one of the walls. Dark, reddish-brown marks that looked like blood spatter adorned part of the surface. He called out to one of his men and told him to get onto the forensic technicians and secure the area until they arrived.

With the powerful beam of his flashlight illuminating the way, he made his way down the hall and stopped at the first room on his left. It was small and bare of furniture and looked like it had once been a bedroom. The beam of light fell on something on the floor across the other side of the room. He strode forward and picked it up.

He trained the light on his find and his heart skipped a beat. He reached out for the nearest wall to steady himself and stared down at the object in his hand. A small flip flop. Silver, with sparkly bits stuck to the sides. Just like Ellie had described.

Olivia Munro had been there.

Yelling out to his men, he told them of his discovery and shouted orders for lighting plants so that they could comb every inch of the house. Striding down the hall, he checked the second bedroom for further evidence of Olivia, but found none. The bathroom offered nothing but a wisp of fabric he spied lying on the floor.

Once again, Lane held his discovery up to the light. This time, his jaw dropped in shock. Turning the scarf over in his hands, his gut churned with anger and disbelief. Gray with delicately embroidered silver thread, it was as familiar to him as if he'd seen it only yesterday. In fact, he *had* seen it only yesterday—around the neck of Zara Dowton.

She was involved. She had to be. Somehow, she and her illustrious father were involved. It was the only explanation that made sense.

What didn't make sense was *why*. What did either of them have to gain? If the AG was to be believed, Brittany was the original target. Lane couldn't for the life of him conjure a reason why arranging the kidnapping of his daughter would be to his advantage. *Unless he was lying.* Unless the AG had offered that information up to put them off the scent. To misdirect the course of their investigation to enable him to get away with whatever it was he was hoping to achieve.

It was possible Brittany had nothing to do with it; that Olivia Munro had been the target all along. But what did the AG have to gain by snatching Clayton's child? None of it made sense. He was missing something. The only thing he was sure of was that Zara Dowton was also involved.

He shook his head, still stunned to discover the innocent-looking woman he'd spent far too much time thinking about was in cahoots with a notorious outlaw biker gang. Along with her father. The Attorney General. A man who could end Lane's career with a click of his fingers.

"What else did you find?"

He spun around and found Jett staring at the scarf in his hands. "Er, um...this." He handed it to Jett who fingered it for a few moments and then held it up to catch the wide swathe of light provided by Lane's flashlight.

"What is it?"

Lane drew in a deep breath and let it out slowly. "It's a scarf. A woman's scarf."

Jett frowned. "Olivia Munro's?"

Lane shook his head. Realizing Jett probably couldn't see it, he spoke again. "No. It belongs to Zara Dowton."

"*Zara Dowton?*" The shock in Jett's voice mirrored his own. "The *AG's* daughter?"

"Yep."

"But... I-I don't understand. Has she been abducted too?"

Lane shook his head. "Not that I've heard."

"Then why would a scarf belonging to the AG's daughter be in a shithole owned by the president of the Redbacks?"

"I don't know," Lane replied, his voice grim. "But I sure as hell intend to find out."

Zara pulled her BMW into the drive and switched off the ignition. A tension headache pierced her temples. She'd tried to ward it off with a couple of paracetamol tablets she'd dug out of her handbag on the drive back, but the headache had hit her with a vengeance a few blocks from home and it had been all she could do to park in the garage and stumble into the house.

"Miss Zara, your father—"

Zara waved the housekeeper aside and hastened up the stairs, her head throbbing. Running cold water into the sink in her bathroom, she filled her hands and threw it over her face. Riffling through the medicine cabinet, she located another packet of painkillers and tossed a couple more down.

She stared at her reflection in the mirror and couldn't believe the state she was in. Her eyes were huge and dark and full of bewilderment. Her hair looked like it had been set upon with brushes and fine tooth combs wielded by a roomful of pre-schoolers. Her neck was...bare.

Her hand went to her chest and then over her shoulder. She looked around the bathroom. *Nothing.* She spun on her heel and hurried back into the bedroom. The pale blue carpet was clear and so was her bed. She flung open her door and retraced her steps, all the way back to her car.

It wasn't there. Her scarf wasn't there. With a feeling of dread cementing her to the spot, she prayed it had blown out of her car on the way home and that she hadn't left it in the ramshackle cottage on Scarborough Road. The thought of leaving anything belonging to her in a house that was possibly connected with a notorious biker gang member filled her with unease.

Knowing there was nothing she could do about it now— after all, there was no way in hell she was going back for it— Zara sighed with resignation and slowly made her way back upstairs. Her headache had worsened. Dampening a wash cloth with cold water, she collapsed onto her bed and draped it across her eyes.

Minutes later, the sound of her cell phone ringing on the nightstand made her groan. Trying to ignore it, she turned onto her side and pressed the cloth harder against her forehead. The ringing continued and she cursed the extra-long ring tone she'd set up on her phone. With a groan of frustration, she rolled over and snatched at the handpiece and glanced at the Caller ID.

Lane.

Her stomach somersaulted with a mix of emotions. Excitement, eagerness and anticipation warred with dread. She wanted to hear his voice, to speak to him about anything and nothing. To laugh and joke and flirt. To be young and single and available.

But she couldn't. She couldn't do any of those things. He was investigating the abduction of her sister's best friend and she still didn't know if one of the men he was looking for was her father.

The dread in Zara's belly intensified and the sudden urge to vomit propelled her upright. Last night, she'd been desperate to talk to her father, to demand to know the truth, but this morning, confronting him was the last thing she wanted to do. After going to the house in Scarborough Road, she was more confused than ever, but what she did know was that she couldn't put it off any longer. She had to confront her father about the notepaper and its contents. She had to beg him to tell her the truth.

Before it was too late.

Lane listened to the phone ring out and cursed when his call went through to voicemail. Although the dulcet tones of Zara's voicemail message glided over him like the way single malt scotch slid down his throat, he forcibly pushed the feelings aside and ended the call without leaving a message.

He didn't know if she was purposefully avoiding him, but he was sure as hell about to find out. A little girl's life was at stake and every minute counted. He wasn't in the mood to take no for an answer.

The sun was much lower on the horizon when Zara eventually made her way downstairs. Although a remnant of her migraine remained, she felt better after her nap. Guilt assailed her for wasting time on sleep when every moment might make the difference between Olivia being found alive or dead.

The door to her father's office stood slightly ajar and she braced herself for the confrontation, determined not to be put off again. Squaring her shoulders, she took a step in that direction.

The sound of someone pounding on the front door snagged her attention. She halted mid-stride and debated about whether to open it. She glanced around for Mrs Harrow, but the housekeeper was nowhere in sight. The pounding came again, the knocks loud and urgent. She changed direction and reached for the doorknob and pulled it open.

Her heart hammered at the sight of the man who stood on the other side. "L-Lane? Wh-what are you doing here?"

His face was chiseled granite. He pushed past her without a word. She closed the door and tried to contain her alarm. Spinning on his heel, he turned to face her, brandishing something in his fist. Pale and gauzy, he held it inches away from her nose. She looked down and gasped, paralyzed with shock.

"W-where did you find it?"

"Where do you think?" he bit out, anger radiating off him in palpable waves.

She shrugged and tried to come up with an answer. Her mind raced. With a sinking feeling of dread, she closed her eyes.

"That's right, princess. That's *exactly* right. I found your scarf in the very same house that, until very recently, held Olivia Munro captive."

Shock ricocheted through her. Her mouth gaped. She'd searched that house from top to bottom. She'd seen no sign that indicated Olivia had been there.

She stared up at him, dazed. "H-how do you know?"

"That you were there, or that Olivia was?"

"O-Olivia."

"I found a piece of her footwear in one of the rooms, right before I found your scarf. We'll run tests on the flip flop for DNA to make sure, but we don't have time to wait for that, at the moment. Right now, I'm going with my gut and my gut tells me it belongs to Olivia Munro."

Zara shook her head, still feeling poleaxed.

Lane moved closer, crowding her with his body. She instinctively stepped back and came up hard against the front door. Her breath came fast, both from apprehension and nervousness at his nearness.

His grin turned feral. "We also found blood, but you already know about that, don't you?"

She stared at him, aghast. Not for an instant had she considered he might think she was involved. *Oh, God! How had it come to this?* How had things spiraled so quickly out of control? All she'd wanted to do was protect her father and find a scared little girl, but nothing was turning out the way she'd planned.

Lane stood so close, dominating her with his superior strength and size. She struggled to breathe. He stared at her, cold suspicion narrowing his eyes. Her heart filled with dread. There was nothing she could say to alleviate it.

"What were you doing there?" Coated with anger, the deadly words were bitten off between gritted teeth.

Zara prayed for a way to respond, trying not to notice the fresh, woodsy scent of his cologne. It tickled her nostrils and smelled way too good. She turned her head away from the distraction.

She couldn't believe he'd found Olivia's footwear. Zara had checked the place from top to bottom. Well, as good as she'd been able to without a flashlight. And he said there was blood. *How the hell had she missed that?*

She should have taken her suspicions to Lane in the first place. He was a trained police officer. He knew how to look for evidence. Then she wouldn't have dropped her scarf and she wouldn't be staring him down now, trying desperately to find some way to convince him she had nothing to do with Olivia's abduction.

The implication of what it meant, now that they knew Olivia had been in the house on Scarborough Road, suddenly hit her. Pain spread through her chest. She gasped and covered her face with her hands. The address she'd found in her father's locked drawer was everything she'd prayed it wouldn't be. She now had irrefutable proof. He was involved in—maybe even responsible for—Olivia Munro's abduction.

The horror of that weakened her knees. She leaned forward and would have fallen if Lane's arms hadn't come around her and held her upright. She clutched at the steel in his forearms.

"You can cut the shock and surprise act, princess," he said, his voice harsh. "I know you're in this up to your elbows. The only thing I don't know is *why*."

Chapter 17

Sunday, 28 January, 3:12 p.m.

"**O**h, my God! Where is she? Let me see her. Where's my *baby*?" Allison Dowton flung open the front door and flounced into the entryway in a flurry of designer clothing and a cloud of expensive perfume. Her gaze darted wildly around the foyer. She pushed Zara aside, not even taking the time to acknowledge her.

Zara landed up against Lane and stiffened. His hands came up reflexively and broke her fall. An instant later, they dropped away and he stepped sideways, putting distance between them. The anger on his face eased and his expression became composed. It took Zara a good deal longer to recover from her stepmother's sudden arrival.

Lane cleared his throat. "Mrs Dowton, I presume?"

Allison spun on the heel of her bright yellow Christian Laboutins and looked Lane up and down. A spark of interest lit the pale blue depths of her eyes. "And you are?"

"Detective Senior Sergeant Lane Black, from Chatswood Police. I'm part of a joint taskforce between the State Crime Command and the Australian Federal Police investigating the kidnapping of Olivia Munro."

"The State Crime Command and the Australian Federal Police? Wow, I'm impressed," Allison answered with a teasing smile.

Zara's fists clenched. Lane's lips tightened. "Your husband's been assisting us with our enquires. I understand you've been away?"

Allison frowned and then waved him away. "Yes, yes. That's right. I've been waiting for like *forever* to get a flight home. I was visiting my sister in Hervey Bay. She…she's not well."

Zara swallowed her surprise. Knowledge of Aunty Patricia's illness was news to her.

"I'm sorry to hear it, Mrs Dowton. I wish I had more time to commiserate with you, but I'm sure you'll appreciate, time's marching on and I have a little girl to find."

"Of course, Detective, of course." Tears welled in her eyes. She took a lace-edged handkerchief from out of the top of her Prada dress and dabbed at the moisture. "Such a dreadful, dreadful business. I can't imagine what Ellie Munro must be going through. I thank God every second that my little Brittany was spared." She sighed dramatically. "How, why—they're questions only God can answer."

Zara went to argue, but clamped her mouth shut. Years of experience had taught her that arguing with her stepmother was an exercise in futility. Lane's expression turned grim.

"I wish it was that easy, Mrs Dowton. Unfortunately, the Almighty is playing his cards very close to his chest. I appreciate your sentiment, but I'm sure Olivia and her parents will be comforted to know my team and I don't intend to wait around until He reveals them to us."

The door to her father's office opened and Zara's father joined the small gathering in the entryway.

"What's going on? Zara? Detective? Oh, Allison. I see you've made it home." He stepped forward and pecked her on the cheek. With a wail, Allison threw her arms around his neck, and pressed herself against him. It was all Zara could do not to roll her eyes.

"Oh, David, I can't *believe* it! How could this *happen?* Our little girl! I'd never forgive myself if she'd been harmed. Where is she? I need to see her!"

Gently extricating himself from his wife's enthusiastic embrace, Zara's father stepped away. "She's resting in her room," he murmured.

With another wail, Allison turned and headed toward the stairs. For a few moments, her father's gaze followed her progress. His wasn't the only one.

Lane also tracked her ascent. His gaze stayed on her stepmother's enviable figure and Zara felt an immediate and entirely unwelcome stab of jealousy. Aided by the skills of the best plastic surgeon money could buy, Allison looked a decade younger than she was. Much to Zara's chagrin, men never seemed to be any the wiser. To them, Allison Dowton was a unique and ultra-rare butterfly: beautiful, delicate and completely unattainable.

Zara turned away, unable to watch another man fall under her stepmother's spell. The motion caught Lane's attention and he turned to her. His gaze hardened.

"We need to talk."

She glanced at her father. Emotion warred within her. She owed her father another chance to explain. *Didn't she?* He'd lied to her about Draco and the other man who'd met with him in his study, but was he really involved in the kidnapping of his daughter's best friend? It was too much to bear considering the implications that such actions would have for her father, his career and family. She'd already given him not one, but two opportunities to come clean, to tell her the truth. Both times he'd chosen deceit.

Lane stood still and silent, his eyes challenging her to disagree. Despite the graveness of the situation, a thrill of excitement coursed through her at the thought of spending time alone with him.

Ignoring the curious gaze of her father, she nodded decisively and whispered, "Call me."

———————

Lane's text came barely five minutes later. Zara had left

her father in the entryway looking melancholy and confused and had headed back up the stairs to her room to freshen up.

Lane had given her the name of a café with an address in nearby Double Bay. "Christina's on the Bay" was small, but private. She'd been there before with her father and recalled the delicate, wrought iron garden furniture surrounded by shrubs and flowerbeds and ancient fig trees. It was like picnicking in a secluded garden and she'd been told it was a popular spot for illicit lovers seeking a discreet place to meet.

That thought sent heat rushing to her cheeks and she silently castigated herself. Lane worked in the northern suburbs. This wasn't his neighborhood. It was unlikely he had any idea about the establishment's reputation. Even so, the thought of spending time alone with the handsome detective had her feeling a range of unfamiliar sensations.

She looked down at her dress and grimaced. Dust and dirt from the house in Scarborough Road had soiled it in several places. If she hadn't had such a debilitating migraine upon her return, she'd have showered and changed immediately. Lane had demanded she meet him in fifteen minutes. The café was at least a ten-minute drive away.

Moving quickly, she undressed and stepped into the shower. She prided herself on her punctuality, but she refused to meet him while she was filthy. He'd just have to wait.

It was another ten minutes by the time she'd dressed in clean clothes and leaned over the basin to apply a fresh coat of lip gloss. Picking up her hairbrush, she untangled the knots from the long, straight strands and then twisted it into a chignon that caressed the back of her neck.

She wondered about Brittany and hoped her little sister was coping. Zara hadn't stopped in to see her since she'd arrived home and she was immediately filled with guilt. Then she remembered her stepmother had returned and was assured Brittany would be well and looked after.

Her thoughts flew to Olivia, no doubt distressed, hungry and terrified. Zara's guilt intensified. The midnight deadline loomed ever nearer. She sent up a silent prayer that rescue was close at hand. Knowing she might be of help, determination surged through her. It was time to follow the right path to the end. With a clarity that so far had eluded her, she came to a decision.

It was time to tell the truth.

CHAPTER 18

Sunday, 28 January, 3:57 p.m.

Lane sat back against the hard, wrought iron chair and wished he'd found somewhere more comfortable to meet. Like many cafés along the waterfront in the eastern suburbs, comfort had been sabotaged by fashion and he longed for the old, but relaxing booths that filled the café around the corner from where he lived. They may have been covered with cracked red vinyl, but they were big enough for a man to spread out on, to stretch his legs and take a break from the world.

Not that "Christina's" didn't have atmosphere or a view of the harbor that was less than spectacular, but it wasn't the kind of place he felt comfortable in and he wished he'd suggested someplace else.

He glanced at his watch again and tried to contain his impatience. She was late. Or ignoring him. He scowled at the thought. A moment later, she materialized in front of him and his irritation dissipated in the warm summer breeze.

She wore a different dress from the one he'd seen earlier and her hair was damp from the shower. Instead of being loose, it was now pulled back behind her ears and secured low at the back of her neck. Soft pink lipstick glistened in sun, emphasizing the lusciousness of her mouth.

His gut tightened in response. He stood when she

approached, hoping she wouldn't notice his body's reaction.

"Thank you for meeting me," he said, remaining upright until she'd taken a seat.

She stared at him, a myriad of emotions filling her dark eyes. "I had no choice. It was the right thing to do."

Surprise coursed through him. He leaned forward in anticipation. *She was going to confess.* A part of him felt disappointment, even as he braced himself for her admissions.

"Are you admitting you're involved in Olivia's abduction? That you've been involved from the outset?"

A frown marred the smooth skin of her forehead. She shook her head and her eyes narrowed in confusion. "Me? Involved?" She laughed without humor. "Oh, God. You couldn't be further from the truth."

Now it was Lane's turn to feel confused. "But, you knew where she was being held. You were there, in the very same house. I found your scarf."

He watched in silence while she closed her eyes and drew in a deep breath. Tension gripped him. He waited for her to speak. It seemed to take a lifetime.

"You're right about some of it. I *was* there and somehow I dropped my scarf, but I didn't know it was where they'd been hiding Olivia."

"Bullshit. Why the hell else were you there? You live in Point Piper. No one heads out to Milperra and especially not to a place like that, for the sake of a morning drive."

Zara held his gaze steadily. "Please understand how hard this is for me. I-I want to do the right thing. That's why I'm here. I could have ignored your text—"

"And I'd have hauled your sweet little ass across town and put you in the lockup," Lane growled, impatience once again surging through him. "You're in this up to your ears, princess. Now, start talking before I change my mind and slap some cuffs on you."

Her eyes widened with anger that was also laced with fear. Her shoulders rose and fell in time with the rate of her breathing. Lane refused to soften his hard stare. When she spoke again, he had to lean forward to hear her.

"As much as it pains me to tell you, it's...it's my father. He's the one involved in this." The increasing burden she'd felt over the last few days suddenly lifted as each whispered word fell from her lips. While she fully understood the implications of what she'd revealed, she no longer felt inhibited.

Lane's eyes narrowed. He sucked in some air and tried to still his racing heart. "How do you know?"

She drew in a deep breath and released it on a heavy sigh. "A couple of weeks ago, my father met with two men at home in his office. They were rough looking men—unshaven, leather jackets, dirty jeans. They looked so out of place. When I mentioned them to him, he told me they were undercover DEA officers."

Lane made no comment. His gaze continued to drill into hers. She broke the contact and shrugged. "It seemed like a reasonable explanation. I left it at that."

"What happened to change your mind?"

"Two things: Olivia's abduction and Dad telling me he thought the kidnappers had made a mistake—that Brittany had been the target."

"He told me he'd received a threatening phone call from someone identifying with the outlaw motorcycle gangs," Lane said.

"I don't know anything about that, but I recognized two of the men in your photo line-up. One of them was Boris Vukovic, the same man Brittany identified. The other one was Draco Jovanovic. You told me they were members of the notorious Redbacks biker gang."

Lane nodded, his body taut. He waited for her to continue. At last, she spoke again.

"They were the men I saw a few weeks ago in my father's office."

Shock ricocheted through him. It explained her reaction when she'd looked at the photo line-up. He couldn't believe the Attorney General hadn't said a word about that meeting. The thought made him frown. "How do I know you're telling the truth?"

She met his stare without flinching. "You don't. But I have a sister the same age as Olivia. I can't imagine the horror her parents are going through. I want to help. I *need* to help."

She looked away, her breath coming faster. After a few moments, she looked back at him.

"After you left the second time, I questioned Dad again. Again, he denied the men in his office had anything to do with outlaw biker gangs." Her shoulders rose and then slumped. "I knew he was lying. And what reason could he have to hide the truth…? I've run out of reasons to defend him."

She looked bereft and defeated, but Lane quashed the urge to offer her comfort. He was in the middle of a breakthrough in the case. A little girl's life depended upon it. The seconds were ticking by. Anger stirred inside him.

"Why didn't you call me?"

Her eyes scrunched closed. Her teeth bit into her bottom lip. Lane tried to contain his impatience.

"I should have. I know that. I thought about it, but you have to understand. I still didn't know the extent of my father's involvement. I wanted to protect him as much as I could. When I found the note with Draco's name on it, I thought—"

Lane tensed. "Hang on a minute, what did you say? What note?"

"I-I snooped around in Dad's office. I found a piece of paper with Draco's name on it and an address."

"The house in Milperra."

"Yes."

Lane let the information settle inside his head. It made sense. It explained why the ransom note offered no contact details. It explained how she'd known about Draco's hideout. *It explained what she was doing there.* All of a sudden, a different kind of anger surged through him.

"How could you have been so stupid? I can't believe you put yourself in such danger. How did you know the place wasn't crawling with armed and dangerous criminals? If you really thought it might have been where they were hiding Olivia, surely it occurred to you that you were putting your life in danger by going there? Do you really think that little of me and my colleagues?"

Zara winced and pulled away from the anger in his voice, but he didn't care. He couldn't believe she'd been so foolhardy. The men that ran with the Redbacks were violent criminals, some of the worst the State had to offer. And she'd waltzed into their hidey-hole alone and unarmed.

"Did you have the sense to tell anyone where you were going?"

Color bloomed in her cheeks. Tears glistened in her eyes. She looked away and shook her head. Pity tightened Lane's chest when he saw the desolation that flooded her face.

"I-I thought I was doing the right thing. I wanted to protect my father, but I also wanted to help that poor little girl." Her voice broke. She swiped at her eyes and then riffled through her handbag and finally withdrew a tissue.

His anger died. What she'd been trying to do was heroic, admirable—even if it was the stupidest thing he'd ever heard. She weighed no more than a grasshopper. If Draco or his men had still been inside the house, they'd have squashed her like a bug. She'd have disappeared like so many of the gang's enemies, never to be seen again.

Anger once again ignited low inside him, but this time, he did his best to contain it. He believed she'd had the best of intentions in her heart. She couldn't have known the danger she put herself in. At least she'd come out of it unscathed.

On impulse, he leaned across the table and reached for her hand and gave it a reassuring squeeze. She gasped softly, but didn't pull away.

Though the late afternoon sunlight was plenty adequate, sometime during their conversation, a waitress had approached and lit the candle that was centered on their table. The flame flickered and danced in the light breeze, but he hardly noticed. Zara stared at him, her eyes huge in her delicate face. He couldn't take his gaze off her.

His heart pounded hard against his chest. His throat tightened. He opened his mouth, but found he couldn't speak. She was so beautiful, she took his breath away.

There had been women in and out of his life, but none that had affected him like her. He could drown in the depths of her midnight eyes. They beckoned him to look deep within her, encouraging him slowly, until once committed, he'd be powerless to resist her and there would be nothing more he could do but surrender.

Delicate laughter from a nearby table snapped him out of his reverie. This wasn't the time to let his emotions take over. The timing was all wrong. Loosening his hold on her hand, he slowly released it and returned it to the table. She curled her hand into a fist.

He cleared his throat. "I'm sorry. I shouldn't have done that. You're a beautiful woman. I…" Heat raced up his neck and spread across his cheeks. He turned away.

What the hell was he doing? He was acting like a teenager, not a grown man of thirty-one. Besides, he didn't do serious. Women and commitment just didn't work for him. Not after what had happened to his mother.

He swallowed a sigh and readied himself to leave. As much as he wanted to spend more time in her company, time was a commodity in short supply.

He cleared his throat and refused to look at her. "I have to go. Thank you for telling me. I'm sure it will make a difference."

"Do you think you'll find her?"

"Well, we have more to go on than we did before. I'll go back to the station and make some plans. Our raid on Vukovic's place yielded nothing but confirmation of the house in Milperra. Let's hope a raid on Draco's place of residence will give us more. I'm sure he's not stupid enough to move her there, but we might shake a little more information out of him. Who knows?"

"It's worth a shot," she murmured.

Suddenly impatient to get things moving, Lane shoved

back his chair and stood. "I'm sorry. I'd really like to stay, but I can't. I need to get back."

Zara nodded, her expression grave. "I understand. Call me if you find her. Please."

He stared down at her, wanting to memorize the sweetness of her features. His gut tightened with resolve.

"I will. I promise."

———

Olivia slowly regained consciousness and became aware of her surroundings. She still lay sprawled across the back seat of Boris' car, her hands tightly secured. She still wore the blindfold and her breathing continued to be labored through the gag. Every part of her body ached and her head pounded so hard it felt like it would explode. She didn't know how long she'd been out of it, but the air that blew in from the car's opened window felt cooler.

Please, Daddy, please hurry. I need you to find me. Now. I'm so scared. Tears burned behind the blindfold. Even the sight of Ellie would be welcome.

At the thought of her stepmother, Olivia bit her lip against a sob. Ellie had shown her nothing but kindness and love. From the time she could remember, Ellie had treated her like her own child. Until the boys arrived, she'd been their only child. She hadn't once felt unwanted or unloved.

But the older she got, the more she became aware of the loss she'd suffered by losing her real mother. The more she thought about it, the angrier she became. It wasn't fair that her mother had died so young. It wasn't fair that Olivia couldn't remember her. If it hadn't been for the photos her father kept, she wouldn't even have known what Lisa Munro looked like.

The unjustness of it ate away at her like a disease and made her madder and madder still. With cold purpose, she set her sights on Ellie and took out the brunt of her anger on her. At first, it was little acts of defiance, a tantrum here and there, but the more she realized how much it affected Ellie, the more determined she became to keep it up.

She was waging her own personal war against God and the unfairness she'd been served. But God was out of her reach and Ellie was much more accessible.

Hot shame burned through Olivia at the thought of how she'd treated the only mother she'd known. Ellie had been so good and kind and loving—everything she assumed a real mother was. She hadn't deserved to be treated so badly. She hadn't deserved the attitude. She hadn't deserved any of it. Olivia could see that now. She only prayed she'd be given the chance to apologize.

The vehicle swerved suddenly and took a corner fast. Olivia slid across the seat and banged her elbow against the armrest. She gritted her teeth.

It was a moment before she realized the car had come to a halt. Boris opened his door and she tensed. The sound of the backseat door opening reignited all of the fear that for a brief moment had subsided. Now, it exploded through her like fire.

Two meaty hands grabbed her ankles and hauled her out of the car. Unable to use her arms, she braced herself as best she could against the jarring impact of the ground. She fell hard and the breath was knocked out of her. Pain radiated through her hip and up into her spine. Fresh tears burned behind her eyes. *Where, oh where was her daddy? Where, oh where was her mom?*

If God ever let her see them once more, she'd never be mean to Ellie—her mom—again. She'd picked the fight with her mom on purpose and God was punishing her for it. And she deserved it. She deserved everything that happened to her.

The ground beneath her cheek was grassy and moist and there wasn't even a glimmer of light. She could only assume it was nighttime again. They must have been driving around for hours. Her bladder was painfully full and she did her best to ignore it. The blindfold was still pulled tightly across her eyes, making it impossible to see even the slightest of shapes in the darkness, then hope flared inside her at the sound of a woman's voice.

"What the fuck are you up to, Boris? The coppers have been here. They're lookin' for you. You'd better not be in fuckin' trouble. Last time you went to the clink I had to put Emma into foster care. Couldn't afford to look after her."

"Shut the fuck up, Sandra. You hear nothin', you see nothin', understand?"

"What the fuck happened to your face?"

"Nothin'. I ran into somethin', all right? See this girl? She's our ticket to the big time. Just you wait and see. Now, go and open up the trapdoor."

Olivia's courage collapsed at his words. Her body trembled. Rough hands lifted her off the ground and forced her to walk forward. She stumbled in the darkness and earned a string of curses from Boris.

"For fuck's sake, just walk, would you?"

With fear continuing to surge through every part of her body, Olivia did her best to do as he asked. Her bare toe connected with concrete, causing it to bend backwards. She grimaced pain.

"Lift your fuckin' feet, girlie. We're goin' up some steps."

Concentrating all her efforts on staying upright, Olivia counted the three steps that led into a building. A door slammed behind her and Boris dragged her further into the room. She shuffled along beside him, feeling the softer tread of carpet beneath her feet. The sound of a television on low came from the other side of the room. Her best guess was that she was in another house.

The bindings that held her wrists cut into her skin. She'd given up trying to loosen them. It only made the pain worse. The creaking of old dry wood snagged her attention. Boris pushed her forward, toward the noise. Two steps, five. And then...*nothingness.*

The ground went out from underneath her. Her feet flailed. Her arms reflexively moved upwards, but were cruelly restrained by the bindings. Air whistled around her. She screamed and fell into a black pit of terror.

It seemed like forever, but it was probably only a few seconds before she hit the hard ground with a thud that knocked the breath out of her. Gasping, she leaned away from the arm she'd fallen on and prayed it wasn't broken.

With her other hand, she felt along the floor and walls of the tight enclosure as best she could. Her fingers scraped over crags and eddies along the earthen surface. It felt like some kind of cellar under the house. The smell of damp earth permeated the air and filled her nostrils. The tears swelled as she tried to fight off the nausea that suddenly threatened.

She hiccupped and sobbed through the choking gag and prayed for the nightmare to be over.

CHAPTER 19

Sunday, January 28, 4:18 p.m.

Allison smoothed back the hair off her daughter's face and thanked God her baby was safe. Never in her wildest dreams had she thought it would come to this. When David had told her about the unexpected visit by the two bikers, she'd been alarmed—of course she had—but there had been threats in the past and they'd never come to pass. A fortnight ago, Draco had even struck her and yet she hadn't once imagined he'd threaten her child.

She couldn't even feel guilty about the fact Brittany had been spared and someone else's child hadn't. That was the luck of the draw. Still, she was pissed at Draco for making the attempt. If he hadn't mistaken Olivia Munro for Brittany, Allison would be feeling a lot less ambivalent about the whole fiasco.

Brittany. Sweet, baby Brittany. Thank God she was all right. Allison would die before she let anything happen to her daughter.

The phone in her jacket pocket vibrated against her hip. With a grimace, she eased it out and checked the Caller ID. It was blocked. Wanting to ignore it, but not quite brave enough to do so, she stepped away from Brittany's bed and answered the call.

"Just because Boris fucked up, don't think I've given up. You should know me better than that."

Allison's knees weakened at the venom in Draco's voice. "Wh-what are you talking about?"

"The girl. I know he took the wrong one. I told him to get rid of her. She's of no use to me. As if you're going to pay for the daughter of some fucking copper. Next time, I'll do it myself. Next time, there won't be any mistakes. And be warned, there'll be a next time."

"Please, Draco. I-I'll get your money. I promise. David is trying to liquidate some assets. He…he needs more time."

"I've already given him a fortnight. He's had all the time he's going to get."

Alarm sent cold shivers down Allison's spine. She bit her lip and tried to keep calm. "Come on, Draco. There's no need to be like that. You know me. David will find the money."

"Seems to me like he might need a bit more incentive," Draco growled. "Something to hurry him along. Perhaps if his trophy wife's life is on the line, he might liquidate a bit faster."

Allison could barely hear him over the pounding of her heart. Her fear intensified. "No, not me," she answered quickly. "You've got it all wrong. I'm not the one he adores." She paused. Something that felt suspiciously like guilt pricked at the edge of her consciousness, but she pushed it aside and decisively forged on.

"Take Zara. His firstborn. There's nothing in the world he wouldn't do for *her*." She proceeded to enlighten Draco about her stepdaughter, providing him with all the details he needed to aid him in his quest.

She held the phone in her hand for a few brief moments after the call ended and replayed every word of their conversation. It was done.

Satisfying herself Brittany was still asleep, she left the room and closed the door quietly behind her. At the end of the long corridor, she entered the master suite and headed straight for the bathroom. With the door closed, she pulled open the bottom drawer of her vanity and tugged out a bag of ice. Tipping a small amount into the glass smoking apparatus she kept hidden beneath her sanitary pads, she added a few drops of water and then heated it with her lighter.

Sucking on the end of the glass pipe, she drew the smoke deep into her lungs and sighed in relief. Within minutes, the world was a better place. Afterwards, she returned the components of the drug paraphernalia to their hiding places. She checked her appearance in the mirror. Her pupils were slightly dilated, but after the distress she'd been through, people would understand it. Nodding once, satisfied she'd pass close inspection, she returned to her daughter's side.

David poured himself another finger of scotch and took his time replacing the lid. Setting the half-empty bottle back on the shelf, he collected his glass and returned to the chair near his desk.

It had been nearly two hours since he'd spoken to Allison in the front foyer. With Zara and the detective standing nearby, he hadn't been in a position to do more than offer her a strained greeting. She'd gone upstairs to sit with Brittany.

He understood her need to reassure herself that their daughter was safe. But enough was enough. She'd had her time. Besides, she'd taken her own sweet time getting home. He didn't believe for an instant every plane out of Port Douglas the day before had been booked out. It was obvious she'd been delaying her arrival—and with it, their inevitable confrontation.

Well, she'd had plenty of time to come to terms with it. The moment of truth had arrived and she better be darn well prepared to accept responsibility for her part in the whole debacle; to take ownership of the problem; and to come clean to the police.

He'd done what he could to steer them in the right direction. It was the reason he'd fabricated the threatening phone call. The police would never have thought to connect Jovanovic with the Munro child otherwise.

He'd hated to deceive Zara and worse, to omit certain other details to the police, but he hadn't been able to bring himself to betray his wife.

Yes, it was her fault this had happened, but she was sick. Deep down, she was a good person and he loved her, despite what she'd done. He'd loved her from the first moment he'd met her.

Allison hadn't warmed to Zara, but then, being a stepparent was difficult for anyone, let alone a stepparent to a teenager. It hadn't been easy. And then in no time at all, little Brittany had come along and it didn't seem to matter so much anymore. He should have tried harder; he should have insisted Allison make more of an effort, but his love for Zara hadn't wavered and somehow, he'd justified to himself that this was enough.

Besides, his firstborn daughter was tough as she was smart. She was a fighter and she knew how to take care of herself. He was never more proud than when she decided to follow in her grandfather's and her father's footsteps and carve out a career in law. Even now, the knowledge of her success lit up his heart.

Taking a sip out of his glass, David relished the taste of the single malt whisky on his tongue. It slid smoothly down his throat and burned a pleasant path to his stomach, easing the tension that had taken up residence there for the last fortnight.

He'd known, of course, that Allison's drug addiction was getting out of control. The signs were there when you knew what to look for. As far as he was aware, Zara and Brittany were clueless to it, but then, his wife was very clever at concealing her habit.

It had started out innocently enough—a tablet here and a tablet there. She said it helped her relax, be more social— especially in a roomful of dignitaries and government officials. He hadn't liked it, but he'd accepted her explanation and it had alleviated some of the guilt he felt for dragging her to so many high-profile events.

As she so often pointed out to him, she hadn't signed up for any of this. When they'd married, he'd been a partner in a very successful law firm. While they enjoyed a healthy social life, it was nothing on the scale or level of importance expected of the New South Wales Attorney General.

Allison had played his guilt to her advantage and had used it more times than he could remember as an excuse for her need to take drugs. He knew her dependence upon them had escalated. It was the reason he'd booked her into an exclusive rehabilitation center at Port Douglas in far north Queensland. He'd told everyone she was visiting her sister.

But until Draco's evening visit, he'd had no idea about the amount of money she'd been spending on her habit. He'd been shocked again to discover the Redbacks' president had allowed her to take drugs on credit and Allison was a good and loyal customer.

That created one gigantic problem: Accounts had to be paid. David had been stunned beyond words when Draco had told him the tab was a million dollars.

How could she possibly have consumed so much? There had obviously been many, many occasions when she'd been high and he hadn't realized it. He could see that his frequent interstate and overseas travel in his role as Attorney General had only made the problem worse.

Not that he could do anything about it now. He had the money, of course. If Draco had been just a little more patient, the whole messy business could have been resolved with only minor inconvenience to everyone. But Draco wasn't patient, and a little girl had been taken—a little girl that by all rights should have been *his* daughter.

Once again, relief flooded through him, followed swiftly by searing guilt. He prayed his delay wouldn't cause the loss of Olivia Munro's life. If he'd acted quicker, sold shares sooner, he'd have made Draco's first deadline.

But he'd dragged his feet and taken his time, furious that

Allison had put him in such a position. He'd been angry about liquidating assets he'd worked hard to acquire in order to satisfy her drug debt and before he knew it, the deadline had come and gone.

The next thing he knew, he was taking a phone call from Ellie Munro. Almost hysterical, she'd told him about the kidnapping. He'd immediately thought of the visit he'd had from the bikers a fortnight before.

His guilt had forced him to steer the police in Jovanovic's direction. Of course, he hadn't been able to tell them the real reason why a member of the Redbacks had abducted the Munro child. The fabricated phone call had given the biker gang a motive and he'd made it clear his daughter had been the target. At least it gave them a fighting chance of finding Olivia.

Pain twisted in his stomach and he grimaced. The stress of the last two weeks had taken their toll on his ulcer. The effort to keep up the facade was wearing him down and the thought of admitting Olivia might never be found—or not be found alive—left him shaken to the core.

Guilt surged through him again, along with renewed anger. Allison should be the one feeling scared and guilty. She was the one who'd put them in danger, to the point that she'd endangered her own daughter.

Tugging his phone out of his pocket, he dialed his wife's number. After several rings, she finally picked up.

"Come downstairs. We need to talk. *Now.*"

Lane looked over his shoulder in both directions and checked that the men waiting behind him were ready. Speaking quietly into the handpiece attached to his shirt, he confirmed the team of officers assembled at the rear of Draco's residence were also ready and waiting for his command to enter.

The TRG squad he'd hastily pulled together contained

many of the men who'd raided Boris Vukovic's house a day earlier and they were once again primed and ready to go. A quick meeting at the Chatswood station had brought everyone up to speed. There wasn't an officer among them who wasn't keen to see this scene played out.

Straining to listen for signs of danger over the distant sound of a television that murmured behind the closed door, Lane at last gave the order to his men. Simultaneously, he yelled into the handpiece.

"Go! "Go! Go!" Men in dark police-issue overalls stormed Draco's house. The sound of a gunshot curdled Lane's blood and he prayed the victim wasn't one of theirs. Forcing open doors and pushing over furniture, he at last came upon Draco lying on the floor of the bedroom with his hands cuffed behind his back.

Lane nodded an acknowledgement to the officers who had come in from the rear. "Good job, boys. Any casualties?"

"No, Lane. Draco got a little excited. Put a bullet through the ceiling."

Lane looked up and saw the hole in the plasterboard. "Nice shot, Jovanovic."

Draco spat at him. "Fuck off, pig. This is police harassment. I'm not hiding anything. You've got no right to break into my house like this. I'm going to the fucking media with this."

"Talk to whoever you like, Draco. But first, you're talking to me. We're taking you back to the station."

"I've got nothing to say to nobody."

Lane smiled without humor. "Let's just see about that, shall we?"

Two hours later, Lane's temper had reached the boiling point. Despite all his efforts and those of a couple of his AFP colleagues, Draco refused to budge. A knock on the interview room door drew his attention. His boss met him in the corridor, his expression grim.

"It's no use, Lane. He's lawyered up and he's not going to give us anything. Time's up. We can't hold him any longer. We're going to have to cut him loose."

Lane cursed savagely and his hands clenched into fists. "The asshole knows where she is. She was in his house in Milperra, for Christ's sake. There's no way he's not in this up to his stinking armpits."

"That may be so, but we have nothing on him. Footwear similar to Olivia Munro's was found in a shack owned by him. That's it, and unless we can get DNA off it, we can't even prove it's hers. We have no evidence tying him to anything. You know as well as I do, that's not enough. We have to let him go."

Lane groaned and swore again. Helplessness and frustration engulfed him. He was so close to a breakthrough. He knew it. But the smug bastard on the other side of the door knew it, too. He knew they didn't have enough evidence to charge him; if they did, they would have done it the moment they'd brought him in. Draco knew it. Lane knew it.

With everything inside him screaming in protest, he opened the door to the interview room and eyeballed Draco and his lawyer.

"All right, Jovanovic, you're free to go." Catching sight of the triumphant gleam in Draco's eyes, Lane turned away, only managing to keep his fury in check until they'd left the room. Slamming his fist into the worn desktop, he winced at the pain reverberating up his forearm.

"I understand how you feel, Lane, but that probably wasn't a good idea. Your arm won't thank you for it in the morning."

Lane looked at Michael who'd followed him into the room and grimaced. "Where do we go from here?"

His boss frowned as he thought. "The Attorney General's daughter saw Jovanovic and Vukovic in her father's office a fortnight ago. What that means is anyone's guess, but the man had Jovanovic's name and address hidden inside a locked drawer. Why didn't he mention that he knew Jovanovic? He was the one who pointed us in the direction of the Redbacks, after all. Something doesn't fit. You need to have another chat with the AG. Take Jett with you." Michael glanced at his watch. "It's just after nine. You'd better get a move on. I'll call the AG and let him know you're on your way. Have you checked in with Clayton Munro?"

Lane sighed. Exhaustion was setting in. He'd gone home last night and snatched a few hours' sleep before returning to work that morning. The strain of the investigation was beginning to take its toll. He spared a thought for Clayton and Ellie and shook off his fatigue. There wasn't time for fatigue. The deadline was less than three hours away.

"No, I haven't. I'll do it on my way over to Dowton's."

"Okay. We need to know how much money they've managed to get together, in case the AG falls a little short. Find out if Dowton has any more information about where the exchange is going to take place. We can only hope that if Draco's involved in this, he might just extend the deadline. He's been a little busy himself, tonight."

Lane nodded. "Let's hope so."

Chapter 20

Sunday, January 28, 9:13 p.m.

Allison shifted her position in the chair in her husband's office and stared at her fingernails. She needed a manicure and she needed a painkiller. She always ended up with a vicious headache when she was coming down off a high.

After being summoned by David a few hours earlier, she'd come downstairs feeling relaxed and calm. Her husband had taken one look at her and had cursed long and loudly.

"You're fucking high! I don't believe it! How could you? A little girl was abducted yesterday. The police may never find her alive. It was supposed to be *our* daughter. And *you're* the reason behind the kidnapping!" he yelled, his face turning purple with rage.

"You and your drug habit are the reasons Olivia Munro is in the hands of some of the worst criminals this State has to offer. And what do you have to say for yourself?" He spun on his heel and then cursed again.

It was probably his cursing that frightened her the most. It was so unlike the man she knew. Her silence infuriated him further, but she had nothing to say. All she wanted to do was lie down and go to sleep.

As if he could read her mind, he shook his head in disgust.

"Get out of here. There's no point talking to you in this state. Come back when you're able to comprehend the seriousness of this situation."

When she didn't move, he turned on her again.

"Go!"

Now, nearly three hours later, she'd slept off most of her high and once again found herself in his office. Her husband paced a short distance away, becoming more and more agitated.

"I don't understand how you spent a *million dollars* on drugs!" he shouted, turning to face her.

She shrugged, refusing to feel perturbed. He was well aware of the reasons she needed the confidence and security the illegal drugs gave her. She'd been upfront about it right from the start.

Okay, maybe she hadn't been quite as forthcoming about the fact she'd been getting her drugs on credit or that she'd moved on from a pill or two every now and then or the occasional line of speed, to smoking ice on a regular basis. Still, she'd been using for years. He had to know that the more she took, the more she craved. He wasn't an idiot.

He turned on his heel once again. His breath came fast. With his hands on his hips, he glared at her.

"I don't know why you're so upset," she said as calmly as she could, hoping to deflect his anger. "We have plenty of money. Some people like to spend their money on fast cars or race horses." She lifted a shoulder. "I like to do crystal meth. There's no harm in it."

His face mottled with rage. "No harm in it? We're talking a million dollars and that's what you owe. God knows how much you've already spent over the years."

She made a bigger effort to pacify him. It wouldn't do to make him too angry. She ignored the pain in her head and tried a gentle smile.

"You're making too much of this, David. We'll pay the debt and that will be that. I'll even go back to rehab, if that's what you want."

"You seem to forget the minor issue with young Olivia. She was kidnapped and still hasn't been found. Does that not concern you even a *little*?"

"Of course it does," she snapped, losing her patience. "What do you think I am? Totally self-absorbed?" She shuddered. "I'm just so thankful it wasn't Brittany."

"Well, it could have been. In fact, I'm very sure it *should* have been. I told the police as much as soon as I heard about it."

Surprise struck her hard. Her jaw fell open. "Why would you do something like that?"

Her husband stared at her and then slowly shook his head. "Who are you? I don't even recognize you anymore."

The defeat in his voice alarmed her. This was her husband, the dragon slayer, the man who stopped at nothing to achieve his dreams, the man who loved her more than his life. She stood and went to him, pressing a hand to his cheek. He flinched and turned away. Panic surged through her.

"David, please. You know who I am. I'm still the woman you married. I'm still the woman you love, just like I love you. We're a team, you and I. We're in this together. Please don't say things like that. You're scaring me."

He gave a short bark. "*You're* the one who's scared? Really? How do you think that poor kid feels?" He spun away from her. "Our daughter's friend was abducted from the mall and taken God knows where to be held for ransom for a debt that has nothing to do with her or her family. An innocent girl, probably terrorized beyond belief, who may never recover from the ordeal. And that's if they find her alive."

He turned back toward her, his eyes like flint. She gasped at the fury contained in them. He stared at her hard.

"It's over, Allison. It's time to tell the truth. I'm going to call the police and tell them everything. Before it's too late."

A protest bubbled up in her throat, but one look at his face and she swallowed it.

"Don't. Say. Anything. Don't. You. Dare." The words were bitten off and spat at her with such venom she recoiled as if he'd struck her.

"I mean it, Allison. I can't take anymore." He turned his back on her and made his way over to his desk. Taking a seat, he reached for the phone and dialed.

———————

Boris lumbered across the living room and pushed the shabby coffee table out of the way. Bending over, he tugged at the iron ring that was fixed into the wooden trapdoor. It resisted momentarily and then gave way, creaking in protest.

Switching on his flashlight, he aimed the beam into the darkness and smiled. The girl was lying on her side with her knees pulled up against her chest. The blindfold was still in place, as were the bindings around her wrists.

"Sandra, get over here and help me," he yelled at the woman lounging on the couch nearby.

Grumbling and complaining, she at last stood beside him, next to the opening.

"What are you doin'?" Her voice was surly.

He narrowed his eyes at her. "I need to talk to the girl."

"What about?"

"About her parents, you stupid slut. I already told you. She's our ticket out of here."

Sandra peered down into the darkness. "Who is she?"

"She's the girl who was taken from the Westfield Mall in Chatswood yesterday mornin'. Draco told me to nab her. He was holdin' her for ransom, but it turns out he doesn't need her anymore." He turned to his wife and smiled. "He gave her to me."

Sandra stared at him, her eyes gleaming with suspicion and curiosity. "What are you goin' to do with her?"

"Ransom her myself, stupid. Draco doesn't want her anymore. It doesn't mean we can't make a few dollars out of her."

A smile tugged at Sandra's lips. "How much is she worth?"

Boris shrugged. "Draco was askin' for a million, but I don't think her folks could come up with the coin. I say we drop it down a few thou—maybe half a million? Her father's some hotshot federal cop. He's got to be good for that much, don't you reckon?"

The smile faded. "A cop? Fuck, Boris. The pigs were here yesterday, I already told ya. They barged in here fuckin' yellin' and shoutin' and asked me where you were. Of course, I told 'em nothin'. I didn't fuckin' know where you were, anyway." She narrowed her eyes and Boris looked away, resisting the questions in her eyes. The less she knew, the better for both of them.

"It's good you told 'em nothin' and the fact they've already been here will play in our favor. They won't be quick to come lookin' again when they were here only yesterday and found nothin'."

Slowly, Sandra's smile reappeared until it showed all of her sadly neglected teeth. "You're right." She threw her arms around him and hugged him hard. "You're a fuckin' genius, Boris. A bloody, fuckin' genius."

Boris nodded, pleased with her praise. There was no way he was telling her how he'd fucked the whole thing up. She didn't have to know about it. Besides, he liked the way she made him feel all competent-like. It made him feel invincible.

"Here, take the flashlight and shine it down the hole. I'm goin' to reach down and see if I can drag her up from here." He handed Sandra the light and hunkered down beside the opening.

With his arms outstretched, he managed to snag the girl's T-shirt and hauled her up toward him. She whimpered and tried to move away. He tightened his grip. The fabric of her T-shirt tore and he almost dropped her. He cursed and readjusted his hold. Taking her by the arms, he dragged her up through the opening and deposited her onto the floor.

Sandra shone the light over the girl's body. "I didn't get much of a look at her before. Boris. She's only a fuckin' kid," Sandra said.

"So what? I'm sure someone'll pay to have her back. You'd pay if someone pinched Emma, wouldn't you?"

Sandra shrugged. "Yeah, I guess so. But you better not ask them for too much."

"Don't worry. I'm not goin' to make the same mistake Draco did. What if we say two hundred grand? That's still a tidy sum to take with us. It'll get us settled somewhere in the country, somewhere away from all this." He indicated the filth and squalor of their surroundings.

"Can I have a little veggie patch and maybe a few chickens?"

Boris smiled and pulled his wife close, pressing a kiss on her forehead. "You sure can."

"Let's do it."

With Sandra's help, he manoeuvred the girl's slight body onto the sofa. He leaned over to untie the blindfold. "If I take off this rag, do you promise not to scream?"

The girl nodded.

"If I hear one word out of you, I'm goin' to whack you so hard you'll wish you'd done as you were told. Understand?"

Again, the girl nodded.

Satisfied, Boris released the knot that held the cloth tightly over the girl's eyes and tossed it onto the couch. She blinked at the unaccustomed light, staring from Boris to Sandra and back again.

"Wh-where am I? Please, don't hurt me. Please take me back to my daddy."

"We're goin' to do just that, Olivia. That's your name, ain't it?"

The girl nodded a third time.

"Matter of fact, I'm goin' to call your daddy right now. I'm goin' to ask him for a few dollars. If he pays, you get to go home. Do you think he'll pay?"

This time, the girl's nod was swift and sure. Boris smiled. "Good. We'll have no problem, then."

"What's his number?" Sandra demanded impatiently.

Olivia looked uncertain and fear clouded her eyes. "I-I can't remember."

Sandra's expression turned menacing. "Well, you'd better remember, girlie. You won't be goin' home if we can't talk to him."

The girl's eyes widened in panic. "No, no. Please, I'll try harder. I-I can't think. I—"

Boris took pity on her. He shot a warning glance toward his wife. "It's all right, Olivia. We've got time. Take a few breaths and think about it. Who do you call if you're sick at school?"

"Th-the ladies in the front office usually call my m-mom."

"Okay," Boris smiled encouragingly. "What's Mom's name and number?"

"She's not really my—" Olivia stopped. "I-I mean, her name's Ellie Munro and her number's 9957 6529."

Boris smiled wider. "There you go. Now, that wasn't difficult, was it?"

Olivia shook her head, her expression still cautious.

Boris eyed Sandra. "Watch her while I make the call." Turning away, he pulled out his cell phone and dialed the number.

Chapter 21

Sunday, January 28, 9:51 p.m.

Lane stared at the Attorney General, unable to believe what the man had just told him. His gaze shifted to Zara who stood stiffly in the corner of the room, looking almost as shocked as he felt. Her eyes were trained on her father who sat at his desk, his head bowed low.

Only Allison seemed unaffected. Swinging her shapely crossed leg back and forth, she looked around at the men gathered before her and smiled.

"Can I offer anyone a drink? Tea? Coffee? Something stronger, perhaps?"

Lane stared at her and shook his head. Was she for *real*? Her husband had just told them she was a drug addict and that the motive behind the kidnapping of Olivia Munro was retribution for an unpaid drug debt. And her response was to offer them a *drink*?

Was she completely unhinged? High? Or so totally self-absorbed that she was unable to comprehend the effect of her actions on others? He didn't know which it was, but he wasn't having any of it and he let his anger show.

"Mrs Dowton, you may have caused the loss of an innocent girl's life. Do you have anything to say to that?" To his disgust and increasing fury, she waved his question aside.

"Oh, Detective Black, I think you're exaggerating. Draco

knows I'll find the money. I always have in the past. I don't know why he overreacted like he did. But he'll get paid and that will be the end of it."

Lane's eyes widened incredulously. "You just don't get it, do you? Olivia Munro hasn't been found. And even if she is, she may never get over what's happened to her. Imagine if it had been your daughter who was kidnapped. Would you be so quick to brush it off?"

Her only response was to lift a slim shoulder in a half-shrug. Lane turned away in disgust, unable to face her a minute longer. He caught Zara's eye. Her gaze was dark with anger and that anger was directed at her father's wife.

At least the psychosis didn't run in the family. For that much, Lane was grateful.

"Tell me, Allison," Zara spoke, her voice trembling with emotion. "Is Aunty Patricia really sick, or is that another lie?"

Surprise surged through Lane at Zara's use of her stepmother's given name. *So, she didn't call her 'Mom.'* He stored that interesting tidbit of information away for later dissection.

Allison waved Zara's question away. Her father's gaze remained leveled at his desk.

"Of course she isn't ill. At least, not as far as I know." She narrowed her eyes at her husband. "Your father made me check into rehab. I've been up in Port Douglas for a fortnight. The weather, mind you, was quite divine, although the humidity...*whew!* It takes some getting used to. Just as well the rooms were air-conditioned. I don't think—"

"You make me sick," Zara interrupted, her voice trembling with shock and anger. She advanced on her stepmother and came to a halt only feet away from the woman who eyed her disdainfully.

"I can't believe I didn't know you're a drug user. How could I have been so blind? You were probably high right under my nose and right under little Brittany's." She spun on her heel and faced her father, her eyes shooting fire.

"You knew, didn't you, Dad? You've known all along. You knew she was an addict. You'd have never sent her to rehab if you didn't. Did you know about the drug debt? Did you know Draco wanted it paid?" She shook her head and Lane could tell she was slowly piecing it together.

"That's why Draco and that other man were in your office a couple of weeks ago. It had nothing to do with undercover DEA officers or your so-called political persuasions. They were there to collect their money. Weren't they, Dad?"

The room was charged with tension. Zara's breath came fast. At last, the AG lifted his head and nodded, his face ravaged with pain and devastation.

It was nothing compared to the look of horror and disbelief that flooded Zara's features. Lane's gut clenched at the shock and desolation on her face. She crumpled into the nearest chair. He resisted the urge to go to her. This had nothing to do with him. He was in the middle of a kidnapping investigation. He had a terrified little girl to find. He stepped forward and took charge of the room.

"None of this is getting us anywhere. Mrs Dowton, we have until midnight to find Olivia Munro. It's now going on for ten. We have a little over two hours. Can you provide us with anything of relevance that might actually help us find this little girl—before it's too late?"

Despite Zara's outburst and the quiet sobbing that came from her direction, once again, Allison offered a nonchalant wave. "Look, let me call Draco and get this sorted out." She pulled out her cell phone. "I'm sure he'll hand the Munro child over and we can all put this nasty little incident behind us."

Anger ignited inside him, beyond anything he'd ever experienced. He clenched his fists and glared at her.

"We've already questioned him. He denied knowing anything about it."

"Oh, phooey, that's just nonsense," she replied, waving a deprecating hand in Lane's direction. "Of course he knows about it." She scrolled through her contacts, a slight frown marring the smooth skin of her forehead. Lane breathed through gritted teeth, his jaw clenched.

"Ah, here it is." She smiled triumphantly. "Now, let's see if he's going to answer."

Ellie twisted her hands in her lap and stared for the umpteenth time at the clock on the wall of the living room. The television blared tunelessly in the background. She was grateful for the noise that filled the otherwise silent room. Clayton sat close beside her on the couch.

The boys had gone to sleep hours ago, oblivious to their parents' distress. It was well after ten. Less than two hours until the deadline. They'd gotten together all the available cash they could find. Clayton's brothers and parents had all contributed. All up, they had a little over one hundred thousand dollars. She just hoped the Attorney General had been able to find the difference.

Lane had called Clayton a little earlier and explained the progress they'd made. Ellie hoped desperately that Lane was calling to tell them they'd found Olivia. The disappointment was crushing when she realized that wasn't the reason for his call.

The conversation had been brief: They were doing all that they could; they had a few leads; they were hoping the deadline would be extended.

All the normal platitudes she'd heard and offered a hundred times over to anxious family members during her years as a federal police officer. She now had a real appreciation for how completely ineffectual reassurances were.

Clayton had ended the phone call and relayed the gist of Lane's message. Her heart broke at the pain and despair and anger in his eyes. She went to him and put her arms around his waist, not knowing whether he would accept her offer of comfort; relieved and teary when he did. They held each other and tried not to think about the nightmare that had taken over their lives. Clayton shuddered against her.

"I'm sorry, Ellie. Christ, I'm so sorry. I've been such a prick," he whispered against her hair, his voice hoarse with pain and regret. "These past few months and all the tension between you and Olivia... I don't know how to fix it. I want to, but I don't know how."

She looked up at him. "It's been tough on everyone, Olivia included. I understand she misses her mom. I understand her need to lash out. She's angry that her mom isn't here for her. She's taking that anger out on me.

"And I get that, I really do and I'm trying hard to put up with it because I know where it's coming from, but her mom's never coming back. We both know that. There's no point in pretending otherwise. We need to work together, you and I, to help her to see that, to accept it and move on with her life." Ellie drew in a deep breath and did her best to calm down.

"You're right," Clay said, his voice low. "And I'm sorry for letting her obsession with Lisa go on so long. It hasn't helped anyone, least of all, you. You're her mother, the best one she could hope for. The best one *any* kid could hope for. I pray that one day she realizes it."

Tears filled Ellie's eyes. "Thank you," she whispered. "You don't know how much that means to me. It's been so awful feeling like you're no longer on my side. For so long, I've felt like it was the two of you against me. I always knew there would be challenges, but I never imagined in my wildest dreams it would divide us. I've felt so lonely, so abandoned these past few months—"

Her voice cracked with emotion and she gasped on a sob, unable to go on. Clayton reached for her and pulled her head down to his shoulder. Relinquishing the vice-like grip she'd held on her emotions for too long, she cried and cried and cried.

"*Shh*, sweetheart, please don't cry. I'm sorry. I'm so sorry. I should have tried harder. I should have sought help. I should have taken Olivia to see a counselor when she asked for that damn picture, not just had it enlarged."

Ellie raised her head and stared at him, tears still running down her cheeks. "I wish you'd have talked to me about it, first. You can't imagine what a shock it was to walk into her room and find it. I-I couldn't believe you'd done it and especially not before talking to me about it first." She swallowed and tried to temper the hurt and accusation in her voice. "We agreed we'd be equal in this parenting thing, remember? All of a sudden, it felt like you'd reneged. I-I didn't know what to do. You undermined my confidence; you made me second guess myself. You made me feel inadequate, like my opinion—at least in regard to Olivia—no longer mattered."

Clayton stared at her, desolate. Tears sparkled in his eyes and he shook his head wordlessly back and forth.

"I'm so sorry, Ellie. I never meant to hurt you like that. I didn't know what to do—I sure as hell didn't want to tell Olivia the truth—that her mother had committed suicide. She's too young to deal with the reality of how Lisa died. I don't know that she'll ever be ready."

"She'll find out the truth eventually. She knows how to Google, just like the rest of us. It's only a matter of time before she gets curious and there'll be any number of old news reports for her to discover."

Clayton nodded somberly. "You're right. Christ, I know you're right. I need to tell her. Just...not yet. Not until—"

His voice hitched and he swiped at the tears in his eyes. Ellie knew exactly what he was thinking. She was thinking it, too.

What if it was too late? What if Olivia was dead? What if she never got the chance to mature, to discover the truth about her mother, to realize how much she was loved? *What if they never found her?*

Fresh tears filled Ellie's eyes and together, they cried quietly on the couch. She was relieved that the tension between them had been resolved, but the dread in her belly every time she thought of Olivia weighed heavier and heavier with each hour that passed.

The sound of the phone ringing again jarred Ellie's thoughts. Clayton tensed beside her. Her heart leaped.

Blood ceased pumping and then her pulse took off at a gallop. *Was it Lane? Had they found her?*

No, it was the house phone that was ringing. Lane had called on the cell.

As the implications of the house phone ringing so late in the evening began to set in, Ellie's heart clenched in fear. Despite the fact the Attorney General's daughter appeared to be the target, the technicians were still monitoring the line. Until it was clear who was involved and why, they'd stayed in place in her kitchen. Yesterday, they'd run through the procedure over and over again, of what they were to do if a call came in. They made sure she had it down pat.

At the time, she'd barely paid attention, unable to focus on anything but getting Olivia back. Now she wished she'd listened better. Clayton stirred and pulled away. His eyes were dark with emotion and backlit with hope. A phone call was good. A phone call might mean their daughter was still alive.

The phone continued to ring. All at once, it catapulted them into action. Almost as one, they leaped off the couch and rushed over to where the phone stood in its dock on the other side of the room.

Ellie stared down at it, willing it to be good news. She lifted her gaze to Clayton's and he gave her the tiniest of nods. With a shaking hand, she picked up the handset.

"H-hello?"

"Who's this?"

Ellie frowned at the unfamiliar, heavily accented voice and her heart went into overdrive. She prayed the technicians in the kitchen were still awake.

"Th-this is Ellie Munro. Who am I speaking to?"

"Never fuckin' mind who I am. What you need to know is that the game's changed and I'm now in charge. I have your girl. She says her name's Olivia. If you do as I say, she'll stay safe."

Ellie's legs weakened. She reached out for Clayton and was relieved when he offered her his support. She leaned heavily against him and clutched the phone tightly to her ear.

"Sh-she's alive?" Her voice cracked. She swallowed against the emotion that threatened to choke her.

"For now. Follow my instructions or you'll never fuckin' see her again."

"Wh-where is she?"

"Never you fuckin' mind. All you have to know is that I want two hundred thousand dollars. Pay the money and she's all yours."

Ellie gasped. "Two hundred thousand dollars? We don't have that sort of money."

"Don't fuckin' lie to me. Draco asked for a million. Two hundred K is small fuckin' change. Find it, or the girl dies."

Panic tightened in Ellie's chest. She thought of the money they'd already scraped together and knew there was nothing more. She only prayed Brittany's father would come through, like he'd promised. "Okay, okay. Please, don't hurt her. We'll get the money. I promise. Just don't hurt her. Please."

"Like I said, do as I say and you can have her back. It's easy."

"H-how do we contact you? Wh-where do we leave the money?"

"There's an old Caltex gas station on the corner of Bluestone Drive and Kippax Avenue in Milperra. Leave the money in a bag in the men's toilets at six in the morning."

"*Tomorrow morning?* You have to be kidding? I can't find two hundred thousand dollars in that time. The banks aren't even open until nine."

Ellie heard a muffled curse on the other end of the line and then the man spoke to her again.

"All right, I'll give you until Tuesday morning. Be there with the money at six or your kid dies. And come alone. I know the kid's father is a cop. Keep your mouth shut and keep him away. Any fuckin' cops and you'll never see the girl again."

From the corner of her eye, Ellie saw one of the technicians come into the room and give her a thumbs-up. Relief flooded her. *They'd traced the call.*

Clayton tapped her shoulder and she looked up at him.

He mouthed some words. She nodded and spoke again.

"H-how do I know my daughter's still alive? I-I'll need some proof of life."

"Hang on."

There was silence on the other end of the phone. Ellie's fingers dug into the handpiece. Clayton's face was tense. The wait seemed interminable.

"Mom, it's me!"

Ellie gasped and dragged in mouthfuls of air. "Olivia! Honey! Oh, God, I'm so glad to hear your voice. I—"

"She's gone." The unfamiliar voice cut in. Ellie tried to still her racing heart so she could hear over the blood that pounded in her head.

"If you harm one hair on her head, I'll—"

A harsh bark of laughter grated against her ear. "I don't fuckin' think so." The voice turned even more menacing. "Listen, and listen well. Bring the money and the girl goes free. Try any tricks and the next time you'll lay eyes on her she'll be in a fuckin' pine box."

Ellie gasped. The line went dead.

Clayton grabbed hold of her arms. "Who was it? What did they say? Where the hell is she?"

Shaking her head, Ellie gasped and choked and sobbed. All the years of police training hadn't prepared her for this.

"Give her a minute. She's going into shock." The technician that had entered the room earlier nudged Clayton out of the way and helped Ellie to lie down, cushioning her head on the arm of the couch.

Clayton looked like he wanted to say more, but closed his mouth and came to sit beside her, taking her hand in his.

"It's all right," the technician murmured. "We got it."

Relief flooded Clayton's face. "You got it?"

The technician nodded. "We got it."

"Thank Christ." Clayton pulled Ellie into his arms and hugged her hard against him. A moment later, he gently released her and tugged out his phone.

"I need to call Lane."

CHAPTER 22

Sunday, January 28, 10:41 p.m.

Lane stared at Allison Dowton where she sat in one of the armchairs that stood opposite her husband's desk. Her foot swung back and forth in its bright yellow sandal, as if she didn't have a care in the world. He couldn't believe she was prepared to sit blithely by and wait for Draco to call her. The man was a career criminal, a drug supplier, dealer and worse. She seemed so certain he'd be quick to return her call and that Draco would be just as eager to hand over Olivia Munro.

Jett looked equally dubious. He stood on the far side of the room, not far from Zara. From the expression on her face, she was also far from sharing her stepmother's confidence in the good will of the notorious president of the Redbacks.

Lane had tried hard to ignore Zara, but despite his best efforts, his gaze was drawn to her again and again. She was so delicate, so ethereal, so beautiful. Her eyes were wide and dark with fear and concern for a little girl she barely knew...who was still out there, missing. Her kindness and compassion was so far removed from the cold and narcissistic attitude of her stepmother, it was difficult not to be knocked off balance.

How could a girl so obviously concerned about her little sister's new friend have grown up in a household ruled by a woman such as Allison? It was beyond him to even imagine how she'd learned to demonstrate the tolerance, goodness and mercy she displayed. He could only assume David had more substance to him than met the eye. Right at that moment, Lane was feeling a good deal less kindly toward the Attorney General.

If the man had told them the truth from the beginning, they could have been a long way ahead on their investigation. Olivia Munro might even now be with her parents, safe and sound at home.

Instead, they were here, standing tense inside the AG's office, waiting for a phone call from an infamous criminal; a phone call they had only a drug addict's assurances would come. Lane's lips twisted in derision. *Did it get any better?* When his phone vibrated against the inside of his shirt pocket, he welcomed the distraction. He tugged out his cell and checked the Caller ID.

Clayton.

Turning away, he answered the call and then listened, dumbstruck, as Clayton relayed the events of the last few minutes. When he was finished, Lane ended the call and stared into space, feeling blindsided. Zara was the first to notice.

"What is it?" Her softly voiced question was full of concern. He struggled to speak against a sudden surge of emotion. She moved closer and touched his arm. Warmth seeped through his shirt sleeve and into his skin.

He looked up and held her gaze, unable to look away— until the moment was broken by Jett.

"Who was it, Lane? What's happened?"

Lane blinked to clear his head and turned to face Jett. "It was Clayton. They've received a ransom demand. Another one. The technicians have traced the call to Boris Vukovic's house. Ellie told Clayton the caller was a man with a heavy accent. The stupid asshole was calling from his home phone."

"Vukovic. That's the Redbacks' biker Brittany identified," Jett said.

"Yes. The house we raided earlier and came up empty. Strangely enough, he's lowered the asking price. Two hundred thousand."

Jett frowned and then stared hard at the Attorney General. "What the hell's going on?"

"I agree," Lane said, barely holding on to his anger. He turned a grim look on David.

"First you admit you lied when you said you'd received a threatening phone call about your political stance on outlaw motorcycle gangs and then you expect us to believe the demand for a million dollars is nothing more than for payment of your wife's drug debt. You've almost convinced me Draco Jovanovic is single-handedly behind all of this and now Clayton Munro's received another ransom demand—not from Jovanovic, but from his off sider." Lane paused to drag in a breath. "What the hell's going on, Attorney General? And this time, we want the truth."

Dowton was pale and trembling. He looked like he'd aged a hundred years. In different circumstances, Lane might have felt sorry for him, but right now, sympathy was the last thing on his mind.

"Talk," Lane yelled and Dowton jumped. Zara moved away.

"I-I don't know. Jovanovic was the only one I dealt with. He brought Vukovic with him the night he came here to demand payment, but it was Jovanovic who did all the talking. It looked to me like Vukovic was nothing more than the hired muscle. Until then, I had no idea Allison's addiction had spiraled so far out of control. It's not my fault that—"

"Bullshit," Lane exploded, his temper escaping at last. "You should have gone to the police a fortnight ago, the very minute Jovanovic and his cohort stepped out of your house. You should have told us what happened. Okay, you didn't know they'd kidnap Olivia, but none of this would have happened if you'd gone to the authorities. It's called extortion, Attorney General. We pride ourselves on taking something like that very seriously."

Refusing to temper his tone, Lane got up in the AG's face.

"None of this would have happened if you'd done the right thing instead of pretending you had everything under control. Olivia Munro would still be at home, oblivious to the ugliness in this world, growing up loved and protected and safe, like she ought to. You're responsible for fucking that up. You, and you alone—and I won't waste a second listening to your excuses."

He spun on his heel and included Allison in his hard, angry gaze. The woman still held her phone, presumably waiting for Draco to call.

"Why has one of Jovanovic's henchmen called with another ransom demand? Why has he changed the terms? He's not only asked for a shitload less money, he's also extended the time limit. We now have until six on Tuesday morning to gather the money and he's finally given us a drop-off point. It's as if Vukovic's suddenly been put in charge."

He strode toward Allison, his narrowed eyes never once leaving her face. He leaned over her and jammed his face close to hers, daring her to object. "You told us you owed the money to Draco. Why is Vukovic calling the shots? You know these people better than any of us. What the hell's going on?"

Allison's face turned pale and her expression was scared and confused. "I don't know. It's the truth. I don't have a clue why Draco would hand it over to Boris. He's always making fun of the man and tells anyone who will listen how stupid Boris is." She shook her head. "I don't understand. It doesn't even make sense to me."

Lane bit out an oath and spun on his heel, determined to leave the room. He had to get back to the station and work out their next move.

"What are you going to do?"

Zara's question stilled his progress toward the door. He turned and met her turbulent gaze.

"We're going to do exactly as he says and get that little girl back."

She stared at him. The other people in the room fell away

until it felt like it was only the two of them. For long moments, neither said a word.

"Be careful," she murmured.

Lane nodded once and turned to leave, Jett close behind him.

Draco dragged on his cigarette and then slid lower in his seat. He stared at the parade of cars exiting the Attorney General's residence. Despite the lateness of the hour, the house was ablaze with lights and he could only assume it had something to do with his demand for a million dollars.

First to leave was an unmarked cop car. The detective who'd questioned him earlier was behind the wheel. It was followed shortly by the Attorney General himself, hunkered down in a brand new LFA Lexus. Looking neither left nor right, Allison's husband departed the estate with a squeal of tires.

Draco whistled under his breath, impressed despite himself. No wonder the bitch could afford to smoke ice like it cost no more than a pack of gum and no wonder she'd blithely assured him her husband could come up with the money. By the look of things, a million was small change. The car alone was worth more than half of that and had only just hit the Australian market. The AG had to have some serious coin or some considerable influence. Probably both.

There was a lull in the abrupt departures from the mansion and Draco was just about to leave when a silver BMW Roadster fitting the description of the car that belonged to Zara Dowton, filled the entryway and headed past him.

The roof was up, but as the car reached the street light, he caught a glimpse of a small, pale face and a cloud of dark hair before the driver sped away. His body tightened in anticipation. This was going to be so much fun.

CHAPTER 23

Sunday, January 28, 11:03 p.m.

Thoughts of Lane and Allison and her father crowded Zara's mind. She was oblivious to the steady stream of late-night traffic around her. Her only need was to get as far away from her home as possible.

It was a home she'd lived in all her life. The only home she'd known—and yet, tonight, she realized she no longer recognized most of its inhabitants. She'd listened to her stepmother's casual admissions and her father's shame-faced explanations and had shook her head in horror at what she'd failed to see right beneath her nose.

How could she not have known about Allison's drug habit? Why had she just excused the woman's erratic behaviour, the mood swings, the surliness as merely a poor attitude from a woman who had never taken to the role of her stepmother?

Zara prided herself on being an intelligent, observant person. It was inconceivable that she'd failed to see what was right before her eyes. Her stepmother was a drug addict: An egotistical, selfish, irresponsible drug addict. What was worse, it was obvious her father knew. Had always known. And had done nothing about it. He hadn't even felt the need to tell his adult daughter.

The anger that resonated through Zara threatened to

overwhelm her. Heat seared her cheeks and pressure built up behind her eyes. She blinked hard to keep back the tears.

Crying would solve nothing and she refused to feel sorry for herself. Her father had made a choice when he remarried more than ten years ago. She'd tried so hard to remain unaffected; to be happy that her father had once again found love. She only wished she'd had memories of her real mother to cling to. It would have made it easier to accept that her father had more than moved on.

Over the years, his career had flourished. Not long after he'd acquired a new wife, he also gained a new daughter. He was happy, his life was enviable. At least, that's how it had appeared. Now, she realized all that had been a smokescreen: A carefully crafted, immaculately thought-out pretense. And in one fell swoop, the façade had come crumbling down.

She wished she could feel satisfaction at how far her stepmother had fallen, but she couldn't. Her father was obviously hurting and Zara's heart became heavy at the thought of how the truth about Allison might affect little Brittany. Zara didn't take even the tiniest amount of pleasure from the knowledge Allison's life would never be the same again.

She thought of Lane and longed for his comfort—to go to him; to rest her head against his broad shoulder. She yearned for him to put his arms around her and draw her close against his chest. She wanted to pour out her hurts and disappointments and have him soothe them all away.

It scared her a little how quickly she'd come to rely on him. She wanted to turn to him in her hour of need, even though she'd barely known him a couple of days. It felt something like forever. They had an unfathomable connection—something magical—like they'd met in another time.

He felt it, too. She knew he did. She hoped there could be something between them when this whole sorry mess was over.

Less than ten minutes later, she pulled into the empty car park near The Gap. The nearby streetlights threw dark shadows across the asphalt, but they didn't discourage her. Cutting the engine, she opened the door and breathed in the salty air.

Years ago, the place had been notorious for the number of suicides that had occurred off the ledge of the surrounding cliffs, but for Zara, their sheer beauty and the sound of the waves crashing on the rocks far below had always soothed her. She closed the car door and picked her way carefully through the darkness, trying to use the sounds and her fond, familiar memories of the place to help her recover from the night's ordeal.

Of course, she could no longer get close to the edge. That had been barricaded off long ago in an effort to deter people from jumping, but she slipped off her sandals and made her way as close as she could and sat down amongst the tufts of grass and rock.

The moon was only half-full, but it hung golden and glorious over the ocean. Sparkles of moonlight caught the black of the waves and sent them dancing. A slight breeze caressed her skin and goose bumps broke out on her bare arms. She shivered a little and rubbed at them.

She thought once again of Lane and the sleepless nights ahead of him. He'd be busy forming a team of officers to locate and face off against the kidnapper. They'd been given a slight reprieve, but she was certain there would still be plenty to be done before the deadline arrived. She sent up a silent prayer that Olivia would be returned to her family unharmed.

Well, as unharmed as one could hope after enduring such a terrifying ordeal. Her heart went out to the little girl and she sent up another prayer of thanks that her sister had been spared the same agony.

She wondered about Lane's family. She knew so little about him and yet it felt like she knew everything. Everything that was important, anyway. He was kind and caring and compassionate. The way he was with her sister melted her heart. He was also smart and loyal and had the respect of his colleagues. To top it off, he was gorgeous. His eyes were the color of wheatgrass half-ripe in a wide, vast field. Green and brown-flecked, they really were the window to his soul.

She smiled wistfully at her poetic romanticism and wished life wasn't so darn complicated. She'd been cruising along with her life mapped out before her and until she met Lane, she couldn't honestly have said she was discontent. She had a family she loved and who loved her in return—well, maybe not Allison, but Zara had almost resigned herself to the fact her stepmother would never embrace her. She'd given up trying to please her and had buried herself in her work. It never failed to lift her spirits.

She thought of her job and the well-constructed path she'd created for herself. She'd always been confident and knew exactly where she was going and what she wanted to achieve in her life. It now shocked her to realize she hadn't spent even a minute over the course of the weekend thinking about her job and the files that were piled up high on her desk.

Not that the weekend just gone was normal. In fact, she spent most Saturdays and Sundays bent over her desk at the office, trying to catch up on the myriad of things she hadn't found time for during the week. She couldn't even remember why she'd been home when her father had taken the call from Ellie Munro about Olivia's abduction. He'd called her into his office to tell her. Not that the reasons mattered. Fate kept her home. If it hadn't, she'd never have met Lane.

Lane.

Strong, determined, brave: He was the man who made her heart flutter and her thoughts scatter in new directions. Despite the horror of the circumstances in which they'd met, the thought of never knowing him had now become too awful to contemplate.

With a sigh, she pushed those negative thoughts aside and once again, longed for the next two nights and Olivia's ordeal to be over. For entirely selfish reasons, she wanted the next time she met with Lane to be carefree and happy—to have nothing to do with illegal drugs, outlaw motorcycle gangs or kidnappings. She yearned for the two of them to have a fresh start, one free of the complications and misunderstandings that had marred their encounters thus far.

Her shoulders slumped and she let out another sigh. She whispered a little prayer that they would be given the chance she hoped for. She couldn't put into words what she was feeling for Lane, but it was something she'd never felt before. The thought both thrilled and terrified her.

Determination surged through her. She was through with playing it safe. Every waking moment until now had been given over to her father and her career. As much as she loved her job, it couldn't keep her safe and snug at night or make her feel warm and fluttery all over.

She was nearly thirty. How much longer would she leave her life on hold? It was time for her live.

She glanced at her watch illuminated by the moonlight. It was nearly midnight. After what seemed like an eternally long day, her body was weary though her mind refused to quit. She needed to go home and try to sleep. After all, she had work the next day.

The exchange between Olivia and the ransom money was supposed to happen early on Tuesday morning. With a bit of luck, the day after that might be the start of the new beginning she prayed for. The first day of the rest of her life.

Draco took a drag on his cigarette, careful to keep the glow of its tip concealed behind his fingers. Zara Dowton sat with her knees drawn up to her chest pondering the night. The waves pounded the rocks below her.

His cock urged him to take her now. It was way past late. The Gap was deserted. No one would know. Well, no one except Allison and she was hardly likely to tell.

The detective's raid on Draco's home had infuriated him, but there was nothing he could do about that. The cops did as they pleased. Somehow, they'd connected him to Boris and the hideout. He should have let things lie for just a little while longer. Allison would have come up with the cash sooner or later. She always did. Not that her tab had ever been this high, but he was confident she'd make good on her debts.

But then, she'd disappeared. His sources at the airport told him she'd flown interstate. He'd gotten nervous, edgy, unsure. It wasn't like him to be off balance and it made him angry. That's when he decided she needed an incentive to return.

The kidnapping plot had been a stroke of genius. It would have gone just as he'd planned if that fuckwit Boris hadn't botched it. He was supposed to have nabbed Allison's daughter. Word would have reached her that her little girl was in trouble and she'd have coughed up the money without a whimper.

The plan had been foolproof. Draco had even counted on the fact the Attorney General and his wife wouldn't want any adverse publicity. They wouldn't want Allison's dirty little secret coming to light. Going public would ruin everything. They would have quietly paid up and everyone would have been happy. *And it would have worked, if Boris hadn't fucked it up.*

Renewed anger stirred hot in his veins and he drew hard on the cigarette. Zara turned slightly, hugging her arms around her. The movement pulled the fabric of her dress tight. The moonlight illuminated her silhouette, delineating the delicate curve of her jaw and the generous swell of her breasts. Once again, blood rushed to his groin. His cock hardened almost painfully.

Yet again, his body urged him to nab her. With her head turned away from him, toward the ocean, he could creep up behind her and haul her back against him with his arm around her throat. She wouldn't have an inkling about what would happen next. The knife he always kept in his pocket would provide further deterrence. Besides, she was such a featherweight, it would take no effort at all to subdue her.

He toyed with the thought, liking it more and more. Moving in his seat until he found a more comfortable position, he pulled open the snap on his jeans and slid down the zipper to better accommodate the burgeoning swell of his cock. His hand caressed his erection and he sighed softly in pleasure.

The woman in front of him glanced at her watch. He tensed. Moments later, she stood and slipped on her sandals. Shaking out the skirt of her dress, she turned and headed toward him, picking her way back to her car.

He grimaced and debated his next move. If he was going to take her now, he had to be quick. It would be harder if she made it to her vehicle. She was closing the gap between them. Twenty feet. Then fifteen. Draco's heart pounded in anticipation. Quickly, he tugged up his zipper and readied himself for action.

Glancing in the rearview mirror, he spied headlights coming up the hill behind him. He froze for an instant and then turned back to Zara. His lips thinned in annoyance. She'd reached her car and opened the door.

Cursing loudly, he thumped the steering wheel.

He'd missed his chance.

Chapter 24

Tuesday, January 30, 5:43 a.m.

Lane could already feel the tension headache that stabbed behind his eyes. The sun had barely graced the horizon. His men had been in position hours earlier, waiting for the moment of Vukovic's arrival.

He'd run a check through the Roads and Maritime Services database and had discovered a hotted up Harley Davidson motorcycle and an early eighties model Ford F100 in the name of Boris Vukovic. He'd also run a check on Vukovic's wife, but that had come up blank.

He couldn't imagine Vukovic arriving on the motorcycle with Olivia in tow and the biker would have to be plain stupid to think her mother would be willing to hand over the cash without her being present. Lane had taken a punt that Vukovic would turn up in the Ford.

The more Lane thought about the second ransom demand, the more obvious it became that Draco wasn't involved, or if he'd been involved in the earlier demand, he wasn't involved any longer. Lane surmised the Redbacks' president had discovered he had the wrong girl and had decided to recover his money by other means. From what Allison had said, it appeared she was on friendly terms with her supplier and she appeared as surprised as they were that the man had taken such drastic steps.

Maybe Draco had second thoughts and had backed away from the whole kidnapping scenario? Another possibility emerged: Maybe he'd left it to Vukovic to get rid of Olivia and Vukovic had decided to make it worth his while?

These questions and more had been canvassed by the joint taskforce. They'd gathered at the station for most of the previous day formulating their plan of attack and discussing all possible worst scenarios.

Ellie had told them Vukovic demanded the ransom be dropped off only by her and at the agreed meeting place. Some time yesterday, Lane had filled Clayton and Ellie in on the plan. Right now, they sat tensely inside an unmarked police vehicle about fifteen yards away from the assigned spot. Clayton was to lie low when Vukovic appeared.

Clayton's eldest brother, Tom Munro, a veteran police negotiator had also been brought in and now formed part of the team of officers who paced nervously in the breaking dawn, awaiting Vukovic's arrival.

Lane had cleared the immediate area and undercover officers, posing as members of the general public, appeared sporadically at the gas pumps to fill up their cars. Lane didn't know how long Vukovic would case the place, but if he had any brains at all, he'd turn up ahead of time to scout out the place.

Lane had gone to a great deal of trouble to make the gas station look as normal as possible, even down to the young constable who manned the cash register with his baseball cap on backwards and his best bored expression on his face.

Glancing at his watch, Lane's gut clenched. The appointed hour was almost upon them.

A moment later, as Lane anticipated, Vukovic's pickup truck appeared around the corner and parked on the far side of the gas station. Lane held his breath. The car door opened and the biker emerged.

As instructed, Clayton flattened himself across the back seat and Ellie climbed out of the unmarked car. She slowly approached the man who claimed he held their daughter captive. Nerves jangled in Lane's gut and weighed down his limbs. He sent up a silent prayer that things would turn out right. From across the other side of the road, the early morning air carried the sound of voices. Vukovic's was the loudest.

"Where's the money?"

"In the men's restroom, like you said," Ellie replied, as instructed.

"You come alone?"

Ellie nodded emphatically. "Of course. Where's my daughter?"

Vukovic looked at her and smirked. "All in good time."

"No, I want to see her. I want to know she's all right."

Vukovic stared Ellie down. Lane held his breath. After what seemed like a lifetime, the biker nodded and headed back toward the Ford. Pulling open the trunk, he bent over and lifted something out.

Olivia Munro wobbled on her feet as Vukovic held her upright. She squinted against the rising sun. "Mommy? I'm so sorry, Mommy! I'm so sorry!"

Ellie appeared unsteady on her feet, but somehow held it together.

"I'm here, baby, I'm here." Ellie took a step toward her.

Vukovic pulled a gun and held it to Olivia's head. "Not so fast. I want to check the money, first."

Ellie froze and put a hand to her mouth.

Lane thanked God they'd taken the time to put every dollar of the two hundred grand of marked bills supplied by Clayton and the AG into the gym bag they had been left behind the restroom door.

Vukovic frog-marched Olivia to the side of the gas station where the restrooms were located. They disappeared inside and Lane held his breath. They were the longest seconds of his life.

Vukovic reappeared with the bag in his hands. A smile tugged at his lips. He shoved Olivia toward her mother.

"She's all yours. It was nice doin' business."

The next few moments were a blur of screaming and shouting and the sound of gunfire. Heavily armed TRG officers burst onto the scene with an arsenal of weaponry trained on the biker. Within moments, Lane and his team had Vukovic facedown on the ground, cuffed and under arrest.

It all happened so quickly, Lane barely had time to register that it was over. His breath came fast. Relief poured through him and it was his turn to tremble.

Olivia Munro was safe.

CHAPTER 25

Tuesday, January 30, 11:49 a.m.

Lane couldn't remember ever feeling wearier. After spending more hours than he could count, preparing for the confrontation with Vukovic, he could barely remember what his bed felt like and even though the interception had gone off without a hitch, he'd still spent the rest of the morning debriefing and completing a mountain of paperwork. Boris Vukovic was in custody. Draco Jovanovic soon would be. Olivia Munro was home, where she belonged. All in all, it had been a good day's work.

Rubbing the soreness from his shoulders, he fitted the key into his front door and dragged himself inside. A hot shower and a few hours of uninterrupted sleep would go a long way to making him feel almost human again.

With that thought in mind, he stripped off his shirt and loosened his pants. He seated himself on the couch and tugged off his boots. His socks were tossed next to them. Pants and underwear joined the pile.

The feel of the hot spray on his neck and shoulders was the best thing he'd felt in days. Maybe weeks. He groaned in appreciation and let the water do its magic.

The relief he felt, knowing Olivia was safe, was immeasurable. Ellie had clung to him, crying her gratitude, trying to form the words. Clayton had hugged him hard—the expression of relief and thankfulness on his face conveyed his thoughts. Tom had shaken him by the hand and offered him a few solemn words of thanks.

While Lane appreciated their gratitude, he didn't need it. Knowing an innocent little girl was safe from harm was enough for him.

During the exchange, Vukovic had gotten off a shot. Fortunately, it had gone wide. His men had quickly and efficiently done what they'd been trained to do and made sure the thwarted kidnapper was given no second chance. Clayton had bolted from the squad car and Olivia had collapsed against her parents, surrounded by their embrace and protected by the wall of their love.

Lane had left them laughing and crying and talking over each other, as the stress of the past few days and their indescribable relief took over. He would interview Olivia a little later, once she'd been checked over at the hospital and had a chance to recover from her ordeal.

Pouring a generous blob of shampoo into his hair, Lane scrubbed at it long and hard before dipping his head back to rinse. Repeating the process with the conditioner, he eventually turned off the faucets and stepped out.

After toweling dry, he took his razor out of the bathroom cabinet and lathered his cheeks. It seemed like a waste of precious sleep time, but it felt like weeks had passed since he'd had any semblance of normalcy and at that very moment, having a shave was something he felt he needed to do.

Slapping on some aftershave, he looked at himself in the mirror. He looked the same. And yet, everything was different. His life had been turned upside down and inside out. First, with the kidnapping of his friend's daughter and then meeting the first woman he couldn't get out of his mind.

Despite all that had happened, his brain refused to move on from her. Zara was all he could think about. Every moment since Vukovic's arrest, he'd wanted to call her; to hear her voice; to reassure her that it was over, and that everything was all right.

But he hadn't. He'd returned to the station and had kept busy debriefing, answering questions, interviewing Vukovic, writing reports. Clayton telephoned him at one stage and told him about Sandra Vukovic and her part in the ransom demand. Lane had consulted with Michael and a pair of officers were dispatched to her home. She'd been arrested and charged and had been put in a cell adjoining her husband's. Officers from child welfare had taken custody of the baby.

Vukovic had been presented with overwhelming evidence that he and he alone had instigated the abduction of Olivia Munro. Despite the fact Lane and the other members of the taskforce were convinced Jovanovic was the mastermind behind the scheme, they only had the evidence of Allison Dowton's drug debt and the meeting with her husband and it wasn't enough. Jovanovic would claim he'd called upon the AG about payment for a debt and no one could dispute that fact. Without more, they'd never prove he had anything to do with Olivia's kidnapping. Their only chance was to force something from Vukovic.

So, Lane had showed the biker the security tape of him entering Myer moments before the little girl had been abducted. He'd told him of the eyewitness who had identified him out of a photo line-up. He'd talked about Olivia's ability to give evidence as to the identity of the man who had abducted her. He'd reminded Vukovic about the call he'd made from his home phone to Ellie Munro and that he and he alone had arrived that morning with the girl in exchange for the ransom money. Lastly, he reminded him of the sentence he could expect for kidnapping a child.

Vukovic's initial brashness quickly dissipated. Within moments, he'd spilled his guts. No surprise—he insisted it was all Draco's idea. The tension in Lane's shoulders didn't ease until the last of the evidence had been recorded. Another team of TRG officers was immediately put together and plans were made to arrest Draco Jovanovic.

Lane wanted to be part of it, but his boss had insisted he go home. He'd been working around the clock with only the briefest of rest breaks in between and it was in everyone's interests that he go home and get some sleep. There would be plenty to do once Jovanovic had been brought back in for questioning. Michael wanted Lane alert.

Of their own volition, Lane's thoughts circled back to Zara. If Draco implicated her stepmother, things would get messy for the AG and everyone connected with him. Draco would have nothing to gain by publicizing his connection to the AG's wife, but scum like Jovanovic didn't care about how their comments might permanently damage the reputation of innocent people. Zara and her father would be sullied by their proximity to the woman who'd sold her soul to the devil.

Once Allison's relationship with the president of the Redbacks became public knowledge, her candid admissions of illegal drug use couldn't be overlooked by law enforcement, no matter how much more pain and humiliation the laying of criminal charges against Zara's stepmother would cause her family. And there was nothing Lane could do about it.

With a sigh, he dropped his wet towel on the bathroom floor and strode naked, down the hall. Without bothering to draw the blinds, he threw himself across his bed. Stacking his hands behind his head, he was once again bombarded with images of Zara. He'd never met a woman like her and he was struggling with how to deal with the unfamiliar feelings she stirred inside him—and what they meant for his long-term plan to remain single.

His father had died in the line of duty when Lane was very young. It was only when he was older that he'd come to fully realize the effect his father's early demise had on his mother. She'd been widowed in her early thirties and left to raise four young sons on her own. It had been a constant struggle and one Lane hadn't really appreciated as a child.

When he became an adult, the world around him began to look different, became clearer and he'd determined then and there to never put another woman in the position his mother had been placed. That he was going to follow in his father's footsteps and go into policing had been indisputable, but he'd vowed never to take the risk that a stray bullet would end his life prematurely, leaving behind a wife and children who depended upon him.

The decision made all those years ago now weighed heavily on him. Up until now, it hadn't been a problem. He'd dated on and off, enjoying casual relationships when they presented themselves. He appreciated the company of women and had been largely unconcerned when none of those relationships ever moved to the next level.

His decision never to have a family wasn't an issue. It was just the way it would be. He'd deliberately dated women who felt the same way. Katie Leeds was a prime example.

And then he met Zara.

Everything about her was different. From the outset, before a word was spoken, he'd been drawn to her—felt connected to her. The thought of dating her casually and then leaving her to move on, following what was by now a very familiar pattern, tore at him. The thought that she'd move on disquieted him even more. He wanted to bellow in anger and denial when he considered that; he wanted her for his own. But that would break the promise he'd made to himself and he didn't know if he had the courage to do that.

But did he have the strength to let her go?

With a groan of frustration, he threw himself on his side and closed his eyes, willing sleep to overtake him. Instead, his mind crowded with more images of Zara: the touch of her hand, the sound of her voice, the smell of her intoxicating scent. She was everywhere and it was driving him crazy.

He rolled onto his back and stared at the ceiling. He could probably call her and tell her Olivia had been found and was safe and well. Michael had already made a call to the AG, but Lane had promised Zara he'd let her know how things went. A call wouldn't necessarily mean he was instigating anything beyond the investigation. He was merely keeping his word. That was all.

With that decision, he bounded out of bed. His heart beat fast as he strode back to the bathroom, retrieved his cell from his pants pocket and keyed in her number.

———

Zara pulled the door to her sister's bedroom closed behind her and made her way to her room a little farther down the hall. After her father had given her the news of Olivia's rescue, she'd headed straight upstairs to tell Brittany. Despite the early hour, her sister had been awake, watching the television with the sound muted. Brittany had been overwhelmed with relief and gladness at the news and had insisted Zara tell her every detail, but Zara didn't have more to offer.

Her father had taken the call from the superintendent of Lane's unit and had done little more than pass on the information that Olivia was safe and well and after being checked over by paramedics, was now back home with her parents.

For the first time in her life, Zara had called in sick. Her boss had expressed his surprise and enquired about her health, but she remained purposefully vague with the details. He'd find out soon enough.

She'd been disappointed when Lane didn't call with the news, like he'd promised. She'd checked her phone every few minutes and made sure it was fully charged, but there'd been nothing. Hours later, there was still no word from him.

With a sigh, she opened the door to her room and closed it quietly behind her. No doubt there had been a mountain of paperwork and other details to be attended to by the investigating officer of such a high-profile case. Although she hadn't yet caught a sniff of it on the news, that would certainly change over the next few hours. It was too much to hope it wouldn't become public knowledge. She hoped, when it did, that her bosses at Breakers would understand.

With another heavy sigh, Zara made her way over to her

bed and flopped down on it. The last couple of nights sleep had eluded her and she was more than weary now. Adrenaline had kept her awake and on edge with thoughts of Lane and Olivia at times pushing her close to the edge.

But now, it was over and she gave herself permission to feel relief that things had worked out—for him and for the Munros. Over the coming weeks and months, they could put the episode behind them and do their best to move forward and rebuild their lives.

The news that Olivia was safe had certainly revived Brittany's spirits. She'd wanted to call her friend right away, but Zara had gently cautioned against it, telling her Olivia would need a little time alone with her family to come to terms with the ordeal she'd endured and the realization that it finally was over. Brittany nodded her understanding, her eyes wide and solemn and had seemed content to wait.

The sound of her phone ringing jerked Zara from her reverie. Tugging it from the pocket of her shorts, her heart skipped a beat when she recognized Lane's number. With shaking fingers, she drew in a deep breath and answered the call.

"H-hello?"

"Zara, it's Lane." His familiar, smooth tones glided over her senses, leaving her breathless and shivery.

"Lane, it's...it's good to hear from you. Dad told me about what happened; that you found Olivia. Congratulations, that's fantastic news."

"Yes, thank you. I'm...I'm sorry I didn't call sooner. I've been snowed under since it went down."

She smiled and stretched out on the bed. *It was just as she'd imagined.* He'd been busy wrapping up the investigation. It wasn't that he hadn't wanted to call.

"Well, I appreciate you taking the time to phone me now. I'm sure you still have plenty to do."

"Actually, I'm home. I finished up about an hour ago. The boss gave me the rest of the day off. Said I'd earned it."

"I'm sure you have. I'm guessing you haven't managed much sleep these past few days."

"You're right. With everything going on, sleep wasn't high on the agenda."

There was a pause in their conversation. Zara listened to the sound of his quiet breathing on the other end of the phone. The silence extended. Nerves tightened her throat.

"I can't stop thinking about you." His quiet, husky admission caused a tingling sensation to ignite low in her belly, soon followed by a radiating heat.

"In fact, you're *all* I can think about and it's driving me crazy. It sounds like something out of a corny movie, but... I've never felt like this with anyone before. I want to spend time with you. I want to get to know you. I want to know everything about you."

The fire inside her intensified. Her cheeks flushed from the heat. She squirmed on the bed and tried to speak. "I...uh... I don't know what to say," she managed.

"Say that you know what I mean, that you feel the same way."

The quiet intensity in his voice, coupled with his raw honesty touched her. Neither of them were teenagers. There was no need to play games. He'd been upfront with her. He deserved the same.

"I-I know what you mean. I can't stop thinking about you, either," she admitted just as quietly. "My stomach's been twisted in knots all morning, waiting for you to call, wondering why you didn't. We barely know each other. It seems too soon to be feeling like this, but I can't help it." Her breathing quickened at the thought of what she was about to reveal, but she was tired of playing it safe. The traumatic incident involving Olivia had shown her that. Life was too short to spend it being a passive spectator. She drew in another breath and continued.

"Whenever you're near, I can hardly think straight. I'm scared and nervous and excited all at the same time. I-I don't know what it is or what to call it, but I... I want to see where it goes. For too long, I've played it safe and lived my life treading a trail, tried and true. Up until now, I've never wanted to deviate from the path I'd set myself. Now, I wonder every moment what it would be like to throw away my well-thought-out plans and embrace a little spontaneity; embrace a little fun."

Lane was quiet and for a moment, Zara wanted the floor to open up and swallow her. *God, had she come across too strong?* Had her frankness frightened him away?

"I want to see you." His quiet admission sent a surge of relief coursing through her, but nerves quickly followed on its heels. *What was she thinking?* They'd known each other for a little over three days. It was crazy.

"When?" The words fell out of her mouth. She almost gasped in shock.

"Now. I need you."

Heaven forbid, she needed him, too.

After taking down his address, she bid him a hasty good-bye and bolted off the bed. Racing into the bathroom, she stared at her reflection. Her breath came fast. Her face was aflame. The eyes that stared back at her were the eyes of a stranger, wild and wide and glassy with anticipation and desire.

She ran cool water into the sink and leaned over the basin to splash it over her heated skin. Lane needed her. And she was going to go to him. Blowing her breath out on a determined sigh, she dried her face on the hand towel and took out her hairbrush. After applying a couple of coats of mascara and adding a slash of dark red lipstick, she strode back into the bedroom and pulled open the doors to her closet.

Wishing she had more time to deliberate, but keener to be with Lane, she chose a simple cotton dress in her favorite teal blue. It skimmed her curves and emphasized her waist, falling in a swirl of fabric to just below her knees.

Quickly shucking off her shorts and T-shirt, she pulled the dress over her head and tightened the sash around her waist. She spotted a pair of wedges in the same shade of blue, and slipped them on her feet. Taking a moment to survey the results in the mirror, she patted her hair in place and checked that her lipstick hadn't smudged.

Collecting her handbag from the nightstand, she picked up her phone and tossed it inside. Not in the mood to speak with her father, but unwilling to add to his concern by not letting anyone know where she was going, she tugged a notebook out of the drawer of her nightstand and scrawled him a quick note. With nerves and excitement vying for space inside her, she left the room in a rush.

Clayton pulled up the covers over his sleeping daughter and leaned over to press a kiss against her cheek. The relief of having her home, safe and sound, was overwhelming.

After a check-up at the hospital, Olivia was declared healthy and had been released into the loving arms of her parents. They'd left the hospital together and had returned home. They'd spoken to her in gentle tones about the ordeal, but she'd shared very little with them, other than to apologize over and over again.

It saddened Clayton to know that his daughter felt it was her fault. He swore quietly under his breath that he'd do whatever it took to convince her she wasn't to blame. With a last glance at her slumbering form, he turned and left the room, leaving the door open as Olivia had requested.

He found Ellie seated on the couch in the living room. Lines of weariness had etched themselves onto her face and dark shadows colored the skin beneath her eyes. She looked as haggard as he felt and his heart turned over at the thought of what they'd been through.

He took a seat beside her and heard her soft sigh. Looking across at her, he caught a glimpse of fresh tears. He shuffled closer and reached for her.

"It's over, sweetheart. Please don't cry. We got her back. Our little girl's safe and sound and unharmed. Please don't cry."

His gentle words appeared to unleash an avalanche of emotion in the woman he held in his arms. Ellie's shoulders shook with barely controlled grief. Clayton pressed kisses against her hair and held her close, knowing her reaction was a normal response to the release of the pressure both of them had suffered since Olivia's disappearance.

"I'm sorry, Clayton. I'm so sorry," she cried, her ragged voice muffled against his shirt.

"Hey, it's okay, darling. We've talked about this. It wasn't your fault. Don't think for an instant I blame you. Everytime I think about the way I treated you—even before Olivia was taken—I'm overcome with shame. I'm the one who's sorry." He shook his head. "I don't know what I was thinking, letting Olivia behave like that. You love her more than I ever hoped—as much as you love our boys. I should have supported you during the times when she lashed out at you. It wasn't fair and it wasn't right and I'll never let that happen again."

Ellie lifted her head off his shoulder, her eyes red and swollen from her tears. She stared at him, her expression one of sadness that warred with hope. Clayton's heart clenched at the pain in her eyes, the agony of it made worse because he knew he was the cause.

Framing her face in his hands, his voice cracked with emotion. "I can't change what's happened, but I promise you with everything that I am that I'll make it up to you. I promise from now on we'll deal with Olivia and her needs together, united as one. She's our daughter and we love her, but you're my wife and I love you more than anything in the world."

"Oh, Clayton," Ellie gasped. Another wave of tears sparkled in her eyes, but a tiny, trembling smile tugged at her lips, chasing the pain away. "I love you so much."

Tilting her chin upwards, he leaned down and brought his lips to hers. She melted against him, her mouth moving under his, matching the desperate passion that coursed through him.

His arms pressed her tightly against him. He kissed her like a starving man, silently vowing never to let anything come between them again.

CHAPTER 26

Tuesday, January 30, 1:22 p.m.

Lane pulled back the curtain in the living room for what felt like the hundredth time and checked the street below.

Nothing.

He'd spoken to her more than an hour earlier. She should have been there by now. Perhaps she'd taken down the directions wrong? Perhaps she'd gotten lost? Perhaps she'd simply changed her mind?

With a groan, he turned away, unable to believe the state he'd gotten himself in. *What the hell was he?* A randy teenager? Anyone would think he was on his first date, about to go all the way for the first time.

He wiped sweaty palms on the shorts he'd hastily donned and tried to think of something else. *The fact that she hadn't called was good news, right?* Surely, if she were lost or had changed her mind, she'd call him. It was just plain good manners and she struck him as someone who believed manners were important.

He looked around his condo and was grateful he'd taken the time to tidy up a bit. The pile of clothes he'd cast on the floor had been deposited into the laundry hamper, along with his wet towel and last week's newspapers had been tidied away off the couch. He'd even put on a fresh pot of coffee.

A knock at the door drew his attention and his heart stuttered. He wiped his hands again on his shorts and hurried forward to open it.

She was wearing another floaty kind of dress, this time in a bluey-green color that highlighted the golden tones of her skin. Her full lips sparkled with burgundy lipstick. Her smile was shy and hesitant.

"Hi," she said and her gaze skittered away.

"Hi to you, too." Heat crept up his neck. He cleared his throat and then turned abruptly and headed back inside. "Come in," he threw over his shoulder and escaped into the hall.

Get a hold of yourself, mate. What the hell are you doing? She's just a girl. So what if you like her more than any other girl since Sonia Bullan in the fifth grade? She'll go running for her life if you don't stop acting so weird. Now, get a grip.

Lane drew in a deep breath and turned to face her. "I'm sorry. Can we try again? I'm...I'm a little nervous."

Her face filled with relief. She smiled again, this time with more confidence. "Really? I thought it was only me."

He grinned and moved closer. "Nope. I'm so nervous I have sweaty palms and I've lost count of the number of times I've had to visit the bathroom. How's that for impressive?"

She laughed outright and the light sound of it went straight through him, exciting him on so many levels.

Her smiling gaze met his. "I'm so nervous, I took the wrong turn like...five times and I have a state-of-the-art navigation system mounted on my dash. How's that for lame?"

"I wondered what was taking you so long."

Her smile widened and she ducked her head in an effort to conceal the blush that stole across her cheeks. Lane's heart clenched. *God, she was beautiful.*

"Can I get you a drink? Tea? Coffee? Something stronger?"

"Coffee would be great. It smells good."

Lane moved into the kitchen, inordinately pleased when

she followed him. He pulled two mugs out of the cupboard. "How do you take it?"

"White with one, thanks."

He frowned and opened another cupboard, hunting around inside for the sugar. He couldn't remember the last time he'd had someone over who'd asked for it. He grimaced when he realized he had none and turned toward her with a sheepish smile on his lips.

"I'm sorry, but it looks like I'm all out. Sugar's not something I use a lot of."

She smiled back at him and his heart did another somersault. "That's fine. I'll do without."

"Great."

Striding over to the fridge, he pulled the door open and came up short. The shelves were decidedly bare. *Oh, hell, he didn't have any milk.* With cheeks flaming, he faced her again and slowly shook his head.

"Let me guess, you don't have milk, either. Right?"

Grimacing, he nodded.

"Well, I guess I'll take it black." She grinned mischievously. "Let's start again, shall we? Hi, Lane, great to see you. I'd love some coffee. Black would be great." She turned her face up to him, her eyes glinting with laughter. "How did I do?"

He tried not to laugh, but despite his best efforts, it burst out anyway. "Good. You did good. And you wouldn't believe it, but it's your lucky day. Black coffee I can do."

Their gazes locked. For the life of him, he couldn't look away and it seemed, neither could she.

The silence between them lengthened. Her eyes went wide. Then lips parted. The smallest sliver of pink tongue peeked outside and swept across them. His heart thumped. Blood rushed to his groin.

"Zara?" His voice had turned husky with need.

Her chest rose and fell more quickly, with excitement or apprehension, he couldn't tell. But then she took a step toward him, her gaze still on his.

"I want you, Lane."

It was the only encouragement he needed. In two long strides, he closed the distance between them and took her in his arms. Crushing her to him, he lowered his lips to hers, groaning aloud as he finally tasted the softness of her lush mouth. His arms tightened around her.

"Oh, God, you taste so good." He angled his mouth and increased the pressure. His tongue glided over her lips, seeking entry. She gave it freely and he slid his tongue inside her mouth and relished the warmth and softness that met him. She tasted as good as he'd imagined. Better.

Anticipation surged through him and pulsed hot and hard through his veins and immediately centered in his cock. He pressed his erection against her and was gratified when she leaned into him and her arms crept around his neck.

Fire ignited in his groin. He kissed her harder, more urgently. His hands tugged at her clothing, loosening the belt at her waist. It came free and he started on the row of little white buttons that began at her neckline and ran down the length of her dress. His fingers slipped and fumbled and he cursed aloud.

Zara laughed and dipped her head, a blush stealing into her cheeks. "Here, let me," she murmured.

He gazed at her hands, fascinated by the daintiness of her fingers, each nail painted a soft, pearly pink. The buttons opened one by one. Each time one was released, a little more of her smooth, tanned skin was exposed. When she was done, he pushed the dress off her shoulders. It pooled at her feet.

He stared at her.

"You're so beautiful."

When her blushed deepened, warmth spread through him. His heart filled with tenderness.

"You look like you don't believe me," he whispered and brushed a strand of black hair off her face.

She lowered her head, her face hidden behind a curtain of silky, dark hair. "My father's the only man who's ever called me beautiful and everyone knows that doesn't count."

Lane shook his head in disbelief. "What about all your past boyfriends? Were they blind?"

Zara dropped her gaze. "To tell you the truth, there...there haven't been that many who've been in a position to comment. I-I haven't exactly been a social butterfly. My boyfriends have been fairly thin on the ground. I guess I've spent most of my adult life either at university or at work."

Lane couldn't help the surge of surprise and contentment that flooded through him. A rush of protectiveness rushed through his veins. He wrapped his arms around her and drew her close. "I knew right from the start you were special," he whispered against the softness of her hair.

Zara breathed in the warm, manly scent of him and tried to quell her nerves. As much as she wanted this, wanted him, she was scared her inexperience would show and would turn him off.

Not that he seemed to be concerned at the moment, if the rock hard erection against her belly was any indication—but all they'd done was kiss. It might be a different story once they were completely naked.

As if sensing her shyness, Lane pulled back and looked down at her with tenderness and concern.

"Are you sure you're all right with this? We don't have to. We can go back to having coffee." He smiled.

She drew in a breath and shook her head. "No, I want to. I-I think I've wanted to from the moment I saw you."

His eyes darkened with desire and he growled low in his throat. Taking her once again in his arms, he pulled her up tight against him and kissed her softly, teasingly, on the mouth. Desire rekindled in her belly and the ache between her legs intensified, helping to chase the nerves away. She put her arms back around his neck and clung to him, enjoying the pressure of his lips on hers.

Needing to feel the warmth of his skin, she slid her hands down his chest and tugged at the ends of his T-shirt. It came out of the waistband of his shorts and she pushed it up over his head, loving the feel of his taut chest muscles beneath her fingers.

She skimmed over one of his nipples by accident and he gasped. The flat, brown nub pebbled and she was overwhelmed by a sudden surge of satisfaction. She'd never felt so powerful before, so in control. She couldn't quite believe a man who looked like a movie star could find her so desirable. His response gave her the confidence she needed.

Reaching around behind her, she undid the clasp on her bra and let the scrap of black lace fall to the floor. She was immediately rewarded by a flash of desire in Lane's eyes that darkened them to an earthy green. He pulled her hard against him and she sighed at the feel of his warm, firm skin against hers.

"God, you feel so good." Lane nuzzled the side of her neck. She shivered from the contact and tightened her arms around him, crushing her breasts against his chest.

He groaned again and his hands reached down to cup her bottom and lift her up against his erection. Liquid fire pooled between her legs and she moved restlessly against him. Need had built up deep inside her, a need that only he could satisfy.

"Make love to me, Lane."

The words fell out of her mouth and she blushed. *How could she have been so brazen?* She'd never asked a man for sex before. The very idea was too embarrassing to contemplate and yet with Lane, it felt so right.

He set her a little away from him and stared down at her. His eyes were dark with desire, his breath came fast.

"Are you sure?"

She loved that he asked her again. Nerves once again surged through her, but Zara refused to let them distract her. She wanted him—no question. She'd never wanted anyone more.

"Yes," she whispered and was immediately rewarded by a flare of emotion in his eyes. His hands went to her hips and he drew her forward until her belly once again pressed against the length of his hardness.

His gaze burned into hers. "Can you feel how much I want you?"

"Yes."

"Touch me."

Zara gulped. The nerves intensified. It wasn't that she didn't want to. It was more that she didn't know how.

"Don't you want to?" A tiny frown marked the space between Lane's eyes.

She nodded, a little frantically. "Of course I do. You're magnificent. Your body is...beautiful."

"Then what?" he questioned softly, taking her hand in his and lifting it to his chest.

Her hand lay flat against the warmth of his bare skin. His heart pounded an excited rhythm beneath her palm. Her fingers curled through the slight smattering of dark brown hair that covered his chest.

"I-I've never touched a man before. I mean...I've been kissed, but not very many times and it felt nothing like when you..."

Her face was aflame. She couldn't go on. She turned her head away and buried her face against his chest. He held her against him, giving her a few moments to recover.

Sooner than she was ready to have eye contact, he tilted her chin up with a gentle finger and forced her to look at him.

Lane stared down at her and his pulse pumped hard. *He couldn't believe it*. She was a virgin. He should have known. From the moment they'd spied each other across the frilly, pink bedroom that belonged to her sister, he'd known she was different.

He'd spent his life seeking out women who weren't looking for long-term relationships; who were more than happy with a one-or-two night stand. They were women who played the field and that had suited him just fine.

And then he'd met Zara.

She held his gaze, her face still flushed with embarrassment. As the silence stretched out between them, confusion and uncertainty flooded her eyes. He hastened to reassure her.

"Please, don't be embarrassed by your lack of experience, sweetheart. You should be proud of it. Everyone seems to be in such a big hurry these days to sleep with as many people as they can, I think we've forgotten how special making love can be, how special it *should* be."

He lifted her hand off his chest and pressed a kiss against her palm before drawing her over to the couch. Pushing her gently onto the leather seat, he bent and picked up her dress. In silence, he offered it to her. She threw him a grateful look and took it from him.

Tugging it over her head, she stood and shimmied it down her body. When she was once again clothed and sitting on the couch, he sat beside her and put his arm around her shoulders and drew her in close to his side.

"I lost my virginity when I was seventeen," he said quietly. "She was a girl I'd known for a while, but we'd never dated. I'd seen her around, hanging out at McDonalds and down at the local skate park. She'd been a few years ahead of me in school, but despite the age difference, she seemed interested." He paused and drew in a breath before continuing.

"It was a Saturday night. I'd been at the skate park with a couple of my brothers for most of the afternoon. She turned up and sat there, watching. I was getting ready to leave when she came up to me and asked me if I wanted to go and get a coke at McDonalds."

Zara bit her lip, but remained silent. Lane stared at her, trying to gauge her feelings. He didn't know how she'd react to listening to how he'd lost his virginity or if she even cared, but something inside him told him she did and he squeezed her thigh, hoping to reassure her.

"I knew she liked me," he said. "She'd been hanging around for weeks. I liked her, too, although I liked her more when I realized she wanted to have sex with me." He offered Zara a rueful smile and cursed the blush that rose on his cheeks. A smile tugged at her lips.

"Hey, I'm not making any excuses. It was totally all about me. I was seventeen and randy as hell. I wasn't about to turn her down."

"What about your brothers? Weren't they there, too?"

"I sent them home. I told them to tell Mom I'd met a friend and was going to McDonalds for a coke."

Her smile widened. "All of which was true. Did they believe you?"

Lane grinned back at her. "I'm the oldest. My brothers knew something was going on, but I think they were too young to realize I was going to have sex." He grimaced. "Unfortunately, Mom wasn't so naive."

Zara's smile widened. "I'll bet."

Lane cleared his throat. "Anyway, the point I'm trying to make is that sometimes we wish things had turned out differently. Afterwards, I wondered what it would feel like to do it with someone I really cared about. I felt a little cheated. I felt like I'd let myself down."

He stared at her, hoping she'd understand. Her breath hitched and her eyes glittered with emotion. She didn't look away.

He dropped his voice to a whisper. "I'm not going to pretend there haven't been others since then, Zara, but I'm telling you the truth when I say I'm still wondering what it feels like to make love to someone I really, really care about."

Her eyes widened in comprehension. Her lips moved, but no words came, as if she didn't quite know what to say. He leaned toward her and claimed her lips, silencing her efforts.

"I want to love you with every part of my body. I want to teach you everything I know. I want to drive you wild, so wild, you'll hardly be able to stand it. I want to make you mine."

He leaned down and pressed kisses against her forehead, her cheeks, her eyelids before taking her mouth once again. Softly, tenderly, he kissed her. His cock was rock hard.

His body screamed for more, but slowly, gently, he pulled away. He wrapped his arms around her and with his chin resting on her head, fought to regain control.

"I want your first time to be special and it won't be as good as it could be if we rush things. I want us to get to know each other, to spend more time together before we go any further. You deserve dinners and champagne and candles. You deserve moonlit walks along the beach, picnics in the park, dancing until midnight. Call me old fashioned, but I guess that's what I'd like—for both of us."

She moved slightly away and stared up at him, her eyes dark with uncertainty. "I thought you wanted me?"

His gut clenched against the urge to sweep her back into his arms and make love to her like she wanted. But he resisted the temptation and breathed in deeply to regain control. It would be better for both of them if they waited. He only hoped she understood.

"Of course I want you. I want nothing more than to be buried deep inside you, watching you while you come, but you need to trust me on this one, sweetheart. Let's wait a little longer; let me earn my place in your bed. I want to be worthy of the honor."

Her shoulders slumped and she turned her head away, resting it against his chest. A long while later, she spoke, her voice low. "Are you sure? Because, you know, I'd be happy for you to be the first."

"Oh, don't you worry, I'm going to be the first," Lane said possessively, tightening his arms around her. "Let's not make any mistake about that."

She relaxed against him. "I'm glad."

They sat on the couch in silence. Lane breathed in the scent of her hair and tried to ignore the guilt that prodded his conscience. *What was he doing with this beautiful, innocent woman?* He didn't do commitment. He'd never done commitment. She wasn't like the girls he usually dated. She deserved more. Far more.

Anguish burned inside him. *What was he going to do?* Could he put aside his fears that his life would turn out like his father's? Was he willing to take the risk? At that moment, he simply didn't know and the knowledge just about killed him.

Chapter 27

Tuesday, January 30, 7:12 p.m.

Draco took a drag on his cigarette and held the smoke deep in his lungs. When at last he exhaled, only the tiniest whiff of smoke clouded the air in front of him. He shifted in his seat and tapped on the steering wheel with his fingers in an effort to relieve the boredom.

The Dowton bitch had been in there for hours. The first hint of evening had already darkened the sky and still there was no sign of her. He didn't have a clue who lived in the four-storey Chatswood apartment block, but whatever she was doing in there was taking some time.

Irritation surged through him. He scrubbed at his hair and then took another drag on his cigarette. After having his plans to snatch her thwarted the previous night, he'd lain in wait for her outside her house. He knew that sooner or later, she'd emerge and when she did, he'd be ready.

His patience had paid off. Around lunch time, he'd spied her BMW leaving the AG's mansion. He idled in behind her, careful to keep a reasonable distance between them. He didn't know where she was headed, but if he could, he intended to intercept her the minute she stepped from her vehicle.

He'd followed her all the way over the Harbour Bridge and into the northern suburbs. Finally, she brought her car to a stop in front of the unit block situated close to the busy Pacific Highway. Draco looked around him and cursed. It was Tuesday afternoon and the streets were crowded with traffic.

It was madness to even contemplate grabbing her in front of so many witnesses. These days, every man, woman and child had a phone in their pocket and it would have been an act tantamount to signing his own prison sentence if he hauled her into his car then and there and stole her away in front of them. He'd done enough time on the inside not to be leery of heading back and he was certain she'd put up a fight.

So, he'd found a shady spot across the road and settled in to wait. He guessed she was visiting a friend, but it had been too late for lunch and too early for dinner. He'd expected the visit to be brief.

Four hours later, he was forced to revise his initial assessment of the situation. He stretched his legs as far as he was able in the cramped confines of his white commodore sedan and rubbed at the ache behind his knee. During his last stint in Long Bay Jail, he'd copped a savage hit from an iron bar wielded by a member of a rival biker gang. The shattered bones and severed tendons had never quite healed under the oh-so-caring ministrations of the jail's resident surgeon and now, after sitting idle for such a long time in his car, the injury was lodging its protest.

Draco cursed aloud, now encompassing Allison in his increasing irritation. If the stupid bitch had just paid up when he'd asked, he wouldn't be in this predicament. It was all her fault.

He immediately squirmed, knowing full well his own part in the situation. He'd been the one to suggest she cut out her debt on her back. Initially, things had worked out well. He'd given her all the ice she demanded and had enjoyed the classiest pussy he'd ever known.

Despite the regular availability of sluts who hung out at the clubhouse, he'd been drawn to the blond, high-class aloofness of the bitch from the eastern suburbs. Not to mention the finest set of tits he'd ever laid eyes on. His cock had taken over and before he knew it, they were meeting up on regular occasions. She fucked better than any slut he'd known and he was only too happy to keep her supplied with gear. It was only later he discovered she was the wife of the State Attorney General.

At first, he'd shit his pants. The ramifications of what could happen to him and to the members of his club had kept him sleepless and sexless for weeks. Even the most seasoned of the sluts that frequented the clubhouse hadn't been able to get him hard. It was the latter that had really put the fear of God into him.

He finally confronted Allison with his concerns and had been relieved to find out she had no intention of cutting off her drug supply—not to mention their mutually enjoyable trysts in the back of the clubhouse—by disclosing his existence to her husband.

Their mutually beneficial arrangement had gone along just fine until little Miss eastern suburbs had decided she'd had enough of western suburbs biker cock. Almost overnight, she turned mean and nasty and spiteful, accusing him of being stupid, ugly and smelling of gear oil.

It was then he decided the top-shelf pussy she offered him in return for her little bags of crystals wasn't as valuable to him as he'd first thought. Allowing her a modest discount for the sexual services she'd provided, he calculated her drug debt at around nine-hundred and forty thousand dollars. As someone who didn't deal in small change, it didn't take him long to tell her she owed him a million.

She'd scoffed and laughed, of course. He expected that, but it had angered him, just the same. He'd slapped the smirk off her beautiful face with a couple of quick backhands and enjoyed the satisfaction of watching the shock and fear suffuse her perfect features.

Up until then, he'd given her free reign over his body and to some extent, over his mind. He'd enjoyed buying her expensive trinkets, designer clothing and so many handbags she could have opened her own shop. She'd repaid him enthusiastically with imaginative and physically challenging sex. He'd never been with a woman whose sexual appetite exceeded his own and it had become as addictive as her crystals.

But now, in the privacy of his car, Draco grudgingly conceded he should never have mixed business with pleasure and especially with someone who had the power to destroy him. One word in the ear of her husband or his police cronies and Draco could be put away for the rest of his natural life.

He'd been willing to take the risk when he was having the most uninhibited sex he'd ever enjoyed, but when the pussy was shut down, his outlook took a turn for the worse. His usual sense of self-preservation kicked in and had sharpened to the point where it could no longer be ignored.

When Allison failed to pay what she owed, he stormed around the clubhouse for more than two days before he came up with the plan to kidnap her daughter. He was thankful he'd caught a glimpse of the child in a photo Allison kept in her wallet, or he'd have never known the kid existed.

Allison had emptied her handbag onto the coffee table in his office at the clubhouse one evening, hunting around for a lipstick. The slut's purse had fallen open in the process. He picked it up and glanced at the photo that was inside a plastic sleeve in the wallet.

She noticed his interest and had puffed up with pride. He duly listened while she raved about the girl in glowing terms. It was obvious she loved her.

It was during his furious rant to his sergeant-at-arms in the back of the clubhouse, when he'd considered and discarded several options to force the eastern suburbs' slut to pay, that his mind had latched onto the image of her daughter. All at once, it was clear what he could do. There was nothing Allison wouldn't do for the girl, including repaying what she owed.

Everything would have worked out just dandy, too, if Beefcake hadn't fucked it all up. The kid would have been snatched, the ransom demand would have been issued and the stuck up bitch would have paid. Simple as that—they would have been square.

Only, it hadn't turned out that way. After their meeting at the clubhouse where he'd warned her she had a fortnight to pay up, the slut had fucked off north without a single word. Okay, he may have treated her a little roughly, but he hadn't expected her to flee. He'd been forced to threaten the AG—something he'd hoped to avoid. And who could have foreseen that on the very day they'd planned the kidnapping, Brittany Dowton would be in the company of another kid who happened to look just like her?

Could the gods have screwed any more with his head? He would have killed himself laughing if the joke hadn't been on him.

Draco growled low in his throat and thumped the steering wheel of his car. Nobody made a fool of him and got away with it. He glanced around to check that no one had noticed and was glad to see that, apart from a couple of youths loping along the sidewalk about thirty yards in front of him, he was alone.

His phone call to Allison after the botched kidnap attempt had been meant to frighten her and it seemed like it had done the job. She'd begged him to leave her kid alone and had promised to get him the money. She'd even offered him Zara as an incentive to get the AG to pay.

Naturally, he'd been suspicious at first and had wondered at her willingness to allow her oldest daughter to be subjected to a violent abduction—and worse. He wondered whether the bitch had been setting him up.

But then he'd done a little research on the Internet and had discovered Zara wasn't Allison's biological daughter. Suddenly, the slut's willingness to aid him in the recovery of his money by offering the other child made sense. The cold malice of the woman he'd once been half in love with stunned him, but she'd assured him Zara's father would pay anything to have her returned. At the end of the day, all Draco wanted was his money.

He looked at his watch and cursed again. *What the fuck could the girl be doing in there?* He quelled the urge to storm into the building and knock on doors until he found the right one. That would be stupid and if there was anything he wasn't, it was stupid. He hadn't gotten this far in life by being a fuckwit.

With a sigh of resignation, he shifted his bulk in the seat and prepared to spend a little more time in the cramped confines of his car. He'd waited this long. *What was another hour or two?*

CHAPTER 28

Tuesday, January 30, 7:26 p.m.

Lane threaded his fingers through Zara's and gave her hand a tender squeeze. They lay on their sides on the wide leather sofa, sharing stories about their pasts, including Zara's less-than-amiable relationship with her stepmother. He now understood why she called the woman by her first name.

He was doing his best to keep his mind off the fact that Zara's warm, lush body was pressed up close against his, since he'd promised both of them he'd keep his hands off her. Despite his best efforts, he couldn't prevent the hard-on that was doing its best to be noticed. The rumble of Zara's belly was a welcome distraction.

"I'm sorry," she murmured. Her face flushed in the dim glow from the lamp on the side table he'd switched on a little earlier. Night had set in and he'd barely noticed.

He waved her embarrassment away. "Don't be. It could just as easily have been mine. I haven't eaten all day."

Her brow furrowed in concern. "You should have said. We could have eaten earlier."

"And missed out on hearing about your attempt to be the prima donna of the Point Piper ballet school for infants?" he teased.

Her blush deepened and tenderness swelled in his chest.

She was beyond adorable. Everything she'd shared with him over the course of the afternoon only drew him further under her spell. He was falling for her and falling fast. He shook his head at the wonder of it, even as a shadow stole across his heart.

Watching him, Zara's expression turned serious. "What is it, Lane? Talk to me."

He pursed his lips, wishing he hadn't remembered all the reasons he'd vowed to remain single. He'd made those vows before he met Zara, before he met the woman who could light up every corner of his life—if he let her. She made him see how cold and lonely his life had been and would continue to be, if she weren't around to share it.

He wanted to brush off her concern and would have if he'd been with anyone else. But he cared for her too much to casually ignore the growing confusion in her liquid dark eyes.

What the hell was he going to do?

Despair settled like lead in his heart. Uncertainty tightened his gut. Slowly, Zara's gaze filled with hurt and disappointment. In silence, she withdrew her hand and tucked it against her side. She inched away from him and sat up, putting distance between them.

"What is it, Lane? A minute ago we were both feeling like the world could never be more right and now you look like the dog you've owned since you were a kid has just been run over on the freeway. What's going on?"

Her voice had lowered to a tortured whisper, confusion plain on her face. He wished he had the words to make this go away.

"Lane, talk to me. Please. You're scaring me. Did I say something wrong?"

"No. Please, don't think that. It's not you; it's me."

There, he'd finally admitted it. He risked a glance in her direction, expecting to find her gaze filled with pity. Instead, he found resignation tinged with a quiet anger.

"Would you care to explain what you mean?"

He stared at her and couldn't for the life of him work out

what she had to be angry about. He'd just admitted he was the one with the problem. *Hadn't he?* Perhaps she misunderstood.

"There are things about me you don't know. Things I've never told anyone." He drew in a breath and then rushed on. "I...I'm never going to get married. I don't intend to have a family." He shrugged and forced himself to add, "I don't do long-term commitment. I have nothing to offer you."

Her voice was filled with surprise and disbelief. "Marriage? Children? We've only known each other since Saturday. Surely you can come up with something better than that?" She shook her head in disgust and leaped off the couch and then hunted around for her shoes. Lane's heart clenched when he caught sight of the tears that glistened in her eyes.

"Zara, I'm sorry. I'm not explaining this very well. Let me—"

"No, no. Don't bother. It's all right, I get it. Your invitation to come over was a spontaneous, heat-of-the-moment thing, a by-product of the relief both of us felt at having found Olivia alive and well. It was nothing but two adults coming together for a few hours of relaxation and companionship. Nothing more, nothing less. Well, thank you for your time, Detective Senior Sergeant Black and for your efforts where both Olivia and Brittany are concerned. I wish you all the best."

She spun on her heel. Lane's hand snaked out and snagged her elbow, holding tight. She gasped and came about face, her dark eyes shooting fire.

"Let me go."

"No."

"Lane, I swear, let me go or I'll—"

"You'll what? Scream? I'll scream louder. Cry? Believe it or not, I can manage that one, too." He gentled his hold on her and lowered his voice. "Please, Zara, sit back down. Please give me a chance to explain."

She resisted his tug on her arm, still staring at him defiantly. He held her gaze and hoped like hell she could see how much he cared for her. It was a long moment later, but finally she relented. Lane swallowed a sigh of relief and released her. He patted the space next to him, silently urging her to join him.

Grudgingly, she did as he asked, but the tension in her body indicated she was a long way from understanding. Lane braced himself with a deep breath and spoke again.

"I told you about my childhood, my mother and my brothers. I told you about some of the escapades my brothers and I got up to during our teenage years. What I didn't tell you about was my father. Warren Black was a police officer, a senior detective in the DEA. That stands for the Drug Enforcement Agency, in case you don't know."

She stared at him with narrowed eyes, her lips compressed. Lane flushed. *God, could he mess this up any more?*

"I'm sorry, of course you know. You're a lawyer. I didn't mean to imply…" The heat in his cheeks intensified. He bit his lip in consternation and looked away.

"Just get on with it." Her expression was still closed, but her tone was gentler. He took encouragement from it and continued.

"I'm the oldest of four kids. My father died when I was seven. He was shot in the line of duty by some drug-crazed idiot he'd been trying to help off the street. Literally. The man was lying in the middle of the road. Dad was bent over him, trying to get him to move out of the way of the traffic when the asshole drew a gun on him. My father died at the scene."

Zara's eyes widened in shock and her mouth fell open. The color leached from her cheeks. Lane cut her off before she could say the words.

"Tragic, yes. Sad as hell, you betcha. He was given a hero's burial. Even the Police Commissioner was there." He shook his head, trying to ward off the memories. "But it didn't matter. None of it did. The only thing that mattered was that we'd lost our dad and my mother had lost her husband."

His voice cracked. Tears welled up in Zara's eyes, but he didn't want her pity. She reached out to him, but he brushed her hand away.

"I'm not telling you this to make you feel sorry for me."

"Then why *are* you telling me?" Her soft query nearly did him in, but he forced aside the temptation to unload his long-pent-up grief and anger and instead, forged ahead.

"I'm telling you because it shaped who I am, who I became. My mother worked two jobs to keep food on the table. Sure, there was a payout from the Police Service for Dad's wrongful death, but it was a pittance when faced with the reality of supporting four children. My youngest brother was only six months old when Dad died.

"Mom put the money into a trust fund for us kids—to pay for college or whatever other educational options we wanted to pursue when the time came. Every cent of her wages went to pay the day-to-day expenses, including the monthly car and mortgage payments."

Lane drew in a ragged breath, hating the thought of dredging up the memories, but unable to stop until he was finished.

"I watched my mom go from a pretty young housewife and mother who met regularly with her friends for lunch and who was always around when we needed her, to a woman who aged a decade overnight and worked sixteen hours a day just to keep her family alive. None of that sacrifice would have happened if Dad hadn't died. Her life would have been so different."

Zara's eyes were full of compassion. "Accidents happen, people die. You can't help that, Lane."

Anger surged through him and he pushed away from the couch, suddenly unable to sit still. "You think I don't know that? That's the reason I vowed to never get married, to never have a family. I love being a cop. It's what I was born to do. I'm not prepared to take the risk that my job gets me killed and leaves another woman to struggle on alone to raise our family."

Zara stared at him, her eyes dark and stormy with emotion. He knew what she was going to say and he didn't want to hear it. He'd heard it all before from his mother, when he'd confessed to her late one night a few years ago, how he had felt when she questioned him about his unwillingness to settle down.

He held up his hand. "Please, Zara, don't say it. I don't want to hear about what ifs and wherefores and maybes." His voice rose as he tried to make her understand.

"Don't you *see*? I can't take the risk! I chose policing because it was in my blood. It was all I wanted to be and so far, it's lived up to every single one of my expectations. But I chose it, knowing it meant I would never have a family to call my own." He began to pace across the thick woollen rug that covered the tiled floor of the living room. Zara watched him in silence.

"I've lived with my decision for more than a decade and I've been fine with it. Did you hear me? I've been *fine* with it! Girls have come and gone through my life—I've enjoyed them and they've enjoyed me—and that's been fine. I've never wanted anything more permanent. I've never yearned for a family of my own. I've never once thought I might have made the wrong decision."

He spun on his heel and faced her, his breath coming hard. Zara stood and came toward him, her cheeks wet with tears. He drew in a huge breath and exhaled. The air escaped and with it, his anger. His shoulders slumped. She reached out. Her fingers grazed his chest. He sucked in another breath and dragged her to him, burying his face in her hair. His voice was rough, muffled, defeated when he spoke again.

"I've never once thought I'd made the wrong decision," he whispered. He lifted his head and stared down at her. "Until you. You've turned my world upside down. You're all I can think about, even in the middle of a nightmare investigation where my friend's ten-year-old is the victim, you were in my thoughts, my dreams, in almost every waking moment."

He stared at her, confusion, uncertainty and wonder warring inside him. "For the first time in my life, I'm questioning who I am and what I believe about myself. And it scares me. It scares the hell out of me, but there's nothing I can do about it. I want you. I need you. I yearn to have you in my life. Every hour. Every day. But that means putting you at risk. It means risking leaving you alone, to fend for yourself and perhaps our children, to grow old and tired decades before your time."

He framed her face in his hands, imploring her to understand. "I care for you too much to do that to you."

"Do you care for me enough to try?"

Her quiet words shocked him to the core. He dropped his hands and stepped back, dazed and confused. *How could he try?* Didn't she understand anything? Hadn't she listened to a word he'd said?

He shook his head, but she was having none of it.

"Don't give me that nonsense, Lane. You're terrified of trying. You're terrified of even *thinking* about trying. You're terrified of something that may never happen. Are you really willing to throw away what we could have together for something that may never come to pass?

"People die every day, from all sorts of things. Some of them die at work, absolutely—but most of them don't. That's life, it's a gamble. Nobody said it wasn't. But you either choose to live or you choose to die."

She dragged in a breath. Lane braced himself for another bout. She didn't disappoint. Her eyes flashed with passion and fire and determination and the tiniest spark of hope. He couldn't look away.

"So far, you've chosen *life*. But it comes with risks. It comes down to whether you care enough about the outcome to take that risk. You either want to take it, or you don't." She stared him down. "It's your choice."

Lane was torn. One part of him yearned to take her in his arms and promise her the world, promise her that he was willing to take the risk that what they found together would be enough...but deep inside, he still had doubts, grave doubts and they killed the words in his throat before they could even form.

Zara must have sensed his withdrawal because her face closed. She ducked her head and a curtain of dark hair shrouded part of her face from his view. As she turned away, he caught sight of fresh tears.

His gut clenched in agony. His hands fisted by his side, but he didn't move, didn't speak, didn't even murmur. His own silence and inability to comfort her nearly killed him.

She'd walked less than ten feet away from him when she turned on her heel and stalked back, closing the distance between them. Her eyes spat fire.

"Do you know Lane, from the moment I met you, I believed in you. You exuded confidence, courage, determination and kindness. You cared about a little girl who'd been kidnapped; you cared about her family who were depending on you to bring their baby home. You cared about the little girl who'd had a lucky escape and her family who were relieved she'd been spared."

Her voice cracked. He stood, cemented to the ground, feeling helpless. He wanted to reach out to her, to comfort her, but his limbs were leaden.

She lifted her chin and stared him down. Despite the turmoil inside him, a burst of admiration flooded through him.

"I-I think I fell in love with you right there, in Brittany's bedroom, when you treated her with such kindness and concern and caring. You were under pressure and every second counted, but you took your time and coaxed my sister with gentleness until she was able to give you what you needed and all along, you never lost sight of the scared, little girl who needed you more. Olivia Munro has no idea how hard you worked to find her."

She swiped at the tears that now stained her cheeks, but didn't break his gaze. Her voice was softer, calmer when she spoke again.

"In all of those long, tense hours when none of us knew if we were ever going to see that little girl alive again, when I prayed to God with gratitude that my sister had been spared and with hope that Olivia would be found unharmed, my faith in you never wavered."

Her hand clenched into a fist and she thumped him on

the arm. He gasped, but more from surprise than pain. Then she hit him again.

"Not *once*, do you hear me? Not even for an *instant* did I doubt you. I believed in you. I believed in your courage. I believed in your strength. I believed in your determination."

Her shoulders slumped as she finished and the fight went out of her. Lane ached from the tension in his body. His eyes burned from unshed emotion. Unable to stand it another second, he reached for her.

She flinched and stepped away from him, her eyes hard. "I never dreamed how wrong I was, that beneath your confident, courageous exterior there's a coward." Tears filled her eyes again and rushed down her cheeks. Her voice hitched on a sob. "If you ever find the man I'm beyond certain you can be, you know where to find me."

She turned and stumbled, bending awkwardly to collect her shoes and handbag. With her head held high, she strode out of his home. He stared at the empty doorway—for what seemed like a lifetime—in an agony of pain and indecision.

Chapter 29

Tuesday, January 30, 7:49 p.m.

From a distance, Draco saw the woman stumble down the steps that led out of the unit block and hurry along the sidewalk toward her car. The night had fully descended and if it weren't for a couple of conveniently placed street lights, he'd have missed her.

"Fuck, she's coming." He peered behind Zara, checking to ensure she was on her own. Her car was where she'd left it, fifty yards or so ahead of her. Draco checked behind her again. Still no one. His mind worked furiously. He spent a few seconds debating his next move, but there was nothing for it. He might not get another opportunity and he was sick to death of sitting.

Pushing open the car door, he climbed stiffly out of his vehicle and hurried across the road. He reached into the back pocket of his jeans and was relieved to feel the reassuring hardness of his snubnosed revolver. His blade was also handy.

He found a thick shrub growing a few feet away from her silver BMW and silently congratulated himself on his luck. Crouching low in the shadows, he waited.

Tears rolled down Zara's cheeks and she let them fall unhindered. She wanted nothing more than to crawl into bed and cry her pain away. Over and over, she replayed the conversation with Lane until she could recite nearly every word by heart.

She couldn't believe he was willing to throw away the promise of what they could find together because he was scared—scared of something that in all likelihood would never come to pass. She'd meant it when she'd told him she'd never imagined he was a coward, but he'd let her walk away without even a murmur of protest.

Her heart clenched again at the memory, but she'd done the right thing to leave. He had to be the one to decide she was worth the risk—that *they* were worth taking a risk. He had to come to the conclusion that his fears were irrational, that, when compared to the potential joy and love and enrichment they could bring to each other's lives, his anxiety about a premature death were as insubstantial as cotton candy.

With her gaze determinably fixed to the concrete beneath her feet, she hurried along the path that led to her car. The night had settled in and the pavement was dimly lit. Sifting through her handbag, she found a clean tissue and wiped at the tears on her cheeks.

With some degree of decorum restored, she drew in a deep breath and hunted in her handbag for her keys. Her car was still where she'd left it. In the darkness, it looked forever away, but she'd taken the closest parking spot she could find when she arrived at Lane's condominium, hours earlier.

Had it really been only a matter of hours? So much had happened, so much had changed. Hopes had been raised and then dashed. It felt like a monster roller-coaster ride that she'd taken a lifetime ago.

She took another deep breath and released it slowly, determined to put this behind her, at least for now. She had to go home and get some sleep before heading to work in the morning. She felt guilty enough about taking two days off, knowing someone else had to cover her clients and any other crises among her cases that needed to be resolved.

She smiled without humor. She knew all about crises.

Her fingers closed over her car keys and she heaved a sigh of relief. Her BMW was only a few feet away. At this time of night, it would take her less than an hour to get home where she could climb into bed, pull up the covers and do her best to forget all about Detective Senior Sergeant Lane Black.

With that resolution firmly in her mind, she pointed her remote at the car. Before she could press the unlock button, a heavyset man leaped out from behind a bush. A millisecond later, a gun was shoved in her face.

Zara froze. *She was being robbed.* She couldn't believe it. Adrenaline surged through her. She could hardly hear over the pounding of her heart but she did her best to maintain her composure, refusing to let her attacker see her fear.

The man stepped closer and hauled her against him. One thick, hairy arm pinned her against his chest, the other hand held the gun hard against her temple.

"One word and you're dead," he growled against her ear.

Zara tried to get her brain working through the shock and fear that paralyzed her. He'd already half-pushed, half-dragged her to the side of the highway. A car whooshed past, its lights almost blinding her. The driver was intent on the road in front of him and didn't even glance in her direction.

Her captor started forward. Zara tensed and tried to resist, but she was no match for the brute strength of the man who held her. Before she knew it, they'd shuffled across the road and he'd thrust her up against the side of a vehicle that was half concealed by the darkness. With the gun still trained on her head, he let go of her and pulled his keys out of his pocket.

Oh, God, he was going to abduct her. Any minute, she'd be forced into the car and taken to who knew where.

Thoughts spun through her mind—frantic, scattered thoughts that refused to cement into actions.

Staring at her through narrowed eyes, he tugged the rear passenger door open and waved the gun toward her, indicating without words, that she was to climb in.

Her heart thumped harder. Time was running out. If she was going to make a run for it, she had to do it now. She might never get another chance.

She eyed the man who looked vaguely familiar and then eyed the gun. The headlights from another passing car glinted off its shiny metal barrel. She'd never been this close to a gun. She shuddered and prayed silently for the courage to challenge its deadly promise.

Knowing it was now or never, she flung up her arm to ward off the weapon and spun around, ducking under the meaty arm the man swung in her direction. Tensing, she took off at an awkward run, her wedges making progress difficult. She'd barely made it past the end of his car when she turned her ankle on the loose road base that lined the shoulder of the highway.

She yelped in pain and then in fear when her captor hauled her up by the hair and turned her to face him. Seconds later, his fist hurtled toward her. It connected with a loud smack against the soft skin of her cheek. Fire exploded across her face. Her mouth filled with blood. The fist came out again. This time when it connected just above her ear, she felt nothing.

Chapter 30

Tuesday, January 30, 8:28 p.m.

Lane picked half-heartedly at the ham and pineapple pizza he'd had delivered a little earlier. Despite his hunger, the weight of confusion and uncertainty in his gut now prohibited even the smallest bite.

He sighed heavily and wished for the thousandth time that he wasn't so damaged. He'd resisted the urge to tear off after Zara and beg for her to stay. He knew she needed time alone. They both did.

He'd replayed their last conversation until he was exhausted and determined to claw back a semblance of his sanity. Coupled with the stress and lack of sleep he'd endured over the past forty-eight hours or so, it was all he could do not to push away from the table and head down the hall to his bed.

He stood and dragged himself over to the couch. Weariness dodged his every step. The smell of her perfume hit him the moment he sat down. His single-minded efforts to push aside memories of their time together evaporated like fog in sunlight.

All at once, she surrounded him. Her smile, her laughter, her warmth. His body tightened at the recollection of her pressed against him and he groaned aloud.

He wanted her: now, tomorrow, forever. And yet, the

promise of what could be wasn't enough for him to take this leap of faith. His parents had loved each other to distraction. He'd only been a child, but he'd still been aware of the soft looks, the tender words, the close embraces. His parents had loved as much as anyone could and it hadn't been enough.

Zara's words came back to taunt him. He couldn't deny she was right. It *was* cowardly to be unwilling to take the risk, but it was also supremely unselfish. *Why couldn't she see that?* He was thinking of *her* in all of this. *Wasn't* he?

Shucking off his shorts, he tossed them to the floor and headed toward the bathroom. The sound of his phone ringing pulled him up short. Hope flared inside him and his heart skipped a beat. *Zara.*

The next instant, he was shaking his head, telling himself not to be stupid. There was no way she'd be calling him after the way they parted. Besides, she was probably still on the road.

Picking up his phone from where he'd left it, he glanced down at the screen. He couldn't help the rueful smile that tugged at his lips.

"Hi, Mom, how are you?"

"Lane, I'm fine. More importantly, how are *you?* I just saw the late news. I recognized you and your men from the footage. I'm so glad everything turned out all right."

"Thanks, Mom. So am I. We were lucky."

"It was more than luck, Lane. You're a fine detective."

He instinctively ducked his head. "Thanks," he mumbled.

"I'm so proud of you, Lane. That little girl and her family don't know how lucky they were to have you on their case."

"Mom..." he protested. "It wasn't just me. We all helped out."

"I'm sure everyone did their bit, but some people go above and beyond. That's just the way it is." She paused and her voice roughened with emotion. "Your father was like that, and so are you."

A lump formed in Lane's throat. He tried to say something, but found he couldn't. He swallowed and tried again.

"Mom, you don't have to say that."

"I'm not just saying it, Lane. I mean it. Your father was a man of honor and integrity, a man of determination and courage. He always gave everything he had, every single time. It didn't matter who needed help. He gave it freely, without complaint and came home after every shift a contented man."

"Until he didn't."

His bald statement was met with silence. Guilt surged through him and then he immediately felt angry for feeling guilty.

It was the truth, wasn't it? His increasingly heated thoughts were interrupted by his mother's resigned acceptance.

"You're right, Lane. You're absolutely right. One night, he didn't come home. I don't know what you want me to say."

"Why weren't you mad? I never saw you yell or shout or cry at the injustice of it. I never saw you throw plates or slam doors or...or hit something. How come, Mom? How come you never got mad?"

"Who says I didn't? You were only a child, Lane. You couldn't have possibly understood everything you saw or didn't see. There were plenty of times when I ranted and cried and yes, I even threw a few plates, but I made sure I did it when you and your brothers were out—either at school, or at the park. There were a handful of times I even did when you were asleep.

"There was a long, long time when I was mad at everyone—and particularly your father. What had he been *thinking*? How could he have left us all alone, to fend for ourselves when we needed him so badly?"

Her voice cracked. She dragged in a deep, shuddering breath. He wanted to tell her to stop. He wanted to offer her comfort. But he couldn't. For far too long, he'd wanted to ask the questions that had circled in his head for so many years.

Respect and love for his mother, and fear of the answers, had held him back but he couldn't hold back any longer. He had to know. He *needed* to know. For his sake, and for Zara's.

"Would you have done things differently if you'd known?" he asked.

"No." Her answer was swift and decisive.

"How can you say that?"

She sighed heavily. "Your father and I loved each other more than we thought possible. We met when we were just out of high school. Within months, we were married. Of course, there were plenty who criticized us, told us we'd never last, but we ignored them all and got on with our lives.

"I went to secretarial school and your father entered the Police Academy. It was hard, but we managed and we had each other, and a few years later, you, the first of our boys arrived. We had no need for anything, but each other. Our family was all that mattered." She gave a sad, little laugh. "It sounds like something out of a sappy old movie, but it's the truth. We were happiest when we were together."

"It must have made it that much harder to go on without him."

"Absolutely. There was a long period when I didn't think I'd survive on my own. My heart had shriveled and died and was buried in the ground right alongside him. If it hadn't been for you boys, I don't know what I would have done. I knew I had to live for you. And so, I did."

"It makes us sound like such a burden," Lane said.

"*Never!* Lane Francis Black! Don't you *ever* say a thing like that! I loved your father more than life itself, but I loved my children, too. Even in the depths of my grief and despair, during the darkest time of my life, I never once wanted to leave my boys or relinquish any burden. Our family was worth my all."

Tears pricked Lane's eyes. He drew in a deep breath and bit his lip against the surge of emotion that tightened his chest.

"Do you believe me, Lane?" Her question was pitched low. He strained to hear it. A sob escaped his tightly compressed mouth and he bit his lips harder.

"*Do you?*" This time, her voice was louder and tinged with panic.

He nodded and then verbalized his response. "Yes, Mom, I believe you."

She breathed a sigh of relief. "Thank you. I'm so glad. You don't know how much that means to me. I-I've never talked to your brothers about this. Perhaps, I should."

"Perhaps," Lane agreed, "but I think you should wait until they ask. It might not be the right time for them."

"Why now, Lane? Why are *you* asking, after all these years? Is it the right time for you?"

Images of Zara crowded Lane's mind and the tightness in his chest eased. Love and tenderness filled his heart. All of a sudden, he knew he'd found the woman he'd love until the day that he died. Whenever that would be.

"I've met a girl."

"Oh, Lane! I'm so pleased. I'd almost given up on you finding someone to settle down with. I take it that things are serious?"

Lane filled his lungs to capacity and then blew it out. "Yes. I think I'm in love with her."

"And does she love you?"

"I'm not sure, but she definitely cares."

"I'm so happy for you. I had begun to wonder if your father's death had affected the way you felt about a family. You're thirty-one and so far, I've never seen you date a girl longer than a week or two. I was hoping it had nothing to do with how things turned out for me."

Lane shouldn't have been surprised by his mother's perceptiveness. As a kid, he'd never been able to keep anything from her.

"I can't tell you that hasn't been a part of it," he admitted quietly. "In fact, up until now, I honestly didn't think I could handle the risk of dying young and leaving a family behind to struggle onward without me. But after talking to you, I think my outlook has changed. For the first time, I can see it from your point of view. That the short years you and Dad had together brought you more happiness than a lot of people have over a lifetime and that's something to be cherished and celebrated and remembered."

"Lane, you're a police officer like your dad and there's always a chance you won't come home. We both know that. But you have to remember the thousands of officers who go to work every day and *do* come home. Focus on them, the ones who make it, not on the handful who don't."

"I want to." His voice was a husky whisper. He cleared his throat and tried again. "You don't know how much I want to."

"There isn't a day goes by that I don't wish your father was still here beside me, but I never regret a single moment of our time together." She paused for a moment and then said, "Do you remember how much I like Fleetwood Mac?"

Lane frowned and tried to keep up with his mother's sudden shift of topic.

"Yeah, I guess so. You used to play their CDs until we were ready to leave home."

His mother chuckled in memory. "I did, didn't I? Anyway, what I wanted to tell you was, Stevie Nicks sang a song called *Love's a Hard Game to Play*. Do you know the one I'm talking about?"

"I don't know. Maybe."

"It's a great song and I played it a lot during the years after your father died. There are a couple of lines toward the end of that song that helped me through the darkest times."

Lane's chest tightened. "Okay."

"I'd sing it for you, but we both know I wouldn't do it justice. The gist of it is you're richer for having known love than to go through life never experiencing what it feels like, no matter that it might end in pain."

Emotion surged through him. Tears spilled over and ran down his cheeks.

His mother's sweet voice sounded softly in his ear. Emotion surged through him. Tears spilled over and ran down his cheeks.

"That's how I feel about your dad," she whispered, her voice choked with tears. "That's exactly how I feel."

"I love you, Mom."

"I love you too, Lane, and I hope this girl comes to love you as much as you deserve." She paused and then her voice lowered on a ragged sigh. "If she loves you even half as much as I loved your father, it will be enough."

CHAPTER 31

Tuesday, January 30, 8:42 p.m.

After what seemed an interminable amount of time being jostled, bound and gagged, on the back seat of the kidnapper's car, the vehicle turned into what looked like an industrial area. From Zara's prone position and through her uninjured eye, she caught glimpses of large sheds lit with security lights. The headlights picked up the shape of a low building hunched away from the others behind a high wire fence. The driver headed the car toward it.

Their approach was met by the sound of a pack of barking dogs. Although she couldn't make them out in the darkness, it seemed like they were right outside her door. Minutes later, the man brought the car to a stop and hauled her out. Her cheek burned from where he'd struck it with his fist. One eye was swollen shut. Her legs wobbled at the unaccustomed rough handling and she struggled to gain her balance. Her captor spun her around. It was then that she saw it.

Emblazoned across both of the double entry doors was a logo of an enormous Redback spider. Zara's heart jumped into her throat and all of a sudden, she knew why her captor had seemed familiar: She'd been kidnapped by none other than Draco Jovanovic.

Yelling at the dogs and with his hand tight around her elbow, Draco dragged her across the parking lot and through the doorway of what she presumed was their clubhouse. Despite its rundown exterior, inside, the walls were lined with newly painted plasterboard. A handful of expensive leather couches were scattered haphazardly throughout the large open space. Men in jeans and black leather jackets lounged around, talking with glasses of alcohol in their hands. Only one or two of them looked in her direction and then indifferently turned away.

A well-stocked bar, hewn from enormous planks of pine took up most of one corner of the room. Its smoothly polished surface sparkled from numerous down lights positioned strategically in the ceiling. Light also glinted off row after row of glittering glassware housed in brass racks above the barman's head.

The barman himself looked like a carbon copy of Draco— an over-large package of beef and brawn who emanated an underlying air of menace. Biceps as big as grapefruit were paired with a massive chest, closely set eyes and a shaved head that glistened in the light.

The barman's snowy white shirt looked crisp and freshly ironed and had been decorated with an expertly knotted black bow tie. He stared at her with baleful eyes, not a hint of curiosity lighting their dark depths, even after they rested briefly on her bruised and battered face and the bindings around her wrists.

The thought of begging the man for help took hold in Zara's mind. She opened her mouth to speak. Draco's grip tightened painfully on her arm. He leaned in close, his breath warm and fetid against her face.

"One word and I'll put a bullet in your head." He opened his jacket and she caught a glimpse of the gun as light glinted off its barrel. Renewed fear took a stronghold over her body and mind.

"Besides," he continued, his gaze menacing, "Who do you think will come to your rescue? Everyone in here is a member of the Redbacks. And I'm their president."

Zara's mouth closed with a discernible click. Dread cemented in her stomach. Through the dimness, she spied a larger group of biker members lounging across the other side of the room, drinks, cigarettes—or both—in their hands. Unlike the group she'd seen on her way in, one of these men gave her a thorough once-over before catching her eye and winking at her. His suggestive leer sent shivers of unease down her spine. And then he spoke.

"Hey, Prez, the pigs were here lookin' for you earlier." The man sauntered over to where she and Draco were standing. Zara froze.

"Oh, yeah? What time did they get here?" Draco asked, his casual tone belying the tension around his jaw.

"Bit after one. They were all fired up, ready for action. You should have seen their disappointment when I told them you weren't here." The man laughed, displaying a mouthful of tobacco-stained teeth. Zara tried not to breathe in the rank stench from his body.

"Good job I was otherwise occupied," Draco replied. "What were they after, Toothpick?"

The man called Toothpick smiled slyly. "Said they were lookin' for you. Said they were bringin' you in."

Draco's gaze narrowed. "What did you tell them?"

"I didn't tell them nothin'." He hawked up a globule of phlegm and spat it inches away from Zara's feet. "They're fuckin' pigs. What do you think I said?"

Draco shook his head in disgust. "You're a filthy prick, Toothpick. Go and clean that shit up. And you're lucky you kept your mouth shut. I don't need any more trouble from the cops. I've still got business to do."

Draco turned away from Toothpick. With a none-too-gentle shove, he pushed her in the direction of a closed door. Within moments, he'd unlocked it and deposited her inside what she presumed was his office. With eyes narrowed in silent warning, he turned and left, pulling the door closed behind him. She didn't fail to hear the decisive click of the lock on his departure.

As soon as she was alone, Zara strained against the

bindings that held her wrists tight and prayed that by some miracle, they'd loosened since she'd last checked. Gritting her teeth, she ignored the pain in her face and focused all of her attention on wriggling her fingers to loosen her bonds. Her numb hands made her efforts even more difficult. She held her breath and gave it another go.

The bindings didn't budge. Not even an inch. The only thing she felt was a shaft of pain shoot up her arms. She stifled a sob and searched for inner strength. Now wasn't the time to cry.

In order to distract herself, she tried to concentrate on the possible reasons why she'd been kidnapped. The Redbacks' attempt to take Brittany had failed. Why would they risk another? The police were already on their tail. It wouldn't take a genius to work out who had taken her when Lane and her family discovered she was missing.

She groaned in anguish at the thought of Lane. After the way they'd parted, she was sure he wouldn't be looking for her any time soon. She only hoped her father, or even perhaps Allison, would notice her absence and wonder enough about it to raise the alarm.

But what if they didn't? What if no one found her hastily scrawled note? Or worse, what if they found her note, but decided she must still be with Lane? Would they even think to call him and check?

Probably not. Even though she could count on one hand the number of times she'd spent the night at a friend's house, she was an adult, free to come and go as she chose. It could be some time tomorrow, when she failed to show for work, before anyone became concerned enough to question her whereabouts.

Panic clenched at her belly and tightened her already-ragged nerves. She fought hard against it. Drawing in a breath, she eased the air out between dry lips and did her best to keep the fear at bay.

She looked around her to distract herself from her discouraging thoughts. The room where she'd been unceremoniously tossed was generously furnished with an expensive-looking leather couch decorated with cushions in hues of red and cream. An enormous flat screen TV was mounted on the opposite wall. An imposing, red cedar desk stood parallel to the back wall and took up almost a third of the space in the smallish room.

While her hands were still bound, her feet were not and she was free to explore her surroundings in what dim light was provided by the small antique lamp on the desk. Thinking quickly, she scoured the room for possible escape routes.

There were no windows and the only door she could see was the one Draco had locked behind him. Despair and rising panic hovered at the edge of her consciousness and she groaned aloud at the helplessness of her situation. The low ache in her belly reminded her it had been a long time since she'd used the bathroom.

Not that she was eager to re-enter the main part of the clubhouse. Memories of the undisguised desire on the face of the man who'd eyed her earlier sent any thoughts of requesting the use of a nearby bathroom, scattering like dandelions tossed to the breeze.

Taking a seat on the couch, she crossed her legs and tried to direct her thoughts elsewhere. The memory of Lane's tortured expression as she walked out of his house flooded her mind. She groaned again, almost preferring the uncomfortableness of her full bladder to recalling the way they'd parted.

After their wondrous time earlier, she'd felt like the luckiest girl in the world. At last, she'd found a man who called to her on every level, who was smart, funny, charming and so damned sexy he took her breath away. At the time, she'd been floating on a bubble of happiness, so light and so giddy she could scarcely keep her feet on the ground.

But then he'd blown it. He'd turned his back on any chance they might have of making something together and she watched and listened as his fear dictated his life. With that, the glorious possibility of building a life with him had been ripped away, leaving her bereft and empty.

It wasn't that she didn't understand his fear. After hearing about the death of his father, she could appreciate how it might affect him and the decisions he made, particularly given that Lane was also a police officer. But everyone faced certain fears in their life and it wasn't healthy to let those fears define who they became. It was just like she'd told him: Bad things happen. But good things happen, too, if you're brave enough to recognize opportunities and reach for them.

Knowing he didn't care enough to take a chance on her, on *them*, should have made it easier to turn her back on him, to clear him from her thoughts, from her memories and get on with her life—a life she'd been satisfied with, until he'd entered it. But it didn't. The pain was just as sharp as it had been earlier, when he'd told her plain and simple there was no future for them.

Zara leaned back against the couch and wished she could wrap her arms around herself and hold the hurt inside. That way, she wouldn't have to deal with it. But the bindings around her wrists made such a thing impossible and she stifled a sob of self-pity.

What was she doing there? Was it about the money Allison owed to Draco? Was Zara now the incentive to get her father to pay? With a sigh of despair, she closed her eyes. That had to be it. It was the only thing that made sense. Allison owed Draco a million dollars and he was waiting to collect. Zara was the bait. Better her than Brittany. It was as simple as that. She could only hope Draco would get the message to her father without delay and that the whole nightmare would soon be over.

CHAPTER 32

Wednesday, January 31, 7:06 a.m.

At the sound of his wife approaching, David looked up from the breakfast table and set aside the newspaper in front of him. He'd opted to sleep in the spare room the past couple of nights and was pleased that he'd done so. Both nights, he'd gone to bed angry that Allison could treat the whole episode with Draco and her drug use and the huge sum of money with such cavalier disregard. He'd spent a nerve-wracking seventy-odd hours, desperately trying to locate Olivia Munro before it was too late, knowing full well the real target had been his daughter and all his wife could do was laugh it all off and promise to make it all better.

That Olivia had been found alive and unharmed was a relief beyond all measure, but it had nothing to do with his wife's claim that she'd sort it all out with a phone call. In the end, Draco hadn't answered and David was more than grateful when Detective Black ignored his wife's claims and had fallen back on his own resources.

With Brittany sleeping peacefully down the hall and Olivia safe back home, he'd retired earlier than usual and had managed to string together a pleasant nine hours of uninterrupted sleep. He'd awoken rested and refreshed and feeling slightly less annoyed at the woman who now filled her plate with fresh fruit before moving to take a seat beside him.

His gaze took in her still-youthful features and he felt a pang of sadness at the thought of the toll her drug use would take out on her face. It hadn't happened yet, but if she continued the way she was, it was only a matter of time. He'd seen the wild look addicts got; he'd seen the ravages on their skin. Ice was the worst for hallucinations. Long-term users were convinced there were insects living under their skin. David had seen documentaries where addicts as young as seventeen were covered in sores and rashes from scratching and gouging at the bugs they were certain were in there.

But Allison showed no signs of that yet and he could only hope she'd been saved in time. She'd only done a fortnight at the exclusive rehab clinic in Port Douglas and that was certainly not enough time. He only hoped she'd be willing to return and stay there until she was well.

She looked up at him cautiously, as if gauging his mood. Sadness flooded through him and he had to blink away the tears. She smiled at him, soft and uncertain and his anger dissipated.

His wife was ill. Her drug addiction was no more and no less than any addiction. He wouldn't blame an alcoholic or a gambler or a smoker for their inability to break their habit. He'd see it for what it was—a medical condition that needed treatment. He'd urge any one of them to seek help. He'd offer assistance, compassion, understanding. Those things were the least he could offer his wife. After all, he'd vowed to stand by her in sickness and in health, until death.

In some respects, he felt responsible. If he hadn't been so preoccupied with his political career, he might have had more time to attend to her. He certainly would have been more aware of the danger she was in of becoming addicted.

It was the drug suppliers and dealers he should expend his anger on. They were the ones who made it possible for vulnerable people like Allison to access the source of their addiction. He shook his head, still unable to believe she'd spent a million dollars on drugs.

At his continued silence, her smile faded and she eyed him a little more warily. "I trust you slept well, David?"

He nodded. "Thank you, I did. How about you?"

She looked down at her plate, as if weighing the authenticity of his improved mood. A moment later, she replied. "Not too bad, thank you. I missed you."

Love swelled in his heart. He reached for her hand and raised it to his lips. "I missed you, too. And I'm sorry. You're not well. I never should have yelled at you."

A smile wobbled on her lips, glistening with ripe red lipstick. "I don't deserve you."

He sighed quietly and pressed a kiss upon the back of her hand. "Of course you do." He set her hand down and then returned to his newspaper. Allison speared a piece of watermelon.

David glanced at his watch and then eyed her over the top of his paper. "You haven't seen Zara this morning, have you?"

"No, should I have?"

"It's just that she didn't come home last night. I checked in on her on my way up to bed and found a note saying she was meeting with Detective Black."

"Perhaps the "meeting" went longer than she planned?" Allison responded with a wink that made David frown. "She's a big girl, darling and from what I saw of Detective Black, he's rather appealing in that young, boy-next-door kind of way." She leaned over and pressed a smooth palm against his cheek. "Personally, I like my men a little more mature."

David relaxed against her hand, enjoying the warm pressure against his skin. Breathing in the heady fragrance of her perfume, his body stirred and he was reminded that it had been more than a fortnight since he'd found relief between her thighs.

As if sensing his need, Allison's eyes widened knowingly and her lips turned up in a satisfied smile. Her hand slid down his cheek and stole into his lap. She squeezed his thickening cock through his suit pants. He gasped and let his legs fall open.

"It feels like you missed me a whole lot more than you said," she murmured, massaging his erection with her fingers. "It feels to me like you need me right here, right now, on top of the dining room table and to hell with the staff."

Excitement surged through him, heating his cheeks. Beyond words, he could only manage a nod.

With a smug expression filling her gaze, he watched, anticipation building, while she strode to the door and turned the lock.

Within moments, she was on her knees and reaching for his zipper. Her lips touched the slick head of his erection. His head fell back and he sighed in pleasure.

———————————

Allison worked the thick shaft of her husband's cock in and out of her mouth and thought of Draco. The last time they'd fucked, he'd been rougher than usual, forcing her to her knees and gripping her hair in his fist while he'd plunged in and out of her mouth. With his other hand, he'd viciously squeezed her nipples. It felt like he was tearing them off her chest. She'd loved it and hated it—hated him. But it hadn't stopped her from spreading her legs wide on the leather couch afterward and begging him to fuck her. He was happy to oblige and she'd come, bucking and screaming with relief. No one fucked her like Draco did.

Replete, she'd smoked a handful of ice and passed out on the couch in Draco's office. Hours later, she woke with his cock once again in her mouth. Afterward, he sent her home in a cab.

Not that she could tell David about it. He'd never understand. He thought she was addicted to drugs. He had no idea that she was just as addicted to the man who supplied them and no rehab clinic could cure her of that.

She hadn't been with Draco for more than two weeks.

Not since he'd gotten all nasty about the money. She thought about Zara who hadn't come home and hoped Draco had snatched her before she met up with the cute detective. The sooner David paid Draco the money, the sooner she and Draco could pick up where they'd left off.

And pick up again, they would. She had no doubt about that. *Who the hell did Draco Jovanovic think he was?* The president of an outlaw motorcycle gang. Big deal. He wouldn't tell her when it was over. No, siree. That's not the way it worked. She was the one who called the shots and no one moved on from Allison Dowton without her say so. *No one.*

Cursing silently, she renewed her efforts on her husband's cock. At least one of them would leave the house happy that morning. It had been years since David had made her come, despite his efforts to please her. She wouldn't find relief until the Zara was taken, the debt repaid and Draco back between her legs, where he belonged.

It couldn't come soon enough.

CHAPTER 33

Wednesday, January 31, 7:38 a.m.

Lane dialed Zara's number with fingers that weren't quite steady. The night before, after contemplating the conversation with his mother, he'd wanted to call Zara, but it had been late and he hadn't wanted to wake her. She had work in the morning, after all. Besides, he'd wanted to give her time to calm down a little and remember all the good things that had happened between them: The hours when they'd shared stories from their childhood, mostly funny, some sad. The camaraderie he'd felt, the *connection*. She'd felt it, too.

He'd also, somewhat reluctantly, acknowledged he needed time to find the words to apologize—to somehow make her believe his earlier fears had been resolved. Well, maybe not entirely resolved, but enough that he was now willing to take a risk on them, on life, like she'd asked.

Earlier, he'd called his boss at the station and asked for another day off. Michael readily agreed and then gave him an update on the case. He was disappointed to learn the taskforce hadn't yet located Jovanovic. Not that it really mattered. They'd find him sooner or later. He couldn't hide out forever.

The phone rang out in his ear. He frowned. It was only a little after seven-thirty. She shouldn't be at her office yet.

And even if she were, surely she'd answer her cell phone?

When he reached her voice mail, he drew in a deep breath and left a message. "Hi Zara, it's Lane. I'm sorry. For everything. We need to talk. Please call me."

He ended the call and then cursed. *Sorry for everything?* What the hell was he thinking? What if she thought he meant *everything*—like, the hours they'd spent on the couch?

Biting his lip, he groaned aloud. Short of calling her back and making a complete idiot of himself trying to explain that when he'd said everything, he hadn't actually meant *everything*, he'd have to wait for her to call him. And hope like crazy that she did.

Zara heard the click of the lock opening and moments later, the door to Draco's office swung inward. The man himself sauntered inside and she tensed in fear and anticipation of what might happen. She hadn't seen him since he'd left her the night before and she'd spent countless restless hours running through various scenarios of torture followed by escape plans, until she'd collapsed, exhausted from the effort.

The pain in her face had eased, but her left eye was still swollen almost shut. Her body ached from the awkward way she'd been forced to lie on the couch. She struggled to sit upright and her bladder cramped painfully. She gasped aloud and prayed she wouldn't disgrace herself. It was a humiliation she didn't think she could bear.

Draco moved closer, his smile slow and lazy. She quickly averted her eyes and hoped her fear didn't show. Reaching out, he tilted her chin up and forced her to look at him. She bit down hard on a sob. She wouldn't give him the satisfaction of knowing how terrified she was.

His fingers moved from her chin to stroke the soft skin of her cheek. Emotion darkened his eyes. She held her breath.

"I should have nabbed you in the first place. You're much

more to my taste." His hand slid down her face, her neck and then his fingers opened to cup her breast. The warmth of his skin permeated the thin fabric of her dress. She steeled herself not to react and held his gaze with all the defiance she could muster.

Draco chuckled and squeezed her soft flesh. "You're a feisty, little thing, that's for sure." He squeezed harder, eliciting a gasp. "Just how I like them."

"Please." The word was torn from her. She hated the desperation in her voice, but was powerless to stop it.

"What's the matter, sweetheart? Surely a pretty thing like you has been touched before?"

Zara lowered her gaze, pain and embarrassment burning across her cheeks. She hated him for making her feel guilty, like all of this was somehow her fault.

To her relief, he stepped away and walked toward the desk. "There'll be plenty of time for touching and a whole lot more before I've finished with you, but right now, I need to get my money."

He rounded the desk and searched through the small pile of papers that were scattered on its surface. A frown turned his features fierce.

"*Fuck!* I forgot to get the number off Allison. He looked up at her. "Give me your father's number."

Zara's heart plummeted. It was just as she'd guessed. She'd been kidnapped because of her stepmother's drug debt. No doubt her father was about to receive yet another ransom demand.

"Why did you take Olivia Munro? She and her family have nothing to do with the money my stepmother owes you."

Draco's eyebrows shot up in surprise. "I should have known you were more than a pretty face. I see the slut has been talking." He shrugged dismissively. "I don't give a fuck who she tells. She owes me a million bucks and I'm not letting you go until I get it. I've been led to believe your father will do anything for you. What do you think about that? Will daddy hand over a cool million without a squabble to get his little girl back?"

Zara shook her head, aghast that her stepmother had caused all this grief. If it hadn't been for Allison and her drug habit, neither she nor Olivia would have been taken. She eyed the biker with disgust. "How long have you known Allison?"

A sly look glinted in his eyes and he almost smacked his lips. "Let's just say, me and Allison are old friends. We know each other...*very* well." He gave her a suggestive wink and then laughed loudly.

Zara gasped in shock. *Was he insinuating he and her stepmother were lovers?* He couldn't be. It was ludicrous to think that Allison would be consorting with an uncouth, unkempt, foul-mouthed, filthy biker—and yet, why else would he say such a thing? She shook her head. It was all too confusing. She must have misunderstood.

"Don't you believe me? Don't you think that uppity piece of eastern suburbs ass would fuck a commoner like me?"

She opened her mouth to refute his accusation, but he sneered at her and said, "Don't try and deny it. I can tell from the look on your face that's what you're thinking."

"H-how did you meet my stepmother?"

Draco strolled around the side of the desk and propped his hip against the solid wood. He looked at her, his leg swinging casually back and forth. Light bounced off the bald skin on his head. A little smile played around his mouth.

"Allison and I met through some friends of hers. Her book club group, I believe. They meet once a month to discuss books," he chuckled before adding, "at least, that's what they tell their husbands."

Zara stared at him. Thoughts rushed madly through her head. "I-I don't understand."

Draco gave a short laugh. "Don't you just? Perhaps it's time I gave you an education?"

He stood and came toward her, his eyes darkening with menace and the unmistakable glint of desire. The sound of his booted tread across the concrete floor was obliterated by the sudden pounding of her heart. He reached out to her and she flinched against the sofa. Her actions were met with another chuckle.

"You shouldn't be so touchy, sweetheart. Your stepmother and her friends are certainly not so frigid. They queue up and beg me for it."

Shock and disbelief ricocheted through Zara's head. *Could he be telling the truth?* It was preposterous! Utter madness! She couldn't believe he was telling her anything but monstrous lies.

"Carolyn and Trudy are the greediest. They take turns sucking my cock until I'm as dry as a sandpit. Allison was a bit more reluctant, but only at the start. Lucky for me, she liked a few other things I had to offer. Let's just say we struck a mutually satisfying bargain."

Zara didn't think her brain could cope with any more of his shocking revelations. If Draco was to be believed, her stepmother traded her body for drugs and she'd still racked up a million-dollar debt.

Even so, Zara found herself defending the woman to the disgusting man in front of her. "Are you expecting me to believe my stepmother trades sex with you for drugs?"

Draco's bark of laughter reverberated off the walls. "Of course she does. It was a tidy little arrangement and we both felt more than satisfied. But lately, I've hardly been able to keep the shit up to her." His expression darkened. "That's the reason she stopped fucking me. I refused to give her any more gear. The way she was smoking those crystals..." He shook his head. "That shit's worth a fortune."

He stepped away and moved to the far side of the room. Turning to face her, he leaned against the wall, his arms folded across his chest, a scowl turning down his lips.

"While she was putting out, we got on just fine. I never told her she could have the shit for free, but let's just say she got it at a reduced rate. But after awhile, she couldn't get enough. It was like the more she had, the more she had to have. Ice is like that. Anyone will tell you. I got a bit worried about her. Fuck, I didn't want her dying from an overdose in my fucking clubhouse. So, I told her she couldn't have any more until she paid up."

Zara nodded. "To the tune of a million dollars."

Draco winked at her. "Go straight to the top of the class, baby. You're just as smart as you look."

A sinking feeling weighed heavily in Zara's belly. *Draco was telling the truth.* He had to be. How else would he know about Carolyn Rippling and Trudy Harbord? They'd been among her stepmother's closest friends for years, often over at the house for afternoon tea or a game of bridge. They met once a month for book club.

She shook her head. It was too much. And yet, a small part of her was relieved: relieved that her father wasn't involved. Relieved that all the things she'd thought about him weren't true. That he was as good and upright and noble as she'd always thought him to be.

It wasn't his fault his wife was a drug addict who put out to a biker for her next hit. In fact, Zara couldn't help but admire him for his loyalty, even if it was sadly misplaced.

Anger ignited inside her, burning her earlier fear away. *This was all Allison's fault.* She was the reason Olivia had been taken. She was the reason Zara's father had lied. She was also the reason Zara now found herself at the mercy of a man who appeared not to know the meaning of the word.

She moved on the couch and the pain from her bladder intensified. A moan escaped before she could stop it. Draco frowned and came toward her.

"What the fuck's the matter?"

Heat scoured Zara's cheeks. She refused to meet his gaze, but she was getting beyond desperate.

"I-I need to use the bathroom."

"Why the fuck didn't you say so?" Draco grunted, and strode to the wall behind her. He pushed against it. A door built into the plasterboard, previously unnoticed, opened inward, revealing a small, but clean bathroom.

"Help yourself."

Relief flooded her. She struggled off the couch. "Please, do you mind releasing my hands?"

"For fuck's sake, woman, is there no end to your demands? Turn around."

Zara bit her lip and did as he asked. Within moments, her hands were free. Almost instantaneously, an agony of fire raced up her arms.

"Oh, God," she cried, tears springing to her eyes.

Draco snorted with more than a hint of satisfaction. "You're the one who wanted me to untie them. I could have told you it was going to hurt like shit."

Flexing and wringing and shaking her hands, Zara tried to keep her mind off the excruciating pain as circulation returned to her fingers. Stumbling into the bathroom, she flicked on the light and closed the door behind her.

A mirror hung above a small ceramic sink. It was stained from years of wear. She desperately longed for a drink and to splash water over her injured face, but the needs of her body were greater and she turned a little reluctantly to the toilet that stood nearby.

With gritted teeth, she managed to make her fingers work well enough to lower her underwear. The relief, as she finally emptied her bladder, was unimaginable.

When she was finished, she flushed the toilet and washed her face and hands in the sink. She couldn't remember the last time she'd passed a night without a shower.

Zara stared into the mirror and stared at the face of a stranger. As she'd suspected, the eye that had taken the brunt of Draco's fist was mostly swollen shut. Dark blue bruises surrounded the area, discoloring her skin. A graze on her cheek reminded her of the first punch she'd taken and she dabbed at the redness with cool water. Her long hair was a mess, tangled and unkempt.

A hard knock came at the door, followed by an indecipherable growl. She took quick stock of her surroundings and her shoulders slumped. The room was small and windowless. There was no possible way to escape. With a sigh of regret and a cold wad of apprehension churning in her belly, she turned and opened the door.

CHAPTER 34

Wednesday, January 31, 10:46 a.m.

The phone at David's elbow rang and he frowned at it in annoyance. He was buried knee-deep in draft legislation that had to be reviewed before the next parliamentary sitting and he didn't appreciate the interruption.

The house had been quiet, with Brittany returning to school and Allison out doing whatever it was she did on a week-day morning.

David's frown deepened. He really needed to make more of an effort to be part of his wife's daily life. For too long, they'd let the everyday mundaneness, the kids and his career take over. There never seemed to be enough time for just the two of them. It was probably the reason Allison had felt the need to turn to drugs. At least that had gotten his attention.

He had no reason to feel guilty, but he did, just the same. Vowing to spend more time with her, starting tomorrow, he finally answered the phone.

"David Dowton," he said.

"I was beginning to think you weren't going to pick up."

David's breath caught in his throat at the sound of the all-too-familiar voice on the other end of the line. "Dr-Draco, what the hell? W-why are you calling me?"

"Come now, Attorney General. Surely you didn't think you'd get rid of me that easily? I'm out a fuckin' million dollars. That's not something worth forgetting."

"So it *was* you. Allison was right. That nonsense with Boris was all a smoke screen. He's sitting in jail and you're running around footloose and fancy free—you son of a bitch."

"Talk as fancy as you fuckin' like. It isn't going to change anything and it certainly won't make me go away. Let's try this again: Your wife owes me a million dollars and I fuckin' want it. Get it to me by midnight. *Or else.*"

David blanched at the menace in Draco's voice, but bravely called his bluff. "Why should I care about your threats? One phone call and every police officer within a ten-mile radius will be all over you in minutes."

"Ah, but this is where you're wrong. You're forgetting I have someone dear to you. *Very* dear to you, or so I've been told. She's trussed up like a turkey, spread out on my couch, ready for whatever I might do to her."

A tremor of fear shivered up David's spine, but he ignored it and did his best to sound unconcerned. "I think you're the one with the faulty memory, Draco, and you're way behind the times. Your hired help stuffed up. Boris took the wrong girl. My daughter escaped unscathed and the police rescued Olivia Munro yesterday. She's safe and sound back home, where she belongs."

"Who said anything about the young ones? It's your other daughter I'm talking about."

Icy fingers of dread seized David's heart and squeezed like a vice. Fighting for breath, he forced the words out of his mouth.

"W-what the hell? Z-Zara?"

"Zara." Draco stretched out her name as if testing the sound of it on his tongue. "Such an exotic name. It suits her. I can't wait to fuck her. I bet she tastes as good as her stepmother."

Shock and fury exploded in David's chest. His face burned with rage, tinged with a sharp edge of panic.

"You're lying."

A humorless chuckle sounded in his ear. "You wish."

David clenched his fingers around the phone, his thoughts in a frenzy of fear. "You touch one hair on my daughter's head and you'll wish you were dead."

More laughter greeted his threat. "Seems like Allison was right. She said you'd do anything to get the girl back. Oh, I'm *so* going to enjoy this." A growl of raucous laughter grated against his ear.

David reared back like he'd been struck with a sledge hammer. His heart thundered so hard inside his chest he feared he was having a heart attack. He clutched at his ribs in an effort to stem the pain. Confusion threatened to overwhelm him.

"W-what are you talking about?" he wheezed. "Allison? What the hell does my wife have to do with this?"

David returned the phone to its cradle with a hand that refused to stop trembling. The pain in his chest tightened to an almost unbearable level and he wondered a little more frantically if he were dying.

He sat, paralyzed with shock, in his chair. A myriad of panicked thoughts swirled around his head, each one ramping up the tension in his gut. *Draco had Zara.* At least, he said he did. And apparently, Allison knew about it.

He shook his head with increasing vehemence, unwilling to believe his wife could have anything to do with Zara's kidnapping. It was ludicrous, beyond ridiculous. Allison had a drug problem, but she was still the woman he married. She was still the woman who'd healed his grieving heart, the woman who'd taken a child who was not her own into her arms and into her life—the woman he loved with everything that he had.

He wouldn't entertain such a thought, even for a second. No way. End of story.

Besides, the scumbag biker was probably lying. Zara

might not even be missing. Draco was a man who'd cut his teeth on dishonesty and deception. It would be just like him to say he had her when he didn't—in an effort to make David pay.

And pay he would. He was a man of his word, after all. His wife had run up the debt. He would see that it was made good. He'd always intended to pay, once his fury cooled and would have done so without the kidnapping attempts. It angered and saddened him to know that a little girl had suffered as a result of his tardiness.

Didn't anyone have patience anymore? What kind of a society had they become when one's own importance outweighed good old fashioned consideration?

He sighed. A battle over the current standard of morals was one that would have to wait for another day. He owed the president of the Redbacks a million dollars. As much as he'd tried to avoid it, there was no running from the fact. Draco had to be paid and if he indeed had Zara as he'd bragged, facilitating payment of the debt had just become his number one priority.

With a hand that trembled even more violently, he reached over and picked up the phone. At the same time, he tugged Detective Senior Sergeant Black's business card from his shirt pocket.

———

Lane's phone rang where he'd left it on the kitchen counter. He'd grown more and more anxious as the minutes turned into hours and Zara still hadn't returned his call. But with the ringing of his phone, his apprehension was forgotten and replaced with a surge of relief.

It had to be her.

He strode over and glanced at the screen, anticipation flooding through him. His shoulders slumped. It wasn't her. The number was blocked and with a shrug of irritation, he picked up the phone and answered it.

"Detective Black." His greeting was met with silence and he frowned.

He tried again. "Hello? Who is this?"

"Detective." The caller cleared his throat and spoke again. "Detective Black, it's David Dowton."

Lane's heart skipped a beat and then resumed a staccato against the soft cotton of his T-shirt. He flushed, as if the Attorney General somehow knew of the licentious thoughts Lane had had about the AG's daughter.

"David. What a surprise. Is there something I can do for you?"

"It's about Zara."

Lane stilled at the solemnity of his tone. *Surely, she hadn't gone home and told her father?* He forced himself to speak. "W-what about her?"

"I-I'm trying to locate her. I found a note last night that she left in her room. She said was meeting with you."

"That's correct. We met up about lunchtime." Memories of her body pressed against his on the couch nearly overwhelmed him. He struggled to push the images aside. "Is there...? Is there a problem?"

The Attorney General sighed heavily on the other end of the phone. Lane's alarm ratcheted up a notch, along with his heart rate.

"Zara didn't come home last night. I called her office, but they haven't seen or heard from her. I was hoping... That is, I was hoping she stayed with you. That...that you might know where she is."

Ice slaked Lane's heart. His fingers clenched around the phone. "What do you mean, she didn't come home last night? She left my place before eight."

Lane bit his tongue, but the words were already out. He shrugged off his instinctive concern. He really didn't care that Zara's father knew she'd spent several hours at his house. If he had his way, and if she ever returned his calls, she'd be spending much more time there than that.

"If she left your house last night, where is she now?"

The AG's words crashed through his musings, snapping

him back to the present. Lane strode over to the window that overlooked the street below and pushed aside the blinds. An unfamiliar, sleek, silver BMW was parked several yards down the road. A sinking feeling hit him low in his gut.

"What kind of car does your daughter drive?"

"A silver Z4M BMW Roadster."

Tension gripped Lane's shoulders. His mouth went dry. There was no good reason why Zara's car should still be parked outside his building.

"Fuck." Though he'd spoken softly, the AG immediately reacted.

"What's the matter? What do you know?"

"I don't know anything, but I'm pretty sure her car's still parked outside my building."

"So, you didn't see her leave?"

"No, I didn't." Lane was so not ready to explain in greater detail, especially to her father.

"And you haven't heard from her?" David persisted.

"No, I haven't. The last time I spoke to her was yesterday evening. I understood she was headed home. I take it you haven't heard from her, either?"

There was a pause that David didn't fill. Lane's cop instincts went on high alert. There was something the AG wasn't telling him. After another silence, the man spoke again.

"When she didn't come home last night, I just assumed she was with you. After all, she did leave the note. She's a big girl and...and I was pleased she was spending time with you. You did a good job finding the little Munro girl and... Well, let's just say I wouldn't be unhappy to discover the two of you might have more in common than a missing child."

Lane ducked his head. Heat crept up his neck and he was glad the Attorney General couldn't see the effect his words were having. Lane's feelings for Zara were still so new and he hadn't had the time to sort them out, let along talk to her about them.

As if sensing his embarrassment, David cleared his throat. "Anyway, suffice it to say I wasn't concerned about her no-show last night."

"Something changed your mind." It wasn't a question.

The forthcoming answer was grim. "Yes."

Panic nipped at the edges of Lane's consciousness. He tried to keep the tension from his voice. "What is it, David? Tell me. What's happened?"

"Draco Jovanovic called."

Lane frowned. "The president of the Redbacks?"

"Yes."

"Why?"

"He… He says he has Zara."

The words were said in a rush and for a minute, Lane thought he'd misheard.

"Excuse me?"

"He told me he has *Zara*," the Attorney General shouted, his own fear now evident. "I didn't want to believe him. I thought he was joking, playing a trick on me, pressuring me into paying back his money. I called you. I thought you might know where she is. After all, you're the last person who saw her."

Anger took hold of Lane's body. Dread settled like lead in his gut. He knew before he spoke the words that he didn't want it answered, but he asked the question anyway.

"Are you saying you think Draco Jovanovic has now kidnapped Zara as ransom for Allison's debt? Is that what you're trying to tell me?" Lane's voice rose with every phrase until he was shouting at the other end of the phone. His heart pumped faster. His breath came hard. He held his phone like a lifeline until his knuckles turned white.

"Yes. It's just like Allison said. He was involved in this from the outset. He took the Munro child by mistake and the plan went sideways. The money wasn't paid. Now he's taken Zara."

Shock and fury battled for supremacy in Lane's veins. He spun on his heel, the phone jammed tightly against his ear, his free hand fisted. He wanted to hit something. Hard. His gaze skimmed over the walls, the cupboards, the refrigerator and back again.

Dragging in air through his dry lips, he did his best to get his anger under control. Losing his temper would achieve nothing. He had to find out everything the AG knew. It could mean the difference between finding Zara, or not.

Filling his lungs to capacity, he purposefully held it for a full five seconds before exhaling in a rush. In a voice that brooked no argument, he demanded, "Tell me everything."

CHAPTER 35

Wednesday, January 31, 12:27 p.m.

Draco strode into the room carrying a paper bag that sported the McDonalds restaurant logo. He threw the bag in Zara's direction. It landed awkwardly in her lap. With her hands once again bound behind her, it seemed ludicrous that he expected her to eat.

The smell of the burger wafted tantalizingly close to her nose. Zara's belly growled. She hadn't eaten since breakfast the previous morning and even that was comprised of only a bite of a piece of toast as she'd waited anxiously for news of Olivia's rescue.

As if only just becoming aware of her predicament, Draco sauntered back toward her and pulled a pocket knife from his jeans.

"Turn around."

She did as he ordered and offered him her back. He made short work of the bindings that held her hands fast and then stepped away. Zara breathed a silent sigh of relief and rubbed at her hands to encourage the circulation. They didn't hurt as much as the first time, but the pain was still far from pleasant.

"I've spoken to your father. He has until midnight to pay me the money."

Zara looked up and stared at Draco. He sat in his office

chair with his elbows resting on the desk. From where she now sat, he looked less intimidating, in fact, his tone was almost conversational. Her stomach growled again, this time louder. She flushed with embarrassment.

"Eat. I don't want your father accusing me of mistreating you."

Zara bit back a retort. As if kidnapping and holding her captive for more than sixteen hours didn't constitute mistreatment. Still, his words gave her hope that perhaps he had no intention of harming her, provided the ransom money was paid.

She took a bite of the Big Mac and forced a morsel past her dry lips. She swallowed without chewing. She supposed she ought to be thankful to Draco for bothering to offer her food, but somehow, she couldn't bring herself to feel any gratitude.

Her father would be going out of his mind. First, Brittany and Olivia and now her. She couldn't imagine what he was going through. Well, she could. She'd just been through it herself.

She felt the weight of Draco's gaze on her and looked up. He stared at her from across the room, his expression hooded. A few moments later, he pushed back his chair and came toward her.

She froze. Her heart skipped a beat and then pounded against her chest. Turning her head away, she forced another bite of food into her mouth and did her best to look nonchalant.

He kept coming. She stoically ignored him and held her gaze steadfastly focused on the floor. Jean-clad legs stopped in front of her, his crotch in line with her face. His hand moved to caress the bulge now evident through his jeans.

Fear tightened her throat and she couldn't even swallow the tiny piece of meat that was still in her mouth. She shrank back against the couch in an effort to put more distance between them. Her efforts earned her a mirthless chuckle.

"What, not interested? Your stepmother would have been begging for it by now. It was always best when she was high," he added. "She'd take it from anyone and everyone and come begging to me for more." He rubbed his erection again. "It still gets me hard thinking about her full of cock."

Zara's mouth gaped open. Shock trembled through her limbs and nausea gripped her belly. Draco reached out and ran a surprisingly soft finger down her cheek. She winced and turned her face away, hating the tears of helplessness and despair that sprang immediately to her eyes. With his finger and thumb on her chin, he turned her head back toward him. His eyebrows rose in surprise.

"Tears? Really? If you're anything like your stepmother, you're going to enjoy the next part. I've been looking forward to it all morning."

Zara stared him down. "Don't touch me. I'll scream," she threatened, her words sounding much bolder than she felt.

Draco chuckled again. "Scream all you like. I kind of like the whole idea of taking you spitting and fighting. Besides, there's not a single bloke outside this room who will come in and interfere, scream or no scream."

His hand slid from her chin to her chest and paused to fondle her breast. Her breath halted and then came fast. She bit down on her lip to stifle the groan of fear.

She could tell from the look in his eyes that her fear excited him. With all the courage she could muster, she held his gaze with her shoulders drawn back and her head held high. She was rewarded with a flicker of admiration in the blood-shot depths of his eyes.

"You're a feisty one, I'll give you that." He shook his head, another smile hovering around his lips. "Let's see how feisty you are when I have my cock buried deep inside you. I bet that'll take some of the fight out of you. And that's before I invite a few of the boys to have a go."

Zara quivered from shock and fear. Her chest rose and fell in panic. She looked around her, frantically willing an avenue of escape to materialize. At least her hands were still unbound.

As if reading her mind, Draco shook his head. "The door's locked, babe, and you'll never reach the window. Let's face it, you're stuck here with me for as long as I want it." He squeezed her nipple painfully through the thin fabric of her dress. "And boy, do I want it."

"When's my father due to arrive?" she blurted, unable to believe she'd formed the coherent thought, let alone uttered the words. But they seemed to have the desired effect. Draco's hand fell away and he took a few steps backward.

"Like I told you, I've given him until midnight. It's up to him how soon he gets here. If he knows what's good for him, it'll be sooner rather than later."

The smirk on his face and his slow once-over made Zara's skin crawl, but at least he'd stopped touching her. She didn't know what she was going to do if he made good on his threat.

She scurried as far away from him as she could, perching on the edge of the couch. The discarded bag of food toppled to the floor.

"I promise to tell my father you've treated me well," she said, eyeing him bravely. "He'll be more likely to take it easy on you if he knows I've come to no harm."

Draco grinned. "Is that right? You're a regular little Pollyanna, aren't you? And here I was hoping you and I could have a little fun."

"I'm not my stepmother. I don't know what kind of "fun" you had with her, but I'm telling you now, I don't want any part of it."

"Full of orders, aren't we? You're pretty confident for a little bitch that's locked in a room and at my mercy. I'm sure I've got better uses for that smart mouth of yours."

He strode back toward her with purpose. Zara shrank against the couch. Terror pounded through her veins.

Draco came to a halt in front of her. He unsnapped the catch on his jeans and slid down the zipper. Moments later, his erection sprang free.

Zara cried out in panic and fear. Reaching out for her, he seized a handful of her hair and dragged her head toward his erection. She batted at his hands. His grin widened, displaying his ill-kept teeth.

"This will stop that smart mouth of yours. You won't have any breath for talking." He produced a gun from the back of his jeans and held it to her head. "Now, shut up and suck."

Zara stared at Draco and began to tremble violently. The gun in his hand didn't waver. He looked at her with such malevolence, she had no doubt he'd kill her if she didn't comply. Panic surged through her chest and suffocated her. She gasped for breath, but it wasn't enough. She began to hyperventilate.

Draco's phone rang, momentarily distracting him. The sound of it was loud in the silence. He cursed and moved away from her and she collapsed against the couch, grateful beyond words for the interruption.

Draco growled into the phone and then listened to whoever was on the other end. His face darkened and he swore with vicious intent. Zara curled up in a ball and waited to see how long the reprieve would last. She didn't know what she'd do if he ended the call and returned to take up where he'd left off.

David turned the door knob of his wife's bedroom with a hand that shook. Anger, disbelief, and a tiny sliver of hope that Draco was lying, warred inside him.

Allison sat at her dressing table, an array of hand lotions, eye creams, nail polish, perfume and other girly paraphernalia spread out before her. She stared at him in the mirror, her expression one of surprise. He could understand her reaction: He rarely ventured into her rooms during the daylight hours.

She'd been gone most of the day. He'd expected her home for lunch, at least, but she hadn't shown. It had been nearly three when he heard her come in. He'd spent the next twenty minutes summoning up the courage to confront her and wondering whether he was ready to hear the answers.

With hesitant steps, he drew nearer. As she caught sight of his expression, her eyes widened and a tiny frown marred the smooth skin of her forehead.

"David, what is it? You look like you've just heard your best friend's been killed in a car accident."

He closed his eyes briefly at the callously casual way she offered the comment. *When had she gotten so hard?* She never used to be like that. At least, he didn't think so. He'd been so busy building his political career, a decade had passed and he'd barely noticed.

She looked slim and glossy in a close-fitting black dress that dipped low to display her breasts. Her hair, a thick, shiny swathe of blond, was coiled enticingly around her ears. He drew in a breath and his head filled with her perfume, the same exotic blend of vanilla and frangipani she'd worn for as long as he'd known her.

Little had changed, except, perhaps her eyes. And even then, to see the difference, he had to look closely.

The brilliant blue orbs had lost some of their sparkle and there was an expression of perpetual discontentment in their depths, as if she was still searching for the well of unbridled fulfilment and had almost given up hope.

Why hadn't he noticed it before? Had he really been so self-absorbed? He'd made sure the bills were paid on time, he'd been home for dinner most nights and the nights when he was required elsewhere to lend his political support, she was almost always by his side.

The fact that he knew very little about how his wife spent her time during the day had never been a problem. He assumed she went shopping, got her hair done, had manicures, met up with friends for lunch or the movies. There were numerous ways she could spend her time and the itemized monthly credit card bill bore testament to the fact she knew how to keep herself occupied.

Now he wondered how she'd managed to do all of that and still get high—and even more than that—if Draco's sly innuendoes were to be believed.

Another surge of anger tightened his gut and his hands clenched into fists. His pulse thundered in his ears and he opened his mouth to speak.

Watching him in the mirror, Allison angled her body away

from him, alarm chasing the surprise out of her eyes.

"David, for goodness sake, whatever's the matter? Don't tell me your best friend *has* been involved in an accident?"

He nearly choked on his fury. How could she be so nonchalant? His world was about to be split open and she was still trying to joke with him. It was too much!

"Draco Jovanovic has our daughter."

"Don't be silly. Brittany's over at Olivia's. She was going there straight after school. She wanted to go and see her and make sure she was all right after the...you know." She shuddered delicately.

"I'm talking about our *other* daughter. I'm talking about Zara."

If David hadn't been watching closely, he'd have missed it—the tiniest flare of guilt in the depths of Allison's eyes. Seconds later, it was gone and he wondered if he'd imagined it.

"Zara? What are you talking about? Surely, she's at work. You know how dedicated to her job she is. I was surprised to find her home over the weekend. I guess it was because of Brittany—"

"*Stop!*" David yelled. "Just stop! Did you even *hear* what I said? Zara's been kidnapped by the president of the Redbacks."

Allison lifted a slim shoulder. "I'm not surprised. He wants his money. You know that. Pay him what I owe and I'm sure she'll be fine."

David sputtered with rage, suddenly sure. "You *knew*. Just like he said. You knew he was going to take her, didn't you? *Didn't* you?" Rage flooded his veins and pulsed in his ears. He reached for her, his fingers tightening around her neck.

He struggled to breathe. Black spots danced before his eyes and the scene seemed to play out in slow motion.

Allison screamed and flailed beneath him. His grip tightened...

CHAPTER 36

Wednesday, January 31, 3:44 p.m.

L ane glanced at his watch and drummed his fingers on the steering wheel of his unmarked police vehicle. Even with the sirens and lights blazing, traffic had come to a virtual standstill as police cleared the remnants of an earlier accident.

It had been hours since he'd spoken to David. Hours since the Attorney General had told him Zara had been kidnapped by the notorious president of the Redbacks and was being held for ransom in a second attempt to have his drug debt paid. Obviously unwilling to risk another fuckup, Draco had taken charge himself.

Lane slammed his fist against the steering wheel. "For fuck's sake, how long does it take to tow a vehicle out of the way?"

"Take it easy, mate. We're not going to get there any faster with you hyperventilating."

Lane glanced across at Jett and grimaced. With gritted teeth, he tried to calm down by filling his lungs with oxygen and holding onto it for as long as he could.

"We'll find her," Jett reassured him. "We know where the Redbacks' clubhouse is. If she's not there, we'll interrogate each and every person that is there until one of them gives her up. Someone will know something."

Lane acknowledged his comments with a brusque nod, but remained tense. There was no guarantee Draco's men would point the finger. Most of them were hardened criminals. They were more likely to treat the police with contempt than offer any kind of assistance. Short of arresting every single one of them and throwing them in the cells to re-think their options, there was little any of the detectives could do to force them to talk.

Jett noticed his grim expression and spoke again. "While you were making phone calls and calling taskforce members off leave, I ran a few of the Redbacks through the database. At least five of them have outstanding warrants for minor drug offences, assaults and other misdemeanors. If all else fails, we can take them in on those charges and go from there."

Lane nodded again, appreciating Jett's efforts, but even if they arrested as many as they could, it would take days to bring enough pressure on toughened men like the members of the Redbacks to get them to talk. Even then, there was no guarantee of success. Their loyalty to their colors and to their president was legendary.

Frustration and fear churned inside his gut. The irony of the situation wasn't lost on him. He'd been ready to shout out to Zara and to the world that he was ready—ready to take a risk on life. He'd finally found the woman who'd made him ready—only to have her snatched away from him before he could utter the words. Her life was now at risk.

The traffic in front of him edged forward. He saw an opening ahead and accelerated in an effort to break free of the gridlock. The only thing he was grateful for was that peak hour traffic hadn't yet started. That would have just about done him in. As it was, the tension was eating him from the inside out.

"I hope everyone else isn't caught up in this," Jett muttered, his expression grim.

"At least some of the taskforce are. Anyone coming from the north side. The superintendent managed to get half a dozen TRG members from Parramatta and another three or four from Bondi, so at least those blokes will avoid this mess."

"They'll have to wait for the rest of us, though, won't they?"

Lane compressed his lips and tried to contain his frustration. "Yep."

It was all he could manage.

———————

David watched Allison's face turn red then purple. Her arms flailed, reached for him. One long manicured finger scratched his cheek. He felt the sting of it in some distant part of his mind.

He pushed her backward, toward the bed. His fingers tightened. Her eyes bulged. Gasping, gurgling sounds bubbled out of her throat. Her face deepened to puce.

Pleasure surged through him. Exhilaration. Delight. And then...disbelief. He stared down at her, at his fingers around her neck. Shock ricocheted through him. His hands fell away. Bent over double, he turned away and retched, heaving what little there was in his stomach onto the pale-gray carpet.

He glanced across at his wife, who had collapsed onto the bed, holding her neck in her hands, gasping and choking and crying.

What was he *thinking*? What had he done? Or almost done? He'd nearly killed her. Had wanted to kill her. In the midst of his rage-fueled haze, he'd wanted to make her pay, to see her dead for putting his daughters at risk. First Brittany, and now Zara. His precious Zara.

What good would he be to either of his girls if he'd killed his wife? He'd be locked up behind bars with the very criminals he helped put away. He wasn't the one who'd done wrong. He wasn't the one who needed to be punished.

He stood upright, his chest still heaving and stared at the woman on the bed. She was groaning in a combination of relief and anger. He took another step closer. Her gaze narrowed on him. He shivered from the unadulterated fury that glinted in her eyes.

"How *dare* you!" she croaked, her voice a hoarse whisper.

"Just be thankful I stopped when I did," he shouted, outraged she could feel like she was the one who'd been wronged. "Perhaps I should have another go?"

Fear flashed in her eyes and she scurried further up the bed. "Don't you come near me!"

The fight went out of him. *How had his life come to this?* His wife—beautiful, accomplished, loving—now curled up pathetically on her bed, hatred spewing from her pores. All at once, he felt exhausted. His head ached and his heart was leaden with grief, despair and disbelief. He turned and headed toward the door.

She came off the bed like a banshee, tearing toward him, hair flying, hoarsely screaming. He didn't even see the knife in her hand, didn't feel the blade until it slipped between his shoulders.

Pain, fierce and hot, stole his breath and then his mobility. He crashed to the floor with a grunt.

The unmistakable smell of marijuana assaulted Zara's nostrils and the thick smoke burned her eyes. She averted her gaze from the men who stared at her with unrestrained curiosity and worse. Some stepped nearer for a closer look. Others, fueled with alcoholic courage, came up to her and ran their hands over her lips, her breasts, her belly.

The fortuitous ringing of Draco's phone had spared her the ordeal in his office, but she wasn't naïve enough to imagine that was the end of it. He'd stormed out of the room shortly after ending his call and she'd breathed a sigh of relief, but a couple of hours later, he'd returned. He'd offered her a cheery hello and she was immediately suspicious of his elevated mood. She tensed when he came up close to her where she sat upon the couch.

A moment later, his gun was back out and it was pointed at her head. She gasped in shock, her heart in her throat, and did her best to control her panic.

"W-what's the matter? What are you doing?" She hated that her voice betrayed the depth of her fear, but she was powerless to prevent it.

"You're coming with me. Your father's taking way too long to get here. It's time I gave him a little more incentive to hand over the money before the pigs arrive."

"B-but you gave him until midnight." She glanced at the clock on the wall. "It's only five o'clock. There are hours until the deadline. It takes time to get that kind of money together."

"Yeah, well, the plan has changed. The pigs have got wind of our little exchange. He needs to get here within the hour or it will be bye-bye to you, sweet Zara." He cocked the gun. The sound of it crashed into her head. Her heart stopped.

He laughed uproariously at her reaction and slowly lowered the weapon. "I'm not going to shoot you just yet, you stupid bitch. I told you he has an hour."

He tucked the gun back into his belt and then reached for her. She shied away from him, but there was nowhere she could go. Taking her roughly by the arm, he dragged her off the couch.

"Lift your arms," he ordered and she hurried to obey.

In one swift movement, he grabbed her dress and pulled it over her head. A moment later, he'd unsnapped her bra and had forced her out of her panties. She stood naked and exposed before him and burned with shame and humiliation. During every second of the torture, the only thing she could think of was what he was going to do with her.

It didn't take long to find out.

Pulling out a length of twine from the back pocket of his jeans, he made short work of once again securing her hands behind her. Prodding her forward with the gun, he opened the door that led out into the main room. Zara trembled all over and tears coursed down her cheeks, but she forced her feet to move. He dragged her to a concrete pylon that stood in the middle of the room.

Catcalls clanged in her ears, amid lewd actions and appreciative glances from the men who filled the room. A length of rope materialized and Draco tightened it around her waist and then affixed it to the concrete pylon.

Painfully aware of her nakedness, Zara was helpless to cover herself from the lascivious glances of the burgeoning crowd of Redbacks. The only protection at her disposal was her hair and she shook her head in desperation, pathetically grateful when the long, thick curtain fell and covered what it could. Word seemed to have spread quickly that there was something happening at the clubhouse. Men were standing shoulder to shoulder from the bar at the back, all the way to the front door.

Zara shivered, but it wasn't from the cold. In fact, the room was uncomfortably warm with the mass of men bulked up from studded leather jackets and infinite hours in the gym. Desperation ate away at her. She'd gone past the point of feeling anything more than a cold sense of detachment, even when one of Draco's underlings looked her way, or worse, reached over to touch her.

Draco appeared before her, his phone in his hand. He held it up in front of her and snapped off a few quick shots. She started in surprise and anger when she realized he was photographing her.

"How dare you!" she hissed, forgetting for a moment her determination to remain removed from her situation. "You have no right to do that. When I get out of here, I'll make it my mission to sue you for everything you have. If even a hint of those photos turn up anywhere, you'll regret you were ever born."

Draco merely laughed at her, his shoulders shaking with his mirth. "Oh, you're a little spitfire. You're trussed up like a turkey, naked as the day you were born, and you have the guts to threaten me? I love it."

His expression suddenly turned serious, the speed of it making her gasp. "These pictures are going to your father, sweet Zara. I told you he needed a little incentive. I'm going to tell him that unless he gets here within the hour, I'm going to let my men have a go at you. I'm sure that will make him come running. You want to hope so, anyway."

Tears pricked her eyes, but she blinked them away. She refused to give in to his intimidation. She clenched her jaw and cursed under her breath. To show weakness before such a crowd would be the end of her. *Where, oh where was her father?* Where, oh where was Lane? Had everyone she knew and loved abandoned her?

She refused to believe it. Lane, maybe. Her father, never. He was frantically doing what he could to get the ransom money together. She was sure of it. Any minute, he'd arrive and hand it over and she'd be free to go on her way.

She clung to the fantasy, knowing she had no choice but to believe in it. To think otherwise, even for an instant, would be devastating. She would spiral into a place so dark, she'd likely never escape from it.

The bulk of a large man stepped close, blocking her view of the door. She looked up and tensed. The man Draco had called Toothpick smiled at her and leaned forward. He cupped one of her bare breasts, as if testing its weight, then his thumb scraped over her nipple. He chuckled when it tightened.

"Looks like she's enjoying that, Toothpick," Draco chuckled and snapped off a couple more pictures.

Zara cursed her body's reflexive physical reaction. She held Draco's gaze, trying to put as much defiance as she could into her hard stare, telling him with her eyes how much she hated this, hated him.

"Who'd have thought your father would take so damned long to find a million bucks," he mused. "The way Allison spoke, I expected him here hours ago. I'm beginning to wonder if you're as important to him as she led me to believe." His face darkened. "If that slut has lied to me..."

Shock at his words paralyzed her. She couldn't believe

what she'd heard. *Had her stepmother been involved with her abduction?* It couldn't be true. Allison had never warmed to her, but surely the woman hadn't wished her harm—or actively encouraged it?

Zara shook her head in confusion. She refused to believe it was true. Draco was messing with her mind, that's all it was. It was all just part of his game. *She was sure of it.* She clung to the thought with a vengeance.

Despair darkened the edges of her vision and she squeezed her eyes tight in an effort to dispel it. *She had to stay positive.* She had to believe someone was looking for her. Lane. Her father. Anyone.

Draco nudged Toothpick out of the way and slid his hand across her taut belly. A moment later, his fingers plunged into the curls between her legs. She cried out in shock and distress, her heart hammering out of her chest. The tears she'd tried so hard to keep at bay crowded her eyes and spilled over. Hot and salty, they coursed down her cheeks.

Draco looked up at her and smiled.

CHAPTER 37

Wednesday, January 31, 5:23 p.m.

Lane peered through the dusty window of the clubhouse from his perch high up a ladder that leaned against the back wall of the shed that housed the Redbacks. Through the dirt and grime that lined the glass and the late afternoon dimness, he counted at least a hundred bikers.

He'd expected the building to be guarded and he hadn't been disappointed. Half that number again had pulled the security detail, but they'd been disposed of quietly and efficiently by members of his handpicked team, along with a dozen savage guard dogs.

Knowing what was at stake and that the bikers wouldn't hesitate to use lethal force, Lane had insisted on putting together a team of the best. It had taken longer to assemble and he'd chafed at every minute of the delay, but in the end, it had been a wise decision and one he was eminently grateful for now.

His gaze swept over the crowded room again. He was sure she was inside. If nothing else, the sheer numbers in the clubhouse was testament to something unusual. It was barely five-thirty on a Wednesday afternoon. Way too early for such an impressive display of numbers.

After another sweep of the building, he noticed many of

the men had congregated around a concrete pylon that stood in the middle of the room. Men jostled each other and craned their necks. The crowd moved and shifted and then he saw her.

Lane gasped and then swore. Anger exploded inside him. His heart hammered and blood pulsed in his ears. His men waited in the shadows for his go ahead, but he was momentarily stunned into silence.

Naked and bound to the pylon, she stood proud and defiant. With her head held high she endured the touch of one man after another. Rage and helplessness flooded through him and he viciously thrust them aside. Now wasn't the time to lose control. What was required was cold, calm calculation. He could only imagine the cache of weapons contained within the walls of the clubhouse. He couldn't afford to get it wrong.

Scaling down the wall, he landed back on the ground with a soft thud and crept back to where his men waited, crouching low in the shadows.

"She's in there," he said.

Jett's eyes went wide. "You saw her?"

He swallowed his anger. "Yes."

Jett nodded, his face grim. "Okay, what next?"

Lane indicated for the men to gather close and went through the plan they'd put together in the squad room, in the event they located her. Every officer was equipped with an ear piece, but Lane wanted to make sure they knew what to do. A mistake by any of them could be fatal.

He listened to their questions as best as he could over the pounding of his heart and answered them in halting sentences. Jett shot him a curious look, but he ignored it and did his best to pull himself together.

"Okay, is everyone ready?"

His question was met with a round of nods and murmurs of agreement. With a thumbs-up, Lane stood and watched while half of his team left to take up positions at the front of the building. He crouched low at the rear, giving everyone time to get into place.

With shields held high, tear gas cylinders in hand and weapons at the ready, he counted down the seconds until, as one, they charged the building.

———————

Tears coursed freely down Zara's cheeks. She'd given up on bravery long ago. It had deserted her the moment Draco had violated her body. It wouldn't be long before the terror of her situation became a reality. She'd given up hope of being rescued and now just prayed that the next few hours would pass without pain.

Draco forced her legs apart with his jean-clad thigh and chuckled when she stood firm.

"Relax, you silly bitch. I'm gonna fuck you whether you're willing or not. You might as well enjoy it."

Zara cringed at his foul language and at the images his words evoked. She was beyond fear. Beyond feeling. Beyond hope.

A shout from behind her caught Draco's attention. More shouts and then the sound of gunfire. Zara screamed, terrified of being caught in the middle of something she had no way of escaping. An acrid smell filled the air. Seconds later, her eyes were on fire.

The men around her fell back, screaming and stumbling and clawing at their eyes. Tears blinded her. Another gunshot rang out.

And then she heard it. She heard *him*.

"Zara! Oh, Christ! Thank God you're all right. Oh, fuck. I'm sorry. I'm so sorry. Let me get you out of here."

"Lane." She breathed his name through the cloud of smoke and fumes and tear gas, hardly daring to believe he was real. The scene in the clubhouse was one of noise and chaos, the world around her ghostly and surreal.

The rope around her belly loosened and fell away. Next were the bindings around her wrists. Circulation rushed to her fingertips and she gasped and cried out, chafing at her hands.

"I'm sorry, sweetheart. I bet that hurts like hell. Hold on to me, as tightly as you can. I'm going to get you out of here."

Zara clung to the back of his shirt, pressing herself against him and doing her best to ignore the fire in her hands, her arms, her eyes. She didn't care. In fact, she welcomed the pain, opened her arms and embraced it. She could take the pain if it meant freedom. With Lane.

CHAPTER 38

Wednesday, January 31, 10:38 p.m.

Despite the fact Zara had taken up the superintendent's offer of a shower and had donned clean prison garb, she still ached all over.

"Will that be all, Superintendent Collins? It's been a long time since I've seen my bed and I'm utterly exhausted," Zara said quietly, fatigue weighing her down.

"Perhaps Ms Dowton can come back in the morning and answer any outstanding questions then?" Lane suggested, looking at his boss.

Zara shot Lane a look of gratitude and swallowed a sigh of relief when the superintendent nodded his agreement.

"Of course, Ms Dowton. I'm sure that will be fine. You've been through a terrible ordeal. I'm sorry you've had to relive it all by giving us a statement, but you'll be pleased to know you've provided us enough with information to charge Jovanovic and a number of his cohorts with several serious charges. They won't be going anywhere for a very long time."

Zara nodded in acknowledgement. "Thank you, Superintendent. A lifetime wouldn't be long enough, but I'll be happy for every year they get behind bars. I hope Jovanovic is never again in a position where he can inflict so much terror upon another person."

Lane's expression darkened at Zara's words and she

couldn't help the warmth that surged through her, knowing that he cared. *He cared.* She hoped he cared enough to give the two of them a chance.

She cleared her throat and looked back to Lane's boss. "Has anyone called my father? Does he know that I'm all right?"

Michael frowned a little and looked across at Lane who shrugged.

"I'm sorry, sir. I've been with Zara since we found her. I'm not sure if anyone else has found the time to notify the AG. I-I'll get onto it right away." He pushed away from the interview table where the three of them were seated. Zara reached out and took hold of his arm to stall him.

"It's all right. I think I'd rather do it myself. Now that I've...recovered, I'd like to be the one to tell him everything's okay."

Lane stared down at her, his eyes shadowed with concern. "Are you sure? I can easily get one of the AFP boys to contact him. They can even drop around and tell him in person, if you'd rather."

She shook her head. "No, no. It's fine. He'll be so worried. He needs to be told. I'd rather do it now." She looked around for her phone and remembered that it had been lost, along with her handbag when Draco ambushed her outside her car. Her heart beat fast at the memory. She looked at Lane and tried to speak, but couldn't make her lips work.

He frowned and squatted beside her, angling his body toward her. "What is it, Zara? What happened? You look like you've seen a ghost."

She bit her lip against the sudden surge of tears and tried to get herself back under control. "I-I... My phone. I don't have it. I lost it when—" The recollection of Draco grabbing her crashed through her mind and with it, the overwhelming feelings of terror. She closed her eyes and bit back a sob, but it burst right through her defenses. Tears coursed down her cheeks. She guessed it was delayed shock, now that the trauma was finally over.

Lane jumped to his feet and drew her into his arms. She stood and clung to him in mindless panic and willed the memories to subside. She barely registered when the door to the interview room opened and closed behind the superintendent, leaving her alone with Lane.

His arms tightened around her, holding her close against his chest. "It's okay, sweetheart. It's okay. You've been through a terrible ordeal. Let it out. I'm here for you. I'm never going to let anyone hurt you again."

His soothing words calmed her fears and gradually her sobs quieted. She listened to the steady thump of his heart beneath her ear and was reassured by the strength of it. He was so good and strong and kind. He was everything she'd ever dreamed. She'd known him less than a week and yet she'd fallen head-over-heels in love with him. It was too bad she didn't know if he'd ever feel the same way.

The thought sobered her and brought her back down to reality with a thud. She pulled out of his arms and returned to her seat, ignoring his look of bewilderment.

She kept her gaze lowered. "I-I'd like to borrow your phone, if that's okay? I need to call my father."

"Of course," he muttered and handed it over.

She felt the weight of his concern. Forcing a deep breath between her clenched teeth, she dialed her father's number.

The phone rang out and eventually went through to his voicemail. She left a message, trying to sound as normal as possible when she assured him she'd been rescued by the police and was safe. She ended the call and handed the phone back to Lane with a soft sigh.

"Would you like me to take you home?" Lane asked, his voice low.

Zara thought of her father. He'd be relieved she was all right. He'd want to see her, to reassure himself she'd come through the ordeal unharmed. Her thoughts then turned to her stepmother and renewed shock and anger poured through her veins. According to Draco, it had been Allison who'd suggested he abduct Zara. She couldn't begin to imagine what kind of person could exhibit such malevolence and she couldn't imagine bringing herself to live under the same roof with someone who could.

She shook her head and looked at Lane, imploring him to understand. "I don't want to go home."

He stared at her. The silence stretched between them. And then he nodded. Once.

"All right. I'll take you home with me."

Relief mixed with nerves surged through her. She glanced up at him and just as quickly, looked away.

As if sensing her uncertainty, Lane spoke quietly again.

"I have a spare room. You're welcome to use it. It's late. You must be exhausted."

Zara's smile was grateful. "Yes, you're right. I'm so tired I can barely keep my eyes open."

"Then let's get out of here."

———————————

As much as Zara yearned for sleep, her body was too wired to relax. She kept stealing little glances across at Lane where he sat beside her, his gaze fixed on the road ahead. The tension in his jaw and the set of his head and shoulders was a reflection of how she felt. Flashbacks to the hours she'd spent a prisoner of the Redbacks kept replaying in her head and she could only guess Lane was also reflecting upon her ordeal.

"I'm okay, you know. I-I wasn't hurt. Terrified out of my mind, maybe, but you got there in time. You saved me."

He spared her a glance, his eyes narrowing on her bruised and battered face and then returned his gaze to the road. A muscle clenched in his jaw. "I just can't help thinking what might have happened if we'd arrived another five minutes later."

She closed her eyes at the fear and anger that still coated his voice and took hope from its presence. *He cared.* She was sure he did. She prayed he'd be willing to admit it.

"Thank you...for everything." The words felt inadequate, but it was all she could manage. He acknowledged her gratitude with the barest of nods.

In less than ten minutes, he pulled over to the curb outside his condo and switched off the ignition. Zara released her seatbelt and climbed out of the car. Lane met her on the pavement. He slung an arm around her shoulders and pulled her in close to his side. His casual action sent butterflies fluttering in her belly. She risked another glance at him and her breath caught.

From the corner of her eye, she spied her BMW. It was parked where she'd left it and looked so normal, she couldn't believe the terrifying string of events that had occurred since she'd last seen it. Lane followed her line of sight and his arm tightened around her shoulders, drawing her even closer. She looked up at him and sent him a wobbly smile of gratitude.

"Let's go inside," he murmured and together they walked in through the gate that led to his building.

A few moments later, Lane tugged out the key to his condo and unlocked the door. Zara followed him inside. Lane walked on down the hall toward the living room, switching on lights as he went. He picked up a jug and began to fill it with water from the sink.

"Coffee?"

She met his gaze briefly and then both of them looked away.

"Thanks," she murmured, although coffee was the last thing she wanted. She watched while he pulled two mugs from a cupboard near the cooktop and then spooned in coffee from a jar. She thought of the last time he'd made coffee and her face grew warm.

His actions slowed and then came to a halt, as if he also remembered. He looked at her, his expression unreadable.

"Do you really want coffee?"

"No. Do you?"

He shook his head. Slowly, he rounded the counter and held out his arms. With a sigh of relief, she stepped into them and laid her head against his chest, taking strength from his solid warmth. Gently, he tilted her chin up and lowered his head until his lips found hers. The kiss was whisper soft and so sweet it nearly brought her to tears.

And then she was crying. She thought she was through with it at the station, but hot wet tears once again coursed down her cheeks as the terrifying memories bombarded her yet again.

"*Shh*, sweetheart. It's okay. I'm here. I'm never going to let anyone hurt you again, I swear." He stared down at her, his eyes bright with emotion. She reached up and pulled his head down to hers.

The need to obliterate the horror she'd endured surged through her. Her lips moved over his, hot and explosive until both of them were gasping for air. Lane broke the contact and lifted his head, his breath coming hard.

"Zara, no. I know what you're doing and I know why. It's normal to want to reach out for something or someone after experiencing a trauma like you have. There's nothing I'd like more than to make love to you all night, but it's not what you need right now, even if you don't agree."

His face was filled with such tenderness and love and yearning, Zara's breath caught.

"Please," he added, his voice husky with emotion. "Please trust me on this."

She dropped her arms and took a step back and kept her face averted. He was right. Of course he was. Her actions were nothing more than the reaction of someone who'd survived a trauma.

But he was wrong on one count. It wasn't just someone, anyone she wanted. It was Lane. It had been only him from the moment she'd first seen him and nothing would change that.

"Zara, sweetheart, please look at me. I need to know you understand."

She drew in a deep breath and released it on a sigh and then bravely met his gaze. "I understand and you're right. I even believe you when you tell me you want me."

A smile tugged up the corners of his lips. "Want you? Christ, if I wanted you more I'd explode. I'm going to have to take a cold shower if I'm to have any hope of sleeping tonight."

She blushed and returned his smile, pleased at his response. "Do you think... Um, I mean... Could you maybe just hold me awhile? I-I don't want to be alone right now."

His eyes darkened with emotion and he immediately stepped forward and claimed her with his arms. He held her in tight against his chest and rested his chin on her head.

"Of course that's all right. I'll hold you for as long as you want. It might kill me, but I'll do it. For you, I'll do anything."

His expression turned fierce and his arms tightened around her protectively. A moment later, he relaxed his hold, but with his arm still around her shoulders, he guided her down the hall.

"You can take the spare bed, but there's more room in mine."

Heat seared her cheeks, but she bravely met his gaze and said, "I'd rather stay with you."

Lane groaned under his breath and pressed a kiss against her hair. "No problem. My bed's right through here."

She walked with him into his bedroom and he released her to switch on a lamp. Soft, golden light illuminated the room and glinted off the polished wooden headboard. His bed was huge—a king-size at least. It was unmade and pillows were scattered around. Lane blushed and looked away in embarrassment and then began hastily collecting clothing, newspapers and other things off the floor.

"I'm sorry, I've been so busy these past few days and I've barely had time to close my eyes before I was heading back to work. I-I make it most times, I assure you. I just haven't had time—"

She reached for his arm and squeezed it. *"Shh,"* she whispered and pressed a finger against his lips. "I know how busy you've been. You've been helping me and my family, remember? What kind of person would I be to complain about the state of your house?"

He stopped and looked back at her and then smiled in relief. "Thanks for understanding. I'm not the tidiest of people, but I try and make an effort most of the time."

She smiled back at him. "Lane, be quiet. I don't care how messy or neat you are. You're so much more than that, I can't find the words to describe it."

Slowly, her smile faded and she was filled once again with need. As if sensing her change of mood, he dropped the pillow in his hand and closed the distance between them.

His lips were warm and firm against hers and she pressed herself up against him. Her arms crept up around his neck and she returned his kiss with as much passion as she could muster.

"Oh, God, you taste so good," he muttered against her lips.

She could only moan in response and cling to his broad shoulders. She relished the feel of him, his muscled arms encompassing her, protecting her from harm.

He gentled the kiss and slowly pulled away. With a tender touch, he drew her down with him onto the bed and lay down beside her. Gathering her in his arms, he pressed a kiss against her forehead.

Zara snuggled into his warmth and sighed. "Thank you."

"You've already thanked me."

Zara lifted a shoulder up in a shrug. "Yes, but it doesn't seem like enough."

"You're safe now, sweetheart. Go to sleep."

He pressed another soft kiss on her lips and her eyelids fluttered closed. She was sore and achy and tired, but she'd never felt so happy.

CHAPTER 39

Thursday, February 1, 6:03 a.m.

Zara came awake slowly, aware of something warm and firm beneath her cheek. A glimmer of light shone through the half-open curtains indicating that morning had arrived. She reached out a tentative hand and connected with a solid wall of bare skin and muscle.

Lane.

He must have stripped off his shirt sometime during the night. His skin was warm and smooth beneath her fingers. He stirred and mumbled in his sleep and his arm tightened reflexively around her. She loved how he made her feel safe and protected, even while he was asleep. She sighed in contentment and snuggled back into his side. Laying her palm on his chest, her fingers skimmed across his nipple. She was immediately rewarded with a soft gasp.

"That's one hell of a way to wake up," he murmured, lifting her hand to his lips. He pressed a kiss in her palm and her belly somersaulted. Time and a sound sleep had taken the sharp edge off her memories of her kidnapping and she shyly smiled back at him.

He winked at her and her pulse took off at a gallop. Rumpled from sleep, she'd never seen any man look sexier.

"How did you sleep?" he asked, his eyes shadowed with concern.

"Great. I slept great. I don't think I woke even once. Th-thank you," she stammered. "If it weren't for you, I don't think I would have slept at all."

A tiny frown appeared between his eyes. "Would you stop thanking me, Zara? I wanted you here. I wanted to help. I wanted to take care of you. I still want to take care of you." His last admission was made in a tone only just above a whisper. She stared at him and he held her gaze, intensity burning in his eyes.

He rolled onto his side, taking her with him until she was lying on her back. He lifted his weight off her with his elbow and stared at her a moment longer, before slowly lowering his head to her lips.

Zara's breath came short. Her heart thumped so loudly, she was sure he could hear it. His lips touched hers with the lightest of pressure and then came back to sample more. Again, his lips grazed hers and again, they moved away. She squirmed beneath him, wanting more, but too shy to come out and tell him.

He held her gaze and his eyes darkened to earthy green.

"I want to make love to you, Zara."

Relief surged through her. *Yes! That's what she wanted, too.* She stared back at him and saw the need in his eyes and was suddenly enveloped in heat. She didn't know if he'd changed his mind about steering away from commitment, but right there and then, it didn't matter. She wanted to love him; she wanted him to love her. There would be plenty of time afterward for reflection and debate about the wrong and right of this.

"I want to make love to you, too," she whispered and was rewarded by a flare of his nostrils and a sudden intake of breath. It was like she'd opened the door on his passion. All of a sudden, it was as if he couldn't get enough. He bent his head and captured her mouth in a searing kiss that left them both gasping. And still, it didn't seem enough.

His lips trailed fire everywhere they touched. Her mouth, her ears, her neck. He even pressed the gentlest of kisses on her still-swollen eye and damaged cheek. Her skin was on fire and still, she craved more.

She clung to him, holding tightly to his shoulders and rejoicing in the feel of his hard body against hers. The feeling was so foreign and yet so totally right that she blinked away tears of contentment.

His erection pressed insistently against her belly, burning right through their clothes. She blushed at the thought of him inside her. Gently, he reached up and unclasped her hands from around his neck and moved his weight off hers. With fingers that weren't quite steady, he inched up the shirt of her prison garb and worked it over her head. When he saw the bruises around her nipples, his expression darkened and his jaw clenched.

As if forcefully removing the images from his mind, he drew in a deep breath and eased it out and then gently reached out and cupped her breasts. The reminder that she was braless beneath her shirt would have embarrassed her had she not caught sight of the sheer wonder in Lane's gaze.

"You're so beautiful," he whispered. "Even more beautiful than I remember."

His words filled her with confidence and she lifted her bottom and took off the loose prison pants. Now, fully naked, she lay there beneath his gaze. The memory of her standing in front of Draco in the same state flashed through her mind, but she set her jaw and forced the image aside. *That was over.* She was safe. Lane had found her. Rescued her. Lane had brought her home.

Emboldened by the desire in his eyes, she reached out and tugged at his suit pants. His belt slipped easily out of its loops and then she started on the button and zipper. He stared at her all the while, his eyes dark with need.

With her help, he shucked off his pants until he was down to his underwear. A moment later, even that scrap of fabric was gone and he laid down beside her and let her look her fill. She placed her palms flat on his warm, firm skin and relished the feel of his strength beneath her fingers. Slowly, she eased herself up above him and then bent low to kiss him.

The feel of his lips, full and soft, kissing her back with a magic that was all his, sent a need so strong surging through her, she nearly gasped at the wonder of it. He increased the pressure and then his tongue sought entry and she gladly let him in. The few kisses she'd had in the past could never compare to this and she was amazed at how wonderful the simple action could be.

Without breaking contact with her mouth, Lane drew her flush against him. Every part of her body touched a part of his. She shivered with desire.With a low growl, he rolled her over once more and kissed her long and hard. His lips lowered to her neck and lower still and he kissed the tops of her breasts.

She gasped at the heat of his mouth on her skin and silently begged for more. As if reading her desperate thoughts, he suckled and nipped and kissed her like he'd never get enough. She knew how he felt.

She moved against him, loving the feeling of his weight and hardness against her. His hands found her breasts and gently he kneaded them and shaped them and teased them with his tongue. She gasped and pressed her legs together against a sudden surge of need.

Lane eased away from her and sat back on his haunches. "I want to look at you," he rasped, his voice thick with desire.

Zara blushed, thankful the early morning sun hadn't yet made a dent in the shadows, but Lane was having none of it. Reaching over, he switched on a lamp that stood on the nightstand near her head.

A soft yellow glow gently illuminated the room, but the heat spread across Zara's cheeks. She closed her eyes and turned her face away and hoped he wouldn't be disappointed in what he saw.

"Look at me, Zara." The order was issued in a tone just above a whisper. She sighed and forced her gaze back to his and was surprised by what she found there.

His face was open and full of tenderness, his eyes were filled with desire. Forgetting her nakedness for a moment, she took in his golden magnificence. The breadth of his shoulders swept into a muscular chest and then tapered to narrow hips. Amidst a thick bush of dark hair, his erection stood proud and impressive. She looked at it with a mixture of curiosity and nerves. He was so much bigger than she imagined.

Everything about him was bigger. When he lay down on the bed beside her, his legs stretched so far his feet were almost off the bed. Her gaze returned to his cock, jutting out from his flat belly and she bit her lip in sudden indecision.

"It's okay, sweetheart. We'll fit."

Flames lapped at her cheeks. She looked away—mortified—but Lane smiled and shook his head.

"Come here."

As he tugged her toward him, she reluctantly sat up and wriggled closer until he drew her against his chest.

"You're so tiny," he murmured against her hair. "I can understand why you might be a little wary, but it will be okay, I promise." He applied pressure to her chin with his fingers until she looked up at him. "Do you trust me?"

She stared at him and read the sincerity in his eyes. "Yes," she whispered, knowing it was true.

He lifted her hand to his lips and kissed her fingers one by one. It tickled and sent ripples of heat and desire through her belly...and lower. He took her hand and laid it flat on his chest and then moved it back and forth, like she was stroking him. She *was* stroking him.

Of her own volition, her fingers moved through the fine scattering of hair on his chest, teasing, caressing, and she reveled in the feeling of his warm, male skin. He groaned with pleasure and moved until he was stretched out on his back, offering himself up to her.

Gaining confidence, she slid her hand lower, across the smoothness of his taut belly. Her finger dipped into his navel and tested its depth. He laid still beneath her hand, but she felt the tension in the muscles that crowded his belly. She glanced at his face. His head was thrown back, his eyes closed. Feeling bolder, she inched her hand closer to the thick length of him that lay stiff against his belly.

With the lightest of pressure, she touched him. He sucked in his breath and she pulled her hand away as if she'd been burned.

"Don't stop. God, don't stop."

Checking to make sure his eyes were still closed, she moved closer and encircled his erection with her hand. Her fingers strained to meet around the impressive width of him and she tried not to think about how it would feel inside her. She stroked her hand inexpertly along his shaft, hoping that was what he wanted.

His hand covered hers and stilled it. Moments later, he moved her hand under his, showing her how to pleasure him. After a little while, he released her hand and at once, she felt bereft. With murmured words of encouragement, he urged her to continue.

Taking a deep breath, she tightened her fingers around his cock and applied pressure the way he'd shown her. She was rewarded by his groan of satisfaction and renewed vigor in his erection.

With her confidence growing, she increased the pace and pressure of her strokes. He moved restlessly on the bed. The tip of his cock glistened.

Without thinking, she flicked at the tiny spot of moisture with her finger and was amazed by how soft and silky and warm the tip of his cock felt. With renewed enthusiasm, she continued to stroke.

Lane groaned again and opened his eyes. "I'm not sure I can take too much more of that, sweetheart."

"You're the one who wanted to show me…" She smiled, feeling incredibly powerful.

"I should have known you'd be a quick learner," he growled.

Before she realized what was happening, he sat up and flipped her onto her back, his weight pinning her to the mattress. She yelped in surprise.

"Two can play at this game. Fair's, fair, wouldn't you say?" A wicked gleam flashed into his eyes. Zara wriggled against him, but to no avail. She sighed in defeat yet her body ached for his touch.

With a gentleness that almost stole her breath, Lane kissed his way down her chest. His tongue found a nipple and teased it, licking and swirling it into a hard nub. She gasped at the torrent of emotion and flung her head from side to side.

Just when she didn't think she could stand any more of it, he switched to the other side. Fiery need kindled low in her belly. Her clit pulsed with pressure. She groaned.

"Do you like that, sweetheart?"

She moaned again, beyond words, almost unable to bear the sweet torment. And then, he moved lower. While her breasts ached for the return of his mouth, her belly tensed with every kiss that drew him closer to the center of her need. She tried to stop him, but he was having none of it.

"Lane, please. I don't think you should—"

"*Shh*, it's my turn, remember?"

She squirmed against him. "I haven't... I mean—"

Lane stopped what he was doing and lifted his head, a smile of tenderness warming his face. "You've never had anyone go down on you before?"

Zara's face burned. She'd never been more embarrassed. How could he treat this kind of stuff in such a cavalier way? Sex was never discussed in her household. She could only guess that in his household growing up with a slew of brothers, things had been a little more...open.

Ignoring her embarrassment, Lane leaned forward and pressed a kiss on her lips. "Relax and enjoy the ride," he whispered.

Trying her best to do as he instructed, she squeezed her eyes shut and willed the tension from her limbs. It wasn't long before the feel of his skillful tongue stroking her tender folds had her hips coming off the bed and her discomfort faded away. She clutched at the sheets, at his head, at anything within reach in order to survive the onslaught.

Never before had she been brought to the edge of such exquisite passion. She felt like she would explode if he didn't cease. And yet, she loved every minute of it.

When he lifted his head and smiled at her, she couldn't help but feel a little disappointed. Her body was taut with unreleased desire, her clit pulsed with need. He'd loved her with his mouth and his tongue and his fingers, but he halted before she climaxed. She was confused and suddenly very, very unsure.

Watching the emotions tracking across her face, Lane's smile evaporated. He frowned. "Zara, what's wrong? What did I do?"

She blushed for what seemed like the hundredth time. No matter how comfortable he was about referring to sex like he was discussing the weather, she was a long way from having such a casual attitude.

"I-I didn't…" She stared at the mattress and tried to ignore her flaming cheeks and wished she was more experienced. *Was it normal for it to be over and still feel so…restless?*

"Talk to me, sweetheart," Lane coaxed, his voice gentle. "What are you thinking?"

Zara drew in a deep breath and spoke again. "I… You know… I haven't…"

Comprehension dawned in his voice. "Come?"

Heat exploded across her face. She sneaked a peek at him and saw the relief in his eyes. She offered him a brief nod.

Lane slid up her body, an intimate smile turning up the corners of his lips. He framed her face with his hands, his eyes warm on hers.

"Good, because I'm not finished, yet. Not by a long shot." He dipped his head and pressed his lips against hers. "I want us to come together."

She stared at him. Heat flared in the depths of his eyes, turning them molten. The hard length of him pressed against her. Flames licked the inside of her thighs and her belly tensed in anticipation.

His cock probed the soft folds between her legs. His gaze

stayed locked on hers. Her legs fell apart of their own volition and her breath came in short pants.

He reached across the bed and opened the drawer of the nightstand. With deft movements, he withdrew a condom and sheathed himself before settling back between her thighs. He nudged against her a second time until the very tip of his cock lay inside her. She gasped. He stared down at her, his eyes dark with emotion. The muscles in his arms strained. His chest expanded on an indrawn breath. His hips eased forward and his cock moved another inch further inside her.

She squirmed against the unfamiliar width of him and blinked against the stinging pain.

"Easy, sweetheart. Take it easy. It won't hurt for long. Let me love you."

She relaxed against him and he slid further inside her. Her heart thumped. The stinging sensation receded and she luxuriated in the feel of him stretching her wide to accommodate him. He moved forward again another inch and then another until he filled her and then he stilled. Dropping his head, he rested his forehead against hers and took a long, deep breath.

"You feel so good. So tight, so wet. So right." The words were growled against her neck. Excitement pulsed in her center and radiated upward. She moved underneath him, silently conveying her growing need.

He lifted himself above her and moved, oh so slowly, against her. Inching out until he'd almost left her and then gliding in again in one smooth, silky movement until he was fully sheathed within her a second time. He shuddered against her and she reached up and tightened her arms around his neck.

"Love me, Lane," she whispered, pressing her lips against his.

He growled low in his throat. "Does it still hurt?"

She shook her head. "No, it feels...wonderful."

His eyes flared with emotion. His body tensed, arm muscles bunched and he plunged into her again. She opened her legs wider and then tightened them around his hips. His movements increased in pace and frenzy and she gloried in the feelings he created.

Her face was hot, sweat gathered across her chest. She lifted her hips to meet each thrust and clung to him, quietly urging him on.

His face tightened, his eyes glazed and yet still he thrust into her. Need spiraled hot and tight inside her and a yearning to find fulfilment began to grow. Her arms strained around him, her muscles aching in protest. She clung to him and rode the tumult of unfamiliar feelings that coursed through her, knowing that any moment she was going to reach the pinnacle and topple over into an abyss of relief.

Lane opened his eyes and stared down at her. Satisfaction flared in his eyes. He continued his rhythmic onslaught and moments later she cried out. Waves of pleasure radiated from deep inside her. When it was over, she couldn't help but marvel at the feeling. Almost simultaneously, he groaned and thrust hard, once, twice, before collapsing against her in a wall of hard male flesh and overwhelming relief.

It was long moments later when he stirred against her and lifted his weight onto his arms. He looked down at her and smiled: a tender, loving look that turned her insides to jelly. Leaning forward, he kissed her.

"Now I know."

She frowned up at him, trying to follow his train of thought. "Now you know what?"

"Now I know what it feels like."

She stared at him and slowly recalled the words he'd spoken two days earlier. Comprehension dawned. Her eyes widened in surprise. "You mean...like how it feels when you...care?"

He nodded. "Just so you know, there's no comparison."

CHAPTER 40

Thursday, February 1, 6:58 a.m.

Lane pressed a kiss against the softness of Zara's hair and pulled her in close beside him. She sighed softly and snuggled into his chest, still caught up in the sleep they'd both fallen into after their bout of lovemaking. Stretched out on his bed with her, he couldn't think of anywhere else he'd rather be. All the years he'd vowed to remain single, to never risk inflicting upon another woman the kind of life his mother had suffered, he never knew what he'd been missing out on; he never knew what it felt like to be loved.

Two days earlier, Zara had told him she'd fallen in love with him. He only hoped it was still true. She'd asked him if he was willing to take the risk, if he cared enough about her to try. Now he knew the answer and his heart swelled with emotion at the thought of telling her.

Now, he *could* imagine a wife and family, if she was the one by his side. It was only because of her that he'd been able to conquer his fear about dying too soon and abandoning his family to their fate. Not that his fears had vanished, and they probably never would, but at least now, he was willing to try; to take a risk on life.

His chest tightened at the thought of a bunch of little girls and boys with their mother's dark hair and midnight black eyes. His heart swelled at what could be and he yearned to ask the woman who lay asleep beside him if she would do him the honor of becoming his wife.

Zara.

She'd come into his life and turned his world upside down. But it felt so *right. She* was so right. He couldn't wait to tell her.

Zara came awake slowly. The morning sunlight was brighter than it had been and there was no longer a need for the lamp. The air was cool around her, caressing her naked skin. Lane must have switched on the air-conditioning sometime after they'd made love.

Lane.

The feel of his steady heartbeat beneath her ear brought a smile of contentment to her lips. He'd been right. They *had* fit and gosh, it had been more than wonderful. She now knew why the romance books she'd consumed as a teenager had been filled with countless pages about the wonder and beauty of being loved. With Lane, it had been magical, beyond anything she had read or could have imagined. And the best part was he was still there, lying beside her, holding her close, protecting her.

He was her knight in shining armor, the slayer of evil, the righter of wrongs. He was Detective Senior Sergeant Lane Black and she'd fallen head-over-heels in love with him.

How could she have such strong feelings for a man she'd only just met? And under such awful circumstances? He'd been in her life less than a week—nowhere near enough time to be contemplating love. She was twenty-five years old. She wasn't a giddy teenager who fell in and out of love as often as she changed her underwear.

Zara smiled and shook her head. She'd never been a giddy teenager. From the time she could remember, she'd worked and studied and worked harder, striving to reach her goal. From an early age, she'd dreamed of being a successful lawyer, of striding through the impressive doors of her father's law firm and taking her position by his side.

Even when Allison had come onto the scene and, a little later, Brittany, Zara's dream had never faltered. Her focus remained absolute. Her father might have sold his share of the law firm and gone into politics, but nothing could disrupt her single-minded determination to achieve the outcome she'd worked toward her entire life.

And it had happened. She had a promising career as a lawyer in one of Sydney's most prestigious law firms. It hadn't mattered that her father was no longer practising. Well, perhaps a little, but she refused to let his move into politics deter her from her goal. By the time she'd finished university, the offers of employment came rolling in. She had her pick of jobs. The fact that her career had taken precedence over her private life hadn't seemed to matter. Until Lane.

Zara sighed softly and ran her hand lightly over the smooth, tanned skin of his chest. Her fingers encountered a slightly raised ridge of flesh that ran more than three inches across his bicep. She turned to look at the scar, a faint pink color in the light, and wondered at its cause.

Her fingers continued their exploration and tangled in the light smattering of dark hair that shadowed his chest, before skimming across the flat planes of his stomach. The muscles tensed beneath her touch.

Seconds later, Lane's hand tightened over hers and stilled its movement. "Careful," he growled against her ear. "If you keep that up, I won't be held responsible for my actions."

Zara giggled, the joy of it bubbling up inside her and spilling out of her mouth. Lifting her face up to his, she pressed her lips against his mouth, loving the feel of his stubble as it scraped across her cheek.

"It's okay," she murmured, as her hand continued to make its way across his stomach. "Trust me, I'm a lawyer. I'm prepared to accept all liability."

Lane grinned down at her. "As if I'd fall for that one. A

lawyer willing to assume all liability is one I definitely wouldn't trust. In fact—"

"Hey!" She pinched him on the arm. "I think I've heard enough."

"You're right." He winked at her. "I know of much better things to do with my mouth than talk."

A blush stole across her cheeks and she ducked her head to avoid his amused expression.

"You look so cute when you blush," he whispered and tilted her face toward him.

Her heart thumped at the desire that burned in his gaze. Seconds later, his lips came down on hers, tasting, teasing, coaxing. She groaned from the onslaught of emotions that surged through her as she opened her mouth to his tongue.

His hand stole down to cup her breast and test its shape in his palm. His tongue stroked deep into her mouth and his thumb imitated the action against her nipple. Fire burned low in her belly. Need weighed heavily inside her. She moved against him, tugging at the sheets that were tangled around them. She needed to feel him, hot and hard and naked against her.

Lane broke off the kiss and gasped for breath. As if reading her mind, he rolled slightly and tore the sheet away from them. Taking her in his arms once again, he drew her flush against him.

Zara's sigh of relief mingled with his. The press of their bodies fueled the fire that raged between them.

"Please, Lane. I need you. I need you inside me." Zara blushed at her forwardness, but was beyond controlling the primeval urges inside her. Now that she knew how good it could be, her body was as desperate for his love as an addict for another hit.

He rolled her onto her back and quickly reached for a condom. Seconds later, his cock pressed against her, seeking entrance.

Zara thrust her hips upward in silent encouragement, urging him on. He stared down at her, his eyelids heavy with need.

"I'm going to explode if I don't get inside you. I'll try to take it slow. I don't want to hurt you, but—"

"I don't want it slow. Please, Lane, I want you."

With a low growl in the back of his throat, Lane surged into her. Her legs clung to his hips and she met his hard thrusts and silently begged for more. She stared at him, urging him on with her eyes and with the gasps of pleasure that were torn from her throat.

Desire built low in her belly and radiated upward. She clung to his shoulders and absorbed the weight of him on top of her. Her orgasm continued to build until it almost overwhelmed her. And then she was toppling over the edge, gasping and crying out, clinging to Lane while her body shuddered and finally was spent.

Taking his weight on his elbows, Lane grinned down at her. "So much better than talking, don't you think?"

Zara smiled back at him. Lane shifted a little and she gasped at the feel of his hard cock still deep inside her. Bending his head, he suckled her nipple, tugging it into his mouth in time with the slow movement of his hips.

Despite her recent orgasm, Zara's clit tingled. When Lane scraped her nipple with his teeth, she moaned.

"You like that, don't you?" he muttered, his voice husky with need. She lowered her gaze and offered him a shy nod.

He directed his attention to her other breast and continued the rhythmic stroking with his cock. His movements had slowed and were deeper, more intense. She stared at him and tightened her legs around his hips and lifted to meet each long thrust. He tore his mouth from her breast and grasped her hips in both hands, holding them steady while he moved inside her.

"I can't get enough of you," he groaned.

Zara clutched at the sheet beneath her, loving the feel of him inside her.

Lane picked up his pace and plunged into her again and again. Finally, his body tensed and his face stilled. Seconds later, he climaxed on a groan of relief.

A little while later, he rolled onto his side, taking her with him. She sighed in contentment, even though a part of her niggled with dread at the thought of all that was still unsaid. They needed to discuss their future, or even if they were to have one. She couldn't bear the thought of turning her back and walking away but the decision wasn't hers to make. Only Lane could decide if he would choose her over his fear.

She turned over onto her back and noticed the strip of morning sunshine had gathered in strength. Another day had begun. Life went on. She didn't want to think about work, but she needed to call her boss. He'd probably caught the gist of it on the news by now, but he deserved to hear it from her.

She thought again of everything she and Lane still had to speak about and wished for just an instant they could stay this way forever—wrapped up in each other's arms, holding the world at bay. But it wasn't realistic and if she was anything, it was a realist.

Moving out of Lane's arms, she went to climb out of the bed. His arm snaked out and caught her around the waist and dragged her back close to his side.

"Hey," she protested lightly. "I-I need to use the bathroom." She looked away, embarrassed.

Lane levered himself up on one elbow and smiled at her. "Okay, but be quick about it. I want you back in here in less than…a minute."

Zara smiled back at him and shook her head and then remembered she was naked. It was one thing to sneak out while he was asleep. There was no way in the world she was going to stroll across his bedroom with no clothes on. *So what if they'd spent the previous hour getting to know every inch of each other?* It was different after… She stayed where she was.

Lane frowned down at her. "I thought you had to go to the bathroom?"

"Yes," she murmured.

"What's the matter? It's right through there."

She ducked her head under the sheet. "I know," she said, her voice muffled.

"Then, what's the problem?" Lane sounded bemused. Zara grimaced beneath the bedclothes. Trust a man not to get it.

"Close your eyes," she demanded, still hidden.

"Why on earth...? What are you talking about?"

"Just close your eyes. Have you forgotten I have no clothes on?" *There, she'd said it.* Her face flamed.

Her announcement was met with choked laughter. Lane peeled back the sheet that covered her head and gazed down at her, his eyes twinkling.

"You're kidding me, right?"

She shook her head and refused to look at him.

"Sweetheart, we just spent the past hour—"

"I know," she interrupted him, her cheeks ablaze. "But..." She stared at the bedspread and shrugged. "You know..."

Lane brushed the hair back off her face, his fingers gentle. "Zara, look at me."

Through a sheer act of will, Zara raised her gaze and met his. Her mouth dropped open at the love and tenderness that filled his eyes.

"I love that you're shy," he whispered. "It reminds me how new you are to all of this and that's so very special."

Zara offered him a lopsided smile. "Thank you. I know it sounds silly after all that we've done, but I...it's kind of different when we're not...we're not..." She couldn't say the words aloud.

"Making love. I know what you mean, sweetheart and if I hadn't grown up in a family of boys, I'd have probably learned to have a little more modesty, too."

She swallowed a sigh of relief. He leaned over the side of the bed and produced the shirt he'd worn the day before. He tossed it in her direction. She caught it and hugged it to her, grateful for his understanding.

"I'll grab you a clean towel and some more clothes." His gaze traveled over her. "I can't say they'll be much of a fit, but they're something. You're probably not keen to pull on the prison garb again."

"Thanks, Lane. I guess I should be grateful the police kept

my dress as evidence. If I never see it again, that will be too soon."

Anger flashed in his eyes, but disappeared just as quickly. He leaned over and kissed her softly on the lips. "Anytime."

———————

A little while later, Zara emerged from the bathroom. Lane looked up from where he stood by the stove. Her wet hair hung down her back in a thick, dark swathe. She wore the clean T-shirt he'd given her, along with a pair of his shorts. He noted she'd made use of the belt from his pants to secure the shorts around her waist. A smile tugged at his lips.

He turned off the heat under the pan of scrambled eggs he'd thrown together for breakfast and closed the distance between them, hardly daring to believe she was here, in his kitchen. Pulling her into his arms, he buried his face in her hair and breathed deeply.

"*Mm*, you smell good. How come that shampoo never smells this good when I use it?"

She smiled. "Thank you, the shower was great. Just what I needed." She pulled slightly away and looked toward the stove. "What's cooking? It smells good, too."

Lane grinned and stepped away. "Just a bit of scrambled eggs I whipped up while you were getting beautiful. *More* beautiful," he added quickly. "The toast should be ready—" As if on cue, the toast popped up in the toaster. "Right about now."

Zara chuckled and the sound of it lightened his heart. "I'm impressed," she said.

He took her hands in his and tugged her close. "Oh, you will be," he murmured against her hair, taking the opportunity to nibble on the sensitive skin behind her ear he'd discovered earlier. She shivered and her arms tightened around his neck and then tilted her head to give him greater access. Taking advantage of her unspoken offer, he kissed his way down her throat, across her undamaged cheek and finally claimed her lips.

Her mouth opened under his and he groaned at the sweet taste of her. His hands cupped her bottom and pressed her against his erection through the thin fabric of his cotton boxers, loving the feel of her softness against his hard cock.

"God, you feel good," he muttered. He kissed her again, devouring her with his mouth. Her tongue met his and joined him in an erotic dance as old as time and he groaned with feeling again.

"I just can't get enough. I need to be inside you again."

Zara turned her face up to his. With her hands cradling his head, she stood on tiptoes and kissed him again. Hard. "I want you, too," she whispered.

His heart swelled with love. Happiness filled him until he thought he might burst. Sweeping her up into his arms, he carried her down the hall and deposited her gently among the tangle of sheets on his bed. Making short work of her T-shirt and shorts, he discarded his boxers and lay down beside her.

Gathering her close, he pressed her against his chest, loving the feel of her body against the long, hard length of him. She fitted so well in his arms, as if she was meant to be there. He breathed in the scent of her and prayed the moment would last forever.

She stirred against him. Her hand slid up his chest, tangling in the smattering of hair. Her fingers grazed his nipple and he groaned.

"Oh, hell, yes. That feels so good."

Her mouth replaced her fingers and his pulse spiked. She lathed the hard nubs with her tongue. Her hand reached down and encircled his rock-hard cock and then moved to slide up and down its length. His balls were tight and heavy. He didn't know how much more he could take.

He reached down and stilled her hand, entwining her fingers with his. Finding her lips again, he kissed her and stroked her mouth with his tongue, loving her with a thoroughness that left her gasping.

Nudging her onto her back, he crouched above her. "My turn," he murmured and bent low to take one of her taut nipples into his mouth. It tasted as sweet as it looked and he suckled it deep into his mouth. Zara clutched at his hair, her eyes closed.

He raised his head. "You like?"

"Oh, yes. I like. I most definitely like."

He smiled at her and then shifted his attention to her other breast. She moved restlessly against him, silently urging him onward.

Lifting himself above her, he pressed her legs open and settled himself between them. The tip of his cock glistened with moisture. They groaned as one when he pressed it against her wetness.

Sheathing himself with a condom, he eased inside her and pressed forward until he was buried deep. She felt so right.

Moving slowly, he set up a rhythm, loving the feel of her around him. He stared down at her, at the wonder, at the passion, at the tension in her eyes.

Her arms tightened around his shoulders, pulling him hard against her. His chest melded with hers and he continued his erotic onslaught. Her breathy moans of desire became more frantic. Her legs tightened around his hips. She bucked against him once, twice, three times—and then cried out in release.

Her muscles clenched around his cock and shattered his self-control. He groaned loudly and toppled over the edge. It was long moments later before he had the energy to lift himself off her and a little longer still before his breathing was under control enough to speak.

"I'll take that over scrambled eggs any day."

She smiled and a blush stained her cheeks. He marveled, and not for the first time, how she could be so unrestrained in the throes of passion and then be embarrassed about it afterward. It was endearing and one of the many things he already loved about her.

He drew her close against his side and pressed a kiss on her forehead. "I love you."

She tensed and then pulled back and looked up at him, her eyes wide with surprise and uncertainty.

"Are you sure? I mean, we've known each other for such a short time. How do you know you don't just love..." Her cheeks turned crimson and she dropped her gaze. "You know," she mumbled, "this."

"You mean the sex?"

She groaned and buried her head in his shoulder. He tilted her chin upward, wanting to put her mind at ease.

"I shouldn't have used the word 'sex'. For the first time in my life, whenever I'm with you, inside you, it feels like so much more than sex; it feels like we're making love. That's cringe worthy, I know, but it's true. Kissing, holding, loving you—it all feels new and special and unique. I've never felt like this before. I know I won't again." He stared at her, willing her to believe him, *needing* her to believe him.

"When we parted the other night, I felt like I was being torn in two. I wanted you so badly, but for so many years, I'd promised never to put myself in the position my father was: devoted to a dangerous career, unwilling to walk away from it, even for the family he loved.

"I'd decided long ago if I didn't have a family, there wouldn't be a decision to make. I'd never wake up in the morning feeling torn, wondering if I'd return that night, then walking out the door, anyway. My father battled like that every day. Not to mention the effect his death had on my mother. Her world was turned on its head. Her life was never the same again. I was determined that wasn't for me."

"So, what happened to change your mind?" Zara whispered.

"You," he said simply. "I want you more. Enough to give up my job, my career and find something safer, something less risky. Something that doesn't involve wondering every day whether I'll see you again, or how you might fare if I don't make it home. I'm going to look for a desk job."

He blew out his breath and relaxed back against the pillows, drawing her close. "I also spoke to my mother. For the first time since Dad died, I talked to her about him and about them. She helped me realize it was the time they had together that counted, that she treasured."

He shrugged. "Being a police officer was what my father was and she loved that part of him as much as any other part. She never once blamed his profession for his early death. Instead, she was proud of the man he was and what he'd done for his family and his community and she cherished the memories of their time together."

"She sounds like a remarkable woman."

Lane smiled and pressed a kiss against Zara's hair. "She is."

CHAPTER 41

Thursday, February 1, 8:47 a.m.

It was a couple of hours later, with the eggs long cold on the stove, that Lane and Zara made it out of the bedroom.

Zara reached for the fresh cup of coffee he'd set on the kitchen table before her and took a grateful sip.

"*Mm*, thanks. That's exactly what I needed."

"I even ducked out for some milk and sugar. See how well I know you already?" he teased.

She smiled back at him, wondering not for the first time how she'd gotten so lucky. Memories of how they'd arrived at this point crashed in upon her and her smile faded.

"I wonder if Dad got my message? I guess he did. I thought he'd call me by now."

"You don't have your phone, remember? Perhaps he's left a message on mine." Lane pushed away from the table and searched through some things on the kitchen counter. "Here it is."

"Oh, I forgot. I haven't called into work yet."

"After all you've been through, I think they'll understand if you don't show up today."

"Yes, I'm sure they will, but I wanted to call my boss and let him know I'm okay. Goodness knows what he's heard on the news."

"I'll just check my messages and then it's all yours." Lane winked at her and pressed a couple of buttons on his phone before holding it up to his ear.

Zara took another mouthful of egg and watched him out of the corner of her eye. A moment later, his smile faded and was replaced with a heavy frown. She felt a foreboding low in her belly. The eggs in her mouth suddenly tasted like grit. She pushed her plate aside.

"What is it? What's happened?" she murmured when he put down his phone.

He took a seat beside her and in silence, reached for her hands. Her anxiety went into overdrive. Fear tightened her throat.

"Lane? What is it? Talk to me. Please."

He lowered his gaze to the table and then drew in a deep breath. Slowly, he raised his head, until his eyes met hers. She winced at the anguish she saw in them and her imagination took flight. Something had happened. Something terrible. Who was it? His mother? One of his brothers?

"Zara," he rasped. "Michael called. It's...it's about your father. He's been hurt."

A moan of pain tore from her and she shook her head in denial. "No, you're wrong. It can't be. What happened? Tell me. Is he alive?"

"Yes, he's alive, but only just. He's lost a lot of blood. He's been taken to the hospital."

Her mind reeled with confusion and shock. "What happened?"

Lane drew in another deep breath and squeezed her hands tightly. "He was stabbed in the back. The knife went deep, but luckily missed his heart. They've operated on him to repair the damage. As far as Michael knows, he'll pull through."

"Oh, my God! He was *stabbed*? Who would stab my father? How did it happen?"

Lane closed his eyes, as if gathering the strength for what he had to say. Zara's heart stopped, the fear almost paralyzing her.

"He was stabbed by his wife."

"*Allison?* You can't be serious?"

"She's been arrested, sweetheart and charged with attempted murder. She's claiming it was self defense."

The shocks kept on coming, hammering away at her head. She could barely process what she was hearing. It sounded like an awful joke. But Lane stared at her, his eyes so serious she couldn't help but believe what he said was true.

How could it have happened? Her father loved his wife to distraction. It was part of the reason she'd been allowed to do as she wanted. He couldn't bear to see her unhappy and she'd always been quick to let him know when she was displeased.

"Self defense?" she croaked. "My father thinks she hung the moon and stars. He wouldn't hurt a hair on her head."

"Nobody's talked to your father, yet. He was taken straight to the hospital for surgery and hasn't regained consciousness." Lane looked away and swallowed, his expression turning uncomfortable.

"What is it? What aren't you telling me?"

"There were...marks and bruises around Allison's neck. It looked like someone had tried to...strangle her. She says it was your father."

Zara dragged in oxygen and did her best to feed her laboring lungs. It wasn't possible. It couldn't be true and yet...

No, she refused to believe it. She wouldn't believe it. Not until her father had confirmed it himself. For all she knew, Allison could have caused the bruising herself to make it look like she'd been attacked. She could have—

"Stop it, Zara. I know what you're doing and it will only drive you insane." He tugged at her arms and pulled her out of the chair. "Come on, let's go to the hospital. We'll wait there until your father wakes up. He's the only one who can tell us the truth."

In the end, it was like Lane had said. Zara's father told them the truth. As hard as it was for her to hear it, she was relieved in a way to bring an end to the interminable questions that had plagued her since she'd been given the news. Her head pounded and her chest was tight when they finally left the hospital. The only thing worth celebrating was that the doctors expected her father to make a full recovery.

When they arrived back at Lane's unit, it was all she could do to drag herself down the hall and into the living room. It was midafternoon and she hadn't eaten since the few mouthfuls of eggs she'd managed before Lane had picked up his phone. She should have been hungry, but she wasn't. All she felt was grief.

She made it to the couch and sank down on it and rested her head on the cushion. Her face was still sore and her bruises were now purple, but she could finally open both eyes. Now, she closed them in weariness and bit back tears—tears she'd managed to hold at bay in the hospital. She felt Lane's weight beside her and was grateful when he took her in his arms. She gulped on a surge of emotion and when he kissed the top of her head and urged her to let it out, the sobs burst from her like they'd never stop.

It was a long while later when the tears subsided and she shakily pulled out of his arms.

"I'm sorry for blubbering all over you like that," she whispered.

His eyes were full of love and concern. He leaned over and brushed the hair from her eyes. "Do you feel any better?"

"Yes. I do. Thank you. I-I'm so glad you were here to...to help me. I don't know how I would cope without you."

He smiled tenderly. "You underestimate yourself, sweetheart. You're stronger than you think. None of this is your fault, Zara. You don't get to choose your family."

She offered a weak smile, grateful for his support. "You're

right, of course, but I still can't help feeling responsible. It's stupid, but there it is. Some part of me thinks if I hadn't been so involved in my life, in my career, I would have seen it. I would have picked up the signs before things got so out of control. I would have seen Allison's mood swings as more than just her way of making me feel miserable. I would have realized there was more to it than that. Maybe everything would have turned out differently?"

Lane's hand tightened around hers and she took comfort from the warm strength in his grip.

"Don't think like that, sweetheart. It will get you nowhere. Take it from me, I've been there. A seven-year-old boy still has a fairly well developed sense of responsibility, especially a son who's the oldest of four. For years, I turned myself inside out with "what ifs" and it nearly broke me. I eventually realized I couldn't continue to think like that and I learned to let the guilt go, but it wasn't easy. I want to spare you that pain."

He leaned in closer, his expression earnest. "Please believe me when I tell you it wasn't your fault. Nobody forced Allison to take drugs. Nobody forced her to barter her body. Not you or anyone could have changed things. The only person who had that power was Allison and as far as we know, she wasn't so inclined."

Zara clung to his words, wanting to believe them, needing to believe them. She could only imagine the weight of guilt her father felt. She had to stay strong for both of them, and for little Brittany too.

"Thank you," she said quietly. "I needed to hear that. The saner, objective part of me knows what you say is true. I need to pay attention to that part and do my best to ignore the guilt that wants to undermine all that I know is real."

Lane brought her hand to his lips and kissed her fingers. "I love you so much, Zara. It kills me to see you unhappy. It kills me to know your family has put you in this position, but I want you to know, I'm here for you. I'm in your corner. Now and forever, or at least, for as long as you want me."

She stared at him and her heart picked up its pace. "W-what are you saying?"

He held her gaze for long moments in silence. Finally, he broke it. "Zara, will you marry me?"

"M-marry you?" she stammered. "A-are you sure?"

He smiled a little uncertainly. "Of course I'm sure. I love you. I want to spend the rest of my life taking care of you. I... I'm hoping you feel the same."

Joy blossomed from deep down inside her and lightened the weight in her heart. Her lips quivered and then broadened into a wide grin. Fresh tears sparkled in her eyes.

"Of course, I do. I'll love you until I die. Like I told you before, I fell in love with you the moment you stepped inside Brittany's bedroom."

Lane frowned. "Then, why are you crying?"

She hiccupped again. "They're happy tears, silly."

Moving closer, Lane took her in his arms. His lips met hers and he kissed her until he'd stolen her breath. She returned the kiss, hoping he could feel the depth of her love: love that had snuck up on her and devoured her until she couldn't imagine a life or a world without him in it.

Epilogue

Two months later

Zara collected the dirty clothes out of the laundry hamper and carried them through to Lane's washing machine. Even something as mundane as doing the laundry brought a smile to her lips these days. She and Brittany had moved in with Lane the same day he'd proposed, unwilling to spend even another night in the house they'd grown up in. Not only was it now a crime scene, but every room in the beautiful mansion brought nothing but bad memories.

It was fortunate Lane had a spare room. After what her little sister had gone through, Zara was never going to leave the girl with relatives. Zara still felt appreciative whenever she thought about how Lane had immediately insisted Brittany come and stay with them.

Both her father and Allison had been charged with attempted murder. Both of them had pleaded not guilty. Both of them were on remand, awaiting a trial date. Zara still couldn't believe how quickly her perfect family had been torn apart at the seams, ripped into so many pieces it was no longer recognizable and would never be put together again.

She was just so glad Lane's family had embraced her and Brittany so warmly and without judgement. Just as she'd guessed, Lane's mother was a remarkable woman. Intelligent, kind and astute, she'd given Zara her blessing, telling her that the only thing that would make her happier than discovering her son had finally found himself a wife was to be told there was a grandchild on the way. Zara had blushed, but Lane's smile had lit up the room and she'd secretly hoped they'd have news of that kind before too much time passed. Brittany would be thrilled, too. She'd love having a baby around.

The sound of her cell phone ringing interrupted her reverie. Dumping the laundry on the floor near the washing machine, she hurried into the living room and collected it from the coffee table. Glancing at the screen, she recognized Ellie's number and smiled. Over the past couple of months, they'd become very good friends. They'd bonded over their shared experiences during a traumatic time in their lives and were both more than ecstatic that things had turned out all right.

Through an unspoken agreement, they both tried hard to keep the girls' lives as normal as possible—well, as normal as they could be in the circumstances. Ellie was a former police officer and she understood the need for consistency. Brittany's counselor agreed. The sooner her life went back to the way it was, as far as possible, the quicker her recovery. Maintaining her friendship with Olivia was just one of the ways to achieve it.

Zara was glad her sister had found such a good friend and one who could understand all that she'd been through. It helped to have someone her own age to talk to, especially during times when she felt the adults just didn't understand.

Zara wasn't kidding herself into believing she could be everything to Brittany and she was more than happy for the counselor and Brittany and even Ellie to play a role in her sister's recovery. Brittany had even opened up to Lane, and about that, Zara couldn't be happier.

She answered the call from Ellie with a smile on her face.

"Hi, Ellie. What are you up to?"

"Zara, I'm so glad I caught you. I just had to tell you. The picture's gone."

"The picture's gone?" Zara repeated in confusion.

"Yes, the picture. Olivia and Clayton and I sat down and talked. We...we told her about her mother, the truth about how she died. There were a lot of tears and she was upset that we hadn't told her earlier, but the end result was, the picture's gone and it was Olivia who took it down."

Ellie had confided in Zara about Ellie's despair over Olivia's obsession with her late mother. Knowing the young girl had at last taken steps to embrace Ellie in her life, Zara could well understand Ellie's relief.

"That's fantastic news, Ellie. I'm so glad. Now you and Olivia will have the chance you needed to bond, really bond. And I'm so glad she knows the truth. It's always better that way."

"You're right. We probably should have told her earlier, but there never seemed to be a right time. First, she was too young to understand and then later, she seemed so obsessed with Lisa—neither Clayton or I knew what to do."

"Well, I'm just glad it's worked out for everyone."

"You and me both. Olivia and I finally have a chance to really connect. It's what I've always wanted and I think, deep down, it's what she wants, too."

"You're lucky it turned out so well."

"Yes, I am. We all are—Olivia, Clayton, even the boys. Our household's so much happier. We're all in love with each other again. It's a nice feeling."

Zara smiled. "Yes, it is."

Ellie sniffed then cleared her throat. "Now, enough about me. Tell me about the wedding plans. How are they coming along?"

"Everything's coming together beautifully and I'm so thrilled you've agreed to be my matron of honor. Britt's beyond excited about being a bridesmaid. It's makes her feel so grown-up. I'm sad that Dad won't be allowed out to walk me down the aisle, but one of Lane's brothers as agreed to take on the role."

"That's great, Zara. I'm so pleased things are working out."

Zara's phone beeped to indicate an incoming call. She glanced at the screen. Her smile widened. *Lane.*

"Sorry, Ellie. I hate to interrupt, but Lane's trying to call me. Do you mind if I call you back?"

"Of course not, silly! Answer the call. I'll hear the rest of the details later."

After issuing a quick good-bye, Zara ended one call and picked up another. Her smiled got wider at his opening line.

"Hello, beautiful. What's my favorite girl up to?"

"Oh, you know. Doing laundry, chatting on the phone. I have a very busy schedule."

Lane laughed. "Well, I'm just glad I managed to persuade you to take some time off work. There's no way you could keep up those hours and plan a wedding—and I, for one, am counting down hours until I can call you my wife."

A surge of love flooded through her and tears of joy pricked her eyes. Although she'd never want to experience those horrific few days all over again, she'd always be profoundly grateful that it had meant meeting and falling in love with Lane. Apart from her friendship with Ellie, he was the only good to have come of the whole awful time.

Wiping at the moisture in her eyes, she answered him. "It can't come soon enough for me, either and talking about work, I'm thinking about a career change—or at least, a change in direction."

"Really? I thought you loved being a lawyer?"

"I did. I do, but I want to do more than succession planning and haggling over the terms of a lease. I want to make a difference; a real difference. I want to be a child advocate."

"Wow, that's a change, all right."

"Do you think it's a good idea?" she asked a little worriedly. "After what happened to Olivia and it should have been Brittany... I want to work with the Department of Family and Community Services and the courts. The pay would be a whole lot less, but I'm guessing the job satisfaction would make it more than worthwhile." She paused to catch her breath and suddenly realized how important this had become to her and how much she wanted Lane to understand.

"Too many kids are living their lives in fear and uncertainty, governed by drug addicted parents who care for nothing but their next fix. I want to help those kids. I want to give them a voice. I want to show them that they matter."

She waited for Lane's reply feeling slightly apprehensive. When he finally spoke, his voice was thick with emotion.

"Do you have any idea how special you are? How loving and kind and just so darn good? How did you ever end up in my life? I don't know what I did to deserve you, but I thank God every day that you're mine."

Tears of happiness coursed down Zara's cheeks and there was nothing she could do to stop them. "I love you, Lane Black," she sobbed. "I love you with every fiber of my being. The way we met might have been far from ideal, but if I was given the choice of wiping those awful days and nights from my memory or losing your love, I wouldn't change a thing."

"Right back at you, darling. Right back at you."

NOTE TO READERS

I do hope you have enjoyed reading Lane and Zara's story. Please feel free to leave a review for The Ransom. Every review is very much appreciated and I thank you for taking the time to leave one.

The Defendant—Book Eight in the Munro Family Series is the next book in the Munro Family Series and is Chase and Josie's story.

Here's a sneak peek:

Detective Sergeant **Chase Barrington** has never forgotten the girl he fell in love with in high school. He and **Josie Munro** planned to marry as soon as they'd graduated. But fate stepped in and Chase made the painful decision to end it without telling Josie the truth...

When twelve-year-old Daniel Logan witnesses the rape of his mother, he grabs a gun and shoots the perpetrator dead. Chase attends the scene and Daniel's arrested and charged with murder.

A decade after graduating high school, child psychologist Josie Munro has recently returned to her hometown. When she's appointed by the court to provide a report on Daniel's mental capacity, it's inevitable that she runs into the detective on the case. Unaware of the real reason why Chase ended their relationship, her anger and grief from all those years ago immediately rise to the surface.

With no choice but to carry on and complete the task she's been given, she determines to keep Chase as far away from her as possible and get the job over with as quickly as she can.

But things aren't that easy. If her report proves Daniel knew that shooting the perpetrator was wrong, his matter will proceed to trial. If he's found guilty, he'll face considerable jail time.

As Josie gets to know Daniel through therapy sessions, she realizes he knew exactly what he was doing: He meant to kill his mother's rapist and he's not at all sorry. She's torn between doing what the law requires of her against what her heart knows is right. She's also conflicted over her feelings for Chase. She wants to hate him, but she can't.

Will she follow her head or her heart?

The Defendant will be released on 15 March, 2015 and is available now for pre-order from your favorite retailer.

If you would like to subscribe to my newsletter to receive news on upcoming Munro Family stories, release dates, book launches and other snippets, please go to my website at www.christaylorauthor.com.au and follow the link. I love to hear from my readers. Please feel free to contact me at christaylor@antmail.com.au Let me know who your favorite Munro family member is.

About the Author

Chris Taylor grew up on a farm in north-west New South Wales, Australia. She always had a thirst for stories and recalls writing her first book at the ripe old age of eight. Always a lover of romance and happily-ever-afters, a career in criminal law sparked her interest in intrigue and suspense. For Chris to be able to combine romance with suspense in her books is a dream come true.

Chris is married to Linden and is the mother of five children. If not behind her computer, you can find her doing the school run, taxiing children to swimming lessons, football, ballet and cricket. In her spare time, Chris loves to read her favorite authors who include Richard North Patterson, Sandra Brown, Kathleen E Woodiwiss and Jude Devereaux.

You can find out more about Chris and sign up for her newsletter at her website:

http://www.christaylorauthor.com.au

www.ingramcontent.com/pod-product-compliance
Lightning Source LLC
Chambersburg PA
CBHW031314210726
48287CB00005B/1544